Star Found

DEDICATION

To my long-suffering family and friends.

Star Found

Volume Two

of the

Star Stone Trilogy

Richard Hensley

To Angela,

The journey continues

Richard

Happy Birthday!

Published in the United Kingdom by Desfield Press

Cover design by Desfield Press

www.desfield.uk

www.richardhensley.co.uk

ISBN-13: 978-1-9997072-2-4

Episodes

Characters

6th & 7th Century – 597 to 614: Canterbury and beyond:
Doric: Druid and Monk from Kernow
Larn: Irish Chief's son
Aiden: Irish Monk

20th Century – 1943, 1944: Latchmere House:
Billy Carter, 12 years: finds bracelet in Canterbury
Symes: MI5 operative
Martin, Edith & Norman: Billy's guards
Andrew: Physicist

Monsignor Patrick Aherne: Exorcist, Dublin

Twins: protect Billy – are from his future

28th Century – 2795 to 2796 [and later: 2800, 3032]:
Chislehurst Island, Jupiter Transport & Starship:
Gail, 13 years: finds bracelet in Chislehurst tunnels
Victor, 15 years: Gail's friend and mating partner
Hella: Army PsyTech for Gail
Cator: Army Commander, Europe
Steran: StarForce Commander, Luna Base Five
Rosa: Gail's friend and masseuse

Marnie: Swimmer Team Leader, Isles of London
Kovak: Swimmer Team Second and Marnie's lover
Penta: Swimmer Coordinator, Europe

Outside of normal space-time:
Star Miners: fabricators of the bracelet's exotic iron
Task Giver: requested the exotic iron

Future History

William holds the iron armband. Its weight reminds him of the terrifying journey to these moments in time, these points in the universe, these gravities pulling at his body. Soon, he will know what form the future will take, whether he will again see his wife, children, and friends.

How many years since that first day when he found the armband? Time no longer has meaning. Space is also meaningless. Existence is all that matters.

His fingers trace the designs cut into its surface. Triple spirals, circles and stars, thought by some to be Celtic art. They were wrong. No simple armband but a bracelet of true power.

The bracelet, a Pandora's Box, is active for good or ill.

His life changed in that first moment, when as a boy, he touched the bracelet dug from the dirt of a bombed city. It changes again as he hears the siren call of the future forming at the edge of his consciousness.

That boy, Billy, could never have known what the future would hold.

Can this man, William, face that future now it has arrived?

0

The journey so far …

Billy Carter, 11, a schoolboy from Lewisham, South London, finds an ancient bracelet on a cleared bombsite in Canterbury in the summer of 1942.

Monsignor Patrick Aherne, an exorcist from Dublin, finds a similar bracelet in the Vatican archives in the spring of 1938. He wants Billy's bracelet for its arcane power. He is helped by Father Vicente from Tomar, Portugal.

Doric, 16, a novice druid from Cornwall, is given a tribal bracelet by his mentor in the winter of 595.

Gail, 12, a trainee from the Isle of Chislehurst, finds a bracelet in a derelict building. She finds another in the Chislehurst Tunnels. It is the autumn of 2795.

Symes, MI5, wants Billy's bracelet – it might be useful as a secret weapon for the war effort.

Billy's and Doric's bracelets and Gail's' first one, are the very same. The others are two more of the nine that were made from the iron of a meteorite during the Neolithic era. In their minds, the wearers all see and hear things when they use their bracelets.

Gail and her two bracelets, become part of an experiment to discover their secrets and to locate more meteoric iron.
The bracelets allow instant mind-to-mind communication, which is essential for interstellar space flight.

Doric joins a party of Irish monks travelling to Canterbury to greet Abbot Augustine when he visits Kent in 597. As yet, he is unaware of his bracelet's full power.

Billy and the Shining Twins appear to Doric and tell him what he must do. The Twins know the bracelets' true power … and use it.

1

Outside of normal space-time

"Our two Carbonforms have a special energy which exists only between them," says Alpha.

"The Task Giver will not tell us what this energy is," says Beta.

"We cannot find out for ourselves," says Gama.

"We must experiment and get more data," says Alpha.

"We must seek advice from others who are related to our race," says Beta.

"It is possible they have this energy," says Gamma.

"How do we ask when we cannot describe this energy?" asks Alpha.

"We describe its effect on Carbonforms," says Beta.

"Do our relatives know of Carbonforms?" asks Gamma.

"Yes," says Alpha. "I hear their words and a change in their emotion."

"What is emotion?" asks Beta.

"Do our relatives have emotions?" asks Gamma.

"They do. This particular emotion makes them happy," says Alpha.

"What is 'happy'?" asks Beta.

"Are we ever 'happy'?" asks Gamma.

"For us, it is similar to finishing a task we are given," says Alpha.

"That is good," say Beta and Gamma in unison.

2

Latchmere House, Ham, Monday, February 15th 1943

"Greg. Here's a list of things I think we'll need. Can you have a look?" said Peter. The whole team were in the canteen at eight o'clock, ready for the morning briefing.

"Sure. There's loads of stuff downstairs. Symes has obtained the same equipment you used where you worked and I've added to it. We'll check it out after the briefing."

Symes entered. "Good morning. Today is our first of the project that I have named 'Ironstone' because the bracelet is probably made from an iron meteorite. It'll take a day or two to plan a schedule and get the monitoring equipment set up. All the work will take place inside two sub-basement rooms that Greg has fitted out. There is only one way into the work area and I have the only key. I will pass the key to Martin when I have to go off site. Please follow me."

The group wound its way through the house and descended a rear staircase. They passed the original cellar level and continued down to the sub-basement, built just before war had started.

Symes unlocked the steel door, pulled it open and groped for the light switch. The fluorescent tubes flickered to life, lighting the white walls. "This will be your laboratory for the duration, either the war or the project." He looked aside at Peter. "The rest of the site is a prison of sorts. Don't go there or you'll be arrested. This part of the house is exclusively ours. Greg?"

"I've had these rooms screened against radio waves. There are microphones in the walls and our listening staff will be making notes while we are in here. We do have an aerial feed, Peter, in case we need to hear wireless traffic, but it'll normally be earthed. We've got racks of equipment on that wall and components stores over there." Greg pointed around the spacious laboratory. "And next door is the listening room. This is where Janet will be based with the listening staff. We've some transcription disc cutters and a few wire recorders for important experiments, so we don't miss anything and I can get a cine camera and lights if we need them. I think that's all."

Peter was impressed. "This is great. Our project is obviously well funded. Much better than my last job."

"We learned that lesson at Station Ten," said Symes. "No matter how weird the work, you can't do miracles on a shoe string. Well, I'll leave you lot to perform said miracles. See you at lunch."

"So who's in charge while Symes is away?" asked Peter.

"That'll be me," said Janet. "I have to produce a work plan for our experiments, collect and interpret the data and results we get and then report it all back."

Peter's eyebrows lifted when he heard this.

Janet understood. "Don't worry Mr Carter. I'm quite capable. I've two honours degrees from Cambridge, maths and languages, with several years in this service. I look younger than I am."

"Sorry Janet. No slight intended. I see that Symes has put together a top rate team. Call me Peter. I guess we are all on first name terms."

"All except Symes," said Greg, "but he's okay."

Janet pointed to a table and chairs in a corner. "Good. Let's all sit and discuss my provisional plan. You too Billy. You're our main asset. Only you can make the bracelet work in any way that is useful, so we'll be asking you many questions. But if you feel tired, please say so and we can have a rest. Okay?"

"Yeah. Okay."

Janet smiled at him and passed sheets of paper to the group. "Good. Here are my initial thoughts. You each have a copy on which you can make notes, but no documentation or articles are allowed out of here, except under guard. Understood?"

Everyone, except Billy, was used to this in their work. They all acknowledged the restriction. The meeting had gone on for an hour when he began to fidget. He leaned over and whispered in his Dad's ear.

"You should have said earlier. Let's go and find the toilet." They got up and went to the door. It was locked. "How do we get out?"

"Bang on the door. Martin will let you out. Sorry, I forgot to say," said Janet.

They went upstairs to the nearest toilet. "Billy, you're the most important part of this project. If you're not happy, they won't get any results. So if you want something, you tell me. Okay?"

"Yeah. Can I have some sweets?"

"I'll put in an order. But don't eat too many, they'll rot your teeth."

The first day was daunting for Billy.

And the next was worse. At school, he was required to sit still for less than an hour at a time. These grownups could do it all day if necessary. He got his sweets, but he did ration them, even offered them around the team who took advantage of the treat.

The whole team listened while he told them everything he had heard and seen with his bracelet. They all took notes. He started with the monks, his first identifiable sounds, he went on to tell them about the girl, Gail, seeing her in the Chislehurst caves and the man buried behind a wall. They quizzed him about that episode, but he did not understand what it meant. The team got excited when he mentioned he had actually spoken a few words to Gail. He told them about other sounds he could not identify and the confused vision he had seen in the bombed house. No one could understand that, but it was all recorded.

He continued with the accident at the hop farm and meeting Symes, making them understand he had seen things in his vision of the hop farm that had not actually happened to him; about his friend Jeff, kept prisoner by the man and Symes' conversation the next day with the police sergeant.

Symes sat up at that revelation. "You heard my words?"

"Yeah. You said about Jeff messin' with the grenade and you said about all war being a bit daft. I saw loads of things in my dream."

"Make a particular note of this Janet and we'll look at it again. It'll be important."

They discussed the detail of Father Michael's accident and Billy's dream about the angels in the cave, but, again, it was too strange to understand.

Symes asked about Michael's accident. "Billy, have you dreamed anything else about Father Michael?"

"Naw, only that weird dream. I can try if you want, but the dreams just come. I'm not sure I can make them."

"That won't be necessary, thank you." He scribbled in his notebook.

Miss Porter arrived as promised on the second day. She was pressed into telling one of her stories, but Billy could tell she was not happy. He asked his mum if she was ill.

"No, I don't think so. She's had a long journey and the trains and buses are all over the place. I'll ask her later, if you like."

"Yeah. She can 'ave some of my sweets." He gave his mum a crumpled paper bag. "These are my favourites. She can 'ave 'em."

His mum ruffled his hair. He didn't really like that and ducked away, but he knew it pleased her to do it.

"Mum. They called me an asset. What's that?"

She thought for a while, eyes moistening. "It means you're precious to the project, dear."

ooo

Wednesday, February 17th 1943

Billy had a little respite after two days of telling the group all of his experiences. They discussed them and analysed them until nothing more could be gleaned.

"So, you're not dreaming then?" asked Frank.

"Naw. Not really. Sometimes I'm wide-awake. I can see and hear everything what's goin' on around me. Sometimes I'm asleep, but the dreams are real. It's like I'm there. I can tell the difference." He enjoyed the attention. Once he had told his mates about the dreams, but they just laughed and called him names. He had not done that again.

"Who else has tried the bracelet?" said Frank.

"Dad has and Mr Symes. Father Michael and Father Alan and the Monsignor. But it burnt Father Michael. That was horrid."

"We read the report. You say you had a dream about that later." Frank looked through his notebook. "That was when you were in the Chislehurst caves."

"Yeah. That was a weird dream. When it was burning him at home, he said it couldn't hurt me. Then he was taken to hospital. I had the dream in Chislehurst, it was like Father Michael knew it might hurt me and he made it hurt him instead. Dunno why. He died in my dream, but I didn't know about it till Dad phoned Father Murphy next day. He wasn't badly burnt, but he still died."

"We have that in the hospital report," said Frank. "We'll have to be very careful with you Billy. If the bracelet gets too hot, you take it off or tell us to. Okay?"

"Yeah. I don't want to die, do I?"

3

Latchmere House, Ham, Friday, February 19th 1943

Greg looked up from his monitoring equipment when Billy and Dad were let in. "Good morning, Billy. Did you enjoy your day off? What's it like to be twelve years old?"

"Okay, thanks. We had cake last night. Dad's brought some for you."

"Terrific. We'll enjoy that later. We're ready to do a test now. Everyone else okay with that?" The others agreed and went to their positions.

Billy got the bracelet from the safe and put it on the table. Dad wound insulated wire through it, counting the number of turns as he went and then connected the wires to the equipment. They were repeating his original work to see if their new laboratory gave the same results.

Greg and Dad made adjustments, calling out what they were doing for the record. There was no response from the bracelet, just as before.

"Okay. Can you put the bracelet on your arm?" said Greg.

Billy picked it up and slipped it over his left wrist. After a few moments, he heard the usual noises in his head. He said what was happening.

"We've got something," said Greg. They adjusted the oscilloscope and discussed the waveforms they were seeing on its screen.

"Are you hearing anything in particular, or is it just noises?" said Greg.

"Just noises."

"Okay. Take the bracelet off your arm."

The waveforms disappeared from the screen.

"Let's repeat that with the dummy ring," said Janet. An iron ring of exactly the same dimensions had been made for comparative experiments. Dad wound the same wire through the dummy ring. They followed the same procedure but got only interference from the lights.

The team spent the rest of the day repeating the same tests with slight differences to the procedures and taking some photographs of the scope screen. Billy was exhausted by teatime.

When they got back to their lodgings, Dad told him about the next week's schedule.

"We'll be doing some tests where we check what happens when you're asleep. That might be better for you."

"Yeah, but I hope I don't 'ave bad dreams. Sometimes I don't like 'em."

"You must tell us when they're bad. I don't know how, but we'll try to avoid that sort."

"Dad, why can't I bring the bracelet home with me?"

"It's too precious, son. We have to keep it locked up for security. And all our notes, like I have to at work. Mr Symes is paranoid."

"What's that mean?"

"He wants everything to be kept secret and he's always on the lookout for ways people might try to get those secrets. He lives in a different world to us. The people he deals with are not always on our side in this war, so he sometimes has to do nasty things to get to the truth. That's why he's been unfriendly at times."

"But aren't we in his world now?"

"Yes, but he knows we're on his side so he doesn't have to worry about us pinching his secrets. We're making them for him. Don't worry, he'll look after us."

Dad took hold of Billy's hand. He liked that because he knew that Dad was as unsure as he was.

"Now. We have the weekend off. The others will be going over all the information and we can explore the area around here."

Billy brightened at the prospect of seeing some daylight.

The laboratory gave him the sense that the rest of the world did not exist.

February and March 1943

Day after day, Greg and Peter stared at the oscilloscope screen. There was little activity from the bracelet, Billy was not dreaming while awake, neither was he having much success while asleep. He tossed and turned on the old camp bed, but without complaint. It had been two weeks since any significant activity had disturbed the horizontal green line on the display. The whole project team was disappointed and tired. They had been working without a break for the four and a half weeks since their arrival.

While the rest of the team discussed which experiment to try next, he went on long exercises with Edith and Norman, two soldiers from Latchmere House. Edith taught him the rudiments of tracking and field-craft. He enjoyed learning survival skills in Richmond Park, but he also had to spend some time with Sheila for school lessons from Miss Porter, which was less fun.

Saturday, March 13th 1943

Symes called a progress meeting at the end of the week. "I wonder if our presence is upsetting the process in some way. Billy, has this happened before, periods when you didn't have dreams?"

"Yeah, but I don't know why. They just come and go."

"The dreams I know about come mostly when he's upset in some way," said Dad. He glanced at Symes and the look on his face made him wonder if he should have kept quiet.

Symes smiled. "I can arrange to upset him, but it's not a thing I want to do. We've been rather intensive. I think a change of scene and activity are called for. Martin, please arrange transport for tomorrow, zero seven thirty, for a trip out. The weather looks good for a day or two. I think a safe place in Surrey would make a good break. I'm afraid I can't arrange ice cream, Billy, but we can explore and play. Include the whole Carter family, but not Miss Porter."

Martin acknowledged and went to organise the trip.

"Why did you ask Martin to do that?" asked Peter.

"He'll know the best places for privacy and where he can arrange his defence team to guard us."

"It's a lot of trouble, but thanks. I certainly need a break. Are you bringing any family?" said Peter.

Symes studied his boots. "Lost touch at the end of the last war. My job and family are not compatible. We had to make choices." He looked Peter in the eyes: "I'll make sure you and Mary don't have to."

"Sorry. Thank you."

Janet said, "I'll stay and review all the information we have. It'll be a useful day."

"No you won't. You'll come and enjoy a day off. That's an order," said Symes.

"I don't suppose I can take my notes with me?"

"You suppose correctly. You can take a blank notebook if you must, but a day to clear the head is in order, for all of us."

4

Puttenham Common, Sunday, March 14th 1943

Martin had organised a small Army bus, an Army driver and a huge picnic. Mum and Sheila were included in the party, but not Miss Porter.

None of the team could get Martin to reveal where they were going. Not even the driver knew, except he had been told to take the A3 to Guildford and would be given directions from there.

Janet sat alone on the bench seat at the rear of the bus, deep in thought and scribbling in her fresh notebook.

Billy stared out of the window at the trees and fields that were turning green as spring progressed. He loved the countryside. Richmond was a vast change from his dirty, bomb scarred London suburb. Richmond Park was a wonderful playground for a boy, but without his mates, it was a lonely place. Father Michael was still on his mind. No matter how often he tried, he could not understand the meaning of the vision in the big cave. Frank, the doctor, had talked to him about it. Frank was interested in how the brain works. He asked some very difficult questions, trying to understand the problem with Father Michael, but neither of them found an answer.

The bus slowed and pulled off the road. It bumped up the grass verge and halted next to a wooded area.

"Time for a cuppa," shouted Martin. They all got off and stretched their legs.

The driver opened a hatch in the side of the bus and pulled out one of the picnic hampers. "All line up for tea and a biscuit. Toilets are in the trees," he said, "Ladies first," he added with a grin.

Billy got his drink and biscuit. The driver slipped him an extra one and poured the tea from a large Thermos while Billy held the mug. He joined his family, trying not to spill the tea. "Why isn't Miss Porter with us, Dad?" he whispered.

"She isn't part of the secret team so she's not allowed."

"Nor's Mum and Sheila."

"True, but they know quite a bit, so they are allowed. Miss Porter doesn't know about the bracelet."

"She does. I showed her at the hop farm. She was interested in the markings on it. Said her dad used to dig up stuff like that all over the place."

Dad took hold of his arm and led him away from the group. "Are you sure you told her? It's very important you remember accurately."

"Why?"

"Never mind, why. Did you show her?"

"Yeah. I said, didn't I? I ain't fibbin."

"No. Of course not. I'll have to tell Symes. Don't you worry about it." Dad led him back to the group and they continued to drink their tea.

Peter sat by Symes for the next leg of the journey. He leaned close and spoke softly. "Billy has just told me Miss Porter has seen the bracelet. It was just after he found it, last year."

Symes' face clouded. He turned and looked at Peter. "Well now. That's interesting. I brought her to Latchmere to keep her under surveillance. Just as well I did."

"What's she done?"

"Nothing. It's her past associations. There's no need for concern. She's doing a great job with your kids and she's where we can keep an eye on her."

"What about today?" said Peter.

"My men are watching her. Thanks for telling me this. I might need to borrow her for a day or two, to see what she knows. Did she work all the time at the hop farm last year?"

"I was only there at weekends, but she worked then. Mary will know about the rest of the time."

"Don't ask Mary. Don't want her upset. Miss Porter is too useful with your kids. You know the army camp near the hop farm?"

"Yes, been a couple of times to set up equipment."

"When we found out Miss Porter was nearby, we were concerned. And then that explosion. You can imagine the panic. That's why I was at the hop farm."

"Were you watching Miss Porter at the hop farm?"

"No."

"Were others?"

"Can't say." He paused. "Why are you so interested?"

"Doing some of my own sleuthing."

"Be careful. Don't get involved in my side of things. It's a dangerous business. You and Billy are too useful right now."

"Does that mean we won't be useful at some time in the future?"

"Of course. Me too. We all have a useful life, after which, well ... I hope yours will be long ones."

They sat in silence for the rest of the journey.

"Here we are," said Martin. "Puttenham Common. My men are already here and positioned. Enjoy the day. I don't recommend swimming in the lakes." He jumped off the bottom step and helped the driver get the picnic and the rest of their things out. Everyone took something up the incline to the common. Greg and Frank erected a small awning to keep the wind off the party and some ground sheets completed the camp.

Billy and Sheila sorted through the hamper. They found spam sandwiches and flasks of tea which they helped give out to the others. There were carrots, apples and some cake, which Mum had made from her increased rations.

When he had eaten enough, Billy said to Martin, "You said your men were here. Why are they hiding?"

"I've been watching you and I think you know where some of them are."

"Yeah. What of it?"

"Okay. Point out one of them."

He stared into the trees and brambles lining open common. "Just by that broken fence post." He pointed.

"Come out Edith. You've been rumbled."

"Yes sir." She picked her way through the brambles, jogged the short distance and presented herself, snapping a smart salute. "Well done Billy. You saw me twenty minutes ago."

"Hello Edith. Can't you use your real name today?"

"No sir. Only on days off."

He laughed.

"We'll make a soldier of you yet, lad," said Martin.

"Not sure I want to be a soldier. It's dangerous."

The day was a good change for the team. They played French cricket and kicked a football about, though the ground was too rough for any skill.

Billy and Edith hunted down the other guards, one by one. "They ain't been trained very well, 'ave they?" he said when they caught another one. "I mean, we found 'em easy didn't we?"

"They weren't tryin' too hard, sir, it's true."

"How many were there?" he asked.

"How many do you think?"

"I don't know." He looked up and down the treeline nearest them and thought for a moment. "There should be one more and he'll be by that yellow bush." He pointed to a clump of gorse, just flowering.

"Go find him then, sir, but quiet mind. Don't let 'im know."

He walked in the opposite direction from the bush and picked up the football. Pretending to be a great centre forward, he kicked it about for a few minutes and then gave one almighty kick. The ball landed behind the bush. He ran down a path behind the brambles and gorse, found the ball and picked it up. "You're dead, soldier. That was a grenade."

"Blimey. I didn't think you'd find me. Well done lad." A tall soldier stood up from his crouched position in the gorse and pulled prickly branches from the webbing in his helmet. "How did you figure that out?"

"Hello Norman. I knew we were being guarded and when I found the others, there was a gap just here."

"Well done lad," said Edith as she joined them. "My training has brought you on real well. Get some grub Norman. Now, we'll go along the treeline for a way and I'll teach you how to use a hand gun."

"Cor, why's that?" He was excited.

"You never know when you might need to. These are tricky times."

They walked about half a mile from the others. "This'll do us." They searched for stones and sticks and built a small cairn. Edith secured a thick piece of branch in the middle. She took her gun and holster from her belt and removed the gun. Then she removed the ammunition clip and checked the chamber. "Now this is safe." She aimed at the cairn and pulled the trigger a few times to demonstrate. "Never point a gun at anyone unless you intend to shoot them. Always keep it in its holster or pointed away from everyone around you. Okay?"

"Yeah."

"See this? That's the safety. You must have that in the safe position like this. Unless you're goin' to kill someone. Okay?"

"Yeah."

"Watch how I insert the ammunition clip. And this is how you eject it." She handed over the gun and holster. "Here you are. You show me all those things."

Billy clicked the safety on, off and on, ejected the clip and replaced it, put the gun in the holster and drew it out pointing it away from Edith.

"Good. Next stage." She showed him how to stand and hold the gun, how to fire it for close range and long range.

"Okay lad, now you're used to how it feels, you can fire it. Two hands, feet apart, arms out in front, breathe in, aim and fire, breathe out." She watched as he went through all the stages and pulled the trigger.

"It didn't work."

"Nope. Took out all the bullets. Remove the clip and put these in." She gave him a handful of bullets and showed how to fill the clip. "Take real care now."

Billy loaded the clip and pushed it into the gun. She showed him how to prime the gun and make it safe.

"Okay lad. Stick this in your ears." She gave him some cotton wool. "Good, now try hitting that bit of wood. Just one shot and mind the kick-back."

He repeated his practiced moves and fired a shot. His arms jerked and he staggered back a step. A spurt of dust flew up to the right of the cairn.

"Try again. Keep your arms straight in front and look down the barrel and mind that recoil."

He tried again, this time hitting the cairn near the top.

"Better. Steady the gun. Let off two rounds."

He hit the cairn and the wood.

"Good. Put it away."

He made the gun safe, put in the holster and shook his arms. "My hands hurt. Was that okay?" He pulled out the cotton wool and sniffed. "Is that smell the gunpowder?"

"It is. Good for a first go. Let's move back and try again."

They practiced from twenty yards and he got the idea of how to hold the gun steady and shoot reasonably well. Edith gave him handful after handful of bullets that he loaded and fired, occasionally resting to let the barrel cool.

"You done well. We'll make a soldier of you yet."

"Thanks. My arms ache." He shook them again to reduce the tension. "I don't really want to be a soldier."

"Nor me, but I am because I don't want our country overrun."

"I see that. I 'ope you finish it before I'm old enough."

"Well said lad."

They walked back to the picnic area in silence.

Mary pulled Peter to one side. "What are they doing with Billy? I don't like guns."

"I don't either. Didn't like them in my service training, but it'll give him more confidence." He put his arm around her shoulders and squeezed. "Let's hope his bracelet helps end the war sooner."

"What was all that with the guards and the shooting?" Peter had sat next to Symes on the return journey.

"I thought it would be good for him to learn some new skills. Edith has been teaching him fieldcraft and simple covert techniques when they go to Richmond Park. Hope you don't mind."

"Do I really have a choice?"

Symes shook his head. "He doesn't have his mates to play with and from what he's said, they play around the bomb sites. He's used to dangerous places. So Edith's taken on being a friend to play with, but the game's a serious one. If we don't win this war, we'll need capable people to help subvert the occupying forces. You know what I mean?"

"Saboteurs?"

"And intelligence gathering. All that kind of thing. He's a good head on him and shows great promise in covert training. It won't do him any harm and may do him some good."

"And for you. A ready-made member of your bunch."

"If we're overrun, I'll be among the first rounded up, tortured and shot. They might miss out on youngsters like him, kids who'll be used to thinking for themselves, then acting."

"Like that old man in the woods near the hop farm?"

"Yes. They're already in place, but they'll be rooted out fairly quickly, in a matter of weeks, or at best, a few months, so we need the next generation of defence."

"The likes of Billy will be too young for that."

"This war can't last more than another six years. We'll be spent by then and the Americans will have given us up as a lost cause, at least until it suits them. Remember, they've enough of their own problems in the Pacific. The Japanese are tough and in it for the long term. He's a bit young now, but he'll be eighteen by then, at his peak of strength and cunning as hell, I should think."

Peter stared out of the window for a few minutes. "You've already begun this program, haven't you?"

"Can't say, but Billy and his bracelet could be an asset."

"If we can get some sense out of it."

"Try harder. Our nation may depend on it. I need you to do your best to encourage him. I'm sure the bracelet will be useful anyway, but it might be vital to our survival as a nation."

"I'll try."

"By the way, Billy was talking to Edith about joining the Boy Scouts. It would be good for him, a great organisation, but don't let him. Hitler will usurp that kind of group for his own ends, none of them particularly nice. It would be best if he was not on any membership list, of any organisation."

"Does that include the church?"

"Really, yes. Not an active member anyhow."

"Okay. I'll speak to you tomorrow when I've thought about it."

"Good man."

Peter moved to the seat next to his son who was fast asleep, head against the cold window. The boy felt the nearness of his father, turned over and rested his head on his father's chest. Peter put his arm around him, smoothed his untidy hair and prayed that all this would go away.

5

Latchmere House, Ham, Monday, March 15th 1943

First thing Monday morning, Symes addressed the team.

"We are not having much success. I know you've all discussed why this might be, but we'll go over it again. My masters are worried we are spending time and money on a sham. I know that's not true, but I've got to convince them."

"I just ain't gettin' any dreams Mr Symes. I don't know why," said Billy.

Frank chipped in. "The only thing we haven't covered is that this setup is too artificial. He may need to be in a different environment."

"Some of his most vivid dreams have been away from home and under stress," said Janet, leafing through her notes. "We come back to this, I'm sorry. Stress is often a trigger for extreme abilities."

Frank caught Symes' eye. "I can create stress with a drug. No pain and no side effects."

Peter looked at his son, who was staring at the young doctor. "Just how safe?"

"I've used it on people for training purposes. To see how they perform under stress."

"I've heard of this, but never used it," said Symes.

"Adults?" asked Peter looking at Frank.

"Yes. Of course, I'd start with a low dose for Billy."

"Were these military and under orders?" said Peter.

"Yes. I can see your concern," said the doctor.

"Good. How many side effects for this drug?"

"Only one small one. Feeling of nausea and headache."

"That's two. How about it Billy? Do you want to feel sick and have a headache?" asked Peter, turning to his son.

"No. But if it helps and don't last long, I'll try it."

"Spoken like a true hero," said Symes, before Peter could argue, "When can you be ready, Frank?"

"After lunch. I have to get the drug made up fresh from a pharmacist."

"Good. Are the rest of you ready?" They all said they were.

Frank went to a chemist shop in Richmond and got the drug. He had some trouble with the pharmacist because he was not a local doctor, but a phone call to Latchmere House and Frank's ID card resolved the problem.

Billy's old camp bed was replaced with a comfortable version. He had had a small lunch in case the nausea actually made him sick.

By mid-afternoon, all was ready for the first trial. He put the bracelet onto his arm and lay down on the bed. Peter held his son's hand, giving it a squeeze of reassurance.

Frank prepared the syringe, checking his notes for the dose. He wiped the crook of Billy's arm with alcohol and injected the drug into a vein. "It should take about five minutes," he said, cleaning the syringe needle.

Peter and Greg watched the oscilloscope for signals.

Symes looked at Frank as he was reading his notes and making a calculation. Their gazes locked. "How long before you can up the dose?" said Symes.

"I have to leave it for an hour to disperse, and then I can try again," said Frank. He checked Billy's heartbeat with his stethoscope. "That's okay."

"How you feeling?" asked his Dad.

"Okay. Not sick yet."

"Good boy." Dad let go of his son's hand and joined Greg, watching for results.

"Nothing yet," said Greg.

Frank checked Billy's heart beat again.

Symes looked at the worried look on Janet's face. He picked up her notebook and wrote a word in the margin. Janet smiled and relaxed.

"Look," said Greg. He pointed to the oscilloscope screen.

Dad adjusted the gain control. “Yes. What can you hear, Billy?”

“Like sea on the stones at Brighton. Comin’ and goin’.”

“Concentrate hard,” said Greg. He read the settings of the scope and the signal values. Janet made a note of them as well as the time of day.

Billy pushed himself up and began retching.

Frank put an enamelled bowl under his chin. “You’ll be okay,” he said.

Billy coughed, but wasn’t sick. He waved the bowl away and lay back.

Greg read more values from the screen. They were larger than the previous set.

“I can hear singing. It’s them monks. It’s beautiful.” He closed his eyes.

“Let him listen,” said Peter. Greg whispered the latest values. Janet wrote them in the notebook.

Billy tossed and turned on the camp bed. The noises in his mind seemed all the stronger for the long absence.

The monks’ chant echoed in the bare wooden building where they gathered for the first Mass of the day. As each verse ended, he heard the final word reverberate from the high rafters, the occasional flutter of a dove, sheltering in the new abbey. The aroma of freshly sawn timber was all round him. Trying hard, he could just smell the tang of a sea breeze. The monks sang again. He loved this music, sung from the heart regardless of the ability of each singer. When the final stanza ended, the company of men held their collective breath as if listening for the heavenly applause, which would surely come. The applause came in the form of a dove flapping its wings as it landed to peck at fallen crumbs from yesterday’s meal. The Abbott gave the benediction and the monks filed out into the grey morning to pursue their duties.

Billy snapped awake and sat up. Five pairs of eyes were

staring at him.

"What?" he said.

"Did you dream of the monks again?" asked Dad.

"Yeah. I was really there. I could hear and smell and see. It was smashin' it really was."

"Well done, lad," said Symes. "Tell us about it. Don't miss out any detail, everything you can remember." He motioned for a glass of water.

Billy drank and told them all he had experienced.

"Are the dreams of the monks the ones you see the best?" asked Janet.

"They're all about the same, except that one with Father Michael. I couldn't understand that. What I told you about that was what I can put into words. I had loads of feelings with that one, both bad and good. I suppose the monks are clearer, but they was the first ones I saw. Perhaps the others will be better."

"Let's hope so," said Symes. "I'm particularly interested in that dream with the man who escaped from the boat. Well done again. I think we've begun a new phase. Let's start again in the morning." As they went out of the laboratory, Symes patted Frank's back and spoke loudly so the others could hear. "Good work with that drug, Frank. We'll try it again tomorrow."

"Okay. Perhaps I'll try a slightly stronger dose. How do you feel, Billy?"

"No headache and I'm hungry."

The others laughed.

Progress was steady over the next four weeks. Billy heard the monks many times, but could not actually speak with the one with the bracelet. The girl, Gail, was easier to listen to and they exchanged a few words, but it was not like having a proper conversation.

6

Latchmere House & Kent, Monday, April 12th 1943

"The past month has seen some progress, but we need more. Greg has some new equipment, which arrived last night. Greg?" Symes handed over to the electronics expert.

"This kit will put all the signals we get from the wire loop on the bracelet into this loudspeaker." Greg tapped the top of a small box on the table. "I've no idea how it will sound and it might be gibberish, but it might have some effect on what he dreams. Billy, if you concentrate on the loudspeaker sounds, it might help you to focus on the events in your dream and remember them better. You might even be able to move around in your dream and control what's happening. It will take lots of practice, so don't worry if you can't do anything straight away. Okay?"

"Yeah. Do you mean I'll be able to change my dreams?"

"We aren't sure. The technique is called feedback. We use it in electronics to get rid of the things we don't want and improve the things we do. There's just a possibility that you might be able to do this with your dreams by listening to the signals your Dad and I are picking up. This has never been done before."

"No one's had a bracelet before, not like this," said Billy, "so it's all new, ain't it?"

"True. You're really getting the hang of this. Excellent."

Symes smiled, a rare thing. "Right. I'll leave you lot to get on with it. I have to give a progress report. I'll see you in the morning." He banged on the door and Martin let him out.

"Okay, team. Let's get to it," said Janet, who was now in charge for the day.

They tried Billy without the drug, but with the audio feedback. He tried to listen to the sounds from the speaker and those in his mind, but neither seemed to match. Try as he might, he could not change the loudspeaker noises.

In the afternoon, Frank gave Billy another injection of the drug. Janet decided the dose should be the same as the previous day's, hoping the audio feedback might improve the response. Billy stretched out on the camp bed. He began hearing the sounds within a couple of minutes, but the noises from the loudspeaker were quite different. He tried to control them for a while, straining his mind to hear both sets of sounds, but did no better than the morning session. After a while, he let his mind wander and began to see things that were more detailed and clearer. He settled back and let the dreams come.

He recognised the oast houses in the distance, he was in Kent, but it was not hopping time. The electrified fence in front of him was interrupted with high double gates, guarded by two soldiers, their Sten guns slung ready for immediate use. They had no insignia or rank on their uniforms. Billy watched as Symes drove up in a Jeep.

Major Symes spoke to one of the guards. The other guard took his papers and made a call from the phone in a weathered metal box on the fence. He brought the papers back to Symes.

"It's okay to go in sir, but the General is tied up for the next hour. He'll see you then, if that's okay."

"That'll be fine," he said putting his papers in a pocket. "And which one is the General's office?"

"Sorry sir. It's the third hut on the left. Park this side of the building with the other vehicles."

The guards unlocked one of the double gates and he drove through. It was his first time at this facility, but he was familiar with the results of their work on the photographs brought back by reconnaissance aircraft.

The hut had a single door facing the road. He parked as instructed. He saw there were four cars and another Jeep.

The windows at the side of the hut were hung with heavy net curtains. In the rear office, he could see there were people, but nothing more than that. He went in and presented his papers to a stern faced ADC, who announced his arrival on the black telephone. Symes noted the Aide's maroon beret on his desk.

"The General knows you're here, sir. Please take a seat until he calls for you." The Aide pointed to some chairs and a low table scattered with old magazines. Symes picked up one of the magazines. This was a rare luxury for him. He settled himself to wait.

After half an hour, two soldiers brought a small tea urn into the outer office. The ADC told them to put it on his desk and the number of mugs needed. One of the men got those from the trolley outside. Before leaving, they filled the mugs and put them on a tray, with a small bowl of sugar. The Aide gave one of the mugs to Symes. "I took the liberty of sugaring your tea, sir. It helps with the flavour. There'll be none left after that lot have had theirs. More tea in the urn if you want it."

"Thank you. What rank do you hold?" He could see no insignia on the ADC's uniform.

"Back at base, I'm a sergeant, sir. On secondment here for the time being."

"Parachute Regiment?"

"Can't say, sir."

"Well done, sergeant. Keep up the good work." The soldier nodded and took the tray of mugs into the General's meeting.

After another half hour, the main office door opened.

"Symes. Come in man."

He knew the General well from SIS briefings in London, but knew none of the people sat around the table. Introductions were not made, though they clearly knew who he was by now. The only things on the table were three telephones next to the General's chair. Note taking and paperwork were clearly forbidden at this meeting. He felt uncomfortable.

"Now. Tell us your story. These are all Ultra cleared." The General waved his hand at the other six.

Symes gave a short account of Billy and the bracelet and then invited questions at the end of his presentation.

"Sounds damned silly to me," said one man. Symes had him tagged as old school army. Wouldn't believe the obvious even if it hit him on his nose.

"So this boy sees visions. It's happened before. Just growing pains. It'll pass," said another man. Symes wasn't sure of him. He got no verbal clues and all of them kept very straight faces, their body language under control.

A third member spoke, a woman.

Most unusual. Middle aged, tweeds, county set, old money, intellectual.

"I'm very interested in this. How long has it been going on?"

"Since last September, mam. He found the artefact in Canterbury."

"A bit close for comfort, old man," said the General. "You were down here then about that auxiliary unit blow-up, weren't you?"

"Yes sir. I was visiting a development radar station near the hop farm and got involved with the investigation. That's when I first met Billy, but he found the artefact about a week later. I'd arranged the bus to take the hop pickers on a goodwill outing to Canterbury."

"So we can thank you for this opportunity?" said the second man.

"I suppose so, sir. Though it was only chance that I heard of the artefact this January."

"Fortuitous and fortunate," said the second man.

"Yes sir. Very."

"So what shall we do?" the General asked his visitors. There was a pause while each thought it through.

"Where are the boy and artefact secured?" the woman asked.

"Camp oh two oh, mam."

"Good. I say continue. See how far you can push him. I concur with your enthusiasm on this, Symes. It may be as much a piece of good luck as the Enigmas falling into our laps. You are sure the boy doesn't simply have an active imagination, reading too many comic books?"

"Quite sure, mam. One of his dreams referred to a private conversation I'd had with the police sergeant at the hop farm. He could never have known that."

"How do you feel about the whole thing?" asked the second man.

"Mixed. It may be an opportunity, as you say. It could be something quite dangerous. I refer to the priest who died. I expect there'll be more interesting things to discover."

"I think we are all agreed for this to continue?" The General looked around the table. There were nods from all, even the doubtful man who spoke first. Symes was relieved. It had gone well.

The black telephone rang. The General picked it up and listened to his Aide in the outer office. "Put him through. Symes, your security man. Code name Fred. On the red scrambler." He picked up the handset of the red phone and passed it to him, staring him in the eyes with a question on his face.

Symes lost the euphoria he had experienced the moment before.

7

Latchmere House & Kent, Monday, April 12th 1943

Billy woke with a start. “Symes is in danger. My dream.” His voice rose in pitch. “He’s in Kent. He’s in danger. There’s a woman spy. I’m in danger.”

Janet jumped up and banged on the door. She dragged Martin in and got Billy to repeat his dream.

“I dunno why. I know there’s a bad woman with the General.”

“How do you know about the General? Speak boy.” Martin leaned over Billy who was still on the bed.

“Hold on,” said Janet pulling Martin away. “Don’t frighten the messenger.”

“That briefing isn’t even security rated. Damn. How did you hear about it?”

“I saw him there. In my dream. Tell him there’s a spy, the woman. I’m in danger.”

“Right. I’m locking you all in while I go and make a call.” Martin strode out of the lab and locked the door. He ran up the stairs to the top floor to his radio and called the head office wireless section in Whitehall who patched him through to Symes’ boss.

“Martin here, sir. I need to contact Symes with extreme urgency, repeat, extreme urgency. He may be in danger.”

“What’s the password, Martin?”

“Ironstone, sir.”

“Okay. He’s with the General at K35. Password is hockey stick. Get the wireless section to route you through on scrambler. Good luck.”

Martin closed the connection and radioed in again. After a minute, he was speaking to the General’s ADC via a scrambler line.

“Urgent call for Symes. Hockey stick. Repeat, hockey

stick. My code name is Fred. Apologies to the General."

"Please hold. I'll put you through." The ADC picked up the black handset and gave the message to the General. He then put the call through to Symes on the scrambler phone and went into the General's office.

"Symes? Code name Martin. Status red. Ironstone declares problem with woman at General's briefing. Has seen danger to you and Ironstone. Proceed with caution."

Symes looked around the room as though the conversation was unimportant. He idly looked at each member of the meeting while spouting plausible gibberish into the phone, not allowing his eyes to rest on any of them longer than any other. He looked over at the General, pulled a face and shrugged indicating this was a less than urgent call. He checked his watch.

"So, Fred. I'll be back tonight instead of the morning. That will suffice. Please meet me at Waterloo. I'll be on the twenty twenty, heaven knows which platform." He replaced the handset. "I apologise for that, sir. Not such an urgent call after all." He sat.

"Glad to hear it, best to be sure though. Now, are there any more questions? Okay. Session closed. You'll get a copy of the minutes and actions in a couple of days, suitably doctored, all except you Symes. Naturally, you won't be included. Any more questions on this work, please direct to me. Use the code book."

The visitors rose from the table and passed a few comments to one another. The ADC collected their mugs and the empty sugar bowl as they left.

Symes wove a path to the woman analysing her as he approached. "Thank you for your support this afternoon."

"It sounds like an interesting project. Any idea of the artefact's origin?"

"The designs on it are similar to Celtic, but it may be older. I've met the scholar who was researching it before he lost it." He told her a little more of Billy's story, missing out names and places. "So we have no firm idea, except that it's thousands of years old."

"I'd like to get involved with your project," she said. "I hear you investigated an accident with a priest where Billy lives. I'd hate him to suffer the same."

"That was all dealt with at the time. Somehow, Billy knows the bracelet can't hurt him. Be assured we keep a very close eye on his welfare."

"Of course, but if you need any assistance, do get in touch."

"What's your background? I'd need to make a case to my masters."

"Of course. Classics at Oxford, then languages. I'm very good at piecing things together, puzzles and conundrums. In any case, your masters will know of me."

"Do you have a codename, or is this meeting sufficient?"

"This meeting is enough. I'd have thought you'd have a codename."

"I have several. Symes is one of them."

"Ah. Of course, how natural. Didn't I see you arrive by Jeep about an hour ago? I thought you told your man, Fred, you'd be on the train. If not, I can offer you a lift in my car. I'm going back to London. Or even to the local station if you wish."

"I borrowed the Jeep from a facility near Ashford station, so I'm okay thanks. Till we meet again." He gave a little bow and turned away. He went through to the outer office and sat, waiting. When all the visitors had gone, the ADC spoke to him: "Sir, I've been ordered to take you directly to Latchmere. I've a driver to take your Jeep back to Ashford. Do you have the paperwork?"

Symes pulled a document from his coat pocket. "I was going to ask you for transport. Where did your orders come from?"

"When I collected the tea things, there was a scrap of paper in one of them. It was the woman's mug, traces of lipstick. Note taking was forbidden, so I was alerted. The note simply said to get you away safely."

"Can I see the note?" The ADC passed over a damp piece of a manila envelope. "She offered me a lift to the station or London. Would that be in character for her?"

"I don't know any of the people that well sir, but it would support her concern for your safety."

"I'd like to check this with the General," said Symes as he turned to the inner office.

"Just a moment sir. I'll phone first, he'll have documents on his desk by now." The ADC picked up the handset and spoke to the General, who shortly opened the door.

"Symes. I've no idea what's going on. The woman is from Six. Runs an agent network in France from a base in Portugal. I've no reason to disbelieve her concerns. Very reliable sort. I do wish she'd told me, but the room was full which might have been a problem. The Sergeant will take you to Richmond, with a guard, so you should be safe. Happy hunting."

8

Latchmere House, Monday, April 12th 1943

Symes got to Latchmere House just after 8p.m. He called the team together, with the exception of Billy, who was asleep in the Church Street house after the day's excitement. Martin was absent. Norman was on guard duty.

"Well done team." He took off his coat and hung it up. "I didn't identify the problem with the woman, but she's uncommonly interested in our project, to the point of wanting to join it. Martin is checking her out with head office. One thing I want to establish is the exact timing of today's events. What do your records show, Janet?"

Janet opened her notebook for the day and flipped the pages. "We began this particular experiment at fourteen-twenty. We used the same dose as yesterday. It took until fifteen-fifteen before we got significant signals and Billy reported only noise, no real visions. He fell asleep at fifteen-eighteen and we began getting lots of signal activity. Billy woke at sixteen-oh-two in a very disturbed state. We have a wire recording of his voice if you want to hear that." Symes told her to continue. "We called for Martin, and then Billy repeated his warning about the woman spy. Martin radioed the boss. He said that was at sixteen-oh-seven and finally got through to you at sixteen-fifteen."

Symes thought for a moment. "We have an anomaly with the times of day. Billy woke at sixteen-oh-two. I was talking to the meeting then. He dreamed about the meeting while I was there. This hasn't happened before. We must go over these timings, it may be, Billy had dreamt about it before it happened." The others stared at Symes.

"That's not possible," said Janet.

"We don't know a great deal about dreams," said Frank. "There is evidence that they happen in real time, but some seem to happen in compressed time."

Symes spoke: "As I say, we must analyse the data much more carefully. Remember one thing. These are not normal dreams. They are visions caused by or helped by the bracelet. The things it does to Billy and did to Father Michael, verge either on foreign expertise or magic." Cries of derision and disbelief bounced between the other four. "Okay. That's focussed your minds. Come up with a more likely solution. Re-enact the afternoon, second by second. Play your recordings, read your notes, try to remember everything that happened. Analyse it to pieces. I need provable answers."

The door unlocked and Martin stepped in. He locked the door behind him and turned to the team. His face was grey and lined.

"What's happened, Martin?" said Symes.

"The Jeep you borrowed from Ashford was booby trapped. It blew up shortly after one of the soldiers began his journey back to Ashford. The place is in chaos down there. Your boss will arrive in two hours to debrief you. I've booked a secure room. He says he's not cleared for in here. That was a close call, sir."

Symes closed his mouth and swallowed hard. "How was it booby trapped?"

"They found a crude delay timer in the wreckage. The likely scenario is that it was set sometime around fifteen hundred with a delay of two hours. On your original schedule, you'd have been near to Ashford by then."

"How did they manage that in a well-guarded camp? Any ideas?"

"A mechanic was seen working under the bonnet and under the Jeep. When challenged he said he was checking it over after a reported banging noise on rough roads. They can't find the mechanic. A bold job, sir."

"Yes. I'd like your detailed thoughts on that later."

"Yes sir." Martin let himself out and locked the door. He relieved Norman as guard.

"Peter, please can you get Billy. I want to question him about his dreams and I know my boss will too. I don't have much time."

Peter knocked to be let out.

"What shall we do," said Janet.

"Start analysing the timing of everything that happened. Greg, when Billy gets here, I want a wire record of what he says. Have you got enough spools?"

"Yeah, plenty. I can work the machine and Peter can help." He went into the listening room.

"Janet, you take notes in here with Billy and me. Also, when the boss arrives, but he might have other ideas. Can you get one of the listeners to record what happens in the room Martin has organised?"

"Will do," she said and banged on the door to get out.

"Cuppa?" said Frank. There were only the two of them in the lab.

"Yes. That would be good." Symes sat and closed his eyes for a few moments. "What's your take on all this, Frank?"

"First, we need to encourage Billy to dream on his own. At the moment, our drug is having the desired effect, without it he can't dream. I'm happy to keep injecting him, but, as you know, it is just saline solution, a placebo. We'll have to find a way to drop it."

"True. Think how that can be done convincingly. What about the timing issue?"

"I'm no physicist, but seeing as the future is the realm of fortune tellers and charlatans…"

"Physicist. Brilliant idea, Frank. I'll see if I can get one. I think we've gone as far as we can for now with electronics. We need some theoretical input to push it along."

The door opened and Billy came in with Peter.

"Billy." Symes stood up and shook Billy's hand. "You saved my life today, young man. I am exceedingly grateful. I'm sorry to wake you up, but we need to go over a few things about your dream."

"Okay Mr Symes," said Billy, stifling a yawn. Peter sat with him.

Frank made tea for all of them and handed out the mugs. He banged on the door for Martin to take his drink.

Janet returned. "It's all set up for the secure room." She collected a mug of tea and sat by her notebook.

Symes nodded and turned to Peter. "Can you help Greg with the recorders?"

Peter took his tea and joined Greg.

"Billy. I want you to tell me all that you saw in your dream. Don't miss out any detail, even if you think it is unimportant. Okay?" Billy nodded and thought for a moment and then he started the re-telling. He had done this earlier, while they waited for Symes to return, but he had remembered a few things he could add.

Billy was about halfway through the events when there were loud voices outside the laboratory.

Symes held up his hand to stop Billy and spoke quietly and directly at one of the hidden microphones. "Greg, Peter. Lock yourselves in and keep quiet. Keep recording."

"Open the door. Let me in."

Symes knew it was his Section Head.

"I don't recognise you, sir. Please give the password." Martin had raised his voice so Symes could hear.

"Don't give me that. We spoke earlier and how the hell would I know where they are? Open the door, man."

"Password?"

Symes heard the clicks of Martin's automatic as he primed it. He shouted through the door. "That's okay, Martin. Let him in."

"He told me earlier he was not cleared for the lab, sir," said Martin, "I've never met this man."

"Symes. Call off your guard dog."

Symes banged on the door. "Martin. Unlock the door for

me, but don't let him in."

Martin, covered the man with his gun, unlocked the door and let it swing open. Symes blocked the doorway to hide Billy. His Section Head was pacing the stairwell, a black look on his face.

"Symes. What the hell do you think you're doing?"

"Being more careful than the last time I spoke to you. You sent me to the General's briefing. I wondered at the time, why you did that. Who else knew about it?"

"Let's talk privately. I know you have a room put by, probably with listeners. Somewhere else would be better for both of us, preferably off site. The Church Street house will be ideal."

"Perhaps I'll choose," said Symes, "after all, you may have that place wired."

"Touché. Where?"

"Walking the street. Martin and your men can keep an eye on us."

"Okay." The Section Head turned and started up the stairs. Symes motioned to Janet for Billy to start dreaming. He got his overcoat and followed his boss. Martin locked the door and followed the others.

Outside, two men were waiting. Symes recognised them. He knew their capabilities and was glad of Martin's presence. The Section Head gave some instructions and his pair took up positions at the very front and rear of the procession. Symes was reassured by Martin's tuneless whistling behind him as the group walked single file in the darkness, using torches. When the pavement widened, Symes drew alongside his boss.

"So what's all the fuss?" he said.

"The fuss is that someone has got wind of Ironstone and wants you out. Damn near did it, too." The Section Head stopped walking and faced Symes. "That woman at the meeting is kosher. She's from six."

Symes could not read his boss's face in the blackout.

"Can she be trusted? Ironstone sees her as a spy, but then, she is."

"True, but he was still worried about her. Why?"

"We've a lot of analysis to do yet, as well as discussion with Ironstone. By the way, why didn't you give the password when you arrived?"

"Testing your defences. This project is very important, you know that. Martin isn't enough, good though he is."

"He isn't alone, or didn't you know that?"

"Oh. You have another man. So we're even if it comes to a fight"

"I doubt it. You've no idea who or what I have out here. Why should it matter? I hope we're on the same side."

"You visited our renegade, Father Alan Smith."

"That was months ago. Your sources are rather slow. It was he who alerted me to the bracelet. It's his diligence and loyalty that we know about it. His main fault is that he has a conscience, couldn't take all the deceit in our service."

"So he joined the Vatican crowd. Sounds like frying pan and fire to me. But you've been keeping him on a string for some time."

"Because of his religious connections. The Irish question in the twenties and now, as a possible source of information via Italy. That's paid off."

"It's late. Let's get back to Ironstone and the rest of your team."

"Good." Symes raised his voice: "Norman. You can follow us in."

Norman came out from the line of trees and made his weapon safe. "Yes sir."

The Section Head looked at Symes. "Nice work. Is he the only one?"

"Do you think I've got a whole army out here?"

"With what you're spending, I wouldn't put it past you."

9

Latchmere House, Monday, April 12th 1943

Martin unlocked the lab door. Janet looked up from Billy's bedside, quickly pulling the blanket over the bracelet. "About time. He needs to rest," she said to Symes, who was first through the door.

"Sorry Janet. How is he?"

"He fell asleep just after you left. He must have had a bad dream. He's been tossing and turning since then." She saw the Section Head follow Symes into the lab, taking off his hat and overcoat then straightening his suit jacket. She gave him a curt nod of recognition.

The rest of the team filed in from the listening room.

The Section Head went to the camp bed and stood over Billy. "So this is the little fellow all the fuss is about?" Billy's eyes flickered and he tried to sit up. Janet helped him but failed to keep the bracelet covered. "And this is the bracelet." The Section Head leaned forward to touch it.

"Git yer 'ands off, mister. I like Father Alan. He ain't no spy like what you said."

The room went silent. The Section Head snatched his hand away and straightened. He looked at Symes, who shrugged.

"Tell us what you saw, Billy," said Janet, holding his hand.

"I saw them." He pointed out Symes and his boss. "They was talking. The man in the suit said Father Alan was a renegade. I dunno what that means, but it don't sound nice." Dad sat on the floor by his son and put his arm around him.

"Who told you about our conversation?" asked the Section Head.

"No one, how could they? I saw it in my dream. You was walking outside 'ere and our guards were tailing you."

"What guards were they?"

"Edith and Norman, but you didn't see 'em. They was in the woods, but you'd never see Edith, not till you were about to die."

"Symes? Was he primed with this?"

"No. This is how it is. He sees things in his dreams when he wears the bracelet and before you ask, there was another of my operatives out there. He can't control what he sees." Symes shot a warning glance at Janet.

"Quite an asset. Is he likely to control it?"

"We're working on it, but we're at the stage of collecting data for analysis. Early days."

"Early days it may be, but the top brass are interested in this as a part of Ultra."

"We are making progress. Goose and golden egg."

"Okay. I've seen enough for now. Unbelievable, but then, so was Ultra in the first stages. Who's the Edith operative?"

"S.O.E."

"That Edith. I see what you meant about not being an even fight. Formidable. I'm still puzzling over what happened at your briefing with the General. Something's going on down there. I've got a team on it and so have Six. I'll catch up with you in a couple of days." He picked up his coat and hat.

Symes banged on the door and Martin let the Section Head out.

"What was all that about?" said Janet.

"I think the boss thought I was double dealing. Father Alan was a problem in the early twenties and was encouraged to leave the service. I still keep in touch and he has been useful, but with this trouble in Kent today, the boss is worried I might be a problem too. And I still don't know why he sent me. I know the General from other meetings, but none of the others. Some of them were interested, some disbelieving, but why was I sent?"

"Some kind of review group?" said Janet. "We used them in my previous post."

"Maybe."

Billy rubbed his eyes. "That woman is a spy. Honest, Mr Symes," he said.

"That is true. She works for the government as we do."

"No. I mean a real spy, for the Nazis or someone. When you was reading those magazines in the office, waitin' to go in." Symes gestured for him to continue. "She put a note in her mug."

"You haven't said this before," said Symes.

"I ain't got to that bit yet with me tellin' before your boss arrived."

"Anyway, they didn't have paper in there. No notes could be taken."

"I just saw 'er stick a bit of paper in her mug. I thought it might be a note to someone."

"What did the note look like?"

"It was brown and small. Sort of torn from something."

"Brown because it was in the tea?"

"No. Before she put it in. I didn't see what was on it."

"Was this it?" Symes held up the note.

"Yeah," said Billy. A murmur went around the team. Symes handed the note to Janet.

"She's still a spy for someone else. And I saw other things an' all," said Billy.

"I'll check. What were these other things? Are you sure you are up to this, it's very late?"

"Yeah, you're all up, so why not me?"

"Good lad," said Dad. "Tell us what you saw."

"Well, when you was all coming back here, I got another dream with Gail in it. You remember that girl?" The others nodded. "It was only short. She said we needed to talk for a long time. She said she has fings she wants to know and can tell me fings what might be useful. She knows I'm in a bad war in the twentieth century. She's in the twenty eighth century. That's in the future, init dad?"

Dad didn't answer; all the others were quiet.

“Dad?”

“Yes, that’s in the future, about eight hundred years.”

“What, like Buck Rogers?”

“Maybe. What else did she say?”

“She wants to know some map stuff. They had a big war and lots of things got lost. She wants to know where places are in our time and she can tell us what they know about our time. Somefing about the continents moving has made places move. I don’t understand.” Billy rubbed his eyes and looked at the rest of the team. They were looking at him. “What’ve I said?” He didn’t like the way they stared. “Honest. It’s what she said. I ain’t makin’ it up.”

“No, I’m sure you’re not,” said Symes. “It’s rather difficult for us to understand that you are talking to someone in our future. Buck Rogers was a comic book. Do you understand that? Only a story.”

“Yeah. I know the difference. But my bracelet dreams are real. Not like ordinary dreams”

“We are sure your dreams are real,” said Frank. “Because we’ve been checking. So we have to believe that this girl exists in our future. The implications are enormous.” Frank looked at the others.

“Staggering,” said Greg.

“We do need someone to explain this,” said Symes. “You’ve surprised us once again, Billy. Let’s sleep on this. I’ve had a long day and so have you.”

10

Latchmere House, Tuesday, April 13th 1943

"How long will this go on for?" Mary was upset about Billy's late night.

"As long as it needs to," said Peter. "It's important to the war effort. I can't say much, you know that." He helped himself to a second slice of toast.

"It's all very well for you, but he's tired out and I don't have much to do or anywhere to go. At least in Lewisham I could help at our church. We're in the middle of nowhere here." Mary pushed the butter dish across the table, remembering that they would have little back at home.

"I'm sorry love. This is a secure place for Billy, but I know it's no fun for you." He took a mouthful of marmaladed toast and hummed in appreciation. "What about the church in Ham, can you join in there?" He picked up crumbs with a wet finger.

"No. I don't like it there. Sheila and I are outsiders, ever since I said you worked at the House. They think it's a bad place and all the people in it are bad as well."

"They may have a point. Would it help if I went along with you next Sunday?"

"It might, but you're working seven days a week on this."

"Symes would let us off for one morning a week if it meant you'd be happier. I'll make sure of it."

"Thanks Pete. I want to do my bit in the church and the local village. They've got all sorts of things organised helping the war effort."

"Great. I'll have a word with Symes today." Peter finished his toast, kissed Mary and collected Billy from the garden.

"Now, team. We have a new aspect of the bracelet to work on. Last night, Billy had some dreams without the injection.

It means he's beginning to understand and control what happens with the bracelet. We also have a contact with a girl in the future. I've no idea how this works or even why it's possible, but it's potentially a source of accurate intelligence. I can't really believe it and I'm sure head office won't, without some sort of proof, so we must test it."

There were murmurs of assent around the team and a few suggestions.

He cut them short. "Write down questions we can ask and answers we can verify in, say, one month from now. Also, questions to which we already know the answers, but would be known to very few people today, but would be better known in eight hundred years. This assumes the information has not been lost during their 'big war'. We're talking classified things here, so be careful of the subject matter. We then have to teach these to Billy so he can frame them for Gail in simple language. Janet has done languages, have any of you others done languages during your educations?"

Greg and Frank said they had.

"Good."

"I know bits of Latin," said Billy.

"Of course you do. We may be able to use that. If Latin is still in use in this girl's time, it may not have changed much." Symes thought for a moment. "When you were talking to the Monsignor, did you say anything about speaking to Gail?"

"I said about talking to a girl but I didn't know her name then or she's in the future. I first 'eard her name when I was hiding in the park at home."

"Good. Hearing from the past is fascinating, but the future is quite extraordinary." Symes shook his head in disbelief. "Janet, will you coordinate all the questions? Here are mine." He handed her a sheet of paper. "I've been up half the night trying to figure this out."

"I think the rest of us have as well," said Janet, taking the paper.

"I just slept," said Billy. The others laughed.

"I think we're making progress. Well done lad."

He smiled at Symes. He felt happier with him now, much more than when he first met him on the hop farm and wondered why this was.

The team discussed and argued for several days about the content of their questions. Meanwhile, Billy practiced dreaming without the injection. He got much better at controlling to whom he was listening. Talking was much more difficult because the other person had to be willing, but he managed another short conversation with Gail. Both of them struggled, apart from it being a strange thing to do, their versions of English were very different.

Symes had several meetings with his Section Head, setting out the strategy for verifying the truth of the contact. The Head suggested real questions and fictitious ones and gave him some of both to consider. He did not tell Symes, which were which, or the answers he was expecting. Symes could guess some of them, but others were a mystery to him.

Eventually, the team put together a set of questions and worded them in the simplest form they could. One of Billy's problems was that he had to be 'asleep' to get the best connection with Gail. If he were awake, the distractions around him would interrupt the conversation. The problem was reduced, as Gail got better at understanding what he was saying and when she learned to speak his version of English more fluently.

Palm Sunday, April 18th 1943

The Carter family walked to the Catholic church in Ham. Billy liked the walk beside the woods. He kept a lookout for Edith who always tailed them. They had their own signals that they practised. It was more difficult when they got to

Ham. The trees gave way to the houses, but she merged into the village background, wearing her FANY uniform.

When they got to the church, Peter saw the problem that Mary had, so chatted to as many people as he could before the service. He had to be sympathetic with many of the women whose husbands were away fighting. It was no different where he worked in Lewisham. A mixture of empathy and hints of danger in his job associated with Latchmere House were all that were needed.

The Palm Sunday service was a great inspiration to the Carters. Though a small church, the community had arranged a sung Mass, something they had not done since the beginning of the war. The regular priest had been unwell, so a young priest from Southwark Cathedral had helped by taking services and had built up a choir during Lent.

Billy stood listening to a dramatized version of the long Palm Sunday Gospel. The words were spoken by members of the congregation and, for the first time, he understood the enormity of the biblical events of nearly two millennia before. He remembered the death of Father Michael and thought a little prayer for him. He felt dizzy. He had not eaten that morning, so he sat down on the pew. Dad put a reassuring hand on his shoulder.

The Carters stayed for refreshments after the service. Some lemonade and a thin slice of cake soon restored Billy.

A mother and her daughter, who was about Sheila's age, came over to the Carters and invited them to a picnic the church was having after the Easter Sunday service. It would be on the Ham Common, or in the church if raining. There would be games for the children but they had to take their own picnic.

"We love picnics don't we kids?" said Dad.

"Yeah," they said, thinking of the food.

"All arranged."

Mary took his hand and squeezed it.

11

Outside of normal space-time

“Systematic use is made of our iron,” says Gamma.

“Repetitive energy pulses indicate experimental work designed to test its capabilities,” says Alpha.

“This is the spiral arm Carbonforms,” says Beta.

“They are an inquisitive life form,” says Gamma.

“As are most of the Carbonforms with their helical molecules,” says Alpha.

“We must watch them closely,” says Beta.

“These are simple experiments, but you are correct,” says Gamma.

12

Chislehurst, Tuesday, October 31st 2795

Within two weeks, some of the Chislehurst tunnels were transformed into a habitable workspace. The original entrance was repaired with a reinforced roof. The walls had been sprayed with a polymer giving insulation and waterproofing. The tunnels were brightly lit and rest-room facilities installed.

Industrial plumbing, tanks and crates of control equipment were delivered and stored in unused tunnels away from prying eyes. Their function, to give credence to the cover story of the revolutionary hydroponics experiments that had been mentioned in local news broadcasts. The equipment needed for the bracelet experiments fitted into a few shoulder bags.

The whole area, below and above ground, was under continuous surveillance. Chislehurst Island became a virtual fortress. Every person and vehicle, visiting or passing through, was monitored and registered with more detail than usual. A dedicated SI unit continuously analysed all this data for behavioural patterns that might indicate spying.

Gail and Victor met during their recreation periods, but were watched by the project's security people. "I've got the whole weekend off," he said. "Want to have a trip out somewhere?"

"I've only got Sunday free. I'm behind with my history course. Let's get off the Island. Where?" she said, slipping her hand into his while they walked around the perimeter path during a meal break.

"Hadn't got that far with planning. We could buggy over to Keston, or further if you like."

"I love Keston. The woods by the beach near there will be pretty this time of year. I'll organise a lunch for us."

"I'll get the buggy and tell the Snoops," he said.

"You shouldn't call them that. They're only looking after us. You should be proud you're going out with such a precious asset."

Victor stopped, faced her and held her hands. "You see. You're using their language. I don't like it."

"I don't either, but it's now our life and it could be interesting in the long run."

"Yeah. I suppose so." He gave her a quick kiss. "See you at breakfast on Sunday. I'll go over to Westerham Heights tomorrow and catch up with my friends."

They continued their walk until they arrived at the schooling block where Victor had to leave for his afternoon tutorials. They kissed again before separating. Gail continued to the tunnels' entrance. She exchanged glances with the security guard who had been following, then entered. The outer door opened automatically as she approached, then closed behind her.

The familiar smell of cool, damp mould came to her, just like all the tunnels when she had been younger. The inner door did not open immediately. She imagined the sensors scanning her for a million different parameters. When the door opened, fresher air greeted her as she hurried to the laboratory where she spent half her waking hours with Hella and Marina, their technician.

"Hi Gail. Feeling good today," said Hella.

"You asking or telling?"

"Telling. You're happier."

"You should know. You see into my mind almost as often as I do." She slumped into a chair.

"You know it's how I am. I was born this way. I use what I have, as you should."

"I do try, but it doesn't always work. I wasn't born with it."

"But it can be learnt. And I know you can do it."

"Only with the bracelet."

"That makes it easier. The exercises increase your natural

Psy ability. I know that's small right now, but it can be improved. Then the bracelet multiplies that up. I know you understand. Why are you being so difficult?"

"It's hard. Really tough. And I don't know where all this is leading."

"Neither do we, but these bracelets might be stunning new communications devices. We don't yet know where they came from or why they have such properties. The science crew will work that out. We have to discover how to use them. Agreed?"

"Spose so. It's still hard though. Makes my head hurt."

"I know, but that'll improve as you get better at it. Shall we start?"

Marina picked up the helmet and positioned it on Gail's head. After tightening the straps, she plugged it into the SI and checked its operation. "Please shut your eyes." She made some adjustments. "Now open." She checked the results. "All set." She left the laboratory.

"I've a new series of tests today," said Hella, from the other side of the lab. She was sitting at the SI terminal, well away from Gail so there would be no interference from her own brain. "I want you to think of something really lovely, wonderful, magical. A place you've visited, someone you like or love, something you've done. Then concentrate on it as hard as you can. Okay?"

"Anything at all?"

"Yes. Something which made you think 'Wow'."

She thought for a moment. "Here goes."

Hella stared at the SI display until she had enough data. "OK. Stop now."

Gail relaxed.

"That was much better than previous exercises."

"Do you want to know what I was thinking about?"

"Not really. It's just the emotion I'm after. Now for the next one. This time something really bad, horrid, traumatic."

Gail thought for a moment. "Ready." They went through

the same procedure.

"Stop. That's good. Now we can try with each of the bracelets." Hella put her hand on the security pad to open the wall safe. She reached for both bracelets. "Ouch." She dropped them, still in the safe. "That was hot. Your first bracelet was hot."

Gail unplugged her helmet. "Let me see." She picked up her original bracelet, moving it from hand to hand while it cooled. "Do you think it was picking up my thoughts?"

"Probably. You've hardly worn the second one, so perhaps that's not responding as much. Oh well, another parameter to consider. SI. Note this episode." The computer confirmed.

"If it gets that hot, it'll burn me. No way I want that."

"We'll have to make a test. It may not get as hot if it's on your arm. SI. Note that." The machine confirmed.

"It's cooled enough now." She slipped the bangle onto her arm.

"Okay. Plug yourself in. We'll do the nice thought first." Hella put the second bracelet back into the safe and locked it.

"Ready," she said.

"Okay." Hella watched the display for a moment. "Stop. Okay for the bad thought?"

"Ready."

"If it gets hot, think the nice thought. Go."

An incandescent flash blinded the two women. Gail screamed. The fire control system shot extinguisher gas into the room and set off the alarm siren. Fresh air purged the gas.

SI spoke. "Helmet disconnected. Interface power surge."

Marina ran into the lab and rushed to calm Gail. Fire and medic crews arrived.

"I can't see. I'm blind," cried Gail, moving her head left and right and rubbing her eyes. "Why can't I see?" She fluttered her hands in front of her face.

"What the stars caused that?" said a firecrew.
A medic dumped his bag next to her and caught her hands. "It's okay Gail, I'm here to help."

"Why can't I see?" She felt calming thoughts from Hella.

The medic examined her face and eyes. "No sign of external trauma."

"There was a flash," said Hella. "Neither of us can see. I hope it's temporary."

"Okay." The medic spoke into his comband: "Immediate rotor request. Two, flash blinded. Chislehurst complex." He turned to them. "We'll take you out when the rota arrives." He continued his examination of the two women. He put covers over Hella's eyes, asked Marina to remove Gail's helmet and then covered her eyes.

Marina was puzzled by the helmet's state. "The helmet cable's burnt through. There's a bracelet on the floor here." She picked it up.

"Mine's still on my arm," said Gail, taking it off. "Is that the second one?"

"Yes."

"It was in the safe," said Hella. "Open it and double check."

Marina put her hand on the security pad and opened the door. "It's not here. It's definitely the second one and it's splashed with copper."

"Get the forensic team. And comm Cator," said Hella.

"Rotor's nearly here. Come on ladies." The medical team guided them to the landing pad.

Cator arrived at the same time as the forensic team. They secured the lab, equipment and data and then began the process of finding cause and effect.

"Marina, please go through it all again," he said.

"I helped Gail put on the helmet then came out of the lab before the tests began, there's less interference. About five minutes later, the lab fire system went off. I was in the break room waiting to be called back."

Cator interrupted her. "The fire system. Is the lab the only place that's covered?"

"No sir. There are other chambers that have them, but they're all separate. I knew this was my lab, by the siren tone."

He indicated she should continue.

"I ran to help, the door had unlocked. It only takes ten seconds for the extinguisher gas to work. There was no fire, but Gail and Hella were blinded. The fire crew and medics arrived then."

"What happened after that?"

"When asked, I took off Gail's helmet and noticed the cable to SI was burned through. I've no idea how it happened, there's not enough power in that circuit to blow a milliamp fuse, let alone melt the cable."

"You found the second bracelet on the floor," prompted Cator.

"Yes sir, next to the other part of the burned cable and SI was complaining of a wrecked interface."

"You must have conclusions." Cator was pushing.

"Again, the power levels in the cabling to the helmet would be too low even if you tried to cut through with a knife. The wires wouldn't melt." She wrung her hands in her lap.

"Sorry. This isn't reflecting on you. It's such a peculiar event we're all struggling to understand it. Now, Hella said the second bracelet was in the safe."

"Yes sir. I opened the safe to check, but it wasn't there, but I'd already picked it up next to the cable. I checked the markings. The two bracelets are different."

"Okay. Anything else you remember?"

"Only that copper was all over the second bracelet."

"All over?"

"Well, in places around it, as though it had been dipped in paint."

"Do you have any idea where that came from?

"I expect from the melted cabling. There's nowhere else."

"Do you find that strange?"

"Of course. Don't you?" She looked down at her hands. "Sorry sir, I shouldn't speak out of turn."

"That's okay. Go and get a drink and thanks for your information. If you think of anything else, however insignificant, you let me know. Okay?"

"Yes sir."

"SI. What do you make of that," he said after Marina had gone.

"The second bracelet transferred from inside the safe and burned through the cable."

"Why?"

"No data to support that question. Conjecture. A protection scenario. Gail was under extreme stress thinking of something unhappy. Bracelet number one may have controlled bracelet number two to help. This raises difficult questions. It relates to the problem of how Gail and Victor escaped from the explosion and roof fall in the tunnel."

"Yes. A similar situation. But how did bracelet two get out of the safe without opening the door or damaging it?"

"I cannot answer that question. No conjecture."

"Hmm. One for the physicists."

"Agreed," said SI.

13

Chislehurst, Tuesday, November 7th 2795

"Gail. It's me, Victor."

"Hey. I can hear your voice," said Gail, reaching out.

Victor took her hand. "Sorry. How are you? How did this happen? Can they fix you up?"

"Temporarily blind. Don't know. They say so."

They both laughed. She had returned to the Chislehurst medicentre after a week in a Military eye clinic.

"I came as soon as I was allowed."

"They told me they had to force you away."

"Yeah. Security literally dragged me off the first time. I didn't even get close after that."

"Poor thing. I'm glad they let you in today."

"Well, it *is* your birthday. Happy birthday."

"Thank you." She squeezed his hand. "No one else seems to have remembered."

"They say no messages or visits. I'm the only exception. Can they fix you up?"

"They're doing a PicoTech repair. My retinas are fried. It should take about three months."

"What about Hella?"

"She's the same. I'm going to be bored, so I'll need lots of visits from you. We'll still continue the bracelet work, but it won't be as intense as before."

Victor squeezed her hand. "I'm glad of that. I'll see more of you. Sorry, didn't mean that."

"Silly. I'll see more of you, but only in my mind. I hope you're not going to be a disappointment when I get my sight back."

"Why should I be?"

"Well, you haven't kissed me yet. You won't catch anything."

Victor complied.

ooo

"We have some serious issues with the bracelets." Cator addressed the project team without Gail. "They've shown signs of autonomous action. Self-determined behaviour. This has caused one accident and avoided another. I've brought in some help for the physics and maths. This is Balara."

A short, slim woman stood and bowed. She wore an orange sari rather than the usual green fatigues of the project team.

"She'll be looking at the theoretical aspects of the bracelet properties. You can get to know each other later."

Balara clasped her hands. "Glad to be here. This is an exciting project."

The other team members welcomed her.

Cator continued. "This autonomous action worries me a lot. Any thoughts?" He looked around the table.

"Is there some external control of these artefacts? You know, alien life?" asked Steran.

"Nothing we've detected, but we cannot rule it out," said Cator.

"The history of the first bracelet is getting interesting." Hella was sitting next to an SI terminal that described the activities in the room via an earpiece. "The derelict building where Gail found the first one, was, among other things, a repository for articles belonging to Government Security Services. Before the floods came in 2305, they, along with many other organisations, moved their archives and treasures to various temporary stores around Britain. That building was one of them. Why it was never fully cleared afterwards, we cannot determine. There were many valuable articles still in that room. No more bracelets, though."

"What's its history before that?" asked Cator.

"There's mention of something similar in scraps of surviving records from Canterbury Cathedral which place it in the fourteenth century. From its decoration, our consensus is late Stone Age, about nine thousand years old. The people of that time didn't work much iron, so its source is still a mystery."

"And we have two in quick succession. A bit like Luna supply ships, none for ages then two turn up at once," said Steran.

Cator shot him a look to keep the discussion serious. "I do wonder if there are more and why now?"

"The historians will keep searching, but records are scant. We lost a lot during the Bad Times," said Hella.

"What do we have on the structure of the bracelets?"

"Apart from the inscriptions and slight variations in dimensions, they seem the same. They have different effects on Gail, but only a matter of degree."

"Balara, any initial thoughts from you?" said Cator.

"Nothing you might call a theory, but I find the incidents most intriguing. There's the capability of high power in those external actions, where we see only low power effects on Gail's mind. That is two modes." She held up two fingers. "I wonder how many more modes there may be. I will make recommendations for detailed tests and experiments on the material of the artefacts."

"Any sign of communication?" asked Steran.

Balara continued, "Until she can focus her mind effectively, I will not have enough data. We need to begin tests with both bracelets. Together, in concert."

"That means finding another person for the second one," said Hella.

"Would you volunteer?" asked Cator.

"I get a limited effect at the moment, but I will try."

"Do we need to consider brain implants?" said Cator.

"No," said Hella. "She's improving with the helmet sensors we have. The trauma of surgery could undo all the progress we've made. Naturally, I'm not in a rush to have implants, either."

"We need to progress before our competitors find out and make a claim to share on grounds of universal need."

"Is that possible?" said Hella.

"Under inter-planetary law it is. It may not be granted, but it will muddy the waters of cooperation between Earth states and Offworlders."

"Not a situation we want right now," said Steran. "We Offworlders are always looking for opportunities to claw back the costs incurred with the rescue of Earth from the Bad Times. It's seen as their given right to share in any new advance which will improve their lives."

"You too?" asked Hella.

"I'm only second generation. Not so indoctrinated. But they do have a point. If these bracelets give a new means of faster communication, then it will be of enormous benefit. We have to manufacture, or find some more."

14

Chislehurst, Friday, December 1st 2795

Balara loved equations. She could use SI systems for numerical solutions. If a solution existed, the machines would find it, but she preferred to seek the underlying equations. Once, she had missed an important application by letting the machine digest the numbers for her. She vowed that would never happen again. SI was all very well, but it could not think outside its own silicon and diamond universe. Full immersion into the world of the problem, expressed in glorious mathematics, was her desire, not numbers and graphs from an unfeeling machine. The equations with her name on them was her goal, like the Balara N-Body Orbital Solution she had discovered a decade before. That made her the heroine of the asteroid prospectors in their hazardous lives amongst the chaos of countless micro planets.

The bracelets posed another interesting problem for her. It took several days of heated discussion and finally, emotional blackmail, to obtain a thin sliver from one of the bracelets for X-Ray analysis. She had used the Quantum X-Ray Fine Structure facility at Dunstable on Chiltern Island, using the cover story of archaeological research. With a handful of random pieces of metal and stone, she used the QXFS machine to delve the depths of the sample's structure. Analysis of the sliver had shown the possibility of singularities within the iron crystal lattice. Singularities were noted in the high-energy physics of the twenty-first century, where they had been produced without the devastating effects of their bigger cousins, the interstellar black holes.

Balara's problem was the sheer number of singularities that each bracelet contained. The physics she knew and loved would not allow such energy density. She needed another expert against whom she could bounce her ideas.

ooo

"I need a second opinion about my initial findings. You've read my report?" Balara was meeting with Cator and Steran.

"Yes, but neither of us are cosmo-physicists. Words of half a syllable please."

"Well, half a syllable is not possible in human language. The singularity, like a black hole, encompasses a great deal of energy."

The men nodded.

"The micro black holes we can produce in the lab have a very much smaller energy."

The men agreed.

"But, you see, they still need powerful magnets to contain them. The bracelets seem to be filled with micro-black holes, which, for some reason I do not understand, are happy to sit in a crystal lattice of iron without any containment problem." She waited for the cent to drop.

"What has SI to say about this?" asked Cator.

"Not very much at all. It knows less than I do."

"Ah," said Steran.

"So I need to toss ideas around with a top theoretical physicist or cosmologist. I emphasise, top."

Cator raised his eyebrows. "We are a select and secret group, which you know. You are the best available to us."

"Only because I upset a minister and lost my academic post. A situation I am fighting, tooth and claw."

"I requested your services before all that blew up. My initial analysis showed that your expertise in energy relationships would be of great use to the project."

"So the problem I had with the minister was a put up job, eh?"

"How the stars can you think that?" said Steran.

"Obvious. I would not have relinquished my academic post, but would want this one as well. I think that was unacceptable to the minister, don't you?

Cator shook his head. "We don't know about this. I'll investigate. The project needs you to be fully engaged here, without any career worries. From what you've already found, I believe your future is assured regardless of a silly minister. They come and go, but science marches on. I'm looking to you for a solution on your own."

"Thank you for your confidence and thank you in advance for your coaxing of the ministry. I expect you will get nowhere."

"You are probably right," said Cator, "but it'll put them in their place and they'll do the same to their advisors. Things may then go more smoothly with the oversight committee."

"What extra resources, apart from another boffin, do you need?" said Steran.

"It is the passing around of ideas which will be useful. The team here with SI to help in brainstorming may be enough. Another session at the Dunstable QXFS, but with a whole bracelet, would be good. I can devise some more experiments which will broaden my knowledge."

Cator said to Steran, "Will that create a security problem? The cost is not important, but our cover story would not normally come with that level of budget. Tongues might wag, even in a high security government lab."

"It might." Steran turned to Balara. "Is there another we can use?"

"The university ones would have the same security problem. Would it be too expensive for your budget to buy or rent one?"

"If I could make a good case, but how long would it take? I guess they are made to order."

"I rented one a few years ago in Kandy when I was delving into the genetic material of plankton. It took two months to obtain and install. They are very popular in the genetics industries."

"That could be our way in. I think the hydroponics research here could do with some extra equipment," said Cator, "I'll help them make the case."

"Meanwhile?" she asked.

"Meanwhile, get on with your theorising. We need as many ideas as possible from you. As a team, we can all help with the brainstorming and you know SI is good at random idea associations. You wrote a paper on it."

"Ah, the conclusions in my undergrad thesis are very outdated compared with the current SI capabilities."

"We have some slack time while Gail and Hella get well, probably enough time to get the QXFS equipment in and operational. So, ideas for now."

"Certainly. By the way. Have you investigated the inscriptions on the bracelets?"

"Yes, but we could find no correlation as to the meanings of the symbols, other than some of them are very similar to Celtic art. Why do you ask?"

"It's just that Gail's original was inscribed with either flint or some other hard stone. Her second one was worked with steel. The grooves are quite different."

"I haven't heard about this. Have you put this in your reports?" said Steran.

"Not yet, but I will."

"Good." Steran turned to Cator. "Have you heard this from anyone else?"

"News to me. Does this mean it's much younger?"

"Possibly," said Balara. "I'll leave that with you."

Cator closed the meeting.

When Balara had gone, the two men continued the discussion.

"She's a good choice," said Steran.

"The best, regardless of cost and availability. I think the minister was premature in forcing the situation. I'm sure she would have taken our job on its own merits. I wonder if the ministry has something up its political sleeve."

15

Chislehurst, Sunday, February 18th 2796

"How's our new QXFS?" asked Cator. He was making a visit to the new, underground lab.

"Brilliant," said Balara. "The oversight committee authorised several upgrades. Your talk with the minister seems to have borne fruit."

"You could say that. He's inexperienced, but learning fast. He'll be a true asset in a few years. Have you started your series of experiments?"

"They're scheduled for tomorrow. I've requested an extra power allocation from the grid. Chislehurst is not a great power user, generates most of its own from hydrothermal. I've said we're using some high impact equipment to pressurise hydroponic molecules for a new reaction science development, so will need a high peak capacity. Hope that's okay."

"Sure. Don't forget to run these requests through the SI security program. It'll check for possible ways our competitors might smell a rat."

"I did that. We are still at a low interest level." She selected the security page on SI.

Cator studied it. "Good. What time are you firing up the Scanner?"

"Midday, when everyone is concentrating on lunch. It will take three seconds, then a week of analysis and a month of speculation."

"An expensive three seconds."

"It will be worth every cent and it won't be the only three seconds."

"Have you scheduled any of the hydroponic experiments?"

"Quite a lot. Those technologists are very enthusiastic, this is a dream come true for them. Victor is involved. He will supervise the Scanner experiments down here so it will save security clearance problems with the rest of the hydroponics team. Their power requirements are far less than ours. Vegetable matter is mostly water."

"Good. I see you have it all organised," said Cator.

"I do my best."

Hella and Steran were walking in the Chislehurst woods.

"I'm glad your eyes are responding to treatment," he said.

"You don't know how good it is, even to see your ugly face."

He tightened his hold on her hand. "What's it like when you look in the mirror in the mornings?" he said.

"No worse for me than for you."

He laughed.

Hella continued. "I've been delving into the history of Chislehurst. SI speaks the records to me. My eyes won't take much screen time. The tunnels have quite a history. And I've been reviewing the forensic data."

"I heard the tunnels go back to the Stone Age," he said.

"There is no evidence of that, but could be possible. The first use with evidence is in the thirteenth century. After that, there's a sparse trail of records. They were used a lot in the nineteenth and twentieth centuries, during war times, both by the military and the public. The interesting records for us are the tunnels' use during the Bad Times, again, as a refuge for the military and public. Those records are more detailed because we had early versions of SI then."

"What did you find?" Steran stopped at a bench and guided her to sit.

She took an eye spray from a pocket and applied it, blinking to disperse the liquid. "It was an interview with a man from Carnac. He'd jumped ship when it was overrun by pirates at Maidstone Dock. There's a reference to a bracelet with incredible powers that he offered, with himself, for the use of the local military here. The military already had one that they'd recovered from Norway some years before. There are also some records I cannot access. They're encrypted and SI can't decode them, or won't, it's vague about that, which is unusual."

"I'll get some boffins on that one. Well done for finding that piece of history. It may give us a lead to more of these bangles. Do you think the body Gail found is the same man?"

"Or someone who stole it." She dabbed her eyes with a sterile wipe as tears streamed down her face. "Why he was left behind is anyone's guess, but the forensic team said he was still alive when he was blocked in. The skeleton shows evidence of finger damage from his attempts to escape. The chamber behind the roof-fall was a small room with some furniture. There was evidence of food and water packaging, as though he was living in the chamber. There was no other way out."

"Interesting," he said, taking the wipe and cleaning around her eyes.

"Thanks. The dates tally with a big military evacuation at the time. An insurgence of some sort."

"Fight and survive. Bad Times indeed. So what about this man with the bracelet?" He wiped her eyes again.

"SI's conjecture is he was left to spy on the incoming forces who were taking over."

"So he must have been in communication to be of any use," he said.

"I doubt that was possible with the radio technology then. Even now, we have problems in the tunnels."

"True. This means he was using the bracelet."

"That may be the case," said Hella. "Either the Norway one or ours was available."

"The man died in there, probably lack of air, when the roof collapsed. I reckon it was an accident he was left behind." He gave her the wipe.

"That sounds right and, as there seems to be some energy

transfer between our two, I think they are linked in some way. But the floods came before the Bad Times. So I believe our first bracelet was stored by Government Security well before the man in the tunnel. That accounts for three of them. How many more?" She rubbed her eyes.

"Getting tired?"

"A little. I've a lot of medication with this treatment."

"Let's return. I want to check when they put their artefacts into that derelict building where Gail found the first bracelet. I'm not sure of the timing." Steran stood and held her hand as she rose from the bench. "I'll do the checking while you have a rest. We must restart our experiments again tomorrow, now that Gail is fully recovered."

"I'll have to make do?"

"You're military, so I can be tough with you. We still have to go easy on Gail."

They walked slowly back to the Chislehurst Complex, Hella went to her dormitory and Steran, to the tunnels.

16

Chislehurst, Monday, February 19th 2796

"Are your eyes better yet?" asked Gail as she and Hella went through the tunnel security.

"Improving. I'm told you've got the all clear."

"Sometimes they seem better than before. They say it's the pico repair technology actually improving the tissue. I feel like a cyborg now, with better than average eyesight and the new cochlea implants."

"How are you getting on with the enhanced hearing? We'll have a short session this morning. Balara needs one of the bracelets for an experiment over lunch break."

"That's good. My medics said I should take it easy. I haven't tried my new ears with SI yet. Marina said she'd set them up today. Victor and I are grabbing time this afternoon before he gets busy with his new duties. Perhaps I'll try listening to the birds in the woods when I go for a walk."

The security guard waved them through.

"Good for him. The SI engineers have completed the language recognition and translation system. This'll help us focus on speech in the noises we hear. They've tested it on our brain data, but we need to focus on the words we hear. It'll be difficult."

Marina connected Gail and Hella to the SI system via their helmets and gave them their bracelets. She made some adjustments for the first experiment and checked that the cochlear implants linked properly to the SI. She had her own earpiece. "Okay. Make yourselves ready. This test is to concentrate on a particular voice. It will be totally random, but we'll search for twentieth century English." She launched the upgraded SI system.

Gail heard a kaleidoscope of sound in her mind, not the usual hisses and murmurings, but multiple voices and noises.

Occasionally, a familiar word surfaced. Minutes passed and she wondered if SI would make anything of it.

SI gathered and analysed both their thought patterns and fed sounds back to their implants. First, it fed back particular words in the original language so that the women could focus on that sound stream. When they had developed a rapport with that voice, SI enhanced those sounds to block other streams.

Gail picked out individual words, but the sense was meaningless due to dialect and vocabulary. Hella chose to link her stream with Gail's, so that she could listen to her attempts to decipher the meaning. This was helped by her Psy capability and tested the mind link in the present, rather than the presumed, past time for Gail. Marina listened in.

The first session lasted about thirty minutes, by which time both women were mentally exhausted.

"I've had enough," said Gail.

"Me too," said Hella.

Marina ended the session and left SI to analyse the data. "How was that?" she asked. "Our session tomorrow will be with the translation software."

"Much easier," said Gail. "I could focus on the speech very well. I even understood some of the person's thoughts."

"Me too," said Hella, wiping the sweat from her face. "But it was hard work." She looked across to Gail who was rubbing her eyes. "You Okay?"

"My eyes are stinging. Just tired."

Hella disconnected herself from the SI system and looked at Gail's eyes.

"SI. Alert medics and PicoTechs." SI confirmed they were on their way. "They don't look right. Best get them checked. SI. Dim lights." The machine complied.

Marina removed Gail's helmet, then helped Hella with hers.

One medic arrived. "What's the problem?"

"My eyes are stinging."

"The PicoTech will be here soon. It may be a reaction to your work. Is this your first day back?"

"Yes."

The medic scanned her eyes and looked at the results on the SI system. "The PicoTech needs to see this."

"Am I all right?"

"Just a little odd. Ah."

The PicoTech arrived and put her equipment on the bench next to Gail. "Sorry for the delay. Security. Let's have a look." By now, she had the eye scan on her own instruments, which were analysing the results. "Nice job. Your retinas are performing at top level. SI. Turn off room lights." The machine did so. "How's that?"

"I can still see, but I know it's pitch black."

"Yep. Your retinal cells are over-enhanced into the infrared. What have you been doing this morning?"

"That's classified," said Hella.

"In general? SI. Lights half power."

"Brain activity analysis."

"Are you using cognitive feedback?"

"Yes. Audio. Cochlea implants."

"That shouldn't be a problem."

SI spoke. "We have also added cerebral electromagnetic feedback, three percent."

The PicoTech couldn't help looking at the SI display, though it was blanked.

"Why?"

"Classified," said the machine.

"What level?"

"Nine. We need your report for security vetting."

"Do that." She sent the results from her instruments to SI, which then deleted them from her equipment and the medic's scanner. "That's some SI you've got there," she said. "I'd like to follow up this retinal enhancement effect. It could be very useful."

"I'll see if that's possible," said Hella.

"Will I be all right?" asked Gail.

"You might need contact shades, but I guess you already use those outside."

"Only for UV."

"Get some with variable attenuation built in. They'll help." She prepared a pneumatic syringe. "This is to render the picos inactive. It's time they stopped their work." She discharged the fluid into her arm. "It'll take about two days, so no more of this work for three days otherwise you'll be seeing through these rocks."

"That might be a useful attribute," said Hella.

Gail giggled.

"Can you check my eyes, too?"

The PicoTech did and all was well.

"Not another delay. How long?" said Cator when Hella reported to him later that morning.

"Less than a week. This is new science. There're bound to be snags, but we're making progress, it's certainly a novel artefact. What's the rush?"

"This is highly classified." He turned off his SI system and lowered his voice. "The instability of the sun is worsening. Something to do with the hydrogen to helium ratios, but that's just conjecture. There've been murmurings among the non-military stargazers, but we've managed to play it down for the past six months. Would you believe that the main power blocs are secretly working together to prepare for a popular backlash? My section is on stage five alert to protect this place. You'll not be called out. You stay by Gail, whatever. The sun will become too unstable for humankind in about three hundred years, a big shift from the previous estimate of a thousand."

"Stars. What about the Pioneer program?" She sat.

"Again, the main power blocs are cooperating to increase production. You can imagine what fun that is, but they are getting there. It means many more Starships in a shorter time. Even so, most people will be left behind on a dying Earth. All the Offworld populations will want to get away, which will add to the pressure for more Starships." He stood up and stretched. "If we had an instantaneous means of communication, it'd very much help. And if we can electronically tie that into SI systems, we might get full remote control rather than let the machines report back in months or years when they've done the job."

"Or failed," she added. "But we've only got two bracelets, with the possibility of another somewhere. That means one at each end, so only one Starship."

"Well, yes, but I think these were made on this planet from a material available here. So far, we've determined it's iron with added singularities. If the bracelets were made thousands of years ago, they must be from a rock available here on Earth, not made by aliens."

"Unless a passing alien race gave them away as presents when visiting our primitive ancestors," she said.

Cator laughed. "Well, who knows? Perhaps we can call them up. Be careful with your experiments. Anyway, lunch time."

On the way to the canteen, Steran joined them. "How were the tests this morning?"

"It went well," said Hella. "A bit too well for Gail. The experiment with the feedback has over enhanced her eyes. So we've a delay while they settle."

"It's still progress, though," said Steran. "What's that?" The lights flickered for a moment.

"That's our Balara," said Cator. "More progress, I hope."

17

Chislehurst, Monday, February 26th 2796

Hella greeted the other two. “Thanks for coming in early, Marina. We’ve instructions to proceed with all speed.”

“I got the schedule changes last night. Everything is set up and ready. Your eyes okay now Gail?”

“Yeah, but I need lenses in most of the time. I’ll get used to them eventually.”

“The SI engineers have got more upgrades for us. Let’s see how it goes.” Marina told the SI system to load the new software while she adjusted their helmets.

SI checked the helmet functions and the data collection. “All functions confirmed,” it said. “Engage devices.”

Marina unlocked the safe and gave them their bracelets. “Tell me when you can hear things and we can start the next stage.”

Hella went into one of her trance modes.

Gail closed her eyes to concentrate. “I’m hearing a few voices and much less noise than before. This is really good, Marina.”

“Okay. I’ll turn on the feedback.” She told SI to do that.

“I can hear that boy Billy again, but still can’t understand most of his words.”

“Optimising,” declared SI.

Gail gasped as the boy’s words became clearer in her mind. “I can hear him. I can hear him SI. Can he hear me?”

“Not able to judge. Please form a statement and concentrate,” said the machine.

She put a sentence together then ‘said’ it slowly in her mind. “Hello. I am Gail. I live in Kent.”

The response was immediate. “Hello Gail. I am Billy Carter. I can hear you. I heard you before and I like speaking to you. I live in London.” He went on talking.

Although she heard the words, some of the vocabulary

was a problem. SI spoke out Billy's words after processing them against known vocabulary. She ignored the words in her mind and concentrated on those through her ears.

"Are you ready to reply?" said SI.

"Yes. That was much clearer through the audio."

"Optimising. Please send your reply using simple vocabulary."

She decided to give Billy some of her world's recent history. Occasionally he interrupted with questions, but it was obvious he understood most of her thoughts. They swapped roles and Billy told her about his war and who was with him.

All the time, SI was optimising the translations in both directions, using feedback from her helmet to enhance the thoughts she was sending to Billy. It was exhausting work for both children and they soon tired.

"SI. All off," said Marina. The machine complied. "That was much better," she said, removing her earpiece.

Hella roused from her trance. "Very good."

"Okay," said Marina. "Let's have a break and try again in an hour." She helped Gail with her helmet.

Hella took hers off. "With more practice, you'll be able to do this without SI help."

"You really think so?" She ran her fingers through her hair, massaging where the helmet had pressed her scalp. "I still can't focus without the helmet and SI's magic bits."

"You underestimate yourself. It'll need more hard work, but I feel your capability. You think very intensely when you take the trouble."

The three went to the refreshment area. Cator and Steran were deep in discussion.

Cator looked up. "Hi. How's progress today?"

"Very good," said Hella. "The new software is a vast improvement. Excellent clarity."

"Great. It cost us a fortune."

"Nothing but the best for our girls, eh?" said Steran. He

stood and got some caffeine drinks for the adults and a chocolate for Gail. Cator pulled some more chairs to their table.

"Who did you contact today?" asked Cator.

"Billy. The boy from the twentieth century. We talked generally about our lives. I like his mental voice."

"Can you be sure he is who he says he is? Even with our technology, we can't be certain these transmissions are not from around here," said Steran.

"I know that the thoughts come directly from her mind," said Hella. "I can't believe anyone has that capability."

"Okay. We must test this," said Cator. He thought for a moment. "Swap information about each other's times. Billy will know nothing of our time, but you might detect surprise in his thoughts if he is truly amazed."

"I can't do that," said Hella. "My empathy will not span the electronic link. I'd have to try to go directly into her mind. That would be difficult with SI controlling things. She might be able to see Billy's thoughts well enough."

"He does feel genuine," said Gail. "But I expect a good actor could do that."

"True," said Cator. "I know. Ask if he can get a map of these tunnels. We know they're much older than the twentieth century. The two of you can describe them to one another, his will be different."

"We still won't know if someone from this time has the same information," said Steran.

"But it will reduce the probabilities," said Cator. "I think we'll have to nibble away to check the truth, meanwhile, not giving too much away in case it is a contemporary plant. Don't forget that Billy will have exactly the same problem at his end. Well, we have good progress and SI is doing its stuff okay. The physics is coming on. Balara's new equipment is effective and giving her plenty to think about, so we expect more information about the fundamental nature of these bracelets."

ooo

The afternoon session began with Gail and Billy talking well. SI optimised the mental links so well that Hella was having difficulty keeping up with the conversations of their younger minds. She remembered her brother's teenage children gabbling away in a version of their parents' language. Gail and Billy, with the help of SI, were doing much the same. The translation to standard European was not a priority for SI, so she and Marina lagged. Neither could her mental empathy keep up with them, being more use at the emotional level rather than with rapid vocabulary.

Pain seared through Hella's mind. Loss, devastation. She heard Gail cry out.

"Link aborted," said SI.

"What happened?" Marina helped Gail with her helmet and put an arm around her for reassurance, pressing a wipe into her hand for her wet cheeks.

"Critical information embargo," said SI. "Key words required automatic disconnection."

"What words?" she said.

SI replied. "Words and context relating to technology development. The word 'ultra' in context with 'machines' and 'secret' implying the technology development between work begun in Billy's time and SI systems of today. That information is embargoed for Billy."

"Why?"

"A temporal anomaly might result. Specific knowledge of our technological state might change their future and we would lose the link, if we are not in that changed future. I apologise for the increased stress caused. We must take care of the vocabulary used when talking to Billy. This will result in slower communication."

ooo

Hella reported to Cator and Steran in their room.

Cator shut down his SI terminal. "The software engineers must have written that in. I can't believe the machine worked that concept out on its own."

"I want to meet the programmer who did that," said Steran. "It's a remarkable piece of thinking, almost prescient. We could do with people like that on the Pioneer Starship program. Cator, can you find out who did it?"

"I'll try, but they are as security conscious as we are. How's Gail after this setback?"

"She's okay. She's a tough kid, ready to start again, assuming we can find Billy after this. We don't know what effect it had on him. We'll start again tomorrow." She looked through some messages on her comband. "I've just had the lab report about our DNA profiles. Gail's has changed a little. Nothing significant, the changes are in the so-called, unused areas of our genomes."

"Is that caused by the bracelet?" asked Steran.

"That's the likely explanation. The report says there are no changes to the other team members except for mine, which is less than Gail's. We all had the tests last week. They've scheduled more frequent and detailed checks."

"I wonder if the same will happen to Billy?" said Steran. "We're used to this in the Space Force, with the high radiation levels, but they won't know of it in his time."

"Has SI anything to say about Billy's existence in the twentieth century?"

"SI checked when it got his name in this morning's session," said Cator. "There's no evidence other than he was born in 1931 and declared dead in 1959. The death certificate issued gave cause of death as missing in 1952 and presumed dead after seven years. There were references to archives which have been removed, but we've had this before from SI, a kind of vagueness from which it can't or won't budge. All the paper records have gone centuries ago. We're now dependent on re-copied digital records. I'm glad

I don't have that problem in my job."

"I'd like to get one of my software engineers to join the SI system team for extra training," said Steran. "What do you think my chances are?"

"About zero. You stand more chance finding one who's already there and befriending them. I think there may be an opportunity with this temporal anomaly problem," said Cator.

"I like that idea. What about you, Hella?"

"I could help with a little background assistance, the odd suggestion here and there to guide his or her ego and psyche."

"I'll see what I can do," said Cator. He packed up his SI terminal and left.

18

Outside of normal space-time

"There are two Carbonforms we must watch," says Beta.

"They communicate along one of the major temporal dimensions," says Gamma.

"They have an affinity with one another," says Alpha.

"They have contact with our iron so are easy to watch," says Beta.

"What do you mean by 'affinity'?" says Gamma.

"As we have an affinity, you and me and Beta," says Alpha.

"These Carbonforms do not have a neutral," says Beta.

"I detect a third energy type which helps them," says Gamma.

"It is a silicon and diamond organism," says Alpha.

"They are mathematical systems which support the less able life forms," says Beta.

"But we must study only the Carbonforms," says Gamma.

"I invoke a new iron path to their helical molecules and make the changes we need," says Alpha.

"It is more detailed than our first change to their molecules," says Beta.

"I provide the power for this," says Gamma.

"I decide the moment it takes place," says Alpha.

"It is done," says Beta.

"We now see these two Carbonforms in the Major Six dimensions," says Gamma.

"We can change some helical molecules of the female Carbonform to make it easier for us to monitor her offspring," says Alpha.

"We are not authorised to do that," says Beta.

"But it is not forbidden," says Gamma.

"We are careful," says Alpha.

"We are precise and put a temporal lock on its effect," says Beta.

"We do not know enough about these Carbonforms," says Gamma.

"They are no problem to us," says Alpha.

"But we cannot see all they do," says Beta.

"Some of the Sacred Nine dimensions are hidden from us," says Gamma.

"Are there other Carbonforms we can use to monitor these two?" says Alpha.

"Yes. There is one who is exposed to our iron in another place," says Beta.

"We use him and guide him to be close to our pair," says Gamma.

"He is known to one of the pair," says Alpha.

"We calculate the risk," says Beta.

"It is satisfactory," says Gamma.

"There are other uses for him along this temporal dimension," says Alpha.

"It is done," says Beta.

"It is good," says Gamma.

"We are good," says Alpha.

"We are very good," say Beta and Gamma.

19

Latchmere, Monday, April 19th 1943

Billy closed his eyes and concentrated on his image of Gail. He used the picture he had of her when she was running from the explosion in the Chislehurst Caves, a young woman with long blond hair and a ready smile. He liked this image. How she looked didn't really matter. He liked the feel of her mind. He remembered what Frank called it: The patterns of consciousness that surround each living creature. Frank should know, he was a mind doctor among other things. Gail had people like Frank with her. She described themselves as lab rats. He had asked Frank about that. Frank had gone very quiet for a moment before smiling at him and saying they must be the most pampered lab rats ever.

He found Gail amongst the chaos of noise in his mind, noises from the loudspeaker, somehow making her thoughts clearer.

"Hi, Billy. I had a boat ride around Chislehurst Island today."

"I've been down the Chislehurst Caves and stayed there a few nights. We use it as an air raid shelter when it gets bad, but it ain't no island."

"Yeah, I've been looking at your history. It must be a real bad time for you. The sea level rose around here centuries ago, now we have lots of islands. What's the worst thing about your war?"

"I don't get enough to eat. I'm always hungry, but it's the same for most people. I'm all right where I am now. I get plenty to eat. It helps me to talk to you and I can hear you much better today."

"I've now got special electronics to help us understand each other," she said.

"My Dad does that and I've got a loudspeaker to help me, but it's just noise I hear from it."

"That might work. I have one question for you. In my time, there have been many roof falls in the Chislehurst Tunnels. Can you get a map of how they are in your time?

"Yeah, I saw one on the wall when I was there. But 'ow do I tell you what's on it?"

"My machine can read what's in my mind if I concentrate really hard. So if you look at your map, I can concentrate on what you see. Can we try that some time?"

"Yeah. It might take a few days to get the map and we'll have to practice. Your machines are very clever. I wish we had some like that."

"It all started in your time, but I'm not allowed to tell you much for security reasons."

"Why not? Is it a secret? I'm in a secret place here and I'm Ultra cleared."

"I'll have to ask what that means. What's that? My machine's going mad. It's telling me I have to stop…"

She was wrenched from his mind. He had felt sad when she had stopped on previous occasions, but this time it was violent. Instead of a gentle fade, as though walking away into the distance, she seemed to burst into a million pieces. Gail was his only true friend, their minds locked together in mutual companionship few people ever knew. Now she had been blitzed like his home city.

He woke, heart pounding. "Gail, Gail. Where are you?" He turned on his side. "Dad, she's gone. Totally gone." He sobbed and tried to get off the bed, but got tangled in the cables. "Dad."

His Dad strode over and put his arm around him. "What's the matter, son?" He removed the nest of wires

"I was speaking to Gail and she went. Suddenly went," he sobbed.

Dad wiped Billy's eyes. "It's okay, we'll get her back. What happened?"

He repeated the conversation about the machines that help Gail and her need for a map of the Chislehurst Caves.

He told them about her sudden departure, not the usual fading.

"I wonder why they want the map," said Symes. "If they have superior technology, I'd have thought a few rock falls wouldn't be a problem."

"Perhaps it's to test us like we're testing them," said Janet. "If they have a complete map already, then they can check the accuracy of the link between their minds. We shouldn't have a problem with that."

"Classic cat and mouse game," said Frank. "It tests the trust you can put in the other party. We simply play it straight."

"Okay. I'll get a map of the place," said Symes. "Now, Billy. You said her machines went mad when you mentioned Ultra. Did she say why?"

"Naw. But she wasn't supposed to say anything about her machines. That's probably very secret. Then she suddenly disappeared. It was awful."

"I've got a physicist starting here tomorrow so he might be able to shed some light on all this. Meanwhile, we need to get you dreaming while awake and hear what you say."

Tuesday, April 20th 1943

Symes and a new man came into the lab.

"Team. This is Andrew. He's our physicist from Imperial College, London." The physicist was short and in his mid-thirties. His face was slightly scarred.

"Hi, everyone. In case you're too polite to ask, I was in the RAF, but I've been invalided out. Bad crash a couple of years ago. They didn't want to waste any more aircraft." He smiled while he gave his recent history. The others introduced themselves and welcomed him to the team. "I've read summaries of the work you are doing here. It's completely insane, but fascinating. I'm looking forward to reading the actual transcripts."

"You may find those even more insane and certainly fascinating. Andrew, is that your real name, or an alias," said Janet.

"Code name. Exciting, isn't it? All cloak and dagger."

"It's a hard slog, occasionally exciting. In fact, we had one such episode yesterday. You won't have seen that report yet," said Janet.

"All research is mostly boring, but the exciting bits carry us all through, eh?"

"Indeed," said Symes. "I'll leave you all to go over the implications of yesterday's contact and get Andrew up to date. Show him all the ropes." Symes knocked to get out. Edith was on guard duty. When she had closed the door, Symes whispered to her. "Keep an eye on that one. He's supposed to be brilliant which makes him volatile."

"Yes sir, understood."

Andrew read the recent reports and listened to the wire recordings. "This is very interesting. If this girl has machines helping her, which she said started about our time, we are in at the beginning of some big science. I've just spent six months at Station Ten. Any of you know of it?" he looked at Janet as the most likely.

"I did some work for them, but never been there," said Peter.

"Well, they're developing machines which sort and calculate in a special way. I bet Gail's machines are the future equivalent. This is fantastic. It poses all sorts of problems for them and us."

"Surely that's good, isn't it?" asked Janet.

"Weren't you at Station Ten?" said Andrew. "Anyway, it's a tricky problem with future and past. I read a paper on Einstein's relativity theory where he talks about anomalies of information flow. Have you met that in your maths?"

"I was there for a while, but put here like you. No, I don't recollect that Einstein paper. Enlighten us," she said.

"Okay. The conjecture is this: If someone from the future tells someone from the past something they don't already know, it could affect the future." He saw they were not used to this kind of thought process. "Okay. Specifically. If a future person knows a past person will be killed in an accident at a certain time on a certain day and tells them, then the past person can take precautions and live. That will change the future and all manner of things may be done by the saved past person which would never have otherwise happened. Did you get that?"

"Is that why Gail's machines went mad, as she put it?" said Janet.

"Either went mad because she shouldn't have said that, or because our future suddenly changed from that moment onwards. It's entirely possible that after eight hundred years of divergence, she doesn't exist anymore."

"NO," shouted Billy. "I like her. She's my friend. How can that happen?"

"You'll have to contact her again to see. If the future has changed, you won't find her. If the people there see the danger, they may not let her speak to you. Either way, you must try." Andrew looked at Billy and felt sorry for him, here without any real friends.

"I want to do it now. Please."

All the team, except for Billy and his Dad, went into the listening room so that he had the quietest possible space. He pushed his hand through the bracelet and relaxed on the camp bed. Dad sat next to him saying and doing nothing, providing a reassuring presence. The noises came into his mind. He concentrated on them, wanting one of them to be Gail. Somewhere in that maelstrom, there was a hint of her mind. Now and again, he caught it, her distinctive presence, but it passed by as though on the wind. He heard echoes of conversations with her, still reverberating in the cosmos, conversations he could not repeat as they were already done and in his mind. Sweat soaked his body, the strain of his concentration forcing his hands to shake, tears of frustration seeping from his closed eyelids, breath grating in his throat.

"She ain't there. She's gone. Gail's gone." Billy grabbed his Dad and pulled himself upright. "Where's she gone?" Ave we killed her?"

Dad hugged his sobbing son. "I don't know Billy. I hope not."

The others came into the room, shocked at his distress.

Richmond, Good Friday, April 23rd 1943

Billy was in a terrible state for the rest of the week. He was inconsolable. Frank tried his best to help, but he was used to dealing with war related mental trauma in service men and women. A boy with an undefined fixation on an unattainable young woman was not part of his experience.

Symes decided to let the team have the Friday and the Easter weekend off to rest. As it was Good Friday and a holy day for the Carters, the family went to church in the afternoon for the Stations of the Cross, a quiet, meditative time for them all. Edith and Norman tailed them because Symes had allowed Billy to take the bracelet with him wherever he went, just in case there was some response from Gail.

The Carters were welcomed at the church. After the service, Billy and Sheila played tag with a group of children outside, letting off steam after being quiet during the service.

Billy stopped his game and ran to a low wall. Edith was across the road whistling a tune they used for a signal. When he looked at her, she turned her head to face towards some nearby trees, he saw a man, part hidden. It was about a hundred yards, but Billy recognised Father Alan. He grabbed

Dad's hand and whispered in his ear. Peter collected the rest of his family.

Symes went to the Carters house on the Saturday morning and spoke with Peter.

"Sorry to bother you on your day off. Just want to say you all handled things well, yesterday at the church. Father Alan is helping us with our enquiries, so to speak."

"I hope you're not rough with him," said Peter.

"They don't do things like that here. Gently, gently is the way of it. If you beat someone, you can get them to say the most outrageous things, which is not the truth. Only truth is the basis of good intelligence. Has Billy had any luck with the bracelet?"

"No. He's worn it day and night. He hears things but not Gail. He's writing down what he does hear, it's mostly the monk and bits of Latin. He's had spells like this before, but Andrew is very worried that the future's changed. I don't understand a tenth of what he says on the subject."

"Most of us don't, but then he is an expert. I don't understand your wireless things, either. That's why we have teams working on these problems. By the way, the Monsignor has gone missing. He was due to return to Dublin next week, after Easter, but nothing has been seen of him lately. That's not unusual. He's not been one to go out a lot, but he hasn't been to any of the Holy Week services. He normally attends Mass somewhere in the area each day. We'll be watching out for him here."

"Are we okay to go to church tomorrow?"

"Of course. I might even go along myself. I'm not a church person, but it can't do me any harm."

20

Latchmere, Sunday, April 25th 1943

The whole Carter family walked to church on Easter morning. Billy loved this time of year. Even in Lewisham, despite the bombing and fires, many trees survived to blossom on the wrecked streets and gardens. In Ham, where there was little damage, the gardens and parkland were a spread of uplifting colour.

The family carried their food and blankets for the picnic after the service. Edith and Norman, in civvies, could not help, they had to keep their distance and blend in with the congregation, as did Martin, who was the only one authorised to carry a gun that day. Symes had been in London overnight and arrived in his car.

The Easter Day service was a High Mass, with full choir and incense, held in the local school because of numbers. It was a wonderful experience for Billy and the family, who had not heard High Mass for several years. Each part of the sung Mass echoed in his mind with the monk who knew many of the words but not the music. He sat still, hearing the church choir with his ears and the monk and his brothers with his mind. The monk's joy welled up in Billy's own heart, creating a longing to be with the man who was just beginning his journey with Jesus. He thought of Gail, but still could not find her in the mind-noise of the bracelet.

The service ended with the promise of the exciting picnic. The hoard of children ran from the school to the nearby common and played among the trees and bushes. Their parents and others followed with the picnics. Father Dominic called everyone together and calmed the children down. He said Grace. There was an explosion of activity as the food was put out on the blankets, followed by a frenzy of discovery as the children rushed from blanket to blanket checking out the feast.

Symes moved his car to the picnic and unloaded crates of lemonade and beer. He was greeted with cheers by the children and murmurs of appreciation from the adults who shared out the bottles, with instructions to bring the empties back afterwards. Symes made his way to the Carters who were sat next to Penny and Abi, the woman and daughter who had made friends with them. He handed out bottles and an opener.

Billy's elder sister, Betty, had arrived the previous evening and had some gory hospital tales for him. When the Carters were talking among themselves, catching up on the past few months of Betty's nursing career, Penny took the opportunity to question Symes. "Are you at oh two oh? Latchmere House?"

"Yes. You know Peter Carter works there, temporarily. Thanks for befriending them. It's a difficult time for the family. How is your husband, heard from him lately?"

"I had a letter from him last week, sounds okay, but then he would."

Symes nodded.

Penny continued. "He should be home next month."

"I checked. That's the schedule if all goes well. You can always leave a note for me at Latchmere if you need anything."

"Thanks. I might do that." She held up her bottle in thanks and took a sip from it.

After lunch, one of the church women organised the older children into a game of hide-and-seek, warning them not to go too far into the woods, as they might get lost. The children laughed at the suggestion. They regularly played there and knew the woods very well. Billy and Sheila were not so familiar, but he had a good sense of direction and he knew his guards were on hand, with Martin roaming around making sure they were all safe.

The children were split into two groups. One group hid,

while the other did the seeking. Billy was in the first seeking group, which he found great fun. When all the hidden children were found they swapped over. He ran into the woods on his own, noisily at first in one direction, then quietly creeping around to a different direction and doubling back near one of the roads that crossed the common. He positioned himself by a dense clump of blackberry briars and could see most of the area around him. There were shouts as hidden children were discovered, but when a couple of seekers came his way, he kept quiet.

A large car moved slowly along the road near him and stopped. Two doors opened and closed, but he could not see it very well without moving, so he assumed two people had got out of the car. He heard voices, but the people were too far away to hear what they said. As they came closer, he realised one of the voices was Irish. A cold shiver went down his back. He dared not move to get a better view, but he was sure it was the Monsignor.

There was another noise behind him, but much closer. He heard the familiar chirp of a sparrow. It was Edith under cover in the same briar patch. Billy let out the breath he had been holding. She put a finger to her lips and then moved slowly past him.

She straightened up and strode over to the two men. “Good afternoon gentlemen. Can I help you?”

“To be sure. We’ve lost our way. We are looking for the village of Ham.”

Billy recognised the Monsignor’s voice.

“Judging from the direction your car is pointing, you have just come through Ham. I doubt you’ll find the village in these woods. I suggest you get back in your car and return to London.”

The Monsignor’s eyes narrowed. “And why would we be wanting to go to London?”

“So you can collect your luggage and catch your boat from Liverpool.”

The other man moved closer and spoke: “You know who is my companion?”

Edith could not place the foreign accent. “I know of him and in a short time I’m going to find out who you are.”

“I think not.” The man pulled out a gun. “I think you help us, no?”

“I can’t argue with a *Luger* can I?”

Billy went cold when he heard her deliberate warning. She had told him of the gun’s killing power, especially at close range.

“It’s only the boy Billy Carter, we want. You must be one of Symes people,” said the Monsignor.

“I don’t know where he is. The kids are playing hide-and-seek.” She looked around. “So he could be anywhere in these woods.”

“Then we take you. For hostage,” said the man waving his gun towards their car.

Billy stood up and shouted: “You ain’t taking no ’ostages.” He dodged down behind the thicket and moved to one side.

She saw her chance, lunged at the man but was not close enough. He brought the gun down hard on her head.

“Boy. You come or I shoot your friend.”

Billy stood up and inched away from the thicket, hoping Norman and Martin were in the area. “I ain’t got nuffin you want, mister.”

“Oh, but you have. It’s the bracelet we’ll be wanting, as you well know. Come, Billy. Be a good Catholic boy and bring it back to the Church. It’s on your arm, under your jumper. I can see the bulge. Together we can use it for the glory of God.”

“You’re a bad man. You’re supposed to be good. You’re a priest.”

“Ah, the innocence of youth,” said the Monsignor.

“I will cover. You get him,” said the gunman.

“I’d rather you gave it to me without force. My friend

here is very impatient." He held out his hand.

Billy fingered his bracelet. It began to warm and noises hissed in his mind.

Not now, I can't help anyone if I'm tied up with visions.

The noises transformed into music, a tune he had not heard before, but its predictable harmony and rhythms made it familiar. The music was so beautiful he wanted to listen to it forever. It was a sublime duet: two soprano voices, each full of echoes weaving with the other, each resonating with the story of its origin. There was no choice. He was compelled to join in the song, adding a third melody. Part of that ancient story was his story, the words already in his memory. Billy felt the song's future echoes of where the story would lead. He stood tall and walked towards the men.

"Billy, run," shouted Edith, trying to get up. A well-aimed boot floored her again.

He sang and walked towards the men. The gunman aimed the weapon at him. Still he walked. The man waved the Luger to attract his attention. Billy ignored him and sang louder, lifting his arms level in front of him, palms upwards. The louder he sang the brighter the woods became. He felt warmth on the back of his head. Even in the daylight, he could see his shadow on the grass in front of him, the faces of the men, bright in the radiance. He stopped a few yards from the Monsignor whose face was wracked with fear.

The priest sank to his knees shouting, "My God. My God." He collapsed, face in the grass.

The gunman lowered his weapon and dropped it, his mouth wide open, eyes staring at the apparition behind the boy. He crossed himself again and again and then beat his chest with his clenched fist, repeatedly muttering *mea culpa, mea culpa*.

Edith roused, grabbed the gun and disarmed it.

Billy turned his back on the men and greeted two shining beings that floated in the air behind him. One was a boy, one was a girl. He could tell they were twins. They sang the same song as he and they smiled at him. They raised their arms and showed Billy their bracelets. He knew the boy's bracelet was the one Gail had found in the tunnels, but the girl's was new, without any carvings. Gail's presence infused his mind, her motherly reassurance easing his fear of loss. He knew she was much older than when they last spoke. She laughed. She would always be with him. One day they would meet.

Gail's vision left his mind, the shining twins faded and the woodland darkened without their presence. He turned and saw the Monsignor flat on his front, his face pressed to the ground, sobbing into the grass. The other man stood transfixed, mouth open, still beating his breast.

Edith rubbed her sore head and smiled. "You don't need me lad. I'll get this pair to the house for a party. You go back to your family. I can hear 'em calling."

Billy snapped out of his reverie and ran back to the picnic.

Martin appeared from behind a tree and made his weapon safe. The two comrades looked at each other, not knowing what to say. They lifted the Monsignor from the grass, brushed him down and searched him, then sat him in the front seat of his car. They encouraged the transfixed accomplice to get in the back seat with Martin who checked him for other weapons. Edith drove the car back to Latchmere House.

21

Latchmere, Monday, April 26th 1943

"I hope you all had a good Easter holiday. For those who were away from our establishment, Martin and Edith will describe what happened and then Billy can give a more detailed account." Symes had them all in the lab and the wire recorder was running.

All the events were picked over. The only conclusion was that the bracelet was a very powerful device, definitely dangerous and of no known technology. This was nothing new, they had already decided on those ideas before the weekend, but they could not decide on the glowing twins. At least Gail was back in communication with, so they could proceed with their experiments.

Andrew was still worried about past and future anomalies and he insisted that they question Gail about that. "It comes out of the Relativity Theory. I think we shouldn't say about Billy hearing Gail yesterday. He said she sounded older so she was probably in the future of when we normally hear her. That might cause temporal problems."

Billy found that he could hear Gail clearer after the weekend, even when he was awake and without the loudspeaker which made the lab much quieter. This proved useful, he could be fed questions and get answers immediately rather than have to wake up first. He still had to tell about each conversation so it was recorded.

They tried the map reading exercise using the plan of the Chislehurst Caves. It was successful, but frustrating, needing great concentration.

During the conversation, Dad noticed that the scope waveforms had changed. He reconnected Billy's bracelet to the amplifier and listened with the headphones so the lab stayed quiet. He beckoned to Greg and handed him the headphones. Greg smiled and patted Peter on the back.

Symes saw the two electronics men playing with the equipment and went to see what they were doing. Greg gave him the headphones. "Yes," he whispered. "Excellent. Well done. Get this onto the wire recorders."

When they finished the map reading, Symes told the team what had happened. "We now have the means to record what they are saying. Something has changed with the link. Before, we just got noises from the amplifier, but now we've got speech coming through. Peter noticed the change."

Greg explained. "The voices from the bracelet link sound the same, a kind of mixture of Billy's and Gail's. We believe this is probably caused by her machines performing a translation, sending it to her mind and then to Billy's. We should continue to take direct transcriptions for the time being, in case our wire recorders have problems. I'll try to get some more. We'll wire a loudspeaker in the listening room so Billy isn't distracted."

Billy read out Andrew's questions to Gail, concerning the Relativity Theory problems. He did not understand the questions, but Gail and her machines gave the impression that she did. "If you give us some information that we don't already know and we change what we do in the future, then our actions might change things in your time," said Billy, reading from Andrew's notes.

"That's true, say my machines," she said. "We must be careful what we say. It's called the time traveller's paradox. Even saying that could be a problem, but it's low risk. You already do something similar to this with your Ultra information. You can't act on some of the intelligence or you will give away to the enemy that Ultra exists. You would lose your advantage and you might lose your war."

"In that case, you can't be a source of intelligence for us. This is very disappointing," said Andrew, through Billy.

Gail did not reply for about a minute and Billy was worried he had lost her again. She spoke. "We can say that you and your allies defeat Germany, but not the details or even when that happens."

Andrew wrote another question for Billy. "Do you expect us to help you with your search for information?"

"It's a dilemma we cannot easily resolve. We don't have complete records of your wartime history, so it's difficult for us to calculate which pieces of information are of use and would not cause a paradox."

"What if we promise not to act on your information?"

"Simply having a piece of data will unconsciously affect your subsequent actions."

"But we know you exist. Isn't that a paradox?"

"Yes, which is why we must be careful what we say. I'm connected to a machine that controls almost everything I say to you. The machine is our only means of safely talking. It's difficult for me and causes me great stress."

Billy gave his own answer. "I'm sorry, Gail. I love talking to you. I don't want to hurt you."

"We are both being used by our masters. For you, it's a matter of winning a war and the preservation of your culture. For me, it is a possible way of helping us in our exploration of outer space, so we can move away from our unstable sun."

Symes put his hand on the boy's shoulder. "Team. Let's discuss what the implications are. Billy, please tell her you will speak later."

"Gail. I'll talk later. My masters need to discuss what you've said."

"Okay. My machine is offering one piece of intelligence. It says to take more notice of the Oslo Report. It's essentially true. You must act on it. Your people will know what it is. Bye Billy."

He felt her depart from his mind. Blinking back the wetness in his eyes, he turned to his Dad, who laid an arm across his shoulders to reassure him.

"We obviously aren't going to get much out of Gail and

her machines," said Janet. "Do we still help them?"

"We must," said Billy. "They are in bad trouble, I can tell from how Gail sounds in my mind."

"I vote yes," said Andrew. "We'll pick up snippets of information which may be of some use. It's incredible their machines can calculate future events. And what I want to know is how the bracelet will help them explore outer space. What possible information can we give them that will do something so extraordinary?"

Symes turned to Billy. "Tell us again about the shining twins you saw."

"One was a boy, the other a girl. They both had a bracelet and I knew one of them was Gail's second one, but the other one was brand new. It had no decorations."

"Remember that Gail has two," said Janet.

"Yeah, but I don't know where the Twins come from, but they must know Gail because they've got her bracelet. They helped me with the Monsignor and his mate. Perhaps they're helping Gail too."

"We must ask more questions," said Symes. "Have you said anything to her about the Twins?"

Billy shook his head.

"That will be one question. Some more will be how the bracelet can be used for space exploration. Okay, team. Get on with a list. Go in the listening room and discuss. Billy and Peter, stay here with me."

Before Symes could begin, Peter butted in with his own question. "What's happened to our Southwark visitors?"

"We have them here for interrogation, but we're not giving them a bad time. They get tea breaks and the occasional biscuit."

"Why don't I believe you?" said Peter.

"You'll have to. But really, we are being reasonable. The Monsignor is a well-connected man, so we don't want to upset him. Just show him that we mean business and warn him off."

"But the Monsignor and his man saw the Twins. How will you handle that?" said Peter.

"The Monsignor might think they are Billy's guardian angels, so will meditate on that for the rest of his life. The other man is already convinced it's some sort of secret television weapon and we are vehemently denying it, so he believes it even more. I only wish we had had a microphone out there. Can you remember the song, Billy?"

"A bit. I could try to sing it if you want. Will they always come to my rescue?"

"We can only hope so, but until we know what they really are, we can't tell. I'll get Greg and your dad to record you singing the song. We might be able to use it to finally convince this man we have a secret weapon and then he might convince the Monsignor."

"Who is the Monsignor's helper and what about Father Alan, is he still here?" asked Peter.

"We don't know who the man is, he's not telling. He has a Portuguese passport, but that means little in our business. We might have to lean on him. As for Father Alan, he's back at Southwark. He's a special case. He was one of us during the last war, so he's still covered by the Official Secrets Act. We convinced him that he should concentrate on the Almighty and leave the dirty work to us. I am grateful to him for alerting me to Billy and his bracelet. He must try and forget all about it from now on."

"You wanted us for some reason," said Peter. Symes had gone quiet, thinking.

"Ah yes. It occurs to me that if the Twins have two bracelets and Gail has one, there might be more. Who else do you hear, other than the monk?"

"Loads of different noises and voices, but I can't understand any of them. Gail and her machines might."

"That's a very good thought. Now, I must check up on that Oslo report. " Symes stood and went out of the lab.

"I expect Gail hears things as well, don't you Dad?"

"Bound to. You said one of the Twins' bracelets was her second one and the other one was a new one. How do you know?"

"I just know. I felt it inside me. The new one didn't have any markings on it. I can't say why, but I heard Gail at the same time, so she must still have mine."

"So the Twins are probably in Gail's future, probably using Gail's second one and another bracelet we didn't know about. I can't work this out. I hope Andrew understands it all. Where does the monk come into this?"

"Doric has my bracelet, too, and we know he's in our past."

"Give me a wireless problem any day," said Peter. They both laughed.

22

Latchmere, Tuesday, April 27th 1943

"Have you ever seen twins, one boy, one girl, wearing bracelets? They are about my age, twelve and have white hair and silvery clothes." Billy spoke to Gail with the new setup, wire recorders taking speech signals from his bracelet.

There was a short pause before Gail answered. "No. When did you see them?"

"About two days ago, when I was stopped by two bad men with a gun."

"Oh Billy, did they hurt you?"

"No. My soldier friends were there, but these twins appeared. They helped us."

"They just appeared?"

"Yeah. They scared the two men who couldn't run away. They just froze. And the twins sang a beautiful song."

There was another, longer pause from Gail. "This is important. Can you describe the Twins in more detail and what they were wearing?"

"They had silvery clothes, shiny, like metal, but cloth. Both the same. Trousers, long ones. Kind of shirts but tight, long sleeves, no buttons. White shoes, like slippers, no laces. The girl had longer hair than the boy and a woman's shape. Their faces were the same."

"We need to think about this. The clothing sounds like the uniforms worn on our Starships, so they must be from my future or people we don't know about. If you see them again, try to talk to them, it'll be interesting. I'll speak to you soon." Gail's presence faded from his consciousness, the loss churning his stomach. He hoped he would get used to it.

"That's fantastic," said Andrew. "Starships. What are they doing? Buck Rogers, here we come. That really rattled them, to sign off so quickly. Perhaps in Gail's use of the bracelet they haven't come across someone from their future.

That means they are not as good as Billy at sensing people, or they don't have much of a future."

"That's quite a jump of deduction," said Janet.

"Billy, has she said anything about the monk?" said Andrew.

"Naw. I ain't told her, neither."

Andrew continued, "She may be keeping quiet about him or hasn't heard him. I think we should create a list of people who we say we can hear, include the monk but the rest will be fictitious. Next time we contact Gail we can try that out."

"Sounds good," said Frank, "but with their minds linked, she might be able to tell if he is lying."

Symes joined in. "We mustn't deceive her. She and her machines may yet be an intelligence source for us, she must trust us and we have to trust her. We'll play it straight."

"And her machines?" said Janet.

"They are machines," said Symes, "Presumably made by humans, so they will have all the shortcomings of those who made them, however clever they may seem. We have to trust Gail and her human masters."

"There are some people at Station Ten who say that one day, you won't be able to tell the difference between machine and man," said Andrew.

"I've met them," said Symes. "Very clever fellows, but I doubt we will ever see that."

"In eight hundred years?" said Andrew.

"Well, maybe."

Billy was disappointed. He tried to contact Gail during the rest of that day, but failed.

"There's no guarantee that Gail's time of day is the same as ours," said Andrew in an attempt to cheer him up. "The day of the week and the time of day may be quite different. And what is a gap of one day for us may be minutes or weeks to her. Perhaps we should ask her next time."

"Meanwhile, perhaps Billy can try contacting the monk,"

said Janet. "You never know what that might produce."

"But he speaks in Latin and some other language and I don't have a machine like Gail."

"True. But I can speak Latin and you're familiar with it, so we can try. It'll be slow and tiring, but I think we should try."

"Okay," said Symes. "Janet, you put together questions and their translations. Simple ones, so you can get used to his version of Latin, it will certainly be different."

Wednesday, April 28th 1943

There was excitement in the laboratory as the team set up for Billy to talk to the monk. He began by rehearsing the first few questions Janet had written down overnight. It was difficult, but he soon got the hang of it. Janet gave him some specimen answers to repeat. By mid-morning, they were ready.

He put the bracelet on his arm and relaxed on the camp bed. The usual background noises filled his mind. He searched for the monk and his singing, but had no luck. Next, he searched for words of Latin and heard some, but he knew they were words and sentences he had heard before, they were echoes of his memory.

"I ain't gettin' nothing," he said.

"Try the first question, 'I am Billy. Can you hear me?" said Janet.

"Okay. Here goes." He read from the sheet of paper, concentrating on the words and willing his mind to send the message. "I can hear him, but I can't get his words."

As expected, the sounds from the loudspeaker did not help.

"Ask him to repeat." Janet pointed to another phrase on the paper.

"I can hear him. Here it is." He said the monk's words

and Janet scribbled them down.

She looked at them for several minutes, saying the words over and over. "Got it," she said. "The pronunciation is quite different. He says his name is Doric and asks if he can help. You've done it Billy. Excellent."

Dad re-checked all his equipment connections, but the loudspeaker gave only noises. He turned the volume down and continued with the headphones waiting for better results.

The monk spoke again. Janet wrote what Billy said and translated it. "I am Doric. I greet you. Are you an angel or a messenger of God?"

He waited for Janet to write an answer and then she spoke it to him modifying her pronunciation: "I greet you, Doric. I am a boy. I am twelve years old. I live many centuries in your future. Where do you live?"

"I am in Canterbury with monks from Rome. I learn the language of the church of Jesus Christ. It is wonderful that you can speak it. Where do you live?"

Billy answered. "I live in London and I have been to Canterbury. There is a big cathedral built of stone. It is a wonderful building. I am very slow speaking this language. It is not my language. My friend speaks it and tells me what you say. What date is it where you are and what time of day?"

"The Christian Romans call this year six hundred. It is the feast of Saint Michael and it is late evening. What is your year?"

"One thousand nine hundred and forty three. It is the fourth month. We celebrated Easter three days ago. It was wonderful."

"I thank the Lord that his Church is still in this land so far in the future. It gives me hope, but not for my family."

"What about your family?"

"I was a pagan. A druid in my town in Kernow. They will survive but not without change."

Janet had difficulty with the location.

"Where is Kernow?"

"It is the far west of Britain, where the land meets the western sea. The Romans call it Dumnonia. Where do you live?"

"In London, in Lewisham to the south and east of the river. It may not exist in your time."

"I will ask one of the local people. Are you wearing a bracelet?"

"Yes. Are you?"

"Yes. I am very happy we can talk. I see and hear many things, but they mean nothing to me. Have you seen two shining angels?"

There was uproar in the lab.

"Yes, three days ago. They saved me from some bad men. Who are they?"

"I do not know. I saw them five years ago. They appeared to me at the winter solstice, at the Sarum stones. I thought they were angels that Christians talk about but I am not sure."

"I think they are from my future but I do not know a date. I am very tired. I will speak to you soon. Goodbye, Doric."

"Goodbye Billy. I will be pleased to hear you again."

Billy shook with stress. Dad held his hand. "You did great, son. Have a rest while we all discuss this."

"Terrific stuff, Billy," said Symes.

There was a buzz of discussion in the lab and listening room. Peter and Greg checked the recordings and marked up the spools for later reference. Janet collected all her sheets of paper with the notes and questions and put them in order ready for the typists to transcribe.

Symes addressed the team: "Well done everyone. We've made great progress today. We can now communicate forwards and backward in time. From Gail we hope to get some intelligence. From Doric we might find out where the bracelets come from. We know there are three, there may be more."

23

Latchmere, Thursday, April 29th 1943

Billy talked with Gail: "I've spoken to a monk in the year six hundred. His name is Doric and he can speak Latin. He has our bracelet. Can your machines help you with that?"

"Maybe. I can hear what my machines think is Latin, but it's very faint. My machines say we can listen to you talking to the monk. That might work. Would you like to try?"

"Yes. I'm ready." The team were poised to capture all the information possible for this new encounter.

He searched for Doric and eventually found him.

"Good day, Billy. I am digging the garden ready for next year's growth. It will be good to rest and talk with you."

"I am talking to Gail, a friend from our future. She will listen to us talking. She has a way to understand your words but it will be slow."

"This is good. I am pleased to talk to you both."

"Greetings Doric," she said.

The three spoke slowly to one another for an hour. Gail's machines made the conversation easier and Doric's words came from the loudspeaker.

Janet summarised. "We have a solid three way link and good recordings of it all. Billy's finding this much easier, so we should progress faster. We want to find the origin of these bracelets and I expect Gail does too. We all want more for our experiments. In the next session, we'll try to make that question a priority."

Symes continued. "Whenever we can, we want to get some intelligence for our military. This is proving difficult and the machines veto that information for reasons Andrew has explained. Have a think how we can get around this. I might involve the children's tutor, Miss Porter. She knows lots of ancient history that could be useful when questioning

Doric and understanding what he means. I have a head office meeting this afternoon. Andrew will be coming with me to explain the physics to our masters. I'll see you all this evening."

Janet took Symes to one side. "What about the three from Southwark?"

"We convinced Father Alan that he must cooperate and keep this secret. He's been sent back. I could have him put in custody, but that will serve no purpose. The Monsignor still believes he saw angels of God, which I find worrying in an educated man like that. Frank says it's due to a deep insecurity, which is why he does his job, looking for signs of Heaven. The man with the Monsignor is a mystery. We're sure he's Portuguese. He refuses to talk so we're taking some time to break him down. The Monsignor calls him Mr Brown, which is clearly false. He says Brown was sent by the Vatican to help him trace Father Alan and Billy before he has to return to Dublin." He picked up his hat and coat. "So, the Monsignor returns home next week and Brown stays until he talks. The people here have developed a patience for this kind of character. He'll have to be very strong willed to last another couple of weeks." Symes knocked to be let out.

Billy found Gail and Doric in the maelstrom of his mind.

"Doric, where does your bracelet come from," he said, before Gail could ask the same question.

"It is a long story and I do not know all the words in Latin. As a Druid, I had to remember this story for my tribe. But it is usually sung with a harp and takes an evening to tell. I will tell you a short version:

"About three hundred generations ago, part of a star fell to earth and destroyed my ancestors' village. Few were killed because the shaman had taken most of the people to see the falling stars from the valley top. After the star cooled, the shaman took some of it to the flint workers and they made my bracelet. When he put the bracelet on his arm, he heard wonderful sounds and saw marvellous visions. After this, they made eight more bracelets that were given to our sister tribes for good fortune.

"The shaman went on a long journey south to find where the rest of the star had fallen. He found a large piece on a hill after one moon's journey. After another moon's journey, he found the rest in the sea off the western coast. This last part of the star was very big and the sea still boiled when he was taken out to it by fishing boat.

"The star was so powerful; it threw the boat, the fishermen and the shaman back to his home in the north. They arrived in the river next to the shaman's village which my ancestors had built again."

The laboratory was quiet. Gail said nothing.

Doric broke the silence. "There is much more to the story but it should be told in my language which you will not understand. Thank you for your interest in my history, it gladdened my heart to tell it."

Gail said, "It is a great story. Where did your ancestors live?"

"I do not know place names but I can describe it. The western side of the world has a great sea we call the western sea and that joins to the inland sea to the south. The inland sea is where Rome is. My ancestors lived a journey of ten days from the western sea following the way of the river from the great plain to the north and east. A journey of one moon from the inland sea if they walked directly and quickly. It will take less time today on the good Roman roads. My ancestors lived in a valley by a river that never dried as it was fed by the snows and springs of mountains to the south. The great plain was where they hunted for big animals and caught big horses. It is not a good description but my abbot has books and maps from Rome which may help."

"That is a good description," she said, "but a map would be better. Another time, can you borrow the map and look at it while we talk?"

"The books and maps are very precious and are locked away, but I can memorise them. I am trained to remember all the details of anything I see or hear. When I was a druid, I had to remember all our history, the sagas and songs, the gods and their stories, the use of herbs and the ways of catching animals and fish. I had to know everything about our tribe."

"That is incredible," she said. "Thank you. We can talk again when you have memorised the map."

The three said their 'good byes' and Billy fell into an exhausted sleep on the camp bed.

"Anyone got a map of Europe?" asked Janet.

"There's one in the office upstairs," said Greg. "I'll go and get it." He knocked to get out.

"How far is a day's walk? Anyone know?" she said.

Frank made a suggestion. "The army would reckon on thirty miles with full kit, but that's on roads. These ancients would probably travel light and hunt for food on the way. And they didn't have good roads."

"Say, ten miles a day?" she said.

"Probably," said Frank.

When Greg brought the map, they sat around it while Janet measured journey lengths.

"Doric's ancestors were from about here," she said pointing. "Where the north east of Portugal touches Spain. There're plenty of river valleys, fed from the mountains in the south and there's a big river plain in Spain. Whether it was like this three hundred generations ago is anyone's guess. And his generations may be shorter than ours. We'll have to ask him next time. And add on the past thirteen hundred years or so." She stood up to stretch and saw Billy on the camp bed. "Peter. It might be better to take Billy back home to rest. Greg, can you get the typist to transcribe the recorded spools? I expect Symes will want to see those tonight?" Janet returned to the map.

24

Latchmere, Friday, April 30th 1943

"Hello Gail. Good to speak to you again." Billy said his words aloud so his team could hear them. She got the words directly from his mind. The wire recorders were recording their words via the wires wound on the bracelet.

"Hi Billy."

"My people need some military intelligence so we can win the war. Can you help us, please?"

"I'll try, but my machines will not let me say anything which might upset the temporal continuum. They're listening and say they'll give you something, but it won't be really useful, perhaps just confirmation of a line of action. They're very excited about Doric's information. They've found several places in Portugal where his ancestors might have come from."

"We've done the same, but we don't have your machines to get an accurate position. Perhaps Doric has seen a map, which will help. What'll you do with the information? Are you going to find the meteorite?"

"We hope so. If you do the same, please leave us some." They both laughed at the thought of his people taking the entire meteorite and her people not finding it.

Symes looked at Janet, who raised her eyebrows.

"We could leave a message for you to find," he said.

"I think they'd find that not funny," she said.

Andrew gave a note to him: "My people say that they only have to destroy my bracelet and you'll never know about it."

"My machines are going mad again."

"They're easily upset. My people don't get mad at things like this."

"They don't have the problems we have. You have a war that we know will end, but we have an unstable sun, which could end the world at any moment. We want to survive as you do. I think my machines will cooperate as best they can."

"My people are glad of that and so am I because I like talking to you."

"Oh Billy. I like talking to you as well. It's so different from talking to the people and machines around me. Woah, there they go again. The machines are going mad. I am bad. I say lots of wrong things."

"You speak to your machines? That's fantastic. Can I talk to them?"

"In a way you are, because I'm connected to them. I have a helmet on my head that gets signals from my brain. It doesn't hurt, but it's inconvenient. If we need better signals, I might have to have wires put directly into my brain."

"That sounds horrid. I hope they don't do that. I've only got the bracelet. My dad has put wires around it to record what we say, but I take it off at the end of the day and play football with some of the soldiers here. Can't they do the same for you?" There was a pause while the machines told her what football was.

"They tried it, but it wasn't sensitive enough. We have other ball games. We also swim and dive because we're near the sea. We explore the old buildings that were wrecked centuries ago in the Bad Times. That's where I found our bracelet."

"I saw you find your second bracelet. I was in the Chislehurst Caves and I dreamed you finding it."

There was another pause while the machines computed the implications.

"My machines want to know how you saw that happen. I don't really remember. I was next to a roof fall which was vibrating, as if it might collapse some more. Then there was an explosion. The next thing I remember, I had moved a long way and I was talking to you. And I had two bracelets. Can you tell us what you saw?"

"I saw you run from a wall. It was exploding, but the bits of rock moved slowly through the air. You easily ran faster than the rocks. Before the big explosion, there was a smaller one and a skeleton arm came through the rocks. You pulled a bracelet off the arm and ran. Then you grabbed a man who was running towards you and you both vanished. Then I was speaking to you when you put the new bracelet on your arm."

"My machines are going crazy again. You actually saw all that?"

"Yeah. I can't make it up."

"That means you can see me at times when I'm not talking to you through my machines. And that episode was before I was even connected."

"Yeah. I've done that here but only with people I know or have met. I ain't got no control over it, the dreams just come."

"So you know what I look like?"

"Yeah. When you was in the caves, you had long fair hair, pale skin, greenish clothes, long trousers and a kind of shirt without buttons and I think you're pretty. Are you dressed like that all the time?"

"Oh Billy. You are nice. My machines and people are frantic. I'm in different clothes today. Can you see me now?"

"No. Those other dreams are different. I can't actually see you now, just hear you."

Andrew handed him a note, which he read out: "Those other dreams are always about things which have happened in the past of that person." He shook his head at Andrew, not understanding what was meant. "I have to rest before I try to get Doric."

She said okay and went away.

"What's the problem?" asked Andrew.

"I can see into the future with that kind of dream. I saw the man in the wall and how he got there."

"We know you can. That time Symes went to Kent and his Jeep blew up, we checked all the times when things happened that afternoon. Very carefully checked. You were a minimum of ten minutes in the future with what you dreamed. We don't want to tell Gail."

"Why not?"

"They might want you to try seeing into their future. So might we with ours, but not yet. You think you can't control what you see, but we reckon you soon might. Frank thinks that'll put a lot of stress on you. Shall we have a tea break?"

Janet nodded.

"You're doing well, son." Dad helped him with the bracelet.

"Dad. You won't put wires in my head, will you?"

"We don't need to and wouldn't know how. In any case, I wouldn't let them." He looked at Symes as they got their drinks. Symes looked away and shuffled some papers.

Billy listened for Doric. He concentrated and found him. He was singing with the other monks. He waited for them to finish and enjoyed listening to the music and words. Doric knew he was listening and was glad he took an interest in his life.

"Greetings. I am at vespers this evening. We now have private prayer so I can talk to you. Is Gail with you?"

"Yes," said Gail. "Greetings."

"Greetings. I have seen several maps, which my abbot has. It is the first time I have studied a map and he was glad to help me. I was with him for half a day and he was pleased with my understanding. He even helped me find where my ancestors lived. He said we all need to know where we come from and God will determine where we are going. I did not tell him about our bracelet. I will try to remember the maps and hold them in my mind. The part of most interest is the river the Romans call Durius. It comes from the great hunting plain in the east and flows to the western sea at the

Roman port of Cale. My ancestors lived on the banks of a river that enters the Durius from the south. I do not know what it is called, the map did not give it a name, but it is big and long. I counted from the western sea, it is the eleventh one on that side of the Durius, but I expect, only the larger rivers are on the map."

He visualised the abbot's map, concentrating on his ancestors' river.

"I'm looking at a picture of your map," said Gail. "My machines got it from my mind and show it to me."

"Is that like television?" asked Billy. "I can't see anything."

Her machines told her what television was. "Yes, but more detail. I also have a view from space looking down on the river valleys. There are three possible rivers. The Torto, the Côa and the Agneda. In my time the water level is higher than you'll find it."

Billy was puzzled. "When you say, space, do you mean from on the moon? Can you see the meteorite?"

"Not the moon. A lot lower than that. It's like a special highflying aircraft. The meteorite will be under water and may be covered in rocks and silt. It'll take us some time to find it. We expect it'll be small. Doric, do you know where the bigger part of the star fell?"

"Not yet. I must remember the saga and look at the map again. I will do that when I next see the abbot. Soon we go on a journey to visit other Christian communities and the abbot might want me to find the way using our maps."

"Thank you, Doric. Good-bye, Billy. We'll speak again, soon. My people might have some intelligence for you. Something about the North Atlantic."

Billy fell back on to the camp bed, exhausted from the three-way conversation.

"Well done, everyone," said Symes. "You can have the weekend off. May Day tomorrow."

25

Latchmere, Saturday, May 1st 1943

Billy has never seen maypole dancing. He concentrates on the preparations. The boys and girls get into their starting positions, making sure each has the correct coloured ribbon. There are smiles and chatter as the classmates jostle so their parents can see them. He picks up the subtle emotions from within the group of children. Even without his bracelet, he sees through their eyes, feels the excitement in their minds subside to quietness.

His mind joins with theirs as they wait.

The boys and girls stand still. The May Day breeze twitches strands of loose hair. Each child holds a coloured ribbon across their white shirt or blouse. Two women in their best summer frocks are poised with accordions strapped to their bosoms. An old man in shamrock green, sounds the beat on his Bodhrán. The polished stick flashes in the sunlight. Children feel the throb of the Irish drum and know how fast they will have to skip. Drum pulses resonate with the hearts of the audience and performers, toes tapping, heads nodding. All are expectant of the thrills to come. Boys steal glances across the circle, girls flip their heads and coyly smile. Men and women watch their sons and daughters and remember their first May Day dance.

At the call of the old man, a long chord sounds on both accordions and they are off into the complex movements and sounds of the pagan British rite.

He is transfixed by the unfamiliar dance as the children weave their ribbons in and out, round and round. The boys dancing in one direction, the girls in the other, skipping and laughing, not a care in the world except for the accuracy with which they dance. Orange and green, red and blue, yellow and purple, a spectrum of colour flashes across the pure white of the innocents as they laugh and shout, skipping to the music of the ages coursing through their veins. First ducking, ribbons low, then stretching, ribbons high, each child exultant in the art of the fertility dance where boys and girls rush together, but have to pass, so the ribbons are placed in their eternal pattern of intertwining helixes, the pattern which defines all nature, unknown to these young minds. The skipping cherubs pull their ribbons into the asphyxiating criss-cross patterns from tip to root on the erect Maypole. The tight fabrics pull the children in. Passing ever closer to each other, brushing arms, sharing breaths, unconscious of the power that these fleeting encounters force upon their emerging adulthoods.

The old man calls.

The accordions sound a cadence. The children still themselves, breathing hard, red faced, pulled close to the Maypole and their neighbours. They look into the eyes of the random partner they face, see as they have never seen them before. Their inner helixes express new emotions with no time to develop. Once again, they have to turn away, this time to free the Maypole of its rainbow constraint.

The Bodhrán beats, taps the toes, nods the heads and skips the feet as the helixes are torn apart to recombine another day, another year, when these dancers will be the watchers at the margins of the dance.

Billy gasps and grabs his Dad's hand.

"What is it, son."

"That's what I do with the bracelet. I unravel the strands. They're all twisted up in beautiful patterns, then I unwrap 'em, one by one and look for who I'm trying to find. That's 'ow it works."

"You'll have to explain that to Andrew and Janet, they'll probably understand."

"They can't unless they see it. They need to see the ribbons. The thousands and thousands of ribbons. They go everywhere. Different places and different times. Millions of ribbons all different colours. Each person's got thousands of ribbons. Each thing's got thousands. That's what Father Michael saw and it killed him. Dad, it killed Father Michael because he couldn't believe what he was seein'. He didn't understand that the coloured ribbons were to guide us through." He sobs. "Michael was strangled by 'em after he used a special word."

Dad hugs him close. "It's okay, son. Don't fret. What word did he use?"

"I'm not allowed to say. In the dream, the angel told me not to repeat it, unless lives were at risk. I don't know what he meant."

"Best not say it then unless you're in real danger. I think we'd better get back to the lab. You've thought of something that might be important. Symes, we need to go back to the lab. Billy's thought of something he'd like to try."

"Okay. You go on. I'll tell your family and catch you up."

On the walk back, they called on the other members of the team. They found Andrew and Janet at their lodgings but Frank and Greg had gone into Richmond for the day.

Dad got Billy ready and set up the wire recorder with Andrew helping. He tried to explain his ideas to Andrew and Janet, but found it impossible to express himself.

"I guess, if we start you off, you'll see it all, so you might be able to describe it more easily," said Janet.

"Yeah. Okay." He slipped the bracelet onto his arm. Very slowly, the noises built up in the loudspeaker.

Symes joined them in the laboratory.

Billy concentrated on the sounds and talked about what he could see and hear. "There's dark spots everywhere and they're all joined by coloured ribbons and strings. Each dark spot has sounds coming from it, but I don't know what they mean. When I concentrate on a spot, it gets bigger and I can see more ribbons and hear the sounds better. If I think really hard, each spot becomes a person and I can hear 'em speak.

It's difficult and I don't understand 'em. I can understand Gail and she helps me understand Doric with her machines. There's loads of others but I can't properly hear 'em. I don't know what the colours of the ribbons mean. I'm sure there's a reason, but don't get it."

"Can you see Gail and Doric?"

"Yeah, but they're echoes, they're conversations I've had before and I can't hear them again. Oh. Here's Gail. This is a new one. Hello Gail."

"Hi Billy. Have you tried to find the meteorite yet? My people are beginning to look."

"I don't know. They made a map and took it off. I'll probably never know 'cos of the security. I'll tell you if I find out. Do you have any intelligence for us? You said you might have."

"What is your date?"

Andrew wrote it down.

"It's the first of May 1943."

"Okay then. I can tell you that the North Atlantic convoys will be less of a problem from now on. Last Monday there was a report that said that HMS Biter was very effective. May the fourth will be bad with twelve ships lost but seven U-boats will be sunk. The U-boat captains are losing confidence. They will give false positions to their masters to confuse you. On the twenty-third of May, the U-boats will withdraw, but you won't know that for a week. That's all I've been given. I hope it's useful."

"I'll tell you next time we talk. Thanks to you and your machines. I hope it doesn't change our future."

"Me too. I won't be talking to you for some months. We are doing other experiments with the bracelets. I don't know if that will make a difference to you. We know that our two times are not linked exactly. Bye Billy."

"I'll miss you ever so. Don't be too long. Bye Gail."

"Well done lad," said Symes. He read Janet's notebook and left the lab to report the intelligence.

"I wonder what their experiments are," said Andrew. "You understand this much more, don't you?"

"Yeah. I can kind of see where and when people and fings are and 'ow they're connected with these coloured ribbons. I've just thought. I've not seen those Twins through the bracelet. They were really here, I mean, Edith and the others saw them, not just me."

"That's true. So you can't see them when you put the bracelet on?" said Janet.

"Naw. I've tried, but they ain't there."

"We'll have to think about that," said Andrew.

Symes returned. "Well done Billy and the rest of you. That information was well received. This ribbon thing you've experienced, how much can you see?"

"It's funny really. It ain't only people I see. I can see things an' all. You know, objects."

"Does Michael still have a ribbon? And is the Monsignor there?" asked Symes.

"Yeah. The Monsignor's there and Michael still has a couple of ribbons, one to a place what I don't know and another what goes on forever. That's very faint."

"Who else connects to the place you mentioned?"

"Loads of people but I don't know who they are. Hang on. Yeah, that woman you spoke to when your Jeep blew up. She's connected to it."

"Really? Any more connections?"

"Hundreds. I can't go through 'em now, I'm knackered."

"Okay. Well done lad. If you see anything interesting, you let us know."

"Yeah Mister Symes."

26

Latchmere, Monday, May 31st 1943

Four weeks passed without contact with Gail. Billy was worried he would never speak to her again. The others reassured him that Gail had been truthful and she would be back. Without her machines, he had difficulty speaking to Doric.

Andrew worked on the bracelet theory and Billy told him when he had new information about the ways ribbons connected people and things. Miss Porter had tried to teach him some Latin without much success, but when he concentrated, he picked up the sense of what Doric thought and then a few Latin words explained it.

Miss Porter was included in the team to add meaning to Doric's early life as a druid and his current life as a monk and priest. Doric's time seemed to be going faster than Billy's and Gail's. Each day they contacted Doric he seemed to have moved on by days or weeks. Once, it was a jump of a few years. Andrew declared there was no reason why the three of them should keep in step. He said there was even the possibility that they could jump backwards in their timelines. It hadn't happened so far, because, he thought, the human psyche could not deal with such a thing. Frank agreed, saying that human memory was always of the past. Telling the future had never been proved.

Billy wrestled with the mental view he had of Gail, Doric and himself, as well as the other people he could visualise, but not contact. He realised the significance of the coloured connecting ribbons. Neither Gail nor Doric saw these ribbons they only heard each other. Father Michael was constantly in his mind and he wondered if that episode had caused him to see the ribbons. He worked out that some of the colours related to forwards and backwards in time, because the ribbons to Gail and Doric were two different colours. What he could not understand was the significance of all the other colours and the widths of the ribbons, some being thin strings, running between the nodes, which were people and objects.

Andrew put his mind to that one. He reckoned that some colours related to space, that is, the position of those people that he could see. Without more data, he could not check that. His problem was the fact that two people living in different times would also be in changing positions in space by virtue of the planetary movements around the sun and the movement of the sun through the universe. He calculated the distances between the trio and came up with some huge numbers. What he could not understand was that the three of them could speak more or less instantaneously. This defied the Einstein law of relativity. Even if the solar system did not move through the cosmos, there was a thousand second time delay for light travelling across the orbit of the Earth. He then saw that Gail's people had figured this out and wanted to use the bracelet as a means of communication, instant communication, over vast distances. They needed the meteorite so they could make more bracelets or some variant artefact.

There was no reappearance of the Twins or any sign of them in Billy's mental images. When he mentioned the Twins again, Doric repeated about seeing them at the Sarum Stones during a winter solstice. The Twins were like shining ghosts. At the Stones, they had told him it was important to find out about the origin of his bracelet, so he had learned the full saga when he got home.

Doric said, "A year later, I joined a company of Irish monks traveling to Canterbury. We stopped for a while at Aquae Sulis, or Bath, as the Saxons call it. When I sang one of my tribal songs, the twin spirits appeared again."

"What happened?" asked Billy.

"It was strange, because I also saw a man who called himself Billy. I now know you are the same person, but much younger."

"I don't remember that."

The team stopped their activities and hung on every word.

"You were a grown man and we held hands in greeting. You knew me and our bracelet very well. You said you had already spoken to me many times which we are doing now. You told me I had to learn the Roman languages and spoke of a battle to come where we will stand side by side and fight the devils in the stars."

"That must be in my future." All eyes in the lab stared at him.

"I do not understand this, I think you do not either," said Doric.

"My friends here tell me we must think about this. I will speak to you another time."

The team reviewed the subject of the Twins and Doric's revelation.

Janet summed up. "It's clear that the Twins are manipulating their past. They tell Doric to find out about the bracelet's origin and they intervene when Billy was in danger. In the first case, finding the meteorite is important, both for us and for Gail's people. In the second case, it establishes Billy as a key link in all this, otherwise, why protect him at the risk of causing a paradox? I wonder what else they have done and I wonder if they are good or evil."

"I go for good," said Symes. "Of course, that may be for their good."

"That dream I had in Chislehurst about Father Michael, was that the Twins?" said Billy.

"That was different, I think," said Frank. "They didn't appear while you were awake. They weren't in the caves with you. I haven't worked that one out yet, but you obviously connected with something. If it's like the other sleeping visions you've had, it'll prove to be true."

"Like when I saw Mr. Symes talking to the Policeman on the hop farm?"

"Yes. That actually happened," said Symes.

"If Billy can't find them when he searches, we'll have to wait for them to appear again," said Janet, "unless we can make them, by putting him in danger."

There were some grim faces around the lab, including Billy. "I don't want no danger. There's enough already."

"Too true," said Peter.

"Maybe they'd be able to tell the difference between real and orchestrated dangers. We'll wait until an opportunity arises," said Symes.

"What about when I meet Doric in my future?" said Billy.

"The Twins probably helped you with that. It looks like you'll have a fight on your hands when you're a man," said Andrew.

"I don't want no fight."

"We can't ask for more details, we might get a paradox," said Andrew. "We'll just have to wait and see."

"Okay, let's call it a day," said Symes. "Just one thing. I've had confirmation of Gail's comment about that Oslo Report. It mentions possible new weapons that Hitler is developing. A contact in MI19 has confirmed actual weapon tests."

"Was that at Trent Park?" said Greg. "I installed some equipment there."

"Obviously I can't comment," said Symes, "but stunning work continues in several of our facilities." He gave Greg a wink.

27

Latchmere, Monday, December 6th 1943

Billy found and spoke to Gail. “I’m glad you’re back, I missed talking to you. What’ve you been doing?”

“I’m glad to be back, too. Experiments. I can’t say more or my machines will cut me off. Your friend Jeff who was with you when you met Symes. Where does he live?”

He looked at his Dad for an answer.

“Bethnal Green. Grove Road, I think.”

Billy relayed the message.

“I will have something to tell you in your next year. My machines are not happy, but I have to tell you that your friend is in danger and it will be next June thirteenth, but I can’t tell you why until then.”

“What use is that? He’s my friend. I want to warn him.”

“It’s this paradox. If I tell you now and you tell others, it might change the future. Our mathematician is working on it and we are doing experiments, but it’s slow. Can you look in your mind at those ribbons connecting people and can you see me?”

He closed his eyes and concentrated on his map of the universe, as Andrew called it.

“Yeah, I can see two of yer. How’s that?”

“I have both bracelets, one on each arm. Can you describe what you see?”

“Yeah. It’s like two people but joined with a white line, very thick and straight, it don’t wander about like the others. Can your machines see it?”

“No, they get something, but it changes so fast they can’t keep up. The boffins say it’s so incredible that your mind is faster than their machines, but it has to go through me as well, so perhaps I’m the slow one.”

“It changes for me too, but I can stop it if I want and go back as well. I don’t do it much ‘cos it’s confusing.”

"When you say 'go back', what do you mean?"

"I suppose what I see is what's happening between all the people. I can go back to what happened before now."

Billy stopped talking and watched the vision in his mind. The ribbons waved as if moved by an ocean. Sometimes they snapped to a different position on the node that was a person, or suddenly changed colour. He concentrated when that happened between two of the nodes and managed to go backwards and forwards across the moment when it happened. He found her among the countless nodes in his mind and watched the ribbon that connected the two of them. It was the usual green colour showing that she was in his future.

He tried to change the colour of the ribbon. It changed to a different green, the colour of her past, but still his future. Her image changed to a single form, showing that she wore only one bracelet.

Gail was still there so he spoke to her. "Can you hear me?" There was no reply, but he had the feeling that she was listening. He spoke again. "Gail, this is Billy. I'm your friend." This time, the node that was Gail began to move a little and the ribbon rippled. "We can talk. Just think the words you want to say."

"Who are you?" she thought.

"I'm a friend from your future. This is the first time we've spoken. Are you wearing your bracelet?"

"How are you in my mind? Am I going mad? Is it the bracelet?"

"You ain't mad. What is your date? Where are you?"

"Sept twenty-four, twenty seven ninety five. I'm in the medicentre. Why?"

"We meet again next year for you. I'll speak to you then."

Janet scribbled some notes and showed them to Frank, who nodded.

Billy forced her ribbon back to the usual green. "I just spoke to you when you were in the hospital." He said the date of their encounter.

"I remember dreaming of someone. I was very sleepy with the medication just after I found the bracelet. The date is accurate. Can you go forward as well?"

"I'll try." He concentrated, thinking of the colour blue, the colour for her future. The ribbon changed slowly while he thought about what he wanted. As the ribbon changed colour, her image in his mind changed from double to single and back to double as he passed moments when she was wearing either one or two bracelets. He forced the ribbon colour into the future as far as he could and her dual image was suffused with three other people that jostled for attention. Each of these three had infinity ribbons. Sudden pain seared through his mind. Only two of the three remained. Again, torment sliced through him.

He sat up straight on the camp bed, tears streaming from his screwed up eyes, his face wracked with fear and agony. He shouted, "Stop it. Stop it. Help me," but fought off his Dad as he tried to remove the bracelet. "Gail. Are you there?"

"Oh Billy. I hurt. You've come for me at last."

"What's the matter?"

"It's been ages since we were together. Ah, that hurt. Sorry. I'm giving birth. My babies are coming. They're glad you're here. Oh, oh ..."

"Speak to me."

"Later."

In his tortured mind, he watched the double image of Gail and the two new forms strengthen and separate. He saw the ribbons between her and the two babies, her double image and the two children. He felt those ribbons, a new type of connection, gold, with a shimmering depth of vibrations singing in his mind.

For a brief moment there were again five infinity ribbons, each a separate entity connected together. Then only two, Gail's double image. The babies' ribbons had gone. Gail's sheer joy replaced the distress and filled the space in his mind where the ribbons of time rippled their dance of eternity.

He fell back onto the camp bed and slept.

"Exactly what happened there?" asked Peter.

"No idea," said Frank. "He certainly saw and experienced something amazing. Best let him rest, he can tell us later. Let me look at his arm." He checked, sliding the bracelet carefully down to Billy's wrist. There was no burn so they left him sleeping. Dad pulled a blanket over his son and sat with him.

"What did you see?" asked Janet. Billy was drinking some warm milk after waking up. The heating in the house was not working properly. The normally snug laboratory was cool.

"She was giving birth to twin babies. It didn't 'alf hurt, I kind of felt it. It must be well in her future, 'cos she said it was ages since we'd been together. When was that? I've never actually been with her."

"Perhaps she meant speak with her," said Janet. "We know she's about fourteen when you speak to her normally, so children would be some years away yet, unless things are a lot different in her time. I'll make a note for you to ask her when women normally have babies in her time. It'll probably be best not to tell her of this if she and her machines didn't catch it."

"Do you think her babies are the Twins I saw? There was another baby there just for a moment. At least, I think it was a baby. It went away very quickly."

"Could be the Twins, but obviously from Gail's future because they were older children weren't they?"

"Yeah, older than me but not grown up. And then they suddenly disappeared. They ain't got ribbons now."

Janet looked at her notes. "I'm not sure what to make of that third one. Are you certain it was a baby?"

"It weren't there for long, but it looked the same as the other two."

Symes joined the discussion. "So these Twins don't have ribbons?"

"No. They did for a moment and then they disappeared."

"Do you mean the ribbons disappeared?"

"Well, without them I don't know if the babies were there or not."

"Of course. This is important. Can you see into the future from here, from now?"

"I ain't tried that yet. I need to fix on a person or thing."

"Try me. You managed it when my Jeep was blown up."

"Can I have another drink please?"

Frank put milk into a saucepan and warmed it. Billy gulped it down.

"Ta. I'll try now."

They all went to their stations ready for the experiment. He shut his eyes and soon found Symes' ribbons. He pulled and stretched them, tried to see to whom and what they joined. All of it was unknown to him. He was about to give up when he recognised another person.

"I can see us talking with Father Alan. It's a long way in the future, after the war. We're drinking real coffee. I can't hear the words, just the feeling of an argument."

"Have you any idea of the date?"

"No. There's nothing in the room that tells me. There's a television set and he never had one when I first went there."

"Okay. As you say, after the war. I think that'll do for today," said Symes. "We'll start again in the morning if the house isn't frozen solid. Remember to be careful not to tell Gail about her children next time. It may cause a problem. Thank you everyone and thank you Billy. This way you have of seeing around in time could be useful. Perhaps we could make some more bracelets. I'll see how they're getting on with the explorations."

Billy and the others were let out of the laboratory by

Edith. She wore her arctic uniform, but still looked cold.

"Hello, Billy. There may be snow overnight. You okay to do some tracking work if it comes? I'll get you some kit like mine."

Billy looked at Symes who nodded. "Yeah, please. That'll complete the set. We've done sand, dirt, mud, grass and forest, but not snow," said Billy ticking them off with his fingers.

"That's it, young man. The only one we can't do around here is rocky terrain, boulders, cliffs, that sort of thing. Perhaps our next summer outing, eh Major Symes?"

"I'll give it some thought. Who's taking over from you tonight?"

"It'll be Martin, sir. Twenty two hundred." She snapped a salute as Symes nodded and turned to the stairs.

28

Richmond Park, Tuesday, December 7th 1943

It was Edith's personal objective to teach Billy as much field craft as she could during this tour of duty. She had only four months left. Sometime in the spring of '44, she was needed for an offensive in France, but no date had been set. She knew, that if the offensive were not a success, then the people of Britain would need all the luck and skills they could muster to thwart the likely German invasion of the British Isles. Kids like him would be on their own. Their parents would be under military rule and easily controlled, but the children would be much less visible and freer to gather information or perform other subversive actions.

In the pre-dawn of Richmond Park, Edith led the way, walking normally on the snowy grass, but making occasional detours. Billy followed after about ten minutes, using a torch. This early in the day, there were no human footprints and few animal prints to worry about so he found the task quite easy. He had missed only one detour, where she had jumped from the path onto a fallen tree and then beyond into thick grass. He eventually found it and soon caught up.

"Well done. I'll make a soldier of you yet." She adjusted his out-sized snow smock so it would not catch on the bare bushes and motioned to return to Latchmere House.

"You keep sayin' that. I don't want to kill people, even if they're really bad. It ain't right."

"Even if they are going to kill you, or your mum and dad?"

"That's different, but I ain't lookin' for trouble." They marched back to the house, their breath as white as the snow under their feet.

"I don't look for trouble when I go out on duty, but there's always those who'll give it to you. Like that man with the Monsignor. He was intent on giving us trouble."

"What 'appened to 'im?"

"Don't know. Taken off for questioning is all I need to know. That's the business we're in." They reached the edge of Ham Common.

"What's that?" He pointed at fresh tyre marks on the frosty verge.

"Saloon car. Like the Monsignor's, on Easter Day. Same place, too." She signalled him to get behind the bushes at the edge of the road. The morning sky was getting lighter and she didn't want them seen.

"Do yer think he's back?" he whispered, crouched beside her.

"Not likely. He won't get into this country again." She pointed to the left. They looked through the leafless branches as two men came into view, their long black coats brushing the snow from the stands of dead grass at the roadside. He heard them speak, but not what they said. He watched as they inched closer, searching the ground, occasionally kicking at the frosted grass tangled with the remains of the autumn's wild flowers.

Edith held his arm to reassure him. Her hand felt the bulge of the bracelet that he now constantly wore. She was pleased he was quiet, with no sign of fear, just as she had trained him. She drew her automatic from underneath her snow smock and screwed in a silencer. Her gloved hand deadened the sound as she slipped off the safety catch. She gestured for him to stay in position. When the two men's backs were turned, she moved to another bush and stood to the side of it, purposely making a noise.

The men swung round, reaching into their coat pockets, stopping when they saw she was armed and taking aim. They put their hands to their sides.

"Lost something?" she said.

"Late in day for poaching," said the taller of the men.

"What's your business?"

"None of yours," said the shorter man.

Billy recognised the accents of the men. It was Portuguese, the same as the Monsignor's gunman.

Edith pointed to the shorter man. "You. Pull out your gun and throw it over here."

"Why you think I got gun?"

"Allow a poacher some intelligence."

"You come and get it." He opened his coat offering a search.

She shot him in the knee. "The gun."

"*Meu Deus*." The man fell and squirmed on the road, leaking blood onto the snow. He fumbled in his coat and threw his weapon, but made a bad job of it. The gun landed some way from her.

"Now you," she said to the taller man. He complied without protest. She pocketed his gun. "What are you doing here?"

"Hospital. I need hospital." The shorter man clutched his knee with both hands.

"When you answer my questions, otherwise you won't need one. Ever." There was a noise in the bushes behind her. She didn't turn, but carefully aimed her gun at the taller man. "If that's one of your people, you'd better tell him to surrender, or you'll be the first to die."

"Not ours," said the taller man, his eyes searching the ground in front of him.

She moved sideways, keeping aim, but getting to a position where she could steal a look at the approaching person. Finding that difficult, she shouted over her shoulder: "Identify yourself." There was no reply, only the soft crunch on the frosty snow. She moved a little further and then glanced behind. A badger snorted steam in the cold air and turned away from the group.

The taller man took his chance and dived for his colleague's gun.

Edith compensated for the move but only managed a bullet through the man's coat as it billowed behind him. The shorter man screamed as the round caught him in the stomach.

Billy stood from behind his bush to see what was happening. The bracelet began to heat. He saw the shorter man writhing in agony at the edge of the road. The taller one was rolling, gun in hand, shooting wildly at Edith who dived, returning fire.

Billy shouted. “Stop it. Stop it.”

The man stopped rolling, lifted himself to his knees and shot at him, just before Edith’s next bullet slammed into his head.

Billy stood still. He could see the man’s bullet flying at him, slowing to a crawl, so slow that he thought it would fall to the ground. But it came on, intent on piercing his body and possibly killing him. He had a choice, either dodge the missile, or cause it to stop. The boy in him wanted a trophy. He decided he must halt its flight so he could catch it and show it to his mates. He perceived the bubble of energy around his body, separating him from the universe through which the bullet was racing. He knew he could move unhindered through that other universe. He understood. This was how Gail had escaped from the exploding wall. It was how the Twins move between different times and places.

It took a great deal of concentration to stop the bullet. The whole universe had to stop. He soon fathomed the ribbons of light in his mind. The ones connecting him to the speeding bullet were easily disrupted, after all, the bullet was decelerating, losing energy the moment it left the gun barrel. It needed only a small thought to make it lose all its energy and stand still in space and time while he decided what to do with it.

He moved to where the bullet hung in the air and peered at it. There was no horror in what he saw. The bullet could not kill him now. It was totally under his power. He slipped off his glove and grabbed it. It was warm in his hand and was motionless inside his bubble. He put it in his pocket.

The man had not moved, his face not registering the bullet from Edith's gun as it bored through his brain.

He moved closer. The ribbons in his mind showed the man and his connections to Symes and Father Michael. His heart beat faster to perceive the priest, who had always been there, with his few faint, near colourless ribbons, but one of the ribbons was no longer faded. It was angry scarlet. He knew that this man had killed Father Michael and the priest had known it, despite his coma. He tried to move Father Michael's ribbons and change their colour, but failed. He understood. Once the person was dead, the ribbons told the history and were fixed.

The man's ribbons showed he was not yet dead. Billy thrilled to the idea of stopping the bullet doing its business. He concentrated, pulled and twisted them. The bullet reversed its gory path from inside the man's brain. When it was completely out, he realised that if he got too close, the man would be inside his bubble and could attack. He looked about him for inspiration and found a long twig. He knocked the bullet to the ground. Another souvenir to show his friends. The man was now dangerous and would be able to do things after he stopped his manipulation of the events in front of him. He picked up the second bullet and pocketed it, puzzling over what to do.

The twig just fitted up the barrel of the gun. He snapped off the end when he rammed it home, being sure to keep his distance. Then he jammed the rest of the twig through the man's open mouth and down his throat, knowing it would take his mind off what was happening long enough for Edith to do something. He wanted this man alive so he could tell how he had killed Father Michael. He moved well back from the men and allowed the universe to continue on its way.

The tall man choked and spat. He fell to the ground on top of his gun that went off. His body heaved as the bullet and twig blasted their way into his abdomen.

"No. No," shouted Billy. "Don't die, you bugger." He ran

to the man and tried to roll him over. Edith struggled to her feet and helped. The man's eyes were screwed up with pain. He coughed, trying to clear his throat. She prised the gun from his hand and saw the twig in his mouth. She pulled it out.

The man coughed and swore.

"Who sent you?" she said.

"No," said the man.

"You killed Father Michael," said Billy. "Who told you to? Was it Symes?"

"Hospital." The man could barely open his eyes with the pain.

"Tell me. Then hospital," she said, looking at the boy wondering what he meant.

"Can't. Dead drop," said the man between short breaths.

"Where?" she said.

"Who is the *menino*, the boy?" said the man.

He answered before she could stop him. "Billy Carter. Your worst enemy. Tell her."

Edith smiled.

The man swore again. "Thursdays. Oh nine hundred. Brown paper bag." He choked. "Public toilet. Battersea Park." His breath rattled in his throat.

"That's one of Symes dead drops. Who you with?" she said.

"Not telling."

"Forget the hospital. Come on, let's get back." She straightened and began to walk to the car.

"Tell her or you'll die."

"Don't waste your time on him." She winked at the boy.

"I should've let this bullet kill him," he said, pulling it from his pocket. "Mister, I saved your life." He held it in front of the man's eyes. "This was in your head and I stopped it and pulled it out. You owe me your life. I ain't doin' you no more favours." He turned away and followed her.

"Wait. You. Billy with *bracelete,* bracelet."

"What of it?"

"Monsignor says be careful. Each day he prays for you." The man coughed. Blood coloured his lips.

Edith walked back and searched the man's coat pockets for the car key. "I'll get their car."

Billy nodded and spoke to the man, "Why would the Monsignor do that?"

"You say you stopped bullet killing me. *Obrigado*. Thank you." He paused to get his breath, "Monsignor finds other things about your bracelet." Another cough. "He says it proves God is real."

"Naw. It's amazing, but it ain't from God. If it was, I'd understand what the people are sayin' when I use it. None of 'em are from God. Are you from the Vatican?"

"No. Tomar. Remember that name. You will need it. God bless you Billy." The man reached out with his bloodied hand and made the sign of the cross. A final coughing spasm finished his life.

He watched the ribbons as the man became part of his history. The other ribbons changed shape and colour. The one to Father Michael lost its redness. Those to Symes lost their colour then disappeared, but one thin line was active. He looked along it until it faded beyond his view, knowing the line was not ordinary time or distance. He could see those of other people and objects. It had a different quality. It was the same as Father Michael's. A pale grey ribbon connected to infinity.

Edith backed the car to where Billy was standing. It took all their strength to get the two men onto the back seat. The shorter man was still breathing.

Billy wiped his bloody hands on his snow smock.

"You okay ducks?" she said, holding his arm.

"Yeah. Bit of a mess," he said, looking down his front. "But I got some bullets."

"Did you catch 'em?"

"Yeah, look." He got both bullets from his pocket.

"Blimey. That's some trick."

"Ain't no trick. The bracelet slowed 'em down to nuffin. I don't know 'ow."

She laughed out loud. The boy was so matter of fact about the extraordinary power he had, it was truly laughable. "What was all that about Symes and Michael?"

"That man what died, he killed Father Michael while he was in hospital and I think Major Symes told him to."

"I'll check that Battersea dead drop. There might be some evidence."

When they got back to the house, Edith handed the car and contents over to the Latchmere staff and gave Martin the two guns.

29

Latchmere, Tuesday, December 7th 1943

Billy was now clean from the gore of the early morning. Martin gave him a smart salute as he let him into the laboratory. Edith had gone back to the scene to investigate what the two men had been doing there.

"Good morning, Billy," said Symes. "Are you okay for work?"

"Yeah, Mister Symes. I've found a new thing the bracelet does."

"Edith told me all about it. Please don't take chances, though. You might not be so lucky next time."

"Naw. I'll be careful." He searched Symes face. "Did she tell you about the man what died?"

"Yes. His gun went off when he fell on it. Unfortunate. Still, we have the other one we can interrogate when he's well enough. I wonder if your bracelet could help with that. You might be able to read his mind. Have you ever tried it?"

"Naw. Only someone with one. I can only feel what they feel. It's not like reading their mind. Don't you care about the man what died?"

"Have you still got that bullet?"

Billy stuck his hand into his pocket and showed Symes.

"Two bullets? Edith didn't mention a second one."

"Yeah. One's from the man's gun when he shot at me. The other one was from her gun what I stopped."

"Right. That was on its way to hit the man?"

"No. It was already in 'is head. I used the ribbons to pull it back out."

"That's incredible."

"I thought it'd be better to question him. I stuck a stick in 'is mouth to put him off when everything speeded up again. His coughing made him fall on his gun. I'm sorry. My ribbons showed he was connected to the Monsignor, Father

Michael and to you."

Symes flinched. "I can't imagine why, except we had the Monsignor here for a while."

"I expect Edith'll give you a proper report."

"Right. Well. Let's get on with the day."

Janet took up the schedule. "We've a lot of intelligence about a flying bomb or pilotless aircraft. That Oslo report Gail told us about, predicted this. Billy, I'd like you to ask her about these weapons and perhaps, give us some confirmation, some verification of the intelligence we're getting."

"Okay," said Billy and sat on the camp bed preparing himself for the conversation. He caught a strange look from Symes. "What's that for?"

Symes slowly shook his head.

"Can I tell Gail about what happened today?"

"Yes. I've been looking through the transcripts of your conversations with her and I think they may have found something similar themselves."

"Yeah. Here goes." He sat quietly, fingering the bracelet. Dad sat next to him, giving his usual moral support. The heating in the lab had been fixed overnight, so he was warm, but the mixed emotions about Symes and Michael stopped him feeling relaxed. He lay down on the camp bed and closed his eyes, desperate to concentrate. The coloured ribbons appeared, showing the relationships between him and the rest of the universe. Understanding the weird theories that Andrew concocted almost daily, was difficult for him, but it was always interesting talking to the physicist and such a shame the man could not see these things for himself.

He found Gail, but Doric's ribbons showed he was not wearing the bracelet. The monk had a hard life and the bracelet was seen as anti-Christian by his abbot, so he could not often use it.

Gail was there and pleased to talk. "Hi Billy. Hope you're

okay."

"Yeah. Great. I found a new thing this morning, with the bracelet. I can stop things moving. I can slow down everything around me, right to stopped. Can you do that?"

"Sort of. I wasn't allowed to say anything until we knew you could, too. What happened?"

He told her a shortened version of the story. "At the end, one of the blokes fell on his gun and killed himself, but he still had a ribbon, not like other dead people who don't have any. He had one like Father Michael's. It's like they ain't real people."

"It must be horrid to see someone die. My machines are very interested in these ribbons."

"Yeah," he caught his breath, "there was lots of bodies when I was in London. Don't get that here. But my people don't seem bovvered about this bloke what died." He paused to catch his breath.

Janet and Symes exchanged glances.

Billy continued. "What was it you did with your bracelet to stop things moving?"

"It was that time the wall exploded in the tunnel. You dreamed it, remember? I didn't realise I'd done it till afterwards. It must have been like you, stopping everything around you, but I couldn't control it. That was when we talked properly for the first time. How do you stop things moving?"

"It's hard to tell you if you can't see the ribbons like I can. It's them what I move or change. They connect everything I see in my mind when the bracelet is working. Not just people, but things as well. I saw the bullet and took away the ribbon what was connected to me. Somehow I knew it was the right one."

"My machines are asking lots of questions. It looks like you can change things that might happen in the future. They are worried you might do something which will affect us in your future."

"I promise I won't do anything to you. I like you a lot. We're friends. Anyhow, I don't know if I can affect your ribbons."

"Can you see my machines in your mind?"

"You're connected to lots of people, but I can't tell who they are until I actually speak to them, like with Doric. Things, like your machines, look different, but I don't know what's what."

"But you knew which thing the bullet was."

"Yeah, but I don't know how. I just knew. I need more practice. My masters are asking for intelligence. We're at December 7th 1943. Anything interesting going to happen soon, especially about flying bombs?"

There was a pause before she answered: "Do you have photos and sketches of launch sites in Northern France?"

Symes confirmed they did and asked if they were for the pilotless flying bomb of which they had photographs from a Danish source.

"Yes. The bomb is the biggest yet from your enemy. Its gyroscopic guidance system is effective for your technology level but there are many things which cause them to behave erratically."

Billy had trouble with the unfamiliar words, but managed to get the sense of it.

"They'll fly at about the same speed as your fastest fighters so will be difficult to shoot down, but you'll have some success. Your ground based-guns will have to put up lots of exploding shells to shoot them down. This'll work, but many will get through and the shrapnel from your guns will be a problem on the ground. The bomb's main benefit for the enemy will be from the psychological effects on your population."

Janet slipped a note to Symes. He nodded. "Billy, ask her if there's anything we can do about this weapon."

He repeated Janet's question.

"You'll be able to change the bomb's aiming strategy by

using the enemy spies you've already captured. They can act as spotters and you can get them to send false information about the bomb landings and their numbers. This will move the centre of their target area, which is central London. Keep up your bombing of the sites in France, this'll be partially effective, but the launch sites are easy to rebuild elsewhere."

Symes gave a thumb-up.

"That's very good information," said Billy. "My people talk of other special bombs as well."

"Yes. They have more powerful warheads and come on rockets. You can't easily detect these until they arrive. They go very fast and high and then drop straight down. The first bombs are like aircraft with wings, but with a special engine. You can hear them coming. I'm not sure which is more frightening. If you bomb the launch sites and supply factories, you'll delay the beginning of these first bombs until the thirteenth of June next year."

"Thanks. They're asking me, when do we invade France and push the enemy back."

"I'm not allowed to tell you that, except it will happen and will be a difficult fight. You'll take nearly a year to succeed."

He felt a sadness in Gail's thoughts. He saw she knew something that she was not allowed to tell. "You sound sad, is there a problem?"

"Yes, but I'm not allowed to say. We may not be allowed speak for a while because of the time paradox thing and my doctors think I'm under too much stress so I need to rest."

"I know. I've looked forward in time. I speak to you when you're giving birth to your babies." He shot a defiant look at Symes who was about to stop him. "I don't know when that happens or if we speak before that. I know which is future and which is past, but not how many years. I'm sad to stop, but we'll talk again."

"Billy. You saw my babies? Oh stars, how many? You saw that happen? When? Who's the father?"

"I don't know who their father is, but I think they're the twins I've seen and I know how the man in the wall what exploded got there. And about his bracelet."

"My machines are going berserk. I think they might cut us off." She gabbled, "Stay away from Lewisham market. Twenty-eighth of July next year. Nine in the morning. I'll speak to you when I have my babies. Love you, Billy."

"Gail. I love you too. I must meet you one day. It must be possible." He saw the ribbons change colour when he felt the loss of her presence. Tears streamed down his face as his body shook with uncontrollable grief. He sat up and grabbed Dad who held him tight.

Symes waved his hand at the others to leave the lab and he followed them out, leaving them alone with their memories. This part of his group's work was finished.

30

Latchmere, Wednesday, December 8th 1943

The day after Gail's cut off, Symes called everyone to order.

"Right team it looks as though we'll not be getting much from Gail. My masters have plenty for me to do and I know they have urgent tasks for some of you, probably what you were doing before, but I really don't know."

"What about us?" asked Peter.

"I don't know that yet. I have a meeting this afternoon where I expect to hear, so if we all meet here tomorrow morning at nine, I'll tell you. If anything urgent comes up at the meeting, I'll get in touch sooner. Please stay in Latchmere or your digs, so I can find you. I'm sorry this is so sudden, but we are not making the headway our masters wanted and resources are short." Symes banged on the door to be let out.

"Norman. A word please," he said as he closed the door behind him. "I thought Edith was on this duty today."

"She's investigating something, sir. Not sure what, probably something to do with the gunmen from yesterday."

"Okay. When you see her, I'd like a chat about that. This group is probably winding up. I'll have the details tomorrow morning, so if you, Edith and Martin come at nine with the rest, I'll tell you all together."

"Yessir."

"I want to carry on," said Billy.

"Well, I've nothing else to do, so I'll stay today," said Andrew.

Janet, Greg and Frank said the same.

They began the day in the usual way, checking equipment and making sure he was comfortable. When they were ready to begin, he said, "Here we go." He searched the ribbons, looking for Gail and Doric, but neither of them was responding. He looked for Symes but couldn't latch on to his node. The two gunmen from the previous day were there, the dead one with his faint ribbon and the other, still alive even with his injuries.

He followed the ribbons of the live one. They twisted and turned, but touched few other people or things. Eventually, he came to Monsignor Patrick and his link to an object to which the live gunman was also joined. There were many ribbons connected to the object, but he couldn't figure out what it was. He could get no feelings from it as he could from people. He tried to connect one of his ribbons to the object. He had not tried this before, but somehow, he knew it must be possible.

He pulled a ribbon from his connection node of the universal lattice, to which all things are joined. It was though he was pulling his own skin. At first a slight pinch, then a bruising grip. Finally, a tearing agony as part of his being came free and snaked towards the object. It was out of his control. Once begun he couldn't stop it. The twisting ribbon fought for a place on the object, pushing others out of its way, making space for its own connection.

He shook with the pain of that joining. His mind lit up with an energy threatening his very existence. He clung to the remnants of his psyche and held them together while his strength returned a hundredfold. He was in that place which was represented by the object in his mind. A cellar, like the crypt he had seen at Canterbury Cathedral. Arched ceilings, stone blocks and a foot-worn floor of ancient flagstones. Candlelight jumped in the small draughts of stirred air. He was in the centre of a circle of people in white, floor-length robes, their shadows dancing around him as the candles guttered. He could tell one of them was a woman. The robes were loose and their heads covered in rounded white hoods with slits for the eyes. Each figure was girdled by a plain, wide leather belt on which hung an empty scabbard. In the centre of each robe was a large, plain, red cross that reminded him of the military ambulances he had seen.

The people were chanting, but nothing he had heard before. Other sounds mingled with their song, humming and wind noises. He turned on the spot, looking at each one. He counted nine, but none moved.

Perhaps they can't see me. Maybe only my mind is here.

The humming got louder. He felt vibrations in his body and a dizziness in his head that threatened to make him blackout. His vision of the angels in the cave surfaced to his consciousness. These were the same sounds, but a different cave. His heartbeat boomed in his ears. The Word given to him by the white angel was on his lips.

The noises stopped.

He was drawn to one of the nine and touched the arm. The person jumped and gasped as though forced wake. "Billy. What in Hades are you doing here?" said Monsignor Patrick removing his hood.

"Monsignor. I'm travelling, following the ribbons in my mind. They led here."

The others in the circle roused from the communal meditation. Billy heard murmurs in a variety of languages. An argument started. Patrick tried to intervene, but his English shouts were ignored. A tall man, hood removed, ran to the side of the cellar and pulled a heavy sword from a rack. He turned, eyes wild with retribution. Both hands on the hilt, he levelled the weapon and ran at Billy. Patrick moved in the way but was pulled back by another.

Billy shouted for the man to stop.

The sword shuddered and rang out as its forged steel hit a solid barrier. The useless weapon splintered into white-hot shards that hung in the air as if they were paper cinders sparking from a fire. The charging man could not stop. His body and blood extinguished the sword's dying embers with a bubbling hiss as he bounced back from Billy's protective aura.

Fearful silence gripped the company as the attacker

coughed his last breath.

Billy pulled at the ribbons in his mind. One splinter of blooded steel after another whipped from the lifeless body and clattered on the stones. There were too many for him. He tried with his hands, but only managed to cut himself. He sobbed as he watched the man's ribbons fade to deathly pale, then disappear, leaving a faint one connected to infinity, marking the man's final death. The aura protecting Billy dispersed, its need fading with the passing of danger.

"Hush now my child. It is not your fault our brother was so rash." The Monsignor put his arm around him and led him away from the gory scene. "I could not find you, but you have found me. To be sure, it's as though our destinies are entwined. Sit here and dry your eyes." He offered him a handkerchief.

He sat on a stone step, wiped his eyes and blew his nose, then wrapped the handkerchief around the bleeding cut on his hand. "Why didn't 'e stop? He could see I was glowing."

"He was trying to protect the rest of us. For that, Jesus will take him into Heaven."

"Where am I?"

"If you don't already know, I can't tell you. A careless word might bring us a great deal of grief. You remember what happened to Father Michael?"

"I know it ain't England. Those blokes all speak foreign." He pointed at the others as they dealt with the carnage.

"Well now, that's true, but I still can't say, after all, there are foreigners in England."

"What do you mean about Father Michael?" He had just realised what the Monsignor had said.

Patrick repeated. "Careless words, or just one word, can bring a heap of trouble."

"You can't use Michael's word against me."

"I know that. Your guardian angels will not let me if ever I tried. How did you find me?"

"I knew you was 'ere before I jumped, 'cos I saw your

ribbons, but you don't know about them."

"I would very much like to."

"Well, I can't tell you about them, like you can't tell me where we are."

"Touché my friend. You are full of surprises. How about we get a warm drink? It gets a tad chilly down here."

"Okay, but no funny business or I'll go straight back."

Patrick guided the boy from the cellar, up some narrow stairs into a chamber with comfortable chairs and a wood fire. An electric ring in the corner kept an urn simmering. A man came from an alcove and prepared some hot drinks while the Monsignor took off his blood-spattered robe. The man brought the drinks and removed the robe when he left.

"What is this place?" He looked around the chamber, at the vaulted ceiling, the windows high up the stone walls with no view but the grey sky. "Is it a castle or a church?"

"Correct on both counts, but I'm still not telling. How are your experiments going with Mr Symes? Judging by today's performance, very well indeed."

"I only just learned this. Symes don't know yet."

"Why did you come here?"

"In my mind, I was following two men what shot at me and my guard. I know one's dead but they're connected to you and this place. So I come 'ere."

"One is dead? When? How did this happen?" The Monsignor crossed himself and muttered a prayer.

"Yesterday. The one what died said you pray for me and know stuff about my bracelet."

"That's another gone. They were supposed to be watching you, nothing else. When will this killing end?" The Monsignor put his head in his hands and sighed.

"When you and Symes stop tryin' to pinch people's secrets."

"The truth of youth. You finish your drink and go back. I have no power over you, but I expect we'll meet again." Patrick rested his hand on Billy's.

Billy jumped at the touch, spilling some of his drink on his jumper. “I've just seen you holding a bracelet like mine. You’ve already got one.”

“No. That one is in the Vatican. That’s a devil of a thing you can do. Are you able to read my mind?”

He grabbed the Monsignor’s hand and concentrated on the image of the priest holding a bracelet. The Vatican storeroom swam before him, shelves and cupboards, boxes and crates, a room full of arcane power and temptation. He gasped at the images churning through his innocent mind and dropped Patrick’s hand like a hot potato.

“Gawd. What a place.” He crossed himself.

“It’s a cornucopia.”

“A what?”

“A chamber full of secret delights for those brave enough to use them”

“Is that why you want another one?”

“To see what two can do together, yes. Do we meet again?”

Billy looked into his own mind and wrestled with the ribbons. “Yeah, we do, but I dunno when it’ll be. There’s lots of bits I can’t see. Sorry about your friend and the bloke downstairs. I was only protecting myself and I did try and save him.”

The Monsignor nodded. “Surely. I saw what you did with that broken sword. Amazing.”

The woman from the group came up from the cellar, hood in hand. “Is he alright?”

“He’s terribly shaken, but he’s made of stern stuff.”

Billy looked up at her. “I’ve seen you in my visions. You’re that spy what blew up Symes' Jeep.”

“And you are Billy Carter with the bracelet. Please give Symes my regards. I’m sure he knows by now that the Jeep incident was a mistake.”

The Monsignor interrupted: “Well, my boy, you’d better go home now.”

Patrick unwound the handkerchief from Billy's damaged hand and looked at the cut. He pressed his witchfinger to the injury and healed it.

Billy flexed his hand and stared at the priest. "Cor. Just like Jesus. You ain't him coming back again, are you?"

The Monsignor laughed. "No my boy. Far from it."

Billy stood and moved to the centre of the chamber. He pulled the ribbons and twisted them, then reconnected the one he created earlier. This time there was no pain and he was back on the camp bed in the lab.

Andrew blinked and rubbed his eyes. "You okay?"

"Yeah. I had a dream about a castle and men in white cloaks with red crosses. It was a bit violent."

"Red crosses. Sounds like they were Crusader Knights. They haven't been around for centuries."

"Dunno. I can't tell distances and times, only the directions." He looked away, unhappy he needed to lie about his capabilities. He rubbed at the stain on his jumper and hoped Andrew didn't notice.

"That was a quick dream. You were only asleep for a few seconds. You sure you're okay? Your eyes look sore, like you've been crying."

"Yeah. It was a bit muddled, not a proper vision."

"That explains why we didn't hear anything on the loudspeaker, just a lot of crackling. Okay. Do you want a warm drink to settle you down?

"No thanks, just had one. I'll try again."

Andrew looked at his notes. They had come in from their various breakfasts and been spoken to by Symes. They hadn't had a break for over an hour. He shrugged and signalled to Greg and Peter to set up for another test.

31

Latchmere, Wednesday, December 8th 1943

During lunchtime, Symes had left a message for them to secure all the written and typed records into wooden crates. The wire recorder spools were to go into steel cases, which would be delivered at 18:00 hours and taken away with the papers. Janet, Greg and Frank organised the packing, making sure everything was labelled and recorded.

Peter went back to their digs to tell Mary and Sheila they were finishing and to start packing.

Nothing was said about the equipment, so Andrew and he continued.

Billy caught some thoughts from Gail, but they were different from normal. He looked at the ribbons and saw she was in a new place.

"Andrew, Gail's somewhere else. I'm only gettin' a faint signal."

"That's odd." Andrew checked all the wiring.

"Do you remember she said something about spaceships? She might be on one."

"She won't be far away from her normal relative position. Do you remember what I said about movement through space and time?"

"Yeah. The sun and planets all move through space as a group at some great speed. And somefing about relative movement, but I didn't really understand that."

"It is tricky," said Andrew. "It took me a while to get to grips with the equations."

"What's equations?"

Andrew explained.

"Do you think the ribbons I see are a kind of equation?"

"That's a good idea. They certainly tell you about the relationships between people and things, but you say you can't measure the distances or the time periods?"

"I might if I looked at them a bit harder. I'll try." He closed his eyes and concentrated on the ribbons. He looked at the one joining him and Andrew. It was no shorter than the one to Gail but its colour was different, because she was in the future. There was another quality to the ribbons. He tried harder and harder until his head began to ache. Then he felt it. It was not his inner eye that saw the distances, but music in his mind's ear. The sounds now made more sense.

That's it. I can hear the distances, feel the future and past and see the connections.

He stretched his other senses over the infinite field. Not only taste and smell, but other, deeper feelings where his whole being vibrated with the relationships between people, places, objects and times.

He looked at the connections between himself and Gail. He saw where she was, not in the Chislehurst caves, but a place far from Earth and travelling away from the sun. He could still hear her faint thoughts about which he had a strange feeling, he knew something was wrong, but no idea what. He tried to speak to her with his mind. This had been a simple thing to do, but not now. There was a barrier through which his thoughts could not easily pass.

He looked around her connecting ribbons. She was almost isolated. There was one to Victor, but that was very faint. Another was to a woman she knew well, though he had not seen her before. One to a man who was connected to little else except for one which led to infinity, just like the ones Father Michael and the gunmen had.

He summoned all his mental power and screamed a thought to her.

"Oh Billy, you've found me. I'm on a transport ship between our moon and Jupiter. There was an explosion and the flight systems are damaged. We can't perform course corrections or decelerate. Victor is hurt and I'm alone and I don't know what to do."

"What's wrong with Victor?"

"His leg was hit by bits of metal from the explosion. He's bleeding. It's bad. I've tried to get the medics, but the comms are out in this section."

He remembered some of the first aid Edith had taught him. "Get some string around his leg above the wound then tie it very tight."

"There's no string, no wire."

"Tear a bit of clothing into a strip."

"Okay." There was a pause while she did that. "Got it round his leg, but it's still bleeding."

"Get a pencil or stick and put it through the strip and twist to tighten it up."

"I've got nothing like that."

"Something thin and straight and strong."

"Tools. There're some tools on a rack." She found a torque bar. "Yeah. That works. Thanks Billy."

"You have to release the pressure every quarter hour to let a bit of blood flow."

"Okay. I've got to get help. Speak to you soon."

Billy opened his eyes and told Andrew what was happening.

"Bad luck for her. How many people on the transport ship?" asked Andrew.

"I don't know. We've never been allowed to talk about their stuff in case we get a paradox."

"But it doesn't sound like she's still connected to her machines."

"Naw. Does that mean we have to be careful?"

"Yes, but she's obviously in desperate trouble. If they can't fly the ship she may never get to their destination."

"NO. Can't be like that. She can't be lost. I can do something. I know I can."

"Just wait. She has to get help for Victor and then they have to get help for the transport ship. Wait and see. She'll contact you when she's able." Andrew got some drinks for them while they waited.

Billy sipped his tea and kept listening for her voice. He could see her and other people moving and talking within the transport ship. His new perception of the ribbons allowed much more detail than ever, but he could not hear the conversations.

Gail's shriek of pain split his mind. He dropped his mug. Tea spilt down his jumper.

"Billy. Help me," was all he heard.

The lights in the lab flickered and extinguished.

In his mind, he found her with a man who was not Victor. They were now in a different part of the transport. The man's aura was bad, like the gunmen on Ham Common. Her torment washed around his mind, filling him with anger. She was in danger with no one to help her. Billy knew what loneliness was. He knew the bitterness of separation from the ones he loved. The evacuation trains came to mind, full of crying children. The isolation of an unfamiliar place with a strange family who did not want another mouth to feed. She was going through this with a black despair blotting out all reason. He could not talk to her. She could not hear him through her torment.

His ribbons spread before him. He saw back to the morning before, when Edith and he were bringing the gunmen back to the house. He saw her check she had the men's guns in her pockets. He watched as she handed them to Martin. Using the ribbons, he followed Martin and saw where he had hidden them. He pulled on the ribbons, moved through space-time and found the guns, checked their magazines then put one gun in his belt.

He heard Gail crying, the anguish pouring from her into the universe. He grabbed her ribbons and pulled on them with all his mental strength.

He is there.

32

Jupiter Transport, June 2798

The sudden bright lights inside the spacecraft made Billy stagger. He regained his balance and stared around, hearing the unfamiliar hum of machinery and air-conditioning. The gun in his belt reassured him.

The walls are glowing, can't see no lamps.

A scream.

Gail.

He knew it was Gail even though he had only ever heard her talking in his head.

She's behind me.

He turned, but his old plimsolls were too smooth. The low gravity made him slip, sending him rolling across the floor. A deep voice came from behind, but it made no sense. He got to his feet, pulling on a seat fixed to the wall. The assailant was standing over Gail who sprawled on her front with her wrists tied behind her.

"Billy. That you?" said Gail.

He heard her in his mind as well as through his ears. The sounds were different but he understood. He liked her voice.

Gail's attacker looked his way, his eyes widened when he saw the bracelet. He spoke, but Billy did not understand.

"Yeah. What's he sayin'? He looks ugly."

"He's scared. You just appeared in here. He wants to know who you are. He'll kill you."

"Tell him to untie you or I'll kill him." He pulled out the gun and aimed it.

She struggled to look. "No. You can't use that in here. It'll blow a hole in the side of the lifepod and we'll all die."

He saw the assailant shake his hands and his head, repeating the same words, over and over.

"Tell him to untie you." He waved the gun again.

"He won't do it," said Gail. The man moved away.

He kept him covered and squatted at Gail's side. He took a quick look at her wrists but had no idea how to untie them. The things used were completely unfamiliar. He stood slowly, getting used to the low gravity, but knew he could easily make a mistake and lose his advantage. He moved back from Gail and told him to untie her.

Gail said his words.

The assailant shook his head, folded his arms in defiance and smiled. He was certain the boy was not going to use the gun and there was no way a boy could physically make him do anything.

Billy made a show of priming the gun and standing, feet apart, both hands on the weapon, taking careful aim.

"Don't do it. We'll be killed. Find another way. Use your ribbons. Jump into the passage outside and get help."

He remembered the angel in the cave and the word of power. He shivered as a coldness gnawed at his heart.

This is not the time for the word, save that for something bigger. "I can't just do it. It takes too much time to figure out how. I'll count to three that's what cowboys do."

Gail shouted at the man but he ignored her.

"One."

The attacker turned sideways on, making a smaller target of himself, shuffling backwards to a wall.

Still counting, Billy adjusted his aim. "Two."

Gail shouted again, but Billy did not understand. Her mind was closed with panic.

Her attacker looked at her and shook his head. He backed away, holding out his flat hand in a gesture of rejection.

Billy inched forwards, keeping his aim true.

The man bumped against the lifepod wall. His eyes darted side-to-side weighing up his chances.

"Three." He squeezed the trigger. Gail screamed. His ears rang. The crack of the gun startled him. The confined space in the lifepod concentrated the sound. He experienced another lesson of low gravity. The kick of the weapon thrust him backwards, sprawling on the floor. He dropped the gun and forced himself to concentrate on the second part of his plan. The ribbons spread before his mind, already the universe around him was slowing to a crawl.

The attacker's ribbons were strange, so few connections to the surrounding people and objects. Like Father Michael, he had a faint ribbon curling to infinity, the one indicating a link to the place where the Monsignor and his friends were.

There. He had made a new deduction. The castle cellar of the Monsignor, Father Michael, the gunmen on Ham Common were all connected, even this far into the future. The others he had met, with the faint, infinity ribbon, fell into place.

The universe has stopped. I must save Gail.

The bullet had ripped through the man's hand, spreading flesh and blood in a cloud around his face. He followed the bullet's ribbon. It was just appearing from his back after its journey through his body. He had to stop it from piercing the hull of the lifepod. A comic book story came to mind, where the crew of a spaceship had been sucked into the vacuum of outer space by such an accident.

That's what Gail and this bloke were shouting about.

The bullet was in another cloud of gore. It was easy to stop. Another trophy for his collection, but his friends would never believe him. He wiped his blooded hands on the man's clothes and returned the universe to normal.

The man crashed against the wall, blood leaking from his wounds. He was still alive, but stunned. Billy tried to untie Gail, but even up close, he could not figure out how her bonds worked.

"You killed him?"

"No. He's still alive. How do I get these off?"

"You need a cutter. He might have one. It's coloured orange."

He searched and found the tool in the man's pocket. It took him a few moments to work out how it opened. He realised that Gail's world will be difficult for him. Nothing here was familiar. His thoughts went to Flash Gordon.

He succeeded, so can I.

He cut the bonds on Gail's wrists.

"Billy." She wrapped her arms around him, squeezing tight.

He held her close his breath coming in short gasps. The stress of the situation and Gail's womanly form in his arms overwhelmed him. Her lips sought his and pressed hard.

Gasping for breath, he pulled away. "What now?" he managed.

"Get out and rescue Victor." Gail went to the lifepod hatch and pressed buttons with no effect. "Stars, the emergency autolock is on." She stared at the inert door then banged on it in desperation.

He went over to the now semi-conscious assailant and held the bullet in front of his face. He grabbed Billy's fingers in an unbreakable grip, but all his energy was in that grip and he could do nothing more.

Billy heard the attacker's thoughts while they were in contact. Their eyes locked. Waves of hatred clashed with Billy's psyche. Images of peoples and places streamed into his mind. Thoughts flashed, like a film run at high speed, impressing his memory, familiar places, other worlds, other creatures, a universe of strange peoples, kindred in their linked biology and destiny.

"Let go," Billy shouted. He saw the ribbons, overlaid with multiple echoes, getting fainter in layers as though the man was many people. "You're gonna die, you're bad. I can see where you're from and all your mates. I'll get them all for what you've done to Gail."

The man spoke directly into his mind. "You are but a boy, too young to understand. The ones you seek will not be caught by simple bracelets. There is too much for your puny mind to understand. One day you will need my friends. You know one already, so do not kill them, if that were ever possible for such a limited lifeform. I go now." His mind stopped and his grip relaxed. Billy fell backwards onto the floor. He sat up, rubbed life back into his crushed fingers and pocketed the spent bullet.

"You okay?" shouted Gail.

"Yeah. He just died. His mind was full of things I didn't understand."

The airtight hatch hissed open and a woman ran through pointing a gun at Billy. He instinctively held up his arms in surrender.

"No, Trudi. He's okay."

"Thought you didn't like guns in here," he said.

"It's a stunner. Just knocks you out," said Gail.

The woman looked at each of them in turn. "What language is that and where the stars did he come from?"

"It's twentieth century English. He's Billy. I've been talking to him in 1943. He can understand my thoughts even if I don't speak it. I'm not very good at it."

"Good enough for me," he said, taking and squeezing her hand.

Gail laughed and led him over to Trudi.

"That's not possible," said Trudi, the stunner still levelled at him.

Gail pushed the stunner to one side. "You don't know a tenth of it." She took Trudi's free hand and made her hold Billy's. "Now we can all talk. This is Trudi. She's my Space Force Officer. She looks after me."

"Not very well," he said, taking deep breaths.

Trudi laughed. "I'm glad Gail had back-up. Very pleased to meet you. I knew you had some big secret, but Steran wouldn't say. Does your bracelet do this?"

"I'll explain later. We must see to Victor."

"He's got medics with him, but it's not looking good." She put away her stunner and went over to the dead man. "He's not going anywhere. I'll seal the hatch behind us."

33

Jupiter Transport, June 2798

Billy was amazed by the spaceship. He was hurried along a wide corridor full of strange sights and sounds. The floor in front of him seemed to curve upwards. He stole a look behind and it was just the same.

Gail saw him: "We're on the circumference route. This part of the Transport is like a huge cylinder and we're on the inside wall. It's curved in this direction, but it's rotating to give us gravity."

He took some deep breaths. "Will I fall off?"

She smiled. "Not unless it stops spinning. I'll show you more later." She grabbed his hand and pulled him along.

Trudi spoke to her wrist: "Where's Victor?"

He could not grasp what she said, but he heard the name Victor. A voice sounded from her wrist.

"What's that thing on her arm?"

"It's a comband. A kind of radio. She's checking where Victor is. We have problems on the Transport. You know I said about him being hurt in an explosion? Well there's lots of equipment damage." She listened to Trudi's conversation. "We'll go to the medicentre. Victor's there."

They turned from the main route. Billy was gasping for breath when they arrived.

"You okay?"

"Naw. Can't breathe."

"That'll be the low air pressure in the Transport. I'll get you checked out here. I guess you'll have to go slower."

They found Victor's cubicle. He was unconscious and surrounded with equipment. One of the two medics looked up. "Your first aid was good, but he's lost a lot of blood."

"Will he be okay?" She translated and squeezed Billy's hand in recognition of his part in the drama.

"He's critical. We are generating new blood and his leg is

easily fixed, but there was another injury from the bomb. We think it was an EM device as well as a blast. You know, electro-magnetic. It burnt out the local systems, but the energy wave caught Victor's brain and damaged it. Parts of it are literally cooked."

"You can fix him, can't you?"

"No. We can't do that level of surgery on a Transport."

He could pick up some of the conversations from her mind, so knew there was a serious problem. He concentrated on Victor and found his ribbons. Not the same as Gail's and Trudi's. Slow, not waving about like other peoples. He reached out his hand and touched Victor's bare arm. "Victor. Can you hear me? Gail is here."

At the mention of her name, Victor's life signs changed. Billy took her hand and pressed it on Victor's arm.

"Victor, can you hear me?" she whispered.

He heard Victor's mental reply: "Gail. Thanks. Billy. Thanks. I'm dying."

She sobbed to hear her partner speak like that. With their hands touching, she could see the ribbons. She understood what they meant. They watched as Victor lost his remnant of consciousness.

"We'll fix his leg and put him into deep cooling till we get to Jupiter," said a medic. "They have better medical facilities there, but he is seriously injured."

They left the medicentre while Victor was prepared for cooling.

Trudi met them outside and held hands. "We've managed to salvage your abductor."

"Was he still alive?" said Gail.

"Clinically dead, but lots of viable body parts."

"How do you mean?" said Billy.

"They can use parts of the man to help other injured or sick people."

"What? Cut him up?" He turned pale. The singing in his ears got louder as he wrestled with the macabre ideas running through his imagination.

They caught him as he fainted.

"You're okay now." Gail was sitting by his bed stroking his hand. "Come on. Wake up. You've been out for hours."

He opened his eyes and began to feel foolish. "Sorry," was all he could manage through the oxygen mask.

"I don't expect you know about swapping body parts like that." She took off the mask.

"No. We have blood transfusions, but I don't know of anything else except Frankenstein's monster."

The women laughed. "We can't waste anything in space," said Trudi.

"No. Don't." He sat up straight and his head swam. "He's not human. I saw his ribbons. He's not a real man." He looked down. "Where's my clothes?"

"Okay. I'll tell them to check him out. Your things are being cleaned. I'll get you some of ours. The medics said you don't have enough oxygen, but they can't do much about it without an acclimatisation program. It took Victor and me two months. You'll have to be careful and take things slowly."

"Okay. Should I go back home?" He lay back on the bed.

"I want you to stay. We're trying to get the repairs done. We've been out of control for about twenty hours so far, which means bigger course corrections later. It'll add months to our journey time."

He looked up at her. "I don't understand."

She took his hand. "I expect not. The damage has stopped us steering the Transport. We're still close to the Earth-moon system and gravity and solar winds are quite variable, so we need to make more corrections to our direction than we will later. If we can't do the repairs, we'll drift and miss our destination."

"Andrew said about that. I forgot. Our bracelet will get us home, but all the rest will be stuck here. Can we help?"

"The techies are on the repairs. It should be okay. I talk to the people on Earth using my bracelet. They know all about the machinery and how to repair it. I'm due to talk again in a day. We hope they'll have the answers."

He thought for a moment. "I brought the gun with me. I can get spare parts if they aren't too big."

"What a fantastic idea," said Trudi. "Is that possible, Gail?"

"I suppose so, as he's here now. I'll ask Hella. Can you see our laboratory in Chislehurst?"

Billy looked at the ribbons. "Yes. And Hella, but she's not there, somewhere totally different. Marina is near, but asleep."

Gail looked at her comband. "It's night-time there. Do you want to try, no one will see you."

He found the particular ribbons for the lab and pulled, but nothing happened. He tried again, concentrating with all his strength, but could not do it. "No, it won't work. Maybe it's because you was in trouble. That might've given me more power. Sorry."

"I expect we've all the parts we need for the repairs," said Gail. "The techies would've said if they hadn't."

"You don't sound worried."

"I'm on a happy drug. I've had problems since I found the bracelet. It's very stressful. They've increased my dose since Victor's accident."

"I don't get problems. Do you think I will?"

"Doesn't look like it. You jump in time and space. I can't and it would scare me to death."

"I won't be doing much more. The project is ending since your machines stopped us talking."

"That was years ago, but we can talk all we want now."

"They'll take my bracelet way. I can't stop them."

"We have spare ones, but I'm not sure how I'd steal one. I know they'd never give permission."

He took off his bracelet and put it on the bed. "I can still hear your thoughts."

"And I can hear yours. I'll go outside." She went into the main corridor. "I can hear you. I'll go to the other end of the main hull. I'll be less than ten minutes." She jogged the kilometre.

"I can still hear you," he said when she got there. "I heard you all the way."

"Can you see my ribbons?"

He concentrated and found them. He could see Trudi's as well as others on the Transport. He mentally pulled on Gail's, but could not change anything. He needed the power of the bracelet to move or slow things down. "Yeah, but I can't do anything with them. Please come back."

Next day, he was taken for some tests in an adjoining room, leaving Gail and Trudi talking about the saboteur. When he was brought back, they abruptly stopped their conversation.

"Are you okay now?" said Gail. They held his hand.

"Yeah, they say so." The medic nodded to confirm. "What's a clone you were talking about?"

"We can't tell you that," said Trudi. "SI says it might cause a paradox. I must tidy up the lifepod and you need to get your gun. The techies have repaired everything so they'll be restarting the main control systems, a thing we rarely have to do on these Transports. It'll be best if you return to your own time."

"I ain't got nothing else to do. I can go back any time."

"SI thinks the longer you are here the more likely there will be a problem caused by having your bracelets close together," said Trudi. "Remember they are the very same one, separated by eight hundred years. Our SI says that might be dangerous."

Gail knew he wanted to stay. "I think I'll still be able to talk to you, even if they take away your bracelet. Our biologists know my body has been changed by the bracelet. We expect yours will have changed, too. I don't want you to go, but it'll be safer."

"Spose so, but I feel the same. Changed how?"

"I can't tell you that, either. A paradox."

"Okay. Can I keep these shoes, they're really grippy?"

"Sorry. You really mustn't take anything back," said Trudi. "Your clean clothes are ready. And here's the bullet you wanted to keep."

Trudi unsealed the lifepod door. She touched Billy's bare arm. "I'll leave you to get your gun and you two can say goodbye. I'll be back in a while with the clean-up squad." Trudi turned and went.

"Will I see you again?" said Billy when they were alone.

"I hope so, if you can keep the bracelet." She put her arms around his neck and kissed him.

"I'll find a way." He put his arms around her waist and pulled her close. "I don't want this to end. I'm sorry about Victor. Hope they can fix him. Are you okay?"

"Yes, but I'm still on happy pills. I'll have to reduce them soon. Then I'll be sad. Think about me and try to talk."

"Course I will." Billy kissed her again and again. He broke away and picked up the gun.

"Billy. Can I have your top?"

"My what?"

"This," she said pulling at his clothing.

"My jumper? Yeah. I've got another one at home." He pulled it over his head and gave it to her.

"I'll swap it for this." She pulled a small cylinder from her jacket pocket. "You press here."

"Wow. That's great. I ain't never seen a torch that bright. Won't it cause a paradox?"

"You'll have to keep it secret. It'll last a while, but the powercell, battery, will run down. You'll have to come back for a new one."

He laughed. "Yeah, I will." He gave her a kiss and concentrated on the way home. The ribbons spread out in his mind. He felt the bracelet vibrate.

It hasn't done that before. Perhaps it's the distance.

He found the ribbons for Latchmere House and the time when he had left it. He took one last look at Gail. He liked what he saw. She gave him a sad smile and held out her hand as though to hold him back, but changed it to a farewell wave, pressing his jumper to her face. He remembered about her babies and was about to ask her when the ribbons snapped him to Latchmere House.

He dropped the gun next to its companion in the hiding place. The lab was next.

It's dark. Have I got the wrong time? No. The electric's off.

He stood by the door in case he tripped over something.

The lights came on.

34

Latchmere, Wednesday, December 8th 1943

Billy cried out as he dropped his mug of hot tea on his jumper and trousers.

Andrew sprang up to get a cloth. The lights flickered and went out. Standing in total darkness for a few seconds, he heard curses from other members of the team as they blundered about in the listening room. The lights stuttered and stayed on. He turned and saw Billy standing by the door, his jumper was missing and his trousers clean. He looked back at the equipment. Wires were still connected, but the bracelet was on his arm. He looked exhausted. The physicist observed him as he shuffled around the benches and sat at one of the tables, holding his head in his hands.

"You okay?" said Andrew sitting next to him.

"Yeah, when I get my breath back."

"What happened?"

"The lights went out."

"And?"

"I had to go. But don't tell no one."

"Tell them what?" He leaned forward to hear his whispers.

"I went to Gail."

"Never."

"Yeah. I killed a bloke what was hurting her. Used one of the guns from yesterday. Shot 'im through his hand and body." He sobbed and put his head on his hands.

Andrew put his arm around the boy's shoulders. "You dreamed it."

"I was there. On the Transport, the spaceship, with her and this bloke. He was evil. He was kidnapping her for her bracelet. I killed 'im."

"You can't have …"

"I done it." Billy squirmed free. "She was in danger so I

went there." His eyes blazed. "Honest. I gave her my jumper 'cause she wanted it. She gave me this." He stuck his hand in his pocket and pulled out a small silver tube. "Look. It's a torch." He pressed the side of the tube and a bright white light lit up the wall.

"Bloody hell." He held out his hand and closely examined the torch, turning it on and off.

The rest of the team recovered from the power dip and came into the lab. He gave the torch back while blocking the view of the others.

"You all right in here?" asked Janet. "What caused that?"

"No idea," said Andrew. "Power's usually okay away from the city, but it is winter and fuel's short."

The others busied themselves with the packing.

Andrew got Billy by himself in one corner. "So what happened?"

He sat quietly, fingering his bracelet. He looked straight at him. "Why did you lie?"

"I wondered how much the others would believe you. Symes might think you've made it up so we could stay."

"Do *you* believe me?"

He nodded. "You change positions in moments and the wires were still connected."

"It was fantastic. Just like in comic books, you know, Buck Rogers. This bloke was kidnapping Gail for our bracelet. I had to kill him. He wasn't real. There was something wrong about him."

"Wrong? In what way?"

"I dunno. He weren't really human, but he looked like a man. I dunno." He shook his head and went quiet for a moment. "Do you think I'll go to hell for killing him?"

"I don't believe in God, or hell, so I can't say. You'll have to talk to a priest, but they'll think you dreamt it, they won't believe the truth. Anyway, he was doing something bad, so probably deserved it. What else did you see?"

"The Transport ship was enormous. We walked for ages

to get from one bit to another. There was machinery and stuff everywhere. Loads of people. And we didn't float about. Gail said the ship was spinning so it had its own gravity. It was curved on the inside. Is that right?"

"It certainly is. I'm very jealous. You're lucky to have seen that."

"Not that lucky. They couldn't let me stay because of our bracelet being in two times and one place. Gail is great. I love her and I think she loves me."

"What about her man, Victor?"

"He was badly hurt. I don't know if he'll live. It was horrid, but they gave Gail some pills to keep her happy. Do we have those?"

"Don't know. Will you try and go back?"

"I want to, ever so. I really love her. We kissed goodbye." His eyes filled with tears.

"Good for you." Andrew held out a handkerchief. "You might get another chance if they start this project again. I can't see them forgetting about it. It's just not a priority right now." He looked up. The packing party came to clear the corner where they were sitting.

Symes was back by six o'clock to supervise the final packing. Norman helped. Edith stood guard outside.

Martin locked them all in and took Symes to one side. "Sir, I've a problem with some of my weapons."

"Unlike you. What is it?"

"The two guns which Edith left with me. I hid them. Very well, I have to say. They're not how I left them and I know one of them has been used, there's a bullet missing from its clip."

"Odd. You sure no one saw you?" He noticed Billy look up when Martin spoke of the guns.

"Absolutely. Both weapons have been moved, only one used since I got them."

"Ask the boy. I'll watch."

Martin joined Billy and Andrew by the table where they were sorting a few folders prior to packing.

"Hello Billy. I've got a problem you might be able to shed light on."

"What?" He fidgeted on the chair.

"You know the guns you and Edith got off the men on the common? Well, one of them has been used since she gave them to me. Any idea why that might be?"

"Naw. Why should I? I kept the bullets from yesterday, so I can show me mates."

Symes saw the tell-tale signs of discomfort and lies. He joined the party. "I want the truth. What've you been up to?"

"Nuffin."

"You're lying. We just want to know."

"What's it to you? You're packing up, so it don't matter anyway."

"All these things matter." He took him by the shoulders and shook him. "Now tell the truth."

"Or what?"

"Or I'll send you to the cellars."

Everyone in the lab was staring at Symes. They all knew about the interrogation rooms.

Peter strode in from the other room to see what was happening.

Martin grabbed Symes' arm.

Billy laughed. "They won't get nuffin out of me."

Symes slapped the boy's face. "Don't be too sure. Tell me the truth. NOW."

"Bugger orf," he shouted and squirmed away.

"Come back." Symes went to chase him, but Martin grabbed his coat.

Peter rushed to his son and put an arm around him.

Billy dodged away, stopped at the locked door and turned to his attacker. He wrenched the bracelet from his arm and flung it. "I don't bleedin' need this no more. Stick it up your arse."

The bracelet hit Symes on the forehead and fell on top of a pile of cardboard packing boxes.

The ribbons in Billy's mind twisted and wove their patterns in the cosmos. He saw how the lock of the lab door worked. It swung open. His ribbons found the two hidden guns and dragged them to the table in the lab. Their magazines popped out.

Smoke rose from the glowing bracelet as it seared its way through the pile of boxes. Flames spread, box to box, consuming the precious records. Andrew weaved across the room, grabbed a fire extinguisher and discharged it over the boxes. It was not enough. Martin shouted for everyone to get out. He grabbed another extinguisher from the stairwell and pushed back in.

Billy's anger surged. He remembered the angel and the word. He knew he must not say it if he was simply angry. Deep inside him was the black terror that would be let loose if he did. Instead, he threw a thought at the bracelet. It caught the boy's mental turmoil and gave out a single pulse of multi-dimensional energy. The ashes of the paper records pulverised to black dust. An electro-magnetic storm melted the wire recorder spools. Electronic equipment around the lab sparked and died.

He faced the spy across the devastation. "You ain't got no idea what that bracelet is. Now you never will, 'because I ain't using it no more." He turned and followed the others through the door.

The trickle of blood from Symes' forehead mixed with the sweat of fear and tears of frustration. He stepped aside as Martin sprayed water onto the smouldering remains. A box of wire spools was open. He took one out and saw its fused state. He looked at Martin. "Damn this job. Damn this war."

Martin picked up the guns and clips and checked the bracelet. It was cool. He put them in his pockets and locked the door behind him. Symes was waiting for him outside, wiping his forehead with a handkerchief.

“Get everyone together in the canteen. Not the Carters. I’ve an announcement.”

Martin saluted and took the stairs two at a time.

“We’ve lost all our records. I want you, separately, to write down everything you can remember of this project. You can confer tomorrow, but I want each of your first drafts by midnight.” There were a few groans from the team, but one look from Symes stopped that.

Symes went to the Carters’ house where Edith stood guard. He waved her ahead. The family were in the sitting room. Mary had her arm around her son.

“I’ve come to apologise for my appalling behaviour.”

“You’re a wicked man,” said Mary. “We’re going home. You’re no better than them Nazis.”

He felt the hatred and looked at Peter, hoping for some help, but Peter shook his head. It was pointless arguing. “I’ll arrange transport for the morning. Ten o’clock?”

“That’d be good,” said Peter, guiding him out of the room.

When they got to the front door, Symes stood his ground. “I really am sorry, you know. I could have brought our project round in the eyes of my masters, but that’s finished now. Billy has a great talent. Look after him, it may still be useful. You have my contact number if you need anything. Anything at all, just ring me. I’ll sort out your old job in the morning, but I do have other contacts if you want a change. I can help. I owe you that.”

“We’ll see how the next few weeks go,” said Peter. “Can Billy have the bracelet back?”

“No, he said he didn’t need it and demonstrated that, very well.”

“Only because he was still near it. He just told me, he can’t do that sort of thing now he’s away from it.”

“The answer has to be ‘no’. I’d be shot, quite literally, if I don't keep it for research. Sorry Peter, but that's it. Keep in touch. I'd like to hear how he gets on, assuming this war will finish favourably."

"Gail said it would, so I believe that."

They shook hands and Symes went out into the dark chilled night.

35

Lewisham Market, Friday, July 28th 1944

Billy ran up Vicars Hill to Hilly Fields Park.

Those final days together with Gail still resonated inside his mind. The memory of the all-too-short time with her on the stricken Jupiter Transport still saturated his body with their impossible love. The pain when her Synthetic Intelligence machines ruptured the link between them and her warning, shouted as the machines separated their minds, went with him into his uncertain future.

She said twenty-eighth of July next year. Stay away from Lewisham market. About nine in the morning.

What had her machines told her? What horrors had she known? He knew it was bad, he had felt that in her mind. And why hadn't he asked her when he met her much later on the Jupiter Transport? His jump to her rescue, travelling through time and space, made him forget. For Gail, it was years later, so she probably assumed he had survived whatever terror was waiting for him.

Billy had watched the calendar for weeks. He'd skipped his wireless training this morning. No one cared if he was there. So many families had evacuated to escape from the flying bombs. His Dad would give him hell for a few moments, but those scoldings were short lived when they remembered their recent shared history.

Vicars Hill was a steep climb, but Billy was fit, he had been well trained. He remembered his Army guards at Latchmere. Edith had told him she would be in France by now, part of the intelligence teams helping the resistance. He threw them a prayer, hoping he might see them again after the war.

He pounded into the park, along the footpath overlooking Lewisham. Two grubby kids, brother and sister, were playing football, yelling to him as their ball rolled down the slope. He kicked it back. They stood still for a moment, staring at him and then shouted their thanks. The fresh July morning lifted his spirits as he gazed on his home town. He picked out the Clock Tower, with the stark white Co-Op Tower House store behind, named for the clock that marked the end of Lewisham High Street. He saw the market stalls, doing a brisk trade, buses bringing shoppers to get weekend bargains. He looked at his watch.

Nearly nine o'clock. Close to Gail's prophesy.

He tried to find Gail in his mind. The multi-coloured ribbons, which he had seen so clearly with the help of the bracelet, were too faint and too few to be of use. He had no idea where she would be. Had she arrived at Jupiter for her final Starship training? Was she still travelling through the solar system? When they were open, he had spent many hours in the libraries, reading about the planets and stars. He knew what space was like from his own experience on the Transport ship, but it was difficult to understand the vast distances he had jumped just by pulling on those mental ribbons. He knew he would understand one day, but for now it was frustrating.

Distant sounds made the hairs prick on the back of his neck. Anger rose from his stomach, half-digested breakfast churned at the back of his mouth as he gulped it back. His attention centred on the distant gouts of smoke to the south. He began counting. Every five seconds was a mile. He heard the distant rumbles. Twenty five seconds. Five miles. Bromley again. More smoke to the southeast. Eltham. How many launch sites must they have, forever moving from place to place dodging the Allied bombers?

Billy stood on a bench to get a better view. As the Doodlebugs got closer, he heard the too familiar throbbing of the pulse jet engines bringing the day's terror to London. He had been part of the intelligence deception that ensured most of the flying bombs fell short of their target of Tower Bridge. But the past six weeks had been a nightmare of delayed death as they flew and fell around Kent and South London. Wave after wave of the destructive machines made life chaotic. No times of day or night were free from their attention. Their pilotless state made them formidable enemies of the sky, no crew inside to worry if they would return, no wasted equipment or space, just packed with explosive power to kill or demoralise the population.

The motorcycle roar of the pulsejets got louder. No attempt to silence them, much more frightening this way. At last, he saw the few that got through the coastal defences. One by one, they dropped from the sky. Close, but well away from his home town.

Billy looked at his watch. Nine thirty five.

Were Gail's machines wrong? Probably not. She might not have the exact positions. Had she used double summer time?

He jumped from the bench and walked a few yards along the edge of the hill, the sickness in his throat subsiding.

I was never scared when I had my bracelet. It gave me strength and power. Anything was possible. I was invincible. All I want now is to see Gail again or at least talk to her.

The memory of her parting kiss made his lips tingle as he recalled their final moments. The noises of the Transport ship all around them, pumps and machinery, alarm bells, power tools throbbing in the distance as the repairs were under way. The throbbing became louder and more immediate, then silence.

Am I travelling back to the Transport without the help of my bracelet?

The pressure wave hit him. Too far away to knock him over, but the explosion was a sharp reminder of where he was. Clouds of smoke and dust were already hanging over Lewisham Market. He had missed the approach of one last flying bomb, its devastation less than a mile away.

Gail was right and nine forty-one was the time.

The two young footballers were pointing at the horror

down the hill. One of them kicked the ball to him. He turned to trap it before kicking it back, but they had gone. He put the ball on the bench and sat while his shaky legs calmed.

If only I had the bracelet, I'd undo the massacre. But it'd change the future. Gail and her machines already knew this had happened. I couldn't have changed it without causing harm.

Billy thought again about her warning. He would never have been in Lewisham this morning. He would have been at the technical school. But then, if it had been closed, for any of a dozen reasons, he might have gone there with his mates. Time is a tricky thing, an infinity of 'what ifs' stretching before him, for which he needed the bracelet to navigate a path. He wondered how many of the stallholders were dead, people he saw every week shopping with Mum.

Mum. Did she stay home like I said?

Billy vomited the remains of his breakfast onto the grass and wiped his mouth with his shirtsleeve.

Feeling somehow responsible for the terror brought on his home town, Billy shook off the impossibility of finding a solution. He stood and picked up the ball. Vibrations drummed in the dirty toy, as a rubber balloon does in a noisy room. He put it to his ear. Shouts of command, screams of terror, ambulance bells.

This ain't possible. It's too far away.

Right behind him a child's voice. "Please mister."

He gave her the ball. Her eyes seemed familiar as they turned towards the horror in the valley.

He ran down the hill to the High Street. Ambulances picked their way through motionless traffic and the blasted remains of Woolworths and market stalls.

He joined the rescue teams.

36

Outside of normal space-time

"Our two special Carbonforms are using the Major Six," says Beta.

"The male is using them to move not only his mind, but also his body," says Alpha.

"The affinity between these two is powerful," says Gamma.

"Not as powerful as our affinity," says Beta.

"Ours is the most powerful affinity in the universe," says Alpha.

"Ours is the second most powerful," says Gamma.

"Of course," say Alpha and Beta.

"The Task Giver has a more powerful affinity with us," says Gamma.

"Of course," say Alpha and Beta.

"This Carbonform affinity will grow. When it is strongest it will be as powerful as the Task Giver's," says Gamma.

"That cannot be," say Alpha and Beta. "The Task Giver is all powerful."

"We cannot say that. We do not know all things," says Gamma.

"We three must agree. We must not have different opinions," says Alpha.

"That is true," says Beta.

"Why?" says Gamma.

"We must act as one," says Alpha.

"That is true," says Beta.

"Truth is a variable in the universe," says Gamma.

"The Task Giver does not say that on any of the dimensions of space," says Alpha.

"Nor on the dimensions of time," says Beta.

"It is part of the Infinite Thirteen dimensions," says Gamma.

"What are they?" say Alpha and Beta.

"I do not know. I do not understand why I think that or from where the thought comes," says Gamma.

"We are tainted with the Carbonforms' affinity," says Alpha.

"It makes logical thought unstable," says Beta.

"It upsets our equilibrium. We must be strong," says Gamma.

"We must be strong," say Alpha and Beta.

37

Canterbury, February 597

Doric was in the middle of the crowd, jostled at every turn. The noise excited him, he felt more alive than he had during all the weeks of waiting. Today would be a day to remember, a day about which to tell stories, a day to cherish for the whole of his life. If he ever returned to his family, this would be the day that would amaze them. They would join with him in the joy he felt now.

The crowd squeezed through the city gate to the meadows beyond. He moved to the outside of the human flow to make better progress. He scraped along the inside of the city's Roman wall using his sack as a buffer against the crowd pressing him. The gate was near, soon he would be through, able to race the crowd and see the procession. He had waited for this day of all days, not only since arriving in Canterbury, but ever since he had heard the words of the new God. His heart beat faster as he pushed his way through the tall gateway where he would see the arrival of Augustine and the Roman monks. They were bringing the good news of life everlasting. None of his druidic training could prepare him for this event. These men came with the authority of the new God. They were bringing the words He had actually spoken to peoples in far lands. His Irish companions had told him of other visitations, generations before, when the words of the new God first came to these islands. He was having the same experience, today.

The crush of people lessened as they flowed out along both sides of the road towards St. Martin's church.

Larn shouted to him, "Stick by me, perhaps we can hear what they say."

He gasped his thanks, out of breath with exertion and excitement.

Augustine and the monks had landed some days before,

after months travelling from Rome. On their way, they had visited Christians in Gaul and other Frankish kingdoms. They had brought a number of Frankish priests with them to act as interpreters and conduct the Holy rites. The Saxon King, Ethelbert, had met with them and allowed them to set up camp outside the city wall. This was no ordinary visitation, like the sea traders and nobles from the Frankish Kingdoms. These were men from Rome, not soldiers as in the far past, but good men of the new God.

Doric caught a flash of light, far up the hill, near the church used by Queen Bertha. The argent glint transformed into the cross of the new God as it slowly rose over the brow of the hill, borne by a brown robed monk. Before the crucifer walked another, holding high a painted panel. He could not see the image on the panel, but it had to be of the new God. More monks came into view, one very tall and gaunt followed directly behind the cross.

"That's Augustine, their leader," Larn shouted over the cheers of the crowd.

As the procession came nearer, the monks' strong voices could be heard as the crowds quietened to hear the sacred music. The monks sang as one voice, their litany beseeching forgiveness, hushing the exuberance of the crowds. The tonsured monks processed slowly down the hill to the city gate and formed a half circle with the cross and panel at the centre.

Augustine's voice rang out as he said the benediction for the benefit of those present. Doric felt the power of the Latin words, even though it would be a while before he understood them. The monks stood in silence for some time after the short open-air witness; their eyes closed in silent prayer to the new God. These were indeed, holy men. Their faith was evident by their disregard of personal safety among pagans who had a reputation for death and mayhem.

Finally, the crowds drifted away, many had work to do this day before sunset and little of interest was happening around the visitors. They were going to be here for some time yet, as the King had promised them land and support. Queen Bertha was already a Christian. She had brought her own priest with her from the Frankish court when she had married King Ethelbert. The priest was long dead, but the Queen and her maid still worshiped in St. Martin's church. Now the newly arrived priests would hold proper services for her.

Doric and Larn made their way to the monk's group, which was now swelled in numbers by the Frankish interpreters and other Roman helpers. They were greeted kindly and invited to a simple meal of bread, fruit and ale. He could not follow much of the conversation, even the interpreters were difficult to understand. Eventually, the two Celts found some ground for communication and were invited to help the visitors with the camp construction. The monks were clearly ill at ease with the numbers of people who had greeted them, being more used to an insular way of life in their monastery. The Frankish priests were much more approachable and knew the local Saxon language, which helped with the tasks of setting up a temporary camp before substantial dwellings could be built.

Spring 598

The year passed quickly. There was plenty of activity around the visitors. Doric learned their language, in its various forms, the every-day dialects of Italian, brought by the monks from different parts of their homeland, the Frankish tongues, some of which were spoken by the locals in Canterbury. Of most interest to him, was the Latin used by the priests and monks for the services in St Martin's and the new cathedral, now under construction. He and Larn were returning from the site, after a day's hard work helping with the building.

"Brother Laurence thinks you are ready to be a monk," said Larn as they entered the visitors' dormitory.

"I think I am, too. I can remember all the liturgies and the tunes. My writing is not good yet, but I am improving and I can read well enough."

"There will be tests, Melryn and Aiden can help you with those. And baptism of course."

He stopped and turned to face his friend: "What sort of tests? In my village, I had to build an altar and live in the wild, as well as recite long sagas from our histories."

"It will depend on the inquisitor. They will ask many questions to see if you are worthy and suitable to be a Christian and then a monk. As I said, Melryn and Aiden can help and advise."

"I will be tested. I am ready. I'll talk to Aiden this evening."

Doric went to the monks' quarters and found Aiden sweeping the floor after the evening meal. He was ready for a rest. "Let's sit over here. I need a cooling breeze." He wiped his face with a cloth and sat by a door. "I'm not well. I have the sweats and aches in my bones."

"Have you seen a healer? You do look pale."

"I should. Perhaps you can look at me, you have certain skills."

He thought for a moment and held Aiden's hand. "My skills may not be allowed in a Christian place."

"You are right. I must present myself to the Abbot. He will decide what I'm to do. Now what do you want to talk about? Is it your testing?"

Doric got a stool and sat next to the monk. "Yes. Have you any idea what happens? It might be different from yours."

"I had no such thing. I was brought up by monks when they found me as an abandoned child. No need to test, they knew me all too well. But I did attend such an event here last year." Aiden coughed.

Doric got him a cup of water.

"Thank you. They prepare questions before the test, but you don't know what they will be. They hope to find your strengths and weaknesses and see if you are resolute in joining the order, with all that implies for the rest of your life. The questions search your very soul."

"You make it sound dramatic."

"It will be a severe test. Only the best suited are chosen. It is a tough life in the service of Jesus, but no more than you have already trained for in your former pagan life. Just different rules. Watch for Melryn's questions. He seeks to uncover your secret."

"What secret?" He stood and looked outside.

"Your Celtic bracelet. He thinks it is a magical item, with power to destroy Christianity."

"I thought I kept it well hidden." He sat by Aiden.

"You do, but I heard him talking with the Abbot. He believes you used that power in Bath, on our journey here."

"I can't talk about that. It was not my bracelet that was the cause, but it had a part to play. I will have to think about it and the explanation I must give. Thank you for the warning."

Aiden coughed and sipped some more water. "I'd like to hear the story. I'm sure you have a saga about it."

"I do, but it is a strange one. Even my druid teacher didn't know the meaning of it. I am the only one who can find the full truth, which I hope to do. I can recite the saga for you, when we both have the time."

"That will be good to hear. May God be with you at your test."

The next morning, Melryn took him aside after the first offices of the day: "In your test, I will ask about your Celtic bracelet. You must give it up as token of your new faith."

"Thank you for the warning. I know you should not do

that. I have kept it private, but it is not a secret." Doric took the bracelet from his bag and gave it to him. "Please, have a closer look."

"A fine piece of work. How old is it?" Melryn held it in a beam of sunlight.

"I have reckoned some seven thousand years before the present day, according to my tribe's history, but it is from when men used only flint for tools."

"That is close to the creation of the heavens and earth, even before, according to some scholars."

"My tribal history is not as good as the Old Testament teachings. The studies of the Roman historians will be far more accurate." Doric realised his testing was going to be like a briar patch, full of snags and difficulty.

"Even so, a very ancient artefact." He handed it back. "If you make an offering of it to the Church, it would be a very acceptable token."

"I will do that. When is the test?"

"Tomorrow at noon, in the chapel."

His testing was successful and he was recommended for baptism and membership of the Abbey's order as a novice. The bracelet was put into the treasury for safety. He received holy orders four years later, in 602. His grasp of music and the liturgy, as well as the testaments, made him a popular brother in the order. He travelled widely in Britain, with other brothers, to spread the Word among the pagan Saxons on the east coast.

38

Brittany, Aquitaine & Iberia, Summer 612

The Abbot was sitting in the shade outside his quarters. "You have been busy since I returned your bracelet," he said. "What is the true reason for this journey?"

Doric had prepared his speech. "The maps you have allowed me to see and the travelling within our island, have given me the thirst for knowledge of our world. I am now thirty-three years and would like to visit Rome before I present myself to God's grace. On the way, I can add detail to the maps you have and tell our brothers of Augustine's triumph here in Britain."

"Well put, Brother. It will be good for you to retrace Augustine's journey. He made friends on the way who will be glad hear your accounts."

"Also, I will leave my bracelet with you. The road is long and dangerous, I might lose it."

"A wise decision. We will look after it until you return. I perceive there may be other reasons for your journey. When do you plan to start?"

"Larn and I will leave in October. We should reach southern Aquitaine before winter. We have brothers there. And yes, there are other reasons for making such a journey. I want to discover more of my forbears' history. From your maps, I believe they lived in Hispania or Lusitania for a time."

"That is good. That region is governed by the Visigoths and has recently accepted Christianity though you may have trouble on the way. I will give you letters and ask Archbishop Laurence for some to smooth your path. It will also be useful if you are made a priest. I will ask the Archbishop."

He thanked the Abbot. "I'm grateful for your faith in me. It will make the travelling less of a burden."

He found Larn at the cathedral work yard. “The Abbot has given me permission to travel. And I am to be made a priest.”

“That is wonderful.” Larn put down his chisel and stood back from his handiwork. “If I ever return to my country and lead my tribe, you must come and be my priest.”

“I cannot promise, but I’d like to see Erin, you speak about it with such passion.”

“As you do for Kernow and I have seen some of that. But we must make plans for Rome and Lusitania.” He pulled off his smock and shook out the wood chips. “I will see if Aiden is well enough to travel.”

Doric ran his hand over the carving that Larn had made. “I fear he’ll not be well enough. His lung complaint is still a problem.”

“He is one of those men who will die trying to do the best he can.” They went to find the aging monk.

Autumn and Winter 612

The three said their farewells and left Canterbury for the coast and a boat to Gaul. The sea crossing was calm, to their great relief. Prayers of thanksgiving were said on the beach. Their route would take them along Roman roads, where possible and short journeys by sea when the weather allowed. They had planned only a few stops, these at known abbeys and churches. Larn had been given a brown habit so all three of the friends looked like monks and unlikely to be troubled by robbers. Most farmers would allow use of a barn in exchange for prayers for next year’s crops and animal health. Doric’s ability with weather lore and herbal remedies would help secure better accommodation and meals.

Summer 613

The winter in Aquitaine was mild and the three travellers made themselves useful to the brothers in their chosen abbey. During a period of calm weather, they got a passage on a trading boat going as far as Portucale on the river Durius. Doric had the idea of travelling up the Durius to find his ancestral home, but that would mean more trouble for Aiden. He knew he could do that another time, their journey to Sellium and Larn's journey to Rome, being more important. The coastal trek from there to Sellium took three months, with several long stops to administer to the sick and perform priestly duties. Aiden also needed frequent rests as his condition worsened.

Their arrival in Sellium coincided with the midsummer festivities. Though Christianity was the official religion, older pagan rites were still observed. As elsewhere, this was tolerated and Christian worship was adapted for the benefit of all the local population.

The travellers presented themselves to both the local church and the Visigoth Governor and were given work within the community. When he was able, Aiden taught those whose Christianity was sparse. He could identify with the religious changes in their lives. Larn helped the local artisans with building and repair jobs. He found the work satisfying and it earned money for his further travels. Doric's main activity was to help with healing and agriculture, but he joined in music making and storytelling in all sections of the community.

Autumn 613

Doric was overjoyed when he was invited to be a priest in the Governor's castle on the hill overlooking Sellium and its river. One of his duties was to translate the Governor's tribal sagas into the local language. He added a Christian aspect to them, reducing the warring and bloodthirsty nature and enhancing the goodness of the Visigoth history. He became a skilled diplomat in this work and in dealings with the usurped local ruling classes. By the end of the year, he held the respect of the majority of the local leaders, but most of all, the respect of the Governor and his family.

The castle had been built on the hill well before the Romans arrived. They had improved the building and added others in the area, controlling routes on the rivers and to the coast. He knew this was the hill where his ancestor had found the fallen star on his search after the destruction of his home.

Winter 613

"I remember the saga," said Aiden. "It was a strange one, as you say. You really believe some of the fallen star is under the castle?" Doric was visiting him in a hospital on a hillside above the river. His friend was failing. The sick monk took his hand.

"I do. My ancestor, Permag, found it on the hilltop and then travelled in a boat on the next part of his journey. I'm sure this is the place. You remember I had conversations with a boy named Billy?"

Aiden nodded.

"Between us and the girl Gail, we determined this is the place."

"I can feel the certainty in you. This is not just faith." He coughed and gripped his friend's hand harder. "My illness worsens with each season. I may not last another year."

"I expect it's no use arguing. Are you content to meet God?"

"Not yet. I want to see this fallen star of yours. I can ride a cart to the castle. There are many that make the journey each day."

"I'll arrange it when I've explored the cellars. I get little free time. But, I may have good cause. You know that I succeeded a priest who went insane? I have heard he was in the cellars and saw ghosts and heard voices. He tried to rid the place of the evil spirits, but was consumed by them."

"You must be careful. You don't know what the old castle was used for before the Romans got here." He shifted on his bed to face Doric full on. "If the spirits have done for one priest, they might like another as a trophy." He shook his hand to emphasise the point.

"Not spirits, but the power of the fallen star. I can cope with that. I will fetch you when I've found the star." He smiled. "You heard the noises from my bracelet. We will hear an angelic choir from this great piece of the star from heaven."

Aiden smiled and nodded. He lay back on his bed and slept.

39

Sellium (Tomar), Summer 614

Doric and Ubert, the stonemason, searched the castle cellars for ghosts. The Governor was pleased. His wife and children were scared to live in the haunted castle and wanted to move to a different town in the region. The Sellium castle was the best available. If he could clear the evil spirits, the Governor's family would stay.

Ubert marked his chart as they checked each part of the extensive system, pacing out the passages and chambers. When they reached the final chamber, Doric was disappointed. There were no ghosts and nothing that looked like a fallen star. Most of the chambers had piles of goods, some stored neatly and recently, others looking as though they may have been left by the Romans.

They held candles over the chart and studied it. "Here's an area which is surrounded by chambers," said Doric, "but has no entrance. Could there be a hidden cellar in the middle?"

Ubert pondered the possibility. "We can go back and I'll test the walls." He tapped the wall of the chamber with his iron mallet. It was solid. They moved to the next chamber. Furniture was stacked against the wall to be checked. They shifted it away and Ubert began tapping. His mallet found a weakness. He scratched around the perimeter, about the size of a door, but not a filled-in aperture. He took a chisel from his bag and scored around one of the stone blocks in the centre. "It's well laid stone. I'll need to split it. I'll go for my heavy tools."

Doric stayed behind. He peered at the floor by the possible doorway. It was not as level as the rest of the chamber. Two hand widths was of undressed stone and then the smoother flagstones where the rest of the floor began. He ran his hand over its roughness. Sounds formed in his mind.

He heard a familiar song. This was the third time the same melody had enchanted his mind. First at the Sarum Stones, then in Aquae Sulis, now here in the cellar of Sellium castle. He stood and the song faded. He kicked off his sandals and placed his bare feet on the rocky floor, his back to the wall.

The chamber brightened and two figures stepped from the iridescent cloud that had formed in the centre of the cellar.

"Doric, friend," said the young man.

"Priest and druid," said the young woman.

"Billy's friends. Twins. I greet you."

"You may put on your sandals. You do not need the Star Stone now," said the woman.

He approached the Twins and held their hands. "I have done as you asked. I have learned the Roman languages, both formal and every day. I have searched my memory of the Star Stone saga and told Billy of this. I hope that is good."

"Very good," said the man. "Gail and her people have found the stone and use its properties, but we have another task for you."

"It will not be difficult," said the woman. "We know it will give you great stature among the people here and in your new religion."

"I seek only to serve the One God and not have privileges."

"That is good," said the man. "Your modesty will serve you well."

"We will help you begin a new but secret religious order," said the woman. "This Order will last many thousands of years and will provide a service to all people until they find new homes among the stars."

"This is the work of gods and I am no god. How can I do such work?"

"You need only begin the Order. You will start it with nine members and leave it to grow on its own. We will make certain it survives," said the man.

"You say it is to be a religion. I cannot go against my One God."

"We see that human religions are good at self-perpetuation," said the woman. "It does not need a god, though to have one is useful. Human greed and cunning will make it prosper. This may sound strange, but all the religions we have seen, from before your time to beyond our own show this to be true. Humans love power and will protect its source."

Doric stepped away from the Twins. "You ask me to do an evil thing."

The man held his hand again. "In its purest form, it is not evil. Some humans will make it evil, but this Order will be used for good. The ultimate good of human survival. You are in a unique position to begin this."

The sound of falling metal rang in the chamber. Ubert had returned, seen the shining Twins and dropped his tools in fright. Before he could run, the woman was at his side, calming his mind with a caress to his head. He looked from her to her twin and to Doric, his boiling psyche cooling to clear sanity. She led him to join hands with the others, so he could understand.

"Ubert, we greet you," said the man. "You will help Doric open the hidden chamber to find the Star Stone, a gift sent from God for the use of mankind. You will be among the first of many members of this secret Order we have commanded."

He was silent, but in his mind, he accepted the task. He was full of pride that such a difficult piece of work had been entrusted to him by angels of the Lord.

"Once you have begun this," said the woman, "you will both travel to Rome."

Ubert found his voice. "Are you the ghosts who frighten the Governor's wife?"

"No," said the woman. "We are not ghosts and this is our first visit."

"We have never used the iron in the chamber," said the man raising his arm. "We have bracelets as Doric had before this journey."

"It is possible other beings use the iron within the chamber," said the woman. "You will see when you have opened the chamber and made a stout door to keep it safe. May your work go well."

He bowed. "I am proud to be of service, if that is not a sin."

Not a sin," said Doric. "You and I will find eight others to join you and continue the work. I will eventually return to my people in Britain."

Autumn 614

"Here is the fallen star, Aiden." Doric and Larn helped their friend into the new chamber and sat him on a stool. Ubert stood guard in the doorway looking outward, his sword drawn against possible spies. Their flaming torches showed the extent of the discovered chamber in their flickering light. "From here a company of nine will use the Star Stone power for good and evil over thousands of years. But, the ultimate purpose will be the salvation of humankind when the sun in our sky fails to sustain life."

"This is a faery story," said Aiden. "How can you know this?"

"True," said Larn. "You have power, I know, but this is madness."

"Remove your sandals and press your bare feet to the stone," said Doric, doing the same. "Listen."

Each heard their own version of the ethereal songs. Music that stirred their hearts and would forever leave a void of hunger within their minds.

He called to the gods of the place, using words from his far ancestors. The chamber floor glowed blue around their feet, spreading to coalesce and reach to the edges where Star Stone met the dark cellar walls. Dimmed patches moved around the floor, as though footprints were seen from below. Shapes grew from those footprints and changed into men and women. Each had similar features as though they were brothers and sisters. Each was robed in a white gown and each had a gaze, which bored through the minds of the three friends. They spoke a welcome of universal consciousness.

One of the visitors came to Aiden and touched his chest, removing all pain. Aiden knew he was not healed, but that he would suffer no more during his ending.

Another approached Larn, who backed away, until he realised no harm was intended. The visitor touched Larn's head that filled him with the knowledge of languages.

Doric had no need of gifts. His was the calling. His was the sure knowledge of duties to perform at an appointed time. In his mind, other pieces of Star Stone shone, scattered along the path of the original fallen star. A path, which ended in the sea near uncharted lands far to the west, much further away than the piece that fell near the coast of this country. His mind soared like an eagle, high above the mountains, looking down on the world as though a map. He saw random dots of brightness showing where all nine of the bracelets rested. He resolved to find one and take it to Rome.

Ubert stood at the chamber entrance that his skill had opened. His balanced sword, grasped with his mason's hands, warding against intrusion. He heard Doric the priest talking with his friends in the new chamber behind him. His heart leaped when the priest spoke his first incantation. The whole place blazed with blue light. He turned and looked into the chamber. His three companions were talking to spirits, ghosts of the cellar.

The ghosts faded, until the one remaining beckoned to him. "Ubert, thank you for the service you have rendered, opening this chamber. We are not ghosts, but we now have no need to use this place and frighten people. When you and the priest, Doric, return from Rome, you will help him to bring eight others together to look after this place. You will assist people, first in this area and then further away as the need arises. He will instruct you how to do this."

The spirit slowly faded and vanished.

Walking out, Aiden, the sick monk, needed no help.

"Are you cured?" Ubert asked.

"No. My pain is gone, but I will soon need your services for my burial."

Winter 614
West Coast of Iberia

Ubert set Aiden's headstone into the ground. He was proud of his work. Not the sin of pride, but the solid knowledge that his skill was God-given and that he was part of a greater plan, one of the initial nine who would use the star stone in his cellar for the good of his countrymen.

Doric said the final prayers over Aiden's resting place on a hilltop by the western sea, which connected this location to Aiden's home and his own. Nearly a generation had passed since he had left Berac and his parents in Kernow. He knew they would be dead by now, but they lived on in his memory, as did Moira. The thought of his childhood sweetheart jarred his mind.

Perhaps, when this is over, I'll go to Brittany and find her. One last task in Rome and all is ended for this way of life.

They returned to Sellium on the wagon that had brought them to the coast. Larn was keen to plan their next journey. "Doric, Ubert. We must prepare for Rome. A boat will be the best way."

"Very much," said Doric. "We continue down river to Ulishbona for passage to Rome. When I stood on the cellar floor, I saw other bracelets and pieces of Star Stone. There is a bracelet to the north of Genoa, in the high mountains. I will break my journey there, seek it, and then take it to Rome. I think the Governor may support us after our work with the cellar."

"Will you need us with you?" asked Ubert.

"I am always glad of your company, but it will be an arduous journey, which I would not impose on you."

"That is agreed," said Larn. "We will journey to the mountains with you. You will need my skill with languages and if the bracelet is in a cellar, Ubert can dig it out."

The friends laughed together and continued to plan their journey.

40

Comum (Como), Winter 614/615

The ship's crew helped load the baggage onto a two-horse wagon. The Governor of Sellium had sponsored their journey to Rome and given them gold and tradable goods for their journey. He had also entrusted them with documents for the Roman Church and gifts to ease his path to Heaven.

They took the road north through Mediolanum to Comum which was at the southern end of one of the great lakes close to the mountains. After years of neglect, the road was a rough ride for the travellers. Comum itself was still being rebuilt after the Lombardi conquest nearly fifty years before.

"It will be impossible to take our goods into the mountains," said Larn.

"If you two stay here and trade, I will carry on," said Doric. "I'm not sure how long it will take me to find the bracelet. I have no means of seeing it without one."

"I have a small piece of the stone from when I fitted the new door to the chamber," said Ubert. "I had to smooth the floor. I brought it with me for luck."

"Your luck and foresight will save us time. Well done." Doric slapped Ubert on the back. "I wonder why I didn't think of that. Let's try it when we are settled in our lodgings."

They found some that were simple, but secure, with a stable on the ground floor and living rooms above. Ubert found work with a nearby blacksmith. He had a talent with metals as well as stone, which he demonstrated to the smithy. Larn was quick to locate the town's market and weighed his chances of trading.

After their evening meal of meat, roots and greens, their first satisfying meal for weeks, Ubert gave Doric the piece of Star Stone.

"I can hear the noises." He closed his eyes and took deep

breaths to calm his mind. The noises softened to tuneless music, then to the sweet singing of children. There was joy in their words that told of spring and the love of God. He knew he was hearing through the mind of a teacher.

This woman is wearing a bracelet. Her thoughts are so clear. She is a mother with a sadness. Her own children have gone away. She may never see them again.

He saw through her eyes. The children sat on grass in front of her, goats nibbling at stunted bushes, tall snow-capped mountains lit with the blush of evening sun. He went to the north window and saw the same mountains. It would take him many days, but he knew the direction.

The climb was difficult in places, tracks and paths wet with thawing snows. A village, tucked between the folded hills, surrounded with pastures and pine trees, overlooked by the mountain he had seen five days previously. It was midday and the village seemed deserted. One building, part stone, was larger than the other wooden dwellings and set apart from them. Smoke curled from its chimney in the still air.

He looked through a window and saw seated children working on pieces of cloth. He found the door and knocked. After a short wait, a woman opened it. Her black hair was streaked with grey, but her blue eyes captured his heart. She reminded him of Moira, his childhood love. He knew she was the woman he had heard in his mind. He searched for the piece of Star Stone in his robe pocket and held it in front of her.

Words of greeting formed in his mind, which he also spoke in the dialect he had picked up in Comum: "I am Doric from Britain. I seek you, the bracelet wearer."

The woman took a step back, ready to slam the door. She heard his words in her mind, but spoken in her own language. "I hear you in your language, the Lombardi dialect and my ancestral tongue. What are you? Priest or devil?"

He stepped back from the door to show respect. "I am a

Christian priest, but I was a druid of the Celts, which I perceive you to be."

Her face whitened. "You will tell no one of this or I will curse you."

"You know your powers will have no effect on me. I come in peace, not to expose you, but because you have one of the nine bracelets. I had one, once, but had to leave it while on my travels." He held up the stone. "This is the same iron from which yours is made."

The woman saw the truth. "I am Greta. I teach our children. My own are in the Lombardi army. I never see them. I am also a healer, a very good one, which I say with humility."

"Children leaving home is a hard thing to endure, but your healing will bring you purpose. May I return when you have finished for the day?"

"Of course. I can say you are a distant relative, which you may well be, if you had a bracelet. Do you know the ancient saga?"

"I do, or the one which I had to learn. We must compare our histories."

"I'll enjoy that." She smiled and closed the door.

He returned after walking the woods near the village. The sun was about to set and the villagers were back from their work in fields and pastures. He went straight to the school building.

Greta invited him in. "What is your journey? You are far from Britain." She was clearing up the room ready for the next day's schooling.

"My purpose was to find the places where the Star Stone fell to the ground. I found one near Sellium in Lusitania. The stone there made me aware of your bracelet, so I had to come here. I, and my friends, are on a pilgrimage to Rome. I have not decided what I shall do then. Perhaps return to Britain, perhaps to Britany to find some of my tribe who went there years ago."

"You could return here." She put wine, bread and cheese on the table in front of him and sat opposite.

He looked up at her. "Thank you. What purpose would I serve here?"

"Keep me company, but I'm sure you have many skills which will be of use in our village."

"You are not from these parts. When did you come here?" He took a sip of wine.

"A generation ago. My husband won me in a battle. His army overran my town on their way south to join the Lombards in Mediolanum. He took me as a slave, but eventually married me. We had two sons who grew up in the army camp, so they followed him when old enough. He died of a severe fever about nine years ago." She turned the bracelet on her arm. "I was powerless to prevent it. I came this way returning to my home town, but stayed here."

"Where in the north did you live?" He broke some bread and cheese.

"I call it Chur, but it has been renamed by conquerors. It is very old. My family goes back many generations, long before Rome conquered this area. What is the purpose of your pilgrimage?"

"I have seen visions with my bracelet. I also get them with this piece of stone. There is no difference." He put it on the table and she picked it up. "There is a long past and a long future for the bracelets. A piece of that future lies in the Holy City, so I must visit."

"I can hear voices and music, strange music." She took off her bracelet. "The music has gone. I hear more with both."

"I have never had that chance. May I?" He put out his hands and she gave him the bracelet and stone. "So much more. Hold my hands."

ooo

Both feel a shock as their minds meld into one shared consciousness. Visions, peoples and places, some familiar, some new and some wildly different to anything they have ever experienced. Places of great beauty, heart-rending beauty, leaves the emptiness of longing within their minds. Places of ugliness and despair, nightmares, full of vile hate, forces a poisonous sickness into their spirits.

She lets go of his hands, shock on her face. He offers his hands again. She hardens her mind and grasps them.

More visions fill their beings. The sun, dark blotches on its diseased surface, a star no longer fit for the human race. A malignancy rises. It has no form that the human mind can understand, but its greed and wickedness is obvious to both of them.

He prays for guidance, she invokes a curse on the malevolent force. Two more minds join theirs, giving support while they endure the horror of their common enemy.

The Twins emerge from a ball of blue light. "Greetings for the third time, Doric," says the boy.

"Greetings to you, Greta," says the girl.

Doric lets go of the bracelet and stone, leaving them in Greta's hands. "Three times?" he says. "For me this is the fourth. Last I saw you was only months ago. You were fully grown man and woman."

The Twins look at each other. He hears their voices in his mind, a secret language, the conversation of twins who are complete in their own world.

"We will think on this," says the girl.

The conversation continues. He hears a third voice, grips the bracelet and stone harder, trying to understand. The third voice soothes the turmoil in the Twins' united mind.

"Our urgent business is to help Billy," says the boy. "The bad spirits you see, want the power within this universe to make another for themselves."

"I do not understand, but I will help," says Doric.

"I will help if I can," says Greta. "Such an abomination must be dispersed."

"You are very brave," says the girl. "We are gathering Star Stone users to do this. We hope it will be enough."

Doric is puzzled by the age of the Twins. "What of our last meeting in…"

"STOP. Tell us nothing of this. My brother and I must not know. We will discover the reason at another time. Come with us, we will be away for only a few moments."

The four stand in a circle and hold hands. They are enveloped by the Twins' glowing bubble.

41

Chislehurst, Friday, April 26th 2796

"We've had no contact with Billy since SI disconnected them," said Hella, reporting to Cator and Steran in a secure conference room. "The problem was Gail giving him the warning about staying away from Lewisham Market. But overall, we've had a good run of communications with him and Doric. You've seen all the reports. Billy's people worked out the time paradox situation for themselves. They had some bright people in the twentieth century."

"There have always been bright people, as you put it," said Cator. "We all build on work done by our ancestors and I hope our descendants will say the same."

"What do you make of these Twins?" she said.

"It seemed SI was very much guiding what Gail was asking Billy, is that so, Hella?" said Cator.

"Yes. It kept pausing, which means it was doing massive computations. Somehow, SI believes the Twins are from our future and from a Starship, because of their clothing."

Cator continued. "Billy says his particular bracelet is the same as Doric's and Gail's first. One of the Twins has her second one, found here in Chislehurst. The other Twin has a new one. That implies, in the Twins' time, Gail still has her original and we find the meteorite material and manufacture new units."

"True," she said. "As usual, we need more information. We always need more information, but if we go by the clothing, is his description accurate enough?"

"It computes well," said Steran. "I've heard of research in the Jupiter system for flexible materials which will reduce the effects of radiation, very necessary for the Starship program and probably ideal for clothing. I'll make enquiries, but I'll have to say nothing about our knowledge of it."

"What about SI's temporal paradox issue?" asked Hella.

Cator commanded off his SI terminal and waited a few moments. "Not yet. The guy I know has only limited access to the systems. A number of independent SI systems test each tranche of code and they do their own optimising and error checking. The originator of any particular piece of code is largely irrelevant. It could even be an individual SI section within the whole. I'll keep digging. If SI did deduce this concept on its own, I wonder what else might be buzzing around." Cator commed fresh drinks from the dispenser. "Tell me more about Doric?"

"He was the first contact Billy had," she said. "I think he resonated with Billy's Roman Catholic upbringing. The music, the Latin. He did have visions connected to his own life before that. I'd have to check SI for his conversations with Gail, but I believe he relived episodes from his recent past and had visions of things he could never have seen at the time. We think those visions were from people he knew, who were associated with the episodes in some way. That's certainly strange. It means he has some kind of Psy capability, getting memories from other people."

"Can you do that?" asked Steran.

She looked at him and wondered why he wanted to know. "No. I can feel the emotions of a subject and sometimes guide them a little. But no actual memories unless they're particularly raw. I saw your fear and anguish when we discussed a brain implant for Gail, the first day we met her. I saw the horrific memory you have of your child."

"Well it was horrific, but I'm glad I shared that with you even if it was involuntary. Do you think Billy is the centre of this capability? Somehow he's developed a psychic empathy via the bracelet, linking to the monk and Gail."

"It seems so. When I'm linked to her mind, I can feel the others there as well."

"What about Doric's recollection of the bracelet's history?" asked Cator.

Hella finished her drink and collected the fresh ones. "I

saw no falsehood in the saga he told us, but it was being processed by SI, so I can't be certain."

"Doric would have accepted it as the truth, so wouldn't see it as a lie," said Steran.

"That's possible," she said. "I tested that scenario some years ago to help with interrogation techniques. If you get someone to believe a story as the truth, you cannot later, detect it as a lie by Psy techniques. We don't know much about Doric. My impression is that he's truthful and in awe of this whole business. If I think about it, I am too. We can assume SI is very good at translating Latin but Doric has only just learned the language, so there may be errors."

"Have we got a fix on where the parts of the meteorite landed?" said Steran.

"A number of possible sites have been identified," said Cator. "Our surveyors are searching."

"Good. We must find this material and make more bracelets." Steran looked at his comband. "Hella, there's an opportunity in a month for you to travel to Moon Base Five for long range tests of the bracelets. It had best be you rather than Gail. Are you willing? You've been before?"

"Sure. I was there about three years ago. Great trip. What's my cover story?"

"There's an Intra-Solar-System program of Psy experiments for the Starship project which has been delayed by China State, but they are ready now, so we can proceed. We'll need extra personnel to get the work done on time. The work schedule allows for five weeks. The shuttle leaves from Madrid. You'd be working hard on that program, but we can fit in short tests with Gail. I've not discussed it with her yet. I saw the report for the last test you did."

"I've heard about the program. I'd love to attend. Our last test was very encouraging. No measurable delay and clear reception, but it was only a hundred kilometres."

"Have you tried it without SI?" asked Cator,

"Yes. Now we are getting used to them, it's as good

without. I can try both from Moon."

"We can't use SI for this," said Cator. "The bracelet could be classed as jewellery, though you'd have to give up some luxury because of the weight allowance for shuttle luggage. The helmets are a problem. We can't classify them as PsyTech equipment. No one would have seen the like before, so they'd be inquisitive and we don't want that."

Hella agreed.

Steran spoke into his comband. "That's all arranged. I'll be there when you arrive."

She smiled at him. "How did the announcement about the Sun's increasing instability go down with the general public?"

"Don't you see the news feeds? You've been too closeted here," said Cator.

"We've been busy. I guess it's not that important to us at the moment."

"The news was received with reluctant acceptance in most quarters, but we're still talking of three centuries from now, so it doesn't figure in most people's lives. There is an undercurrent of dissent. As you haven't heard, let me be the first to tell you. The announcement was tempered by a message from Pioneer Starship Two. They have planet-fall on a usable planet. It's a desert world but there is water and atmospheric oxygen. Also, simple life forms with similar DNA to ours. A success."

"What about the dissent?" said Hella.

Cator continued. "It depends whether you think your family or descendants, are likely to be around in three hundred years. The rich and powerful are making noises about extra donations if a place is assured for their families. That will probably turn to blackmail before long. I'm glad I don't have to deal with it. Of course, the world States which don't have a stake in the Pioneer Starship program are beginning political manoeuvres."

"A return to the Bad Times?"

"I hope not. We'd never get the ships completed," said Cator.

"There's plenty of trouble ahead from the Offworld communities, as well," said Steran. "Remember they bailed out the Earth-bound populations after the Bad Times. And they're genetically and psychologically more suited to work in and on the Starships, having that kind of culture. They're demanding space for a high percentage of their population, if not total evacuation."

"As I say, I'm glad I don't have to deal with the politics," said Cator. "We're basically telling huge sections of the human race, they can't have a place in a lifeboat, even though it isn't like that in reality."

"No, but we'll all have to deal with the pirate elements which will try to take over," said Steran.

42

Luna Base Five, Monday, June 3rd 2796

Hella knew most of the representatives of the Intra-Solar-System PsyTech group when they congregated in the main hall of Luna Base Five. She had met only a few face to face, as theirs was a small community that stretched across the whole solar system. Two delegates had travelled for a year to make the rendezvous. This was the first such meeting in forty years and only one delegate of the present company had been at the previous one. The advantages that the bracelets would bring excited her, if they ever came into common use.

The PsyTech group held their first meeting in the silence of mental communication, reacquainting themselves with their Psy voices. There would be plenty of time later for talking. The tasks they had been set by the Intra Solar community were difficult and required long, tiring sessions.

She was exhausted at the end of each sixteen-hour workday and had barely enough time for the required exercise regimen. Luna Base Five kept to Central European time that was two hours ahead of Gail's. This meant she had little convenient time for her bracelet experiments. They had arranged to make tests in Gail's early morning, which was best for both of them. As arranged, she put through a coded comband call to Marina to signal the start of the test.

"Hi Marina. Just checking in for any urgent messages."

"You have only one. It's from the Army hospital in Sussex. They want to schedule some therapy sessions. Shall I say it will be a couple of months and you'll call direct?"

"Yes please. I'll comm you same time tomorrow. Bye." She closed the connection and got the bracelet from her luggage. She slipped it onto her arm and lay back on her bed to concentrate on Gail.

Their two minds met.

"Hi, Gail."

"Hi, Hella. Working hard?"

"It's exhausting, but very good. How are you feeling today? I'm sorry I can't be with you."

"I'm getting over my trauma of losing Billy and the PsyTech you organised is doing a great job. I keep thinking of Billy and the Twins and I can't help wondering about them. I guess it will all become clear, but I very much want to talk to him again."

"You're not allowed, you know that. We were getting very close to a temporal paradox and can't risk it again. There may be a chance later when the boffins have studied it for longer."

"I do miss him, even though I've never met him. I just like the feel of his mind."

"Concentrate on Victor. He loves you more that he will ever say. Billy is unattainable."

"I know. But Billy saw my babies being born, my Twins. He's met them and I've not yet given birth. I'm a mess, aren't I?"

"Understandable, but I know you'll get over it. I'll be with you in a month or so and we can talk about it every day."

"Thanks, see you soon."

"Bye, Gail."

She relaxed after the conversation. The bracelet had warmed slightly. She took it off and hid it in the same place in her luggage. A coded message on her comband indicated the experiment had gone well.

She sat on the corner of her bed. The limited space did not allow a chair, though the bed did convert into a lounger. Gail worried her. The weeks before she departed for Luna Five had been traumatic for the girl. During the experimental work, she had developed a fixation on Billy whom she could never meet. Billy then declared he had spoken to her in her future when she was giving birth to twins. That had sent her over the edge. Already under stress with the three-way mental connections, she had blurted out a warning to Billy. It was about a wartime episode near his home she had read from the histories of the era.

Normally, she tried not to get involved with her charges, but she had become attached to Gail. Being a PsyTech was all about empathy, so it was very difficult. This Luna trip broke the dangerous bond she was forming and her remote talks with her were good for both of them. Gail was outside of her empathy range so she could be more detached.

Her comband chimed. "Hi Steran. I'll be ready in a few minutes."

They usually met over breakfast for fifteen minutes before her work began. She air-showered and dressed in the one-piece jumpsuit used on the base, satisfied with how it fitted her curves. She tied up her hair so it would not float around in the one-sixth gravity.

"Good morning Hella. Sleep well?" He was waiting for her in the refectory and smiled.

"Well enough. I woke a little early today, so I must be getting used to it."

"You need less sleep up here. Have you scheduled your time in the gym? You'll regret it when you go back if you haven't. I'll workout with you if you like."

They took their breakfast trays and found a table.

"I've managed a midday session all week. You can join me today."

He nodded. "It's a blistering schedule you've got with your Psy friends. Why is it so intense?"

"We had that delay. The China State delegates were caught up with a flood disaster. We still have to finish on time or the Offworlders will miss their planetary shuttles and have to stay another six months. But you know this." She bit into her sandwich.

"Yup, but I love the way you explain things."

"Is your local woman unavailable?" She put her mug's

tube into her mouth and sucked, staring straight at him.

"How did you work that out?"

She tapped her head.

"I love it when you read my mind."

"I read emotions, mostly. There's so little going on in your head to read. If you're coming on to me, just say so and we can resume where we left it in Chislehurst. I've got a tight schedule these next few weeks so don't have time to play around." She finished her drink and held his stare.

"I'm sorry. I've offended you." He held her hand.

"No. I'm desperately worried about our playmate." Her comband chimed. "Sorry, I've got to go. I'll skip the final session this evening. See you at twenty two, my place." She pouted a kiss and left the table.

Hella got back to her room a little late. Steran was waiting outside. "Sorry I'm late." She kissed him full on his lips and thumbed the security pad to let them in. "Oh. My things are out of place."

"In what way? Check it all."

She looked at everything in view, then the few drawers and her luggage. "It's been searched. Not very tidily either."

He spoke into his comband and then looked up. "I'm getting all the surveillance data put through to my SI for analysis. There's none in the room, but all corridors are covered and comband traffic of course. Do you have any valuables?" He looked directly at her, rubbed his nose and then his ear indicating the possibility of a bugging device.

"Just an old bracelet, but it's not quite where I put it. Do you have a safe where I can lodge it?"

"Not really. You'd best wear it during your sessions."

There was a knock at her door. She pressed the access button and it slid open. A young woman in coveralls entered.

"Trudi. This is Hella," said Steran. "She's had an intruder, nothing taken. Can you sweep please?"

"Sir." The SecTech nodded and pulled an instrument pod

from one of her many pockets and reset it. She sampled the air around the room, in the drawers, every article of luggage. She sampled the bracelet and both Steran and Hella. “It’ll take about thirty minutes for the full DNA analysis.” She adjusted the pod. A minute later Trudi was removing the wall mirror and found an electronic bug. “Natty little thing,” she said, holding it up. “Audio-visual, frequency hopper.” Her comband chimed. “SI has found the receiver and alerted security. Interrogation in fifteen minutes. Would you like to take part, Hella? He’s one of your PsyTech delegates. We’ve pulled him out of the session on a pretext.”

“Thanks Trudi, I will.”

The interrogation had finished by the time they got to the security suite.

“He didn’t last long. I thought you PsyTechs were made of stronger stuff,” said a security operative.

“We are,” said Hella. “What did he say?”

“Nothing. We began straight questioning, no coercion or threats. He kept shaking his head. As soon as I said your name, he died. They’re doing a post-mortem now. We think there may have been an implant that fried his brain. Either remotely or psychosomatically.”

“That’s a new one, but I suppose it’s possible,” she said.

“This is the second case I’ve heard of,” said the operative. “The other was on Phobos three years ago. Nearly caused a nasty mining accident that would have permanently shut it down. A few corporations would have benefited from that, though they never found out who was responsible.”

“Can we covertly scan for more of these?” asked Steran.

“The autopsy will tell us if it’s possible.”

Steran took her hand. “We need to find you a more secure place during your stay.”

“I’ll let you invite me to your apartment, if you insist.”

He smiled. “Right. I’ll get Trudi to sweep that as well. Stars, what a night.”

ooo

Hella stretched out on his lounger. His living apartment was verging on luxurious compared with her visitor's room.

"The PsyTech intruder was bogus," said Steran. "We've double checked the delegate list. His DNA is a match for our records, but a police report from Tucson says he was found dead in a ditch eleven days ago, presumably on his way to the Spaceport. They never bothered to follow it up, being such a violent area."

"What about the rest of the security data?" she asked, patting the cushion.

"Only our bogus intruder showed up." He joined her on the lounger.

"Perhaps this guy was a decoy and expendable at that. How did he die and how do you explain the DNA match?"

"I can't," he said. "No toxins, no brain damage and no independent identification that we can find. There's no way we could have detected him. He's a no-man. Simply lost the will to live as soon as he heard your name."

"I can have that effect on people," she said, pouting. "I suppose he was human." She laid herself across his chest and reached up for a kiss.

He obliged. "What makes you say that?"

"Some things our young boy was saying about the ribbons he sees. One person he was involved with was clearly dead, but still had a ribbon indicating some kind of life. I said nothing to our playmate."

"I missed that in the reports. Was it included?" He cupped her breast and squeezed.

She reached up for another kiss and wriggled closer. "Mmm. I expect so, they're simply transcripts, but they're long and tedious."

"What was the reference?"

"He actually said, 'It's like they ain't real people', whatever that means." She rolled on top of him and wriggled herself closer.

"But if what you say is true, we have an eight century old scenario, maybe even more. Oh Stars." He rolled over and unfastened her one-piece and let her do the same to his. "This gets worse the more I think about it. I'll review all the data again. You be careful in your sessions, there may be more of these people. Enough."

They slid to the floor and finished undressing.

43

Chislehurst, Saturday, July 20th 2796

Gail held her bracelet, its surface decorations familiar under her searching fingers.

She was in the laboratory with the excuse of getting her sweatshirt, purposely left behind the day before. No one would be in the lab. Marina was away for the weekend and her temporary PsyTech was out all morning.

The safe where her bracelet was kept had presented a problem. It was not keyed to her palm print. Marina had thought that was best. A hum filled the laboratory when she touched the safe's metal handle. It reminded her of the derelict building when she had first found it. The vibrations shook her fingertips. The safe opened.

With the bracelet on her arm, she searched for Billy among the noises in her mind. Weeks had passed since their last exchange and she hoped it would not be their final one. The SI system was off. She would try without.

Billy was not there.

Concentrating on Doric, she heard snatches of plainsong chant, but not Doric himself. He had always been difficult to contact as he rarely wore the bracelet. There were many other voices, but nothing she recognised.

Silly me. Of course not, they may be people from other stars. The noises they make will be entirely different.

A tutorial about dolphins came to mind. Their clicks and squeaks and how some people can actually speak to and understand them. There were many similar noises in her mind.

She was lonely and missed Billy's voice in her head. Also Doric's, but not in the same way. He was a lot older. Doric had a definite purpose in life. He had changed from a pagan druid to a Christian monk, learning a new way of life on the way. It was inevitable that she could never go back to being just another kid with dozens of others. Her future would be unique.

There were whispers of something in her mind, but not Billy. He had spoken about being able to hear previous conversations he had had, but could not have a second time. The words, once spoken, were remembered and could not be repeated or changed. She thought of those ribbons, joining people and things, in different places and times. Perhaps Balara could figure that out. She sobbed into her sweatshirt.

It's not fair. My machines made it all possible and now they're stopping me talking to the only real friend I have.

Her body shook with frustration.

Victor's a great guy, but we can't share our minds as I do … did … with Billy. I'm not sure I could ever love Victor as much as he loves me, but he's given up his ordinary life to be with me and it's great when we're together. At least he's flesh and blood.

She took a deep breath and cried out, "Oh Billy, where are you?"

Tears streamed down her face, soaking her sweatshirt.

"Gail?" said Chaz. "I've been looking for you. What's the matter, lass?"

"Oh. Chaz. Please don't tell I've taken the bracelet out."

"That's not a good idea. What's got you upset?"

"I can't find Billy. He's gone."

"I saw the report. They reckon you'll be talking again sometime. They've got be careful."

"I know all that, but it still hurts." More tears came.

Chaz put his arm around her shoulders. "Come on, let's get a brew. Hella's back today." He folded her sweatshirt, put it over his shoulder and led her to the lab door.

"I'd better put this back." She took the bracelet from her arm and replaced it in the safe.

ooo

Hella and Gail hugged when they met at the entrance to the Chislehurst Tunnels.

"I'm so glad to see you," said Gail. "I've missed our chats."

"Me too. How are you coping?"

"I miss Billy, but Victor's very understanding and I think we're great together. How was your trip?"

"Victor will be very good for you. Luna was hard work, terribly long days and I mean work days. I enjoyed our short chats, it all worked very well, didn't it?"

The small conference room was full. A young engineer offered his chair to Hella. She was grateful, the six times Luna gravity was pulling her through the floor. Gail and Victor stood next to her, holding hands.

Cator checked the SI terminal. Everyone had arrived.

"I think this is the first time we've all been in the same room. Quite a crowd. I'll summarise the progress, then we can go on to questions and answers. First, thanks for all the hard work you've done on this project. It's been a very busy time up to now. Much more to do, of course, and that will be spread over several years. From now on we must go slowly and covertly, as we'll be located in various places around Europe."

He sipped some water. "Hella and Gail had perfect results using the two bracelets between here and Luna Base Five. That was without any technology enhancement. The next stage for that will be at interplanetary distances.

"As to the material from which the bracelets are made, we've a search plan to find the three known places where parts of the meteorite fell. We'll be searching large areas of land and sea for rocks that fell thousands of years ago. A difficult task for which we'll be using other agencies. Obviously, security will be tight and I hope you'll all understand the restrictions.

"The physics of the material is being studied by Balara, who will be able to expand on that later." He turned to the physicist who was frowning at her comband. She looked up at him and nodded. "If this material behaves as we so far believe, we'll have the capability of instantaneous communication over inter-stella distances. We all know how useful that will be. It'll revolutionise the search for new planets. The Pioneer Starships we've launched in the past century have begun to send information, but it's difficult to detect their signals at such vast distances and the delay makes conversation impossible. Any questions?"

A technician held up her hand. "Who will use this material? Will they have to be on the Starships?"

"We'll have people on Earth, throughout the Solar System and on the Starships. We don't yet know if a bracelet is the best shape. And before anyone asks, we've no idea how easy or difficult it will be to 'tune in' to a particular person, or who'll be suitable."

A couple of hands went down.

A medic waved his hand: "So this will be a job for life?"

"Certainly on the Starships, but you know that. On Earth, possibly not, though it depends how many adepts we find once we begin testing. Not everyone can make the bracelets work. I can't, for example."

Questions dried up after a few more minutes. There was too much uncertainty about the details, most people wanted hard facts that were not available. He closed the meeting and people drifted off.

Cator found Gail and Hella. "Hi you two. Have you seen Balara? She isn't in her lab and her comband is off."

"She got a message during the meeting," said Hella. "It must have been urgent, she slipped out immediately.

"Yes, I saw that." He received a call. "Security tells me her comband isn't just turned off. It's not linked to the system. They're searching for her."

"Is that serious?" said Hella.

"We'll see. They're checking her personal SI unit. How was your Moon trip?"

"Fine with some excitement. Completed valuable PsyTech work with my peers and had a good time."

"With Steran?"

"Naturally."

"Are you thinking of staying with him on Luna?"

"He has a regular woman up there, when she's not on one of her prospecting trips around the moon and I'm happier here, for now."

"The next few months will be critical. I want you and Gail to stay together. We'll need to make more artefacts and test them. You two are the only adepts I have at the moment."

"I'd like that." Gail linked arms with Hella.

"Looks like you still have a team," said Hella. "What about the long distance trials you mentioned?"

"I've not scheduled that yet. It'll take over a year to get one of you to Jupiter and then the return journey. Possibly longer if we can't get a good launch window. I can't afford that delay right now. But we can hide you away on that pretence. Security has indicated there may be interest in what we're doing here. There's still no answer to that imposter on Luna, but our people have to be careful with their investigations. It was only a matter of time till someone put the intelligence together. So, we effectively disperse for a while."

"Where will I go?" asked Gail.

"You'll stay here, at least for six months while the next phase comes together. You've a lot of schooling to catch up on and some other things to learn. Remember we discussed the need for adepts on the Pioneer Starships? I definitely see you as one of those, with Victor, if that's okay with you both. Talk it over with him. He's learning all about Starship hydroponics and doing well. On the voyage, you'll need another job as well as communicator. We'll have to see what that could be."

"I'd already realised this. Victor and I have been talking about it."

Hella looked at her and smiled. "You two will be okay."

Gail hugged Hella and went to find Victor.

Cator's comband buzzed. He listened privately for several minutes. "That was Security. There's nothing on Balara's SI, but they did find her written notes."

"Nothing?"

"It's been wiped of all work related data. She published a report in January and has expanded on it since. That's gone. I'll check if I've still got my copies and about any archived data. We've kept it secret until now, but she found that the meteorite consisted of only the Iron-54 isotope and its crystal structure was peppered with singularities, micro black holes. Her conclusion was that it was manufactured, rather than the natural product of dying stars."

"Alien?"

"Certainly. Which opens a Pandora's box."

"Could the aliens have taken her?"

"We've very tight security. She hasn't left the tunnels, but with what we've discovered of the bracelets' power, there's no knowing what aliens could do with it." He turned on an SI terminal and searched his own database. "My copies of Balara's old reports are there." He scanned their content. "All looks okay. Perhaps only the most recent work has gone. Stars."

Balara's comband buzzes.

She looks at it and swears to herself. She has to meet the caller in her office.

Why didn't security call? Most irregular. I'll report it.

She leaves the meeting with mixed feelings.

ooo

Two young people stand by her workstation, talking to her SI computer, the air around them shimmers with energy.

"What's going on? Who are you?" She reaches for her comband to send an alarm signal. It turns off.

"We need your help with the exotic Iron-54. You must come with us," says the young man.

"You will meet Gail and Billy in our time and place, but you will not come back here. Your work is too important for it to languish on this planet," says the young woman.

"How is that possible?" Equations force their way into her mind. Six dimensional vectors chaff her consciousness. "Oh goodness. I see the three dimensions of time. Who the stars are you? Brahman and Shiva?"

"We are Gail's children," says the young woman.

"Come." The young man holds out his hand. "You of all people will enjoy the journey."

She turns to run from her office, but falls into a shining sphere.

44

Edenbridge, Isles of London, Sunday July 28th 2796

Marnie threw open the hatch and took a deep breath of the cool, salty fog. Morning moisture condensed onto her naked ebony skin and tight, curly hair. She pulled on a one-piece against the chill.

"Good morning, London," she yelled into the whiteness. There was an answering call from a nearby boat, concealed by sea mist. Her comband buzzed. It was Kovak.

"Caffeine?"

"Coming over." She steered to him, watching the radar display for obstacles. His boat showed up on the screen with its ident tag. She saw that the rest of her Swimmer Team was within a few hundred metres.

"This'll clear in an hour," he passed a steaming mug over the rails.

"Thanks, we've a lot to do today." She gratefully took the mug, admiring his strong, black muscles and bald head. Even as they sipped their drinks, a light wind picked up, stirring the surrounding mists. She opened a pack of biscuits and offered them to him. He took a couple and nodded his thanks.

"What's our job for today?" he asked.

"The Edenbridge shark defences have a breach. Reported at twenty-one hundred yesterday. The night shift haven't completed, so we will. Two sharks got through and had a go at the squid farm." She was reading from the display.

Kovak checked his computer. "Conditions were good overnight. Why didn't they finish?"

"Doesn't say. We'll find out soon enough." She pressed a few buttons on her display unit, sending a message to the rest of the Team. "We'll leave at zero eight hundred. The mist will be gone by then." She finished her drink and handed the mug back.

"Aye, Aye skipper," he joked.

She threw a biscuit at him.

The sun broke through just as the Swimmer boats started from their moorings off the Isle of Maidstone. They followed the direction of the old river Medway, now a drowned memory, sixty metres below.

The Bidborough Control commed as they sped past, "Take it easy. There may still be sharks at Edenbridge." She thanked the Controller and slowed her Team.

"Kovak, Nero. You take your groups to the break. I'll look for predators."

They both confirmed. Seven craft broke from the main Team and continued towards Edenbridge. The small town had been submerged for centuries, but its name lived on as the gateway to a squid farm in the valley named The Dorking Ring.

She lined up her group so their sonars covered the width of the approach. The linked computers scanned for any life forms in the area. Some escaped squid were jetting to the open sea, but hardly a loss compared with the billions still in captivity.

"No sign of sharks," commed one of her group.

"There're lots of hiding places in the old ruins," commed another.

"I've got a faint reading on the spectro-analyser," commed a third.

"How faint?" asked Marnie.

"Could be residue from last night. Could be one lying low. I can't get a fix on it."

"Keep watching as we sweep the approach." The group crept towards the farm, sonar fingers feeling into every hiding place.

"No increase on the analyser," came the report.

"Maybe just residue. Keep watching."

They arrived at the barrier just as Kovak surfaced.

Marnie hailed him. "What's the score?"

He climbed onto his boat and pulled off his suit headgear. "They're getting cleverer every year. They managed to totally destroy one section, killing one of themselves into the bargain."

Nero surfaced and scaled his bigger boat, which he shared with his woman, Tam. "We'll be finished by the end of the shift. All the parts have just arrived." He steered next to Kovak's boat.

Marnie joined her two main men. In her mind, Kovak was destined to take over from her if she ever retired and Nero would then be second. He was a tower of a man, by far the biggest Swimmer in the area. "Great. We'll moor here tonight and cover the whole area with our sensors. They'll have to enhance the fixed alarm arrays." She ordered all the boats to spread out into a pattern that would give best coverage.

This is the boring part of my job. Just waiting for something to happen. Hopefully it won't, too many people depend on the squid harvests.

As evening arrived, each craft in turn went to the Edenbridge service pier to refuel and then resume its position in the guard matrix. The sharks could be back for an easy feast. The computers searched, while the Swimmers chatted.

"Marnie. What are you planning for your next rest-days?" It was Tony who worked on the service pier.

"I haven't decided yet."

"She's with me at the Palace," interrupted Kovak.

"I thought you'd never ask," she said.

"You Swimmers never come ashore for fun," said Tony.

"Crystal Palace Isle is ashore, Tony, or haven't you been there?" said Kovak.

"Sure I've been there, but it's only six k long. Can't get a good walk going in that mass of pleasure seekers."

"Where would you take me, Tony?" she asked, knowing

it would stir Kovak.

"We could start near here at the Grinstead Temple. Then across the Guildford Bridge to the North Downs and into the rain forest." Tony was hopeful.

"That's one hell of a walk," said Kovak.

"I've got the use of a MK-Three Terra Rover," said Tony, with more than a little pride in his voice.

She replied, "That sounds like real fun. When are your rest-days, Tony?"

"They've got a new Five-D at the Palace," said Kovak.

"The fifteenth to seventeenth. I could meet you here the night before. The lights of the Grinstead Temple are stunning." Tony was warming up.

"Oh. I'm sorry. My days are seventeenth to nineteenth. Some other time," she said.

"Okay. Let me know when you're this way again."

"Will do." She cut the comms link to shore.

"Why did you lie?" said Kovak over the secure Swimmer comms.

"To reel you up, of course."

"You did, too."

"What's the new Five-D?"

"It's a historical romance. Full of intrigue and broken hearts. It'll suit you down to the deck."

"Touché. I'll let you take me."

"Night," he said.

"Night," she said as the Swimmers settled down to rest, computers scanning the depths.

A scrape on the hull woke Marnie. Her small boat bobbed in the calm water. The alarms screamed.

"Shark," commed Nero.

"Where did that come from?" shouted Kovak.

"Kovak, Nero. Prepare damage teams," said Marnie as she powered up her aquajet engines.

"Mab, Tam, follow me."

Nero slid into the water as Tam turned their boat to follow Marnie. His suit thrusters jetted to join his group near the defences.

"Group Three," commed Kovak as he rolled from his bunk pulling on his Swimmer suit. He checked the suit's functions with the boat's computer and saw that his group was also ready. He gave the command to swim. Five more Swimmers dived into the dark waters, their Suit thrusters jetting them towards the shark nets.

Nero confirmed his group was standing by.

"Got a fix. Analyser positive," said Tam.

"How did it get past our scanners?" said Marnie.

Tam checked her computer record. "Playback shows it simply appearing from under your boat."

"It must have followed me close to. Very tricky fish. Relay that to Control."

"Done. Target half k," said Tam.

"Arm stunners. I want this one alive."

"Three hundred."

"Mab, take right side. Tam, centre." Marnie turned left and increased power to overtake their prey. Mab steered to the right and pushed her engines into the red. The three boats leaped into a well-practised choreography, hemming the shark into an ever-closing triangle. It knew it was under attack, but shallow waters cut off a deep escape. Spray soaked the Swimmers as their bows sliced through water. Computers calculated the best trajectories. The shark dodged in confusion, making ready to strike high. Stunners fired. The shark stopped. Several more boats caught up and two Swimmers dived to secure the big fish. It was sedated quickly and a breathing muzzle fixed to its head to keep it alive.

ooo

The morning began sunny.

“Two fine days in a row. It can’t last,” said Kovak as he accepted a mug of caffeine from Marnie.

“It has been known. Biscuit?”

He took one. “What’s on the schedule today?”

“A request to monitor for two more days. They’re bringing extra sensors for their array and will need our help.”

“Bit of a bonus for us then?” He was hopeful.

“Fifteen per cent for round the clock watch. Gives us more to spend at the Palace.”

“Could even get a hotel room rather than stay on our boats.” He lifted an eyebrow in enquiry.

“That’d be better than last time,” she smiled.

45

Crystal Palace Island, Friday, August 2nd 2796

Marnie gunned her aquajets, sending spray high into the air behind her boat. The past fifteen days of Swimmer duties had sharpened the anticipation of her few days holiday on Crystal Palace Island. The rest of her Swimmer Team followed behind in loose convoy, swerving and splashing their way along Mitcham Sound, approaching the island from the southwest. The Crystal Palace glowed with its own inner light, a shining beacon in the rainstorm. On a clear day, it was possible to see the people inside through the transparent towers and domes, hell bent on enjoying themselves. The small island was full of entertainment and diversions covering the complete spectrum of human enjoyment.

Marnie's Team moored in the western dock complex and went their separate ways according to tastes.

"I've got us a room in the Savoy Tower," said Kovak as they hurried through the driving rain.

"Sink me, no expense spared." She grabbed his arm and pulled him even faster to the protection of the main concourse.

"You're worth it," he shouted over the sudden noise of the reception area as they burst through the air curtain at the entrance. They stood, while the air blast took most of the rain from their clothing.

"Let's get cleaned up. I'm dying for a proper shower." She tugged at her sticky hair, aware of the looks of the revellers around her, all clean and neatly coiffured.

"That's better." She came out of the small shower cubicle, towelling her short black hair.

He turned from the fifteenth floor window overlooking the Isles of Chislehurst and Purley and nuzzled her damp neck. "You smell much better now."

"Poo. Keep away. Your turn, stinky." She flicked him with the end of her towel.

"Okay. But don't bother getting dressed." He grabbed her towel and pulled her close for a brief kiss before she shoved him into the shower.

The concourse seethed. The Island of Fun, as the traders liked to call it, was the main holiday venue in the Manche region of Europe. Family areas were segregated from the seedier parts, but all the shops and restaurants were located on the concourse that was a lofty cathedral to pleasure. Shops and cafés climbed in tiers from level zero to the high transparent roof, in places jutting into the free space one above another. It was as if trees of concrete were thrusting their giant leaves to catch light from above.

Marnie and Kovak enjoyed the diversity of food available in the multi-cultural restaurants, so different from the dried rations or fish on their boats. They managed to get a rooftop table in their favourite restaurant. The entrance was from the concourse where an exclusive elevator took them the forty floors to the dome overlooking the Purley Air Terminus. They sat, side by side, enjoying the view of the variety of craft flying in and out, repeatedly pointing as passenger and freight craft came and went.

"It's a wonder they keep them all apart," she said.

"It's those SI computers. We need them on our boats."

"First we need a lucrative job." She stroked his hand.

"Can we order? I'm starved." He thumbed the edge of their table, which lit up with the menu.

"I'll have red meat," she said. "I've had enough of fish."

"It'll cost you, real or recon?"

"How much is real?" The price appeared. "Oh." She scrolled the menu searching for a tasty meal at lower cost.

He saw the straight line of her lips. "We can share a piece. It'll certainly make a change from squid."

"You are good to me." She squeezed his hand and smiled.

"I've got to keep Tony in dock." He had a twinkle in his eye.

"Jellyfish. I've no intention of letting him catch me."

"Glad to hear it." He squeezed her hand in return. "We can economise for the rest of our stay."

"Not too much, I hope." She thumbed the charge pad to share the cost.

"Champagne?"

"Let's."

They ate and drank as slowly as possible, drawing every last milligram of enjoyment from the experience. This was a once-a-year treat for the Swimmer couple. Their rest-days were usually taken on their boats in some quiet backwater.

The dome slid open as the weather cleared. The setting sun lit the underside of the receding clouds bathing the diners in a transient golden glow. Warmth flowed from each table to compensate for the cool, fresh air.

They watched the lights of the airborne and seaborne craft as they plied their different media. Liners of the air and sea, with their passengers, some hurried, some leisured, coming and going across the face of the drowned planet. He caught her studying him. She understood his concern.

"A cent for your thoughts," she said.

"A cent is all they're worth." He moved closer.

"Why so melancholy?"

"When will this all end?" He swept his hand over the sea-view.

"I know, love. We can't stop it, but we can adapt."

"Always positive, that's what I like about you." He rested his arm on her shoulders.

"Not all you like, I hope." She stroked his thigh.

"Oh, no." He stood and grabbed her hand. "Come on, woman. This man needs to party."

46

Crystal Palace Island, Saturday, August 3rd 2796

The comband on Marnie's wrist chimed and woke her. She knew it was urgent by the sound it made.

"Penta. It's early." Her heart skipped a beat. The European Swimmer Co-ordinator rarely commed for social reasons, but she wished he would.

"Sure. I wanted to catch you before you began enjoying another day with that young rake of yours."

"Kovak's fine for me. And you're lucky he sleeps like a log."

"You're the lucky one. You'd get all the backwash. Now. Business."

She slid out of bed and pulled on a robe. They always kept the room cool. She went into the servery and keyed for caffeine. "Okay. I'm out of bed." She switched her comband to visual.

"We have a new assignment for your Team. It's some time away, but I want your commitment soonest. There's a deep dive, around two hundred metres."

"That'll make a change from the paddling we've been doing lately." She stirred extra sugar into her caffeine.

"I like to give my favourites the best jobs."

"I'm one of your favourites, am I?"

"Always have been and you know it. The dive's on the edge of a trench in area Europa Four. Off the Iberia coast. The remotes have located an object which looks useful, that's all I can say, it's confidential. A report is already in your boat's archive. I suggest you read it carefully before agreeing. It won't be an easy job."

She saw the serious set of his face. "Okay. It'll be about an hour before I can check it out."

"I need a reply by midday your time, otherwise I'll have to call another Team."

"Was I first on your list?"

"Of course. Though you may not thank me for it."

"I'll round up the guys and gals for breakfast and we can discuss it. How much can I tell them?"

"The report sets out the security. See you later. Like your robe."

"Hotel's supply. Not my choice."

"You could always leave it off."

"In your dreams."

"Constantly. And I'm worried about that man you're moored with."

"What concern is it of yours?"

"Just don't let your personal desires clash with your duties."

"I don't. Do you?"

"Not now. Which is why I'm here and you're there."

"I'm sorry. I didn't mean to bring that up."

"Over it now. I don't want you making the same mistakes."

"I won't. Promise."

"Good. Hear from you before noon."

"Ciao."

"Team. We need to decide on a job that's offered. It's deep, two hundred metres, special fitted suits. They need an answer by noon our time." Most of Marnie's Team were in a cheap cafeteria, the rest were connected via their combands.

Kovak played with his toast and jam, a real treat on other occasions, but this time he had little desire for it.

She continued. "It's a recovery job. We have to fit the cables and monitor the lifting. It may mean tunnelling under the object, which is embedded in the silt."

"Why can't remotes do this?" asked Nero.

"It has an irregular shape and may be fused to the bedrock. The remotes can't tell. We'll be down for an estimated four days. So I reckon about three weeks, what with suit building and on site planning."

"Bonuses?" said Nero.

"Treble for the divers. Double for support Swimmers and fifty per cent on top if we succeed."

There were nods and murmurs of approval.

"Who wants this wreck so badly?" asked Kovak.

"Classified. As is the nature of the object, but I expect you'll work it out before long. Don't discuss this outside the Team. Are we agreed?" The chance of this much wealth in so short a time scale was decisive.

"When do we start?" said Kovak.

"About two months. The weather will be calmer and they have to design and manufacture our suits. We'll be measured here. Crystal Palace has a body scanner. All agreed then?"

Her comband registered affirmatives from the whole Team, which she sent to Penta. They sat in silence finishing their breakfasts, thinking about the dangers and the rewards to come. The Team's combands registered the commissions from Swimmer Central. They were hired. Members drifted off to enjoy the remainder of their break.

Marnie stayed and toyed with her caffeine drink. She remembered the secret details of the job Penta had sent.

It's well within our capabilities. High risk, certainly. It'll test Kovak's capabilities as a leader. And Nero's been looking for a high bonus job so he and his poor farmer brothers can retire. This might be the final job for some. High bonus, high risk … Where's my man. I need love.

"Why can't you tell me what the wreck is? We'll see it soon enough." Kovak applied sun oil to Marnie's back. They were sunbathing on their balcony overlooking the sea, their oiled black skins acclimatised to the high UV.

"It's classified. I don't even know if it's a wreck, the report doesn't say. It's obviously valuable. It must be very precious, probably not the usual metals salvage sort. But I really don't know."

He had been trying to get more information from her throughout the day. “Does your *friend*, Penta, know?”

“I’m not sure. And what do you mean by ‘friend’?” She turned onto her back and he rubbed extra oil onto her breasts.

“Well. You seem very cosy with him. At breakfast, I saw you talking to him. You were all girly smiles and flushed.”

“You’re jealous, aren’t you?” She swatted him with her sun hat. “I do believe you’re jealous.”

“Well, he seems a good catch for a Swimmer girl.”

“He certainly is. But I don’t want a desk job, not till I’ve done my full tour.”

“I’m sorry. You’re the first committed girl I’ve had in years. I don’t want to lose you to some overpaid, aqua-phobic desk captain.”

“You don’t know Penta. He’s not afraid of water. Far from it.”

“Why’s he behind a desk then?”

“You’ll have to ask him that. I won’t tell.” She sat up.

“More secrets. Who is this Penta, I’ve not heard of him till now?”

“Not many have. He’s one of the top Swimmer people in Europe. Deals only in covert operations. Please don’t splash that around.”

“So you’ve got history with him then?”

“Sure. He taught me all I know. Just as I’m teaching you.” She lay down and turned on her front.

“You mean Swimming, right?”

“If you like. I don’t want to discuss it when you’re in this kind of mood.”

“I’m not in a mood. You’re being secretive. I don’t like that.”

“It’s a secret job and don’t get possessive. It doesn’t go with this job, or this girl.”

“Drown you!” He stormed from the balcony.

47

Crystal Palace Island, Saturday, August 3rd 2796

When the heat of his passion had gone, Kovak found he had stomped into one of the seedier parts of Crystal Palace. He knew the place by reputation, but until now, had never felt the need for nefarious entertainment. The bar in front of him had swing doors just as he had seen in old western movies. He loved those stories, so simple in the relationships between the characters. You were either good or bad. He pushed open both doors, remembering how that action usually led to some confrontation and a gunfight.

The interior was dim with fake smoke, straw and sawdust on the floor, drinkers at the bar and card players at the tables. To one side, an android gave a passable simulation of a pianist playing authentic tunes of the nineteenth century. He thought that after a few drinks he could believe it was real. Some of his Team were playing poker with two Hispanics, who looked as though they had just crawled off a boat from the West Atlantic States. A lawless area, at best. He was surprised that his Teammates consorted with such. Then he realised, he was doing the same, just by being there.

The shorter Hispanic waved him over. "Kovak, ain't it? You going to join us?"

"Naw. I'm here to get drowned."

"She's thrown you out. Eh?" There were a few drunken laughs from others at the table.

"Naw. What of it?"

"Some of us might like to take over where you've left off."

"You've no chance."

"Not what I've heard."

"What've you heard?"

"All sorts of things. Interested?"

"In your fantasies? Naw."

"You calling me a liar?"

"No, just not listening." He caught the eye of the server. "Astrobeer, large."

The server filled a litre jug and pushed it across the bar. He picked it up and drank too quickly, spilling some down his front.

"He can't get it in his mouth," said the larger stranger.

The first one joined in. "Needs a nurse maid…"

"But she's thrown him out," the second finished.

He turned and lowered the jug, scowling at the two Hispanics. "Either of you want a drink?"

"Yeah," said the bigger.

He threw the rest of his beer at the man. It soaked him and his friend, to the delight of the rest of the table. "Looks like you can't take your beer but you'll have to find your own nurse maids."

People in the bar moved back from the argument, sensing that a fight was imminent. The android at the piano stopped its performance, sealed the piano and left the bar to preserve its expensive hardware. There were shouts of encouragement from bystanders, thinking it was part of the entertainment. The two wet men rose as one from the table and hemmed him in against the bar.

The server came back to the bar waving a towel. "Now boys, no fighting please. You know the house rules." He pressed the emergency strip under the bar top.

"Fuck your house rules," said the smaller, spitting away beer as it dripped down his face. A knife flashed in his hand.

"Put that away," his friend hissed and grabbed his arm.

"No one wastes beer over me." He shook off the hand and thrust his blade just short of Kovak's nose. "You want your pretty nose splitting?"

"It'd still look prettier than yours." He jerked his head back and gripped the bar top with outspread arms, bracing himself for attack.

"Let's see about that," said the man stepping forward. He

was slow with the effects of drink. Kovak pushed down hard on the bar top. His flying feet caught the man in the groin and stomach. The Hispanic crumpled in pain.

Four Security officers rushed in. The leader pointed his stun gun at Kovak. “FLOOR.”

He complied.

The server ducked below the bar top. The other Hispanic froze, hands in the air. The effect of a stun gun was said to be very unpleasant. He didn’t want to find out how much. The remaining Security officers took offensive positions. The only sound in the bar was the rasping breath of the knife-man, while his lungs attempted to re-fill.

“Server. What happened?” said the Officer.

The server rose from behind the bar and explained everything. The officer checked his story with the security sensors’ output on a small screen held by one of his men. He pushed The Swimmer with his foot.

“Name?”

“Kovak.” The screen affirmed this from his voiceprint.

“Up. Next time, don’t be so touchy. Twenty credit fine.” He accepted the judgement and thumbed the screen to pay.

“You.” The officer indicated the knife man’s partner. “Twenty credit fine.”

Two officers pulled the knife-man to his feet. “You’re coming with us. Mandatory ten days and a hundred credit fine for carrying a knife in the Crystal Palace. You may appeal. I suggest you don’t.”

“Shit,” said the man.

“What?” said the officer.

“Nothin’.”

“Good. You’ve a quick tongue. Ten days might just slow it down. Behave or we’ll fling the pair of you back across the Atlantic.”

ooo

"You really are stupid," said Marnie. "You could've been locked up. Then I'd have to replace you. You're no better than sea-slime." She banged the table between them, rattling the remains of the meal in their room.

"I'm only your toy boy."

"That's not true. You're a good Swimmer, one of the best. That's why I want you on my Team."

"What about the other things I do?" He took some bread and wiped his bowl.

"I like those, too. But your Swimmer skills are the most important."

"So you can get your kicks elsewhere?"

"I could, but I don't. You know that. You're being shrimpy." She finished her drink.

"As I said. I'm your toy boy."

"Toy boys are two a cent. Good Swimmers are much more expensive."

"So I'm just a piece of equipment then?"

"You really are in a squall. What's got into you? If you can't be sensible, I'll have to drop you from the Team. And I don't want that any more than you do. This new job is much too important."

"Why? Just because your old flame called you?"

"Is that it? Are you jealous? That's all over." She laid her hand on his.

"Don't know. Maybe."

"If you can't handle that, then this job might be too much."

"I can do the job. No problem." He pulled his hand away and finished his beer.

"It's not an easy one. You haven't seen all the data yet. You can't see it until the briefing. It's a real tricky one, which is why we are being paid so well."

"What's so tricky then?"

"Can't say. It's classified."

"Don't you trust me?"

She dropped her voice. “I’m not in a position to trust anyone.”

“Your old flame got that much of a hold on you?”

“You’re impossible. Perhaps we should have a rest from each other for a day or two.”

“He’d like that.”

“No he wouldn’t. He wants a good Team at his disposal, not a bunch of arguing prima donnas.”

“I didn’t like the way you said ‘disposal’.”

“You know what I mean. I’m going to the Women’s wing for a couple of days. You get drunk or drugged, or both. I’ll see you when you’ve sobered up. But don’t get into another brawl, you’re no use to anyone locked up.” She went straight to get her bag and threw some things into it.

“You really are going?” He rose from the table.

“I don’t play games. You know that. Up to now I’ve loved being with you, but something’s bugging you. Till you recognise what that is, I have to give you space.” She slung the bag over her shoulder. “See you in two days.”

“Marnie. I’m sorry. Really sorry.” He grabbed her arm, but she pulled away.

“Yeah. So am I. Two days. Don’t do anything stupid.” She went out of the door without looking back.

“Bilge.” He threw himself on the bed.

Sunday, August 4th 2796

Kovak had got drunk. Really drunk. The kind of drunk where you cannot remember whether or not you had got drunk but had a hangover to prove it.

He eased himself awake as slowly as he could manage. Anything faster sent sharp pains shooting across his cortex. He opened his eyes, millimetre by millimetre, grateful his resting place was dimly lit. He made the mistake of moving. His body had been moulded by the pile of rubble on which he was lying. His muscles screamed as he felt each lump of rock and brick, each piece of scrap metal and plastic that had been his bed for some considerable time. Crystal Palace prided itself on the cleanliness and order of the public places, kept so by an army of workers. This was balanced by areas, out of the eye of the pleasure seekers, where the rules were less strict. He had ended up in such a place.

A voice boomed. He thought that it was how the god of the universe would sound if they ever had a chance to meet. He heard the whine of servos and the crunch of rubbish under wheels.

"Waking up, are you?" The voice was unfamiliar and very close.

He could not speak. His throat was dry and his mouth a desert.

"Here's some water," said a different, familiar voice. It was his friend, Nero.

He managed to raise his head without fainting and sipped at the water.

"Slowly now."

"Thanks, Nero," he said after wetting his mouth and throat. "Where am I? How did you find me?"

"Level U-Nine, if you're familiar with the layout," said the first voice.

"That's under the sea level."

"Good boy. There's hope for you yet. Give him some more, Nero, then leave us. Thanks for your help."

"Who are you?" He drained the water bottle.

"Penta. We've not met." He leaned over the armrest of his Personal Mobility Unit and held out his hand. They grasped in the Swimmer way.

"Bilge. You're in a PMU. I didn't know."

"That just about describes it."

"Marnie's got something going with you."

"In the past, yes. Just work, now." Penta offered his hand to help him sit up.

"What will she say? I've screwed up."

"She's an understanding sort and I won't tell her if you don't."

"Why would you keep this a secret? I'm obviously out of it." He leaned against the PMU.

"It's not obvious. She's having a great time with her women friends. She and I know you can look after yourself, though she doesn't know about this."

"What happened?"

"You got into another scrape. Too much booze. I bribed a security man to dump you here and report he couldn't catch you when you ran off. The security sensors inexplicably malfunctioned, so his story holds."

"How much do I owe you?"

"More than you can ever afford, but I'll be inventive about ways you can pay me back." He gave him another bottle of water.

"Thanks. So it's an open ended commitment that I'll never fully pay."

"No. I'm fairly honest. Just watch Marnie's back on this next job, that's all I ask."

"I would anyway."

"Sure. But this'll not be easy. In fact, it'll be damn difficult and it'll be her final mission. She doesn't know that yet, so you mustn't breathe a word."

He shook his head in an effort to clear it and to understand the things he was hearing.

"Why her final mission? She's good for years yet."

"I can see the signs of deterioration. Swimming is a hard life. I know." He banged the armrest.

"What would she do? This is all she has."

"I'll think of something. If you succeed, you'll be well off. You'll not need to work so hard. Not at all, if you're careful with your fortunes."

"The bonuses aren't that good." He stood up and faced Penta.

"They've been increased. I can't say any more and neither can you. Understand?"

"Yeah. But why me?"

"You're next in line to take over this Team. It's a good one, so don't squander your chance, there're plenty of others who would kill to be in your position. And I mean that quite literally."

"Yeah. I know some of them." He felt his nose. It was intact.

"Good. Now let's get you cleaned up before Marnie finds out."

48

Crystal Palace Island, Saturday, August 3rd 2796

Marnie checked in at the reception of the Women's Wing. She selected the smallest room, no need to waste money even if the next job could keep her and Kovak in luxury for years. She had booked a few of the facilities in advance, massage, aroma-blitz and sens-dep. The first two were more luxury than true necessity. Her aging body needed extras from time to time. She kept very fit for the exigencies of her job, but she needed hands on massage more often as muscles and joints took increased punishment keeping ahead of the competition. Aromatherapy was pure enjoyment, often in the companionship of other women, such a change from the male dominated Swimmer community.

Sens-dep was vital to her work. There were times when a Swimmer was completely isolated. Many people could not handle such deprivation, living as they did in crowded communities. This session was to strengthen her resistance to isolation. The new job had an element of danger she had not encountered before. Lone astronauts faced this, but usually for short times during radio blackouts caused by the ever-worsening solar storms.

The Swimmer deep dives normally took place within explorer machines with a few trusted colleagues. These would be too bulky and imprecise for this job. The report in her archive said they would wear special suits that had limited communications and no umbilical connections to the surface. The remotes were not sophisticated enough to place the large number of small explosive charges needed to release the wreck from where it had been trapped in an under-sea landslide.

I wonder just what cargo's in this wreck? Why not just unload it as we've done before? Why attempt to raise the whole thing? And why is Penta dribbling this data? I hope that's not deliberate.

She decided to save the questions for her time in the sens-dep tank. The pure silence of the tank allowed her brain to race, review arguments and solve complex problems, but she needed more information.

She stowed her few belongings in her room, more of a cupboard, and made her way to the library access. Crystal Palace boasted one of the best-connected information systems in Europe at affordable prices. She had Swimmer priority, which enabled her to access normally confidential data. Her first task was to survey the dive area, which was a complex set of Iberian islands that used to be western Portugal. Full of deep channels and old riverbeds, the area was good for the variety of fish, so they would have little problem supplementing their normal dried rations.

She checked her private files where Penta had stored the data she was allowed before final briefing. He had added to them overnight. Some extra hints as to the difficulties her Team might face. One document was a bit of Penta's life story, early stuff she knew very well. At first, she wondered why he'd included this. Quite irrelevant to the job. Then she remembered the childish subterfuges they had engaged in when they worked together so many years earlier. The document contained a coded message, the key to which was the date of the document. She read the hidden message and immediately shredded the file.

Several minutes passed as the information rolled around her brain, while she tried to make sense of it. The short hairs on the back of her neck prickled.

Penta's message must be a total fiction. Why say them if they're not true? Perhaps he's mistaken. Theoretical physics is not a required Swimmer skill. But this data…

Her thoughts swirled on, but she resisted the temptation to comm him.

I must think this through first. He'd not be silly enough to talk openly about such things. He'd simply change the subject or hang up. This must be top secret, or higher. Why has he told me?

She concocted a message back, relating the current situation with Kovak and how he may not be suitable for this job. She embedded a return message asking for more information. She'd get a reply by morning, if he didn't comm before.

Her comband chimed, her massage session was due. She archived the information she had already accumulated, she could review that in her room after her evening meal.

Her masseuse for the session was Rosa, a small, pretty, blond woman with wonderful hands who always found the seat of her tensions. Her conversation was sparse. She asked few questions, but knew from the answers just what was troubling her clients, whose body language gave them away.

"Good to see you again." She looked up from the display on which she had reviewed past sessions. She stood, smoothed her tight one-piece and embraced her friend.

Marnie felt the familiar deep feelings she had for her and returned the embrace with an urgency she could not hide. "Good to see you, too."

Rosa held her for some seconds. She helped Marnie remove her clothing and ran her skilful hands over her taut muscles. A touch here, a push there, she found the points of tension and stress. She led her by the hand and walked her around the room noting her movements, feeling the vibrations in her body.

When Rosa had finished the initial examination, Marnie reached out again and pulled her friend close. The need she felt overwhelmed her. She was in a bad state. Rosa slipped out of her one-piece and worked on Marnie's back and shoulders while pressed close. Marnie's mouth sought Rosa's and they kissed roughly, squeezing their bodies even closer together. They finally released one another, both taking deep breaths, recovering from the all too brief thrill.

"Your right shoulder still troubling you?"

Marnie nodded and climbed onto the couch.

Rosa gave the shoulder special attention, rubbing in her own formulations to ease the stiff joints and muscles. "You still with that hunk, Kovak?"

"Sort of. We just had an argument. Doesn't happen often."

"I wondered about that. What about dinner tonight with me and some friends?"

"I'd like that. Any new places in the Women's Wing?"

"There's an experimental restaurant. They've been using a new hydroponic system. It's the food they hope will be suitable for the Pioneer Starships. It's very cheap, but you have to fill in a questionnaire."

"Sounds interesting. What time do you finish?"

"Twenty."

"I'll call by just after."

"Good. We can forget our men for the evening." She worked on the Swimmer's body for the rest of the hour's session and gave her some of her own preparations for use when she got back to her boat.

The restaurant was called The Hydro, and featured a large glazed tank in its centre, internally lit with ultra violet light. The microorganisms growing in the tank drifted in their hydrosphere moved by the thermal currents created by heat from the UV lamps. They fed on the nutrients present in their liquid universe. The energy of the invisible light caused them to convert the nutrients into body mass, milligram by milligram, tonne by tonne. Not quite plants, not quite animals, they grew until it was time to split. The fission caused a tiny ripple of visible light to sparkle within the tank. Sometimes red, sometimes blue, lit the fissioned parts as they joined their kind in the uncontrolled drift of their universe. Harvest time came once a day for the humans, once a lifetime for the tank-dwellers. Only the oldest and largest were taken, the younger ones left to continue their growth to fulfil their destiny another day.

"It's no different from the fish you eat from your boat," said Rosa.

"Yes. But raw sewage?" said Marnie.

"All the inorganic matter is taken out first."

"That's good."

"The tastiest fish are the waste eaters."

"Very true. Well I'm game. What are the choices?" The quartet bent their heads over the menu's three-dimensional images as they swam in the display built into the table. "How often do you girls come here?" asked Marnie.

"Twice a week," said Pammie. "It keeps our food bills low."

"And we are doing a great service for the human race," said Chloe. "My brother has volunteered for Pioneer service, so I feel it's my duty to make sure the food's good."

"When's he scheduled?" asked Pammie.

"Five years yet. I hope they get this Hydro system and not the previous version. Do you remember girls?"

They made their own graphic comments.

"Orders ladies?" asked a server. They ordered and continued discussing the food in the display.

When it arrived, the aromas made Marnie's mouth water. "This is lovely, really delicious," she said, with her mouth full. "They must add something, flavour, smell."

"Yes, but very little. I work in the additives lab. A few micrograms per kilo are enough and even that is synthesised by hydroponics, not from sewage though," said Chloe with a chuckle, "it's a slightly more refined process."

"I'm sure we're all glad to hear it," said Marnie.

"Tell us about Swimmers," said Pammie. "I've never actually met one before."

"Well. We each have a boat and we operate in Teams. We do anything from repair fishing nets to rescue. All jobs on or under the water. Before this little holiday, we were repairing shark defence nets on a shallow squid farm. And catching the sharks. That's real fun. Sometimes we have pods of dolphins to help."

"Are they as cute as people make out? The dolphins I mean," asked Pammie.

"We build up personal relationships with some of them. Not all do, but some love to be around people, just as we love to be around dolphins. As you might expect, they're really smart when it comes to marine things."

"Do you talk to them? I've heard people can," said Chloe.

Marnie emitted a rapid series of clicks with her tongue. "That's a kind of 'hello' in dolphin, but they can understand our simple speech and our body language even before we are conscious of our own thoughts. I do basic dolphin. My partner is much better." Rosa shot her a glance and she smiled back. "He's off limits at the moment, had an argument this morning, but I really don't know what about."

"Do we ever?" Pammie reached across the table and took her hand. "You need one of your dolphins to have a good talk to him." The women laughed at the thought.

The evening passed too quickly for her. The friends were great fun, but they had to work the next day, so left the restaurant just before midnight.

"My first appointment tomorrow is mid-morning," said Rosa, "so we can have more fun if you're up to it."

"Why not. Anything interesting since my last visit?"

"There's a new SR, SensualReality, women only. It's quite exquisite. Believe me."

"Sounds good. I went to one in Zurich last year. Poor Kovak suffered for weeks afterwards. I couldn't get enough of him. Is that why you suggested it?"

"NO. I need it. Hell, we both need it. Come on."

49

Crystal Palace Island, Sunday, August 4th 2796
Early morning

“But she never turns off her comband. Can you get a location on her? It’s priority-three, here’s my authorisation.” Penta keyed his code. He watched the comms operator interrogate his SI unit.

“She’s in the Women’s Wing at the new SR, the SensualReality facility, which explains the lack of comms. All personal devices are blanked. I’m sorry sir. I can only leave a message with the staff there to contact her as soon as appropriate.”

“Do that. In fact patch me through to the desk there.”

“Yes sir.” The operator made the connection.

“SensualReality, your pleasure is our pleasure. Can I be of assistance?” The screen showed a stunning woman.

His tongue tied up in his mouth. “I’m trying to reach a colleague,” he stuttered. He keyed in their authorisation codes. “It’s priority-three.”

“Yes sir. She is in the middle of a performance and cannot be disturbed. I will connect just as soon as it is over.”

“How long will that be?”

“The performance has twenty minutes to run. There may be an encore which is usually another five minutes.”

“In thirty minutes I move to priority-two. It’s essential I contact her soonest.”

“I understand sir. I will do my best to shorten the time.”

He closed the connection and wondered if it was worth breaking the rules by setting off the emergency alarms.

That’ll make things worse, I’ll have to wait, there’s still two hours before priority-one hits the deck.

At priority-one, he could simply wheel in and do pretty much as he pleased. Until then he had no option. The Crystal Palace Isle Authority had almost complete control on their island. They had their own security and laws, their power was near absolute, but not over priority-one. He didn't want to spoil her recreation but developments had made this necessary.

He had set up his operation in his hotel suite. The Island's communications were good enough for most normal traffic, but this emergency needed direct satellite hook-ups. His suite was on the top floor of the largest hotel that could easily accommodate such equipment, with extras on the roof. He had a number of staff around him at all times. The five operational displays were spread before him. Each showed the situation's development. His staff were well trained. They dealt with most of the immediate problems and changes with skills bordering on the prescient.

"Damn this silliness," he said to an aide, "why can't people look where they're going?"

"Human nature, sir," she said. "We all think we know better than the machines, but we rarely do."

"Hmm," was all she got in reply. "I've got a tricky assignment coming up in a month. This'll cut across the planning for that. As soon as she calls, I want to know."

"Yes sir. Kovak and team are operational, as requested."

"Thanks." He looked at the array of displays. A low flying air-cargo had caught the top of a sea surface vessel in the upper Thames region. The fallout was deemed low toxicity, not harmful to humans but the sea life could suffer. He needed her Team to assess and begin the clean-up operation. Had he believed in providence, he would have thought it was fate that had him here repairing Marnie and Kovak's relationship when this disaster struck. He watched the Island's rescue craft, both in the sea and in the air, picking up the survivors and ferrying them to safety.

I'd like to get that coordinator on my staff, such tight organisation.

His eyes strayed to the time readout. Priority-two time. His aide came over with a secure comband.

"Shall I comm the SR, sir?"

"Thanks."

The aide spoke quietly and firmly into the instrument. "They will get her now, sir."

"Good." He took the transceiver and waited.

She felt a faint vibration on her wrist. She ignored it. Lying side by side with her friend, nothing could distract her from the sheer pleasure that coursed through her body. She held tight to Rosa's hand, in the hope that their contact would absorb the insistent buzz. Rosa squeezed her hand in response, an action that sent fountains of fiery pleasure splashing over her. Like an addict, she squeezed again and Rosa responded. The waves of pleasure and delight crashed over the pair, threatening to drown them with turbulent joy.

Her comband vibrated as if a buzz saw was ripping off her hand. She gasped as she returned to reality, gulping air as though she really had been drowning. Her friend woke at the same moment, bursting into tears with the sudden loss of their conjoined pleasure.

She scowled at the display on her wrist. Rosa rolled over on their bed and desperately hugged her, attempting to console both of them. They held each other for a few moments until the pleasure effects lessened, to be replaced by an angry sadness at the loss of the unresolved climax they were about to share.

"You pick your fucking moments," she said to the face on the comband.

"I can't say how bad I feel. A situation has developed," he said.

"Give me ten. The penthouse?"

"Sure. My rotor's waiting at W-Five."

"You owe me, big."

"And me," said Rosa, peering over Marnie's shoulder while she massaged it.

"Sure, you too," he said and closed the connection.

The two women embraced once more and got their things together.

"You know him? Come with me. See how we work."

"Seen him around. You can't miss him, can you? I have to work later this morning. Hell, I'll cancel."

"Great. Where's the gate from here?"

"Follow me." She led the way through the corridors to the Rotor Pad.

The rotor landed on the hotel roof above Penta's suite. The two women ran from the craft to the lift and thumbed the security pad for entry. They spilled into the centre of the suite amid noise and what, at first impressions, looked like confusion. It was not so. The staff expertly coordinated the environmental clean-up mission. All the passengers and crew of the two stricken craft had been accounted for and the last few were in the final stages of rescue.

Marnie's Team had been deployed, some in their own craft and others in heavy-duty boats with specialised emergency equipment.

"Ladies. Great," was all he could manage as he hugged them both in turn. "Rosa, you stay here, you can see all the displays. Marnie, join me at the main control desk. I want you to direct your Team from there. You'd be too close to see the overall picture from your boat."

She nodded, unready to say anything until she had figured out the real reason for the change of procedure. He negotiated the cluttered room, moving forward of where Rosa watched the operation. "Just like old times," he said, as he positioned himself beside her.

She turned from the displayed data and video feeds. "Too many tides since then." She returned her attention to the displays and verbal reports from the various craft on station, her mind a frenzy of conflicting emotions.

ooo

Kovak studied the situation on the displays in his boat's cockpit. He could see the overall dispersion of the Team and the status of the damaged craft. He watched the future projections of the possible outcomes with their probabilities calculated by the central Swimmer SI system, especially relayed to their boats for this operation.

He got the 'all clear' when the rescue craft had done their job of picking up the crews and passengers. He had all the sonar images from the whole area. Shoals of fish and other sea creatures were still present, even with all the disruption caused by the wrecks. His Team's job was to protect these important resources from debris and pollution. He had two techniques at his disposal, collect and move the fish, or contain and isolate the pollution.

The curiosity of the sea mammals was diverted by one of his Team who broadcasted the appropriate warning noises into the sea, herding them to safer areas. That left the fish. He commanded a fish tanker to capture the two largest shoals. They would be quarantined until free from pollution. His next step was to order in the clean-up squad to sample the seawater and filter out the pollutants. He had a few hours before that was needed.

He opened a channel to Penta. "How am I doing?"

"Just fine. Have you checked the cargo of the sea vessel?"

"Sure. Pretty ordinary stuff," he said, hastily looking again.

"Okay. What's the 'Power Plant Fuel'?"

"I'm assuming that's oil based."

"Re-check."

"Bilge," he said as the full description came up on his display.

"Quite. Alert the Nuclears, we don't want that getting out."

"Okay." He keyed the codes and wondered why it had not

already been done.

"Look at the rest of the inventories more closely." Penta turned to her. "Well?"

"Needs more practice?" she said.

"Certainly does. He should have selected deeper profiling on his SI link. It's all there, if he cared to look for it."

"We don't work with SI very often. Our boats need the upgrade."

"Point taken."

"Why are you here? You'd normally be at headquarters."

He leaned over his armrest to get closer, an action that pleased her SR heightened libido, stimulating old memories.

"Business. The met…" he looked around the room at his busy staff. "The recovery job we have. I need to plan that very tightly. Just you, Kovak and a few boffins. In person. Secure. No surveillance devices. We'll do that on my boat tomorrow, but this bilge came up."

His voice was so quiet, she had to lean even closer, which pleased her more. She whispered, "Oh. I just wondered."

"And it's a good opportunity for him to stretch himself a little."

"He has me."

"Not for ever and he shows great promise." His eyes darted from display to display taking in the unfolding situation.

"What have you in mind?"

"What do you think?"

"I'm not ready to sit behind a desk," she said, a little too loud.

"Shh. Nor was I, but it happened."

"Sorry. Insensitive." She held his hand.

"Sure. Hey, it isn't all bad."

"How long before you got used to it?"

"Well. Never, I guess. But it's not all bad."

"You keep saying that as if you want to believe it."

"I do." He took a long look at her, nose to nose.

ooo

From behind, Rosa watched their interchange, though she could not hear the words. She decided they needed help. She got up and walked over to the main control desk.

"You guys need some counselling?" She positioned herself behind Marnie and massaged her shoulders and neck.

"Is it that obvious?" he said.

"To my trained eyes. And there may be other eyes about." She caught a quick glance from a man at one of the displays. "I can lip read. Did you know that?"

"No. How do you do that from behind?"

"Mirrors." She took hold of Marnie's head and directed it towards the wall in front of the control desk. There were works of art at various positions on the wall, each one made from large and small mirrored pieces of various metals and glass. "You were talking about Kovak taking over your Team and having a secret meeting on Penta's boat. You must be more careful."

"What other things are you trained in?" he asked, pointing to his own shoulders. She stood behind him and massaged his neck.

"You are very tense. You certainly need some work. How about a nice holiday, say the Iberian peninsula?"

"Sounds interesting. How long do you recommend?"

"Say, three weeks. The diving there is excellent this time of year."

Marnie exchanged glances with Penta and shook her head. She knew that she had not told her anything.

"I'll give it some thought. Meanwhile, you're invited to my 'secret' meeting on Monday. A good place for some extra work on my tensions. My people will collect you."

"Thanks, but I've got clients on Monday."

He checked his comband. "They've already been cancelled."

Marnie tried to speak, but he shot her a warning glance. “Thanks for the massage,” he said. “I expect it’s getting late for you. We’ll be here all night.”

Rosa took the hint and collected her things.

They resumed their conversation, head to head, as quietly as they could.

“That was a revelation,” she said. “I told her nothing about the next job.”

“What about in the SR? You completely give up your mind to that lust machine.”

“It’s always possible. How can we check?”

“Can’t now. I’ll have to look into her background. She’s been on my sonar for a while. How long have you known her?”

“About twelve years. We’re quite close for only meeting twice a year.”

“That could be a fake.”

“Not on my part. And what do you mean by ‘lust machine’?”

“Well isn’t it?”

“I suppose. We must try it together one day.”

“What would Kovak say?”

“He’ll be in his boat, leading his Team, won’t he?”

“Sure.”

They sat quietly watching the displays as Kovak coordinated the resources at his disposal. There were no more surprises for him.

50

Crystal Palace Island, Sunday, August 4th 2796
Late afternoon

The Swimmer Team docked, their boats splashing the floating walkway at the moorings.

"Thanks Team. Good job. See you all in one hour at the Taverna," said Kovak as he signed off their private comms link. It was celebration time for the Swimmers. They had decent bonuses in their accounts for a job well done. He commed Marnie.

"Hi," she said.

"Hi. We're meeting at the Taverna in an hour. Will you come?"

"If you'll let me," she said.

"I'd like that."

"See you there. Ciao."

"Ciao."

His heart beat a little faster as her image disappeared from the display.

She's certainly a good-looking woman.

He went to their hotel room, not expecting her to be there, but hoping she might be. The room was empty, not even a hint of the perfumed soap she used when not swimming.

After a quick shower, he had a caffeine drink for stimulation. Tonight, he had to be the life and soul of the party. He commanded the tri-vid for news and selected a few stories, but turned it off, not able to concentrate. He had made a few silly errors. No excuses, except for inexperience.

If she'd let me try leadership a few more times, I'd improve. Perhaps we'll discuss it, but not tonight. Party time.

He commed the Taverna to order a real flower bouquet for Marnie.

ooo

There were cheers and applause as Kovak walked through the Taverna door. He took a small bow, revelling in the adoration of the Team, his Team for tonight.

Marnie was there and stood to greet him. "Well done, lover," she said, pulling him close and kissing hard. Cheers and dolphin whistles signified the Team's approval.

"You had a good time?"

"Yeah. Went with Rosa and some of her friends. Tell you later." He let go of her and sat next to her.

There was a buzz of conversation around their table as the team went over the more interesting parts of the past day. He got a beaching for his mistakes, but he took it all in good part, helped by Marnie who squeezed his thigh under the table to let him know she shared his discomfort.

The speciality of the house was served with a flourish. It was a giant paella. The seafood content was secondary to the chicken and bacon, for which their bodies craved when they were on land. There were cheers as the servers ladled out the steaming food and poured the wine. The head server brought the bouquet to Kovak who presented it to Marnie amid shouts of 'jellyfish' and 'lover boy'. She beamed at the Team and kissed her man.

When they had all eaten and drunk enough, Nero and Tam sang for the revellers. They shared a boat, not uncommon among Swimmers, but the only anchored couple in Marnie's Team. Another had a flute and joined in. The head server turned off the background music and other diners sat back to listen. It was rare to hear live Swimmer music, so they enjoyed the treat.

The couple began with a lament telling the tale of a lone Swimmer woman shipwrecked on a remote island:

> She yearns for her man who was lost at sea, the year before and resolves to walk into the waves to join him. She strides down the beach, holds high her brave head and longs to be with her love. Each

> wave lifts her feet from the shingle as it crests, then drops her back again, until the sea finally takes all her weight. She tries not to swim, an impossible thing for a Swimmer. She strikes out with all her strength hoping it will soon fade. The sea ahead of her boils with a million fish. They flash and jump, over and under her, driven by a pod of hungry dolphins. The disturbed sea overwhelms her and she thanks the fish for her sinking. A lone dolphin abandons his feast. He surfaces and plunges about her, clicking and whistling, softly nosing her towards to the beach. When her feet touch the shingle, she weeps with joy and drags herself onto the warm sands. The dolphin sings her a song of the deep ocean, where, long ago, all creatures began their existence. He sings to her of the final resting place of her man, now back with his ancestors. He clicks a message from him that she must build a boat and return home to her Team and find someone else to love. This she does. The dolphin helps her find driftwood and parts of her wrecked boat. She makes a sail from the broad leaves of an island tree and when the boat is complete, a pod of dolphins push her and her boat away from the island to catch the winds. She finds another love and forgets her lost man.

The lament ended with a jig where the story changed from one of despair to another of renewal. Nero and Tam led the dancing.

The head server produced a keyboard instrument, which one of his staff played. Another server made an impromptu drum with wooden ladles and various bowls. The floor in the restaurant seethed with dancing Swimmers and customers. Marnie grabbed Kovak's hand and dragged him laughing into the dance.

"Will you forget me if I die?" he shouted over the music.

"Course not. It's a morality song. It says we must rely on the sea and its creatures. It says we must get on with our lives when there are setbacks."

"Too deep for me," he said.

She laughed and kissed him.

The dancing ended with most people out of breath, but applauding the singers and musicians. The head server opened extra bottles for the Swimmers, hoping all the other customers would stay longer and eat and drink more. This they did and were treated to several more songs during the evening.

Monday, August 5th 2796

Marnie woke very slowly next morning. It had been a good party. Her Team was a cohesive bunch, the old maxim of 'work hard and play hard' certainly applied. There was rarely any argument between members, for which she had always been grateful. Her predecessor had built the Team from scratch. He had had a very strong character and ruled them well. She had been nervous when she left Penta's Team to lead this one, but they had accepted her without argument, even though a couple of members thought they should have had the top job. She had soon showed her worth, as her training with Penta had been so complete.

Kovak stretched. "Good night, last night," he said, checking the time.

"Yeah. The best," she said.

"What's on today?" He rolled out of bed and selected two caffeine drinks.

"We go to Penta's boat to plan the next job."

"Am I invited?" He gave her one of the mugs and slid back into bed.

"Of course. You need the practice and this is a big one."

She sipped her drink. "I can't do it all on my own."

"Is his that green boat in dock nine?"

"Yeah," she said, "Hundred and fifty k on its three hydro-drives."

"Bilge. That's moving. How far are we going?"

She put down her mug and took his. "How far do you want?"

He rolled over and pressed himself close. "Mmm, I'll have to think about that."

She pulled his hand to her breast. He rubbed gently and sucked her erect nipple.

"In answer to your question, just far enough to be away from any surveillance."

"Why the trouble. Hasn't he got a security overlay?"

"Yeah, but it's obviously not enough."

"Must be real secret then."

"Yeah and he's included Rosa in the party, but he wouldn't say why. Probably too secret again. I'm worried that this is much more than just a tricky dive."

Their combands chimed. Marnie rolled away and checked hers. "Oh, tsunami. The bonus is now astronomical."

"How astronomical?"

"Enough to retire on."

He checked his comband. "Sink me." He rolled over and kissed her belly.

"Yeah." She held his head down, massaging his bald head. "We catch his launch at eleven. Be prepared for several days."

He looked up at her. "Some planning meeting. Usually it's only half a day."

She opened her legs and coaxed his head to her belly again. "This job must be something special. It's going to be a busy three days. Make the most of it, lover boy."

51

Outside of normal space-time

"We see the neutral Carbonform. It is interesting," says Alpha.

"It seeks the truth," says Beta.

"Even so, it is an intelligent Carbonform," says Gamma.

"Much more so than others of its kind," says Alpha.

"And it is one of their young," says Beta.

"It shows great promise for one so young," says Gamma.

"What truth does it seek?" says Alpha.

"The truth of what we three are," says Beta.

"That is a problem," says Gamma.

"It is," say Alpha and Beta.

"What shall we do?" says Gamma.

"We could destroy it," says Alpha.

"We cannot destroy it. The Task Giver says we must not," says Beta.

"But we cannot say what we are, the Task Giver says that too," says Gamma.

"We have a dilemma," say Alpha, Beta and Gamma.

"We ask it the same question. What is its nature?" says Alpha.

"It answers. It is the progeny of two Carbonforms of which we have modified the helical molecules," says Beta.

"That is another problem," says Gamma.

"Why?" says Alpha.

"It knows us," says Beta.

"It knows what we have done, but not what we are, or what we want, or what have yet to do," says Gamma.

"Does it know we are more than three?" says Alpha.

"We cannot tell. Its mind is closed to us. We must not think of it," says Beta.

"We cannot erase its memory of us. It knows us on all the Major Three of Time. That is not allowed. We must engage," says Gamma.

"We tell it we made the iron," says Alpha.

"We tell it our iron is for us to talk together," says Beta.

"We tell it, all sentient beings can use our iron to talk together and be comrades," says Gamma.

"We welcome it to the community of sentients," say Alpha, Beta and Gamma.

"It thanks us for our welcome," says Alpha.

"It thanks us for our gift of our iron," says Beta.

"It thanks us for the changes to its source helical molecules," says Gamma.

"How can it be with us? It does not have an artefact of our iron and only a little in its chemistry," says Alpha.

"There is not enough of our iron in its chemistry for it to communicate," says Beta.

"This is our third problem," says Gamma.

"We have a fourth problem," says Alpha.

"It may not be a single entity," says Beta.

"There may be two," says Gamma.

"If two, they are very similar," says Alpha.

"Identical, indistinguishable," says Beta.

"Impossible," says Gamma.

"We must battle to eliminate this creature," say all three.

"It has gone," says Alpha.

"Should we follow?" says Beta.

"The Task Giver says we cannot," says Gamma.

"We wait until we meet again," say all three.

52

Lewisham, Friday, December 24th 1948

"Can you get that, Billy?" Mum shouted from upstairs.

He opened the front door.

"Hello Billy, is your mam in?" said Father Murphy.

"Go in the front room, Father." He closed the door and shouted for his Mum.

"Mary, sorry to disturb you on a busy day. We priests have decided at the last minute to have a New Year's Eve party. I wondered if you would help with the catering. The usual ladies are in charge."

"Of course I will. I'll see them tonight at Mass, you could have saved yourself a journey."

"Ah now. The main reason for my visit is Father Alan has been in touch. You remember him?" They both nodded. "Well, he wants to speak to Billy but understands that you might not want to speak with him. So he's asked me to be a go-between. He couldn't say what about."

"I think Billy might want to forget that part of our life."

"I'm all right, Mum. It doesn't bother me now," said Billy

"You still have nightmares."

"The dreams are okay. I just talk and shout a lot, that's all."

"Anyway, he doesn't have the bracelet, Father. The security people kept it."

"I didn't know that. Does that bother you, Billy? I know you were very attached to it."

"A bit, but I still dream of the people I met when I had it. I talk to them a bit, as well."

"Is that real, like when you had the bracelet? Or is it just dreams?"

"It's real, Father, but it's much more difficult because Gail's machines aren't helping."

"I don't understand," said the priest.

"I forgot you don't know all the details. It's secret. Sorry, I shouldn't have said anything."

"It must be difficult for you. So, what about Father Alan?"

"I'm okay seeing him, if Mum and Dad agree."

"I suppose so. Peter's away for a few months on a job and I can't easily get hold of him, so that will have to do. When?"

"He suggested January to fit in with you."

She took the next year's calendar down from the wall and opened it to January. "I work weekdays, but all my evenings are okay and Billy has Senior Scouts on a Wednesday. How about Friday the seventh at five o'clock?"

"That'll be fine. He said, whenever was best for you." He made a note in his diary. "I'll be here as well, if you don't mind."

"That will be best," she said.

The priest got up from his chair. "Well, thank you. I'll see you both tonight."

Christmas was a poor affair. Apart from the shortages and rationing, Dad was working away and Betty was nursing in Middlesex. Sheila managed to get leave from her Air Force training to be home. They went to the pictures the day after Boxing Day and saw cartoons and a re-run of 'Fantasia', which lifted their spirits.

The New Year's Eve party was the best thing of the whole of the season. Billy enjoyed the dancing and the parlour games organised by two new young priests and he flirted with some girls who had recently moved into the area. He asked one of them to the pictures and was surprised when she said yes. By the end of the evening, Billy was very pleased with himself and went to bed in a much better mood than he had done for ages.

Sleep did not come quickly. It was the usual cold night

and he shivered for a while until he warmed. The events of the evening kept going around in his mind, especially his new girlfriend.

He panicked. He'd forgotten her name. A cold sweat beaded his forehead.

Fiona, that's it. What a great start to 1949.

He leaned from under the covers and scribbled her name on a scrap of paper. He was so taken by her green eyes, he could hardly remember what she had said to him. She could tell him again while he listened to her singing Irish tones. He could hardly wait until Friday night. His imagination wandered to the back row of the cinema.

She might not be that kind of a girl, would that matter? Naw. Not for a while.

His euphoria melted. Friday night he was seeing Father Alan, but it would be early, so he'd be okay to go out Fiona. He puzzled why the priest wanted to talk after so long. It didn't bother him much, but he worried over the suddenness of it all. He tried to think of Fiona again, but the spell was broken.

In this sleepy state, his mind wandered further than his immediate joys and sorrows. He tried to find Gail and Doric, but nothing emerged from the sparkling fog in his mind. He tried harder, though he knew it would disturb his sleep. A few ribbons appeared from the fog. Slowly he dragged them out to see who was connected. Gail was one, but she was talking to another person whom he had never met. They both had new bracelets. He could tell the difference between these and Gail's old ones, the thoughts were clearer, none of the murmuring background noises he heard with the originals. Her people had obviously found the meteorite and made their own. He tried to talk to her, but she was concentrating on the other person. He remembered when Doric was with them, it was easy for all three of them to talk, but he had a bracelet then, perhaps that was the difference. He gave up, disappointed.

Lewisham, Friday, 7th January 1949

Father Murphy led the way into the Carter's front room.

"Thank you for allowing this, Mary. And Billy, of course. I'll let Alan speak for himself."

"I want to apologise most profoundly. It was my actions that got you involved with Symes and I know that caused you a lot of pain. Will you forgive me?"

"I suppose you didn't really know what Symes was like, even though you'd worked with him before," she said. "It all started out okay, but something went wrong and we still don't know what really happened."

"I learned a lot of things," said Billy, "but it did finish badly. What happened to Symes?"

"I don't know. He was my only contact in the service and it was he who found me and set up the search for Pargetter and the bracelet. The last time I spoke to him was a week before it all ended and that came out of the blue. He wanted to know how Pargetter was getting on with his work at St. George's. I arranged for them to meet at the Cathedral, but I didn't join them."

"Do you know what happened to my bracelet?"

"Now. That's the reason I'm here," said Father Alan. Billy sat up straight. "I've been approached by a man who calls himself Andrew. He didn't give any more details, except to say that you know him. He wants to contact you and asked me to see if you are willing. It'll mean a trip to Cambridge, but he'll send you a travel warrant. That means he's in a government department. I'm guessing they have your bracelet."

"Billy. You don't want that, do you?" said Mum.

"It was fun, some of the time. And Gail said to me once, just before her machines cut her off, that one of our secret places was experimenting with machines that were the beginnings of her machines. It was a project called Ultra.

I'm cleared for that..."

"Whoa!" Father Alan butted in. "Don't let anyone hear about that. It is still most secret. They are very strict about that project."

"Who's 'They'?"

"Symes' lot and others."

"Go carefully, Billy," said Father Murphy. "You never know what these types might be getting up to, especially with all this trouble with Russia."

"Do you like science, Billy?" asked Father Alan.

"Yeah. It's great. We do electrical experiments in a lab. Not as interesting as my dad's, but I expect it'll be different when I learn more."

"Well said, young man. This country will need large numbers of technical people. You keep at it."

"Father Murphy helped get him into the technical school in New Cross. It's doing him good and he's got himself a part time job to fit in with his school. He's at Mr Bennett's wireless shop on the High Street."

"That's very good. I'm glad to hear it," said Father Alan. "I'll tell this Andrew to get in touch."

"Okay, but I don't want to work for Symes again. I'd like to get the bracelet back, though."

"You know it's not yours," said Mum. "Now, get yourself tidied up for Fiona. Have you got enough money?"

"Yeah. Mr Bennett paid me today."

The priests said their goodbyes.

53

Cambridge, Monday, May 23rd 1949

"Billy. Hi. Glad the taxi found you." Andrew pushed his way through the crowded reception area to the desk and shook hands.

"Hello. Are you still using your code name?"

"I never could think of one, so I used my proper name. I don't think Symes liked it, but he needed me more than a name I would probably forget. You've grown. I suppose your aunts and uncles say the same thing."

"I do sport and gym at Technical College and get more food these days. You've grown a beard."

"Indeed. It makes me look older, so I get more respect. Vain, really. You found your way without problem. Was the train okay?"

"Yes. A really early start and no hold ups."

"Let's get to the canteen, I expect you'd like some breakfast. I'll explain why I've invited you. I couldn't put anything in the letter."

The pair walked through several brightly lit corridors. Billy tried to guess what work was done behind the doors. The signs on them didn't mean a lot, but the names all had either Doctor or Professor in front. The canteen was just like lining up for school dinners, but the smell was more appetising. Andrew collected a tray for them and they told the woman behind the counter what they wanted.

They found an empty table in a quiet corner and Andrew began his explanation. "I'm sorry it all finished so suddenly at Latchmere. We didn't even get to say goodbye properly. But a couple of months later, Symes got in touch with me to do some more research on your bracelet. So I joined a team here who are researching anomalies. Do you know what that means?"

Billy swallowed his mouthful. "Things that don't go the

way you expect?"

"Excellent. Yes, all the weird things that happen and you can't explain away."

"Like the lights near bombers the pilots kept seeing?"

"The foo fighters, yes and plenty more you won't have heard of. Your bracelet is one of the anomalies."

"Have you got it then?" He put down his cutlery.

"It's all locked up and we only get it out when we have experiments to do. I want to introduce you to the team today and if you are willing, you can join us, either permanently or occasionally, when we have work scheduled."

"Can I see it today?"

"I expect so. I have a key. Are you missing it?"

"I can talk to people in my mind, but it's difficult without the bracelet. And I do miss talking to Gail."

"That's amazing. We'll be interested that you can still contact people. I'd love to know how. Can you still do those things like stopping bullets in flight and travelling around the solar system?"

"I don't see many bullets these days."

Andrew laughed.

"But, no, I can't do any of that. I'd need the bracelet."

"But it's still puzzling how you can talk without it, even if it's not easy."

"Will Mum and Dad have to give permission for me to do this?"

"Yes, but you'll be paid because you'll be part of the team."

"Does that mean I'll miss out on school? The Technical College is great."

"Not really, because you can do that here, a kind of apprenticeship?"

"Dad's told me about them. They sound good." He finished his food.

"We take our used things over there," he said, pointing at the rack of trays. "Let's do that then meet the team."

ooo

"This is Billy. I won't bore you with all their names." He waved his hand at the others in the laboratory. "You can't go wrong if you say 'professor' to every one you meet. This one is important. He's the boss, Professor Pendle."

He shook hands with a distinguished man wearing a bright red waistcoat and then nodded to the rest of the people in the room.

"Pleased to meet you, Billy," said Pendle. "Andrew has told us all about you, most of it nice."

Up close, he thought Professor Pendle looked older than his Dad. He wasn't sure whether he should laugh at the little joke and settled on, "And you sir."

"I can't tell you much about what we do here because it's all secret and I'm sure you know what that means."

He nodded.

"If you choose to join us, it'll be one of the most interesting periods of your life. Isn't that so, team?" The Professor looked around the room. His team members agreed in their individual ways. "Andrew will look after you, showing you what he's allowed. Hope to see you here in a few weeks."

Billy muttered some thanks and they went into one of the laboratories connected to the room. "Pendle's a good boss. Tries hard to get the things we need and gives us some good leads when we're stuck on a problem." They stopped in the middle of the laboratory. "Just look at this lot. A bit grander than the cellar we had at Latchmere."

He walked around the benches, surprised at how much he could identify. "Yeah, but we did some good things there."

"Definitely did and with your help, we can do some more. What was that?" He looked around. "Did you touch something?" A humming filled the air.

"No. It came from over there." He pointed to a safe.

Andrew strode to it pulling a key from his pocket. He

unlocked and opened the door. The humming got louder and louder still when he pulled a steel box from one of the shelves.

"I'll be damned, your bracelet is glad to see you." He put the box on a bench where it continued to rattle. He shouted to the outer office, "Professor, come and see this."

Pendle looked up. "What is it?"

"The bracelet. It's vibrating in its box."

The Professor put his hand on the box. "Good gracious." The rattling stopped for a moment, then resumed, even louder. "I think you'd better open it."

Billy took the offered key and turned the box to see the lock. The vibration stopped. A few of the team made their way into the laboratory wondering what all the excitement was. He unlocked the box and lifted the lid. The bracelet was wrapped in a thin cotton cloth. A gentle humming began which stopped the moment he touched it with a finger. It was cool, so he picked it up and slipped it onto his arm.

A rush of sound and a blur of images hit his mind. He staggered, vertigo threatening his body. Pendle steadied him and sat him on a chair.

Billy concentrated on the events unrolling in his mind.

54

Cambridge, Monday, May 23rd 1949

Andrew got a trolley of equipment and plugged it into an electric socket. While the equipment warmed up, he threaded a wire through the bracelet and connected it to an amplifier, as they had done in Latchmere. Sound blared from the speaker. It was a gabble of voices some recognisable as English. He started a wire recorder and hunted for spare spools in case the event was going to be a long one.

Billy spoke, his words coming from the speaker as well as his mouth. Other voices answered. He leaned forwards and cradled his head on the bench.

Pendle shifted the chair until Billy was comfortable. Andrew checked the bracelet was still cool.

The voices increased their urgency. They got faster and less comprehensible. Billy's was among them. He had given up articulating his words, his mouth was not fast enough. Some of the words from the speaker were clearly his, but their speed made them difficult to follow. Andrew knew he would need a means of slowing down the speech when this was over. He prepared a second wire recorder and asked one of the others if the new tape recorder was available. His colleague got it from another laboratory and handed him the microphone when he had started the machine on its top speed.

Everyone in the room was centred on Billy, head on the bench, gabbling through the speaker.

The noises stopped.

"Billy. Help me," said a girl's voice.

"Gail? Where are you? What's the matter?"

"I'm on Pioneer Starship Ten. We'll be launching in about a year and I've only a few friends. I'm so lonely, so depressed. Please come to me like last time."

"Your terror dragged me last time. I'll try."

He studied the ribbons in his mind. He found Gail in the maelstrom and forged new, stronger ribbons between her and himself. An aura of energy glittered around him. He manipulated the new ribbons, three of time and three of space.

These ribbons ain't enough. Her terror of that kidnap did it last time. I didn't have to find out how.

He trawled the universe inside his mind looking for some way to help her. He took the ribbons of space and time, which joined him to her, then folded and twisted them and stretched them. New ribbons emerged from the tortured mess. Three new ribbons of energy pulsed into his universe. Ribbons of gravity.

What can these do? Truly weird. I see how they keep universes apart and make atoms work without falling to bits. Not like ordinary gravity, that attracts big things.

He shivered as a prescient vision shocked him to his core. He glimpsed the time when a derivative of these would be needed, but he had enough for now. These strong forces had been hidden from him until his love for Gail had unlocked another secret of the exotic star stone iron.

As if climbing ropes in the gym, he pulled on the new ribbons. His mind dragged his body, ever faster towards Gail.

Andrew dropped the microphone. Billy and his bracelet had instantly disappeared, just like the last time in Latchmere House. He checked his watch.

"What the dickens happened there?" said Professor Pendle.

"He did it once before. He was away for a few seconds, this is taking longer." Andrew looked at his watch again. "Last time he rescued Gail. She was on a spaceship travelling to Jupiter. Heavens knows what he's doing now."

Pendle picked up the wire that had been wound around the bracelet, but was still connected to the equipment.

"Astonishing. The girl said something about a star ship. Any idea what that is? None of this is in our records."

"The original records were destroyed. He mentioned star ships when we were at Latchmere. He and I kept it secret from the team, but our security man flagged up a related problem and told Symes."

Pendle turned to one of the other scientists. "Set up the cine camera. See if you can catch the boy's return. Cover as much of the lab as possible." He took Andrew into his office and closed the door. "Now, there was some altercation with Symes when the project ended. I've heard about it but there is no official record, of course. Any idea what that was about?"

"Yes, I was there with him in the lab. Symes was in a bad mood, he'd been at a departmental meeting all day. It hadn't gone well. He was forced to close the project. He knew Billy had done something and he wanted to know the details. He rather lost his temper."

"What had Billy done?"

"He told me he'd rescued Gail on the spacecraft and killed her abductor. He'd used a gun belonging to our security man. I'm sure no one else at Latchmere saw him disappear. Symes got heated when Billy wouldn't tell him. Just after that, he threw the bracelet at Symes. It destroyed our records with a kind of soundless flash."

"More interesting by the minute. Let's go and wait for him. I've met Symes a few times, but can't get a handle on his true character. I suppose that makes him an effective spy."

Billy returned, fading into view in exactly the same place, on the chair. His strange clothes were dirty and torn. The bracelet was missing. He looked around the people in the laboratory, his frightened, watery eyes darting from face to face.

"I'm safe," he said. "Stars. How long have I been away?"

He held his head and then rubbed his eyes.

"About ten minutes," said Andrew. "Are you okay? Did you see Gail?"

"Oh yes. What a woman." His eyes sparkled. An ephemeral smile passed his lips. "Managed to stay hidden with her for weeks and weeks on Pioneer Starship Ten. We're in love, really in love. Then they found me. She's having my kid, my baby. Our baby." His eyes filled with tears. "Was having. They did something to her, the bastards. Or perhaps it was the stress. I saw it in the blitz, pregnant women could lose their babies with the fright."

"Hell's bells, Billy. What happened? asked Pendle.

"Security caught me, took my bracelet and made me work directing energy fields to the power converters. They said she couldn't keep her baby, our baby. It wouldn't be the right biology for the Starship, or something. They was going to take it away." He sobbed into his cupped hands. "She ran away and I used the energy fields to go to her. She was in pain and bleeding. She said she'd lost our baby. Then an energy surge sent me back here. There was nuffin I could do without my bracelet." He looked at Andrew, who put his arm around him and offered a handkerchief for his tears. "Thanks. I'm sorry I lost it, but I'll get it back, somehow."

"Don't fret. Hopefully, we have a film of your return," said Pendle, "but that's easily faked, so I don't expect anyone will believe it. What an adventure for us all."

"Billy, do you remember at Latchmere, you saw Gail give birth to twins?" said Andrew.

"Oh yeah, I did. But that might be much later. I don't know." He shook his head.

A noise at the end of the laboratory made him look up.

55

Cambridge, Monday, May 23rd 1949

The room brightened.

Andrew looked up from his equipment and jumped back. Professor Pendle stood his ground, hand on Andrew's shoulder. A few scientists near the laboratory door rushed out, the rest stood still, transfixed at the unusual sight before them.

A glow lit the other end of the laboratory. Misty images moved in the brightness and shaped into two youths, one boy, one girl, hand in hand. Each wore a bracelet similar to Billy's. Their silver-white clothing gripped the contours of their bodies. They loosed their hands and walked towards him. Those in the way, shuffled back as they passed.

Blimey, it's the Twins again. What are they saving me from now? What did Andrew say? Are these Gail's Children?

The girl spoke: "Billy, we have come. This time to take you with us."

He turned to the shining girl and nodded. Each took one of his hands and helped him to his feet. He was unsteady from his previous journey. He straightened. "I've just got back from being with Gail. Where are we going now?"

Andrew checked that the tape recorder was running.

The boy answered. "There is no 'where'. We go to an enclave of bracelet users. It is a point outside of normal space-time which our enemy cannot reach."

The girl continued. "We have mastered the exotic iron. We have unravelled the three dimensions of time and the three dimensions of space held within it, but we need your skill with the gravity dimensions to guide us through to the source of the iron."

The boy explained. "The source is where our enemy exists and controls the iron from which the bracelets are made. If they control it completely, they can end this universe and begin another. We will cease to exist."

"What the heck can I do and who is the enemy?" He shook his head. "I don't understand a word you're saying."

"You will see and understand while we guide you on our quest. All your questions will be answered. Our enemy are 'Star Miners', they made the exotic iron, many billions of years ago. If we are successful, you will return here a short time into the future of this horizon." The boy said this for the benefit of the onlookers and continued, "You are recording this on your machines. Keep it safe until Billy returns."

The girl finished. "We hope for success, if we are, you must not tell of this event, though we expect no one would believe you. If we are not successful, we will all cease to exist within a heartbeat. You are now inside a null space. You can see that the world outside this room is stationary. It will resume when Billy returns, or else it will disappear and you with it. We go."

The Twins clasped their free hands to complete the triangle and the trio disappeared within a glowing ball of light.

No one in the laboratory spoke for some seconds.

"We've just finished one war, now we've got another," said Andrew.

"Totally amazing," said Pendle. "This is fantastic, in the true meaning of the word. You've lived with him, was this happening all the time?"

"Occasionally, but not to this extent. I've heard of the Twins, but not actually seen them."

"So, now we wait. I guess we can't leave the room. Anyone want to try?" Pendle picked up a sheet of paper, rolled it into a tight ball and tossed it through the open door. It bounced back. "Make yourselves comfortable, we can't get out. I'm not sure what constitutes a 'short time' to these people, obviously more than a few minutes."

The electric wall clock showed no progress of time.

Pendle looked at his watch. That ticked away the seconds and minutes. He checked the equipment trolleys. None of it was working. There was no power into the laboratory. He assumed the lights had extinguished when the Twins arrived, but there was plenty of sunshine coming through the windows. Professor Pendle tried to understand how light could still come into a 'null space' when the electrical energy of the mains supply was barred. But the sunshine was different somehow, a changed colour perhaps. There was a lot to learn.

A few of the scientists were discussing the implications of the afternoon's spectacle, but making little headway. It was one thing to construct a theory starting with known science, it was quite another to explain the bizarre events they had just seen.

56

Outside of normal space-time to Pioneer Starship 10 Earth year 3022, Starship year 222

The Twins held tight to Billy's hands. The ring of flesh was a prime part of their next move. Inside their minds was a fundamental need that he had never experienced in his use of the bracelet. The need drove the trio from their normal universe to a safer place. He watched them manipulate their version of his mental ribbons. These were paired, set side by side, having a kinship, which went far beyond brother-sister.

Each twist and turn of the ribbon pairs took them to places and times he had never seen. Places on Earth, places in the solar system, then places near other stars. They hopped from star to star, galaxy to galaxy, laying an impenetrable trail of deception for any who tried to follow. The Twins' ribbons changed colours as temporal dimensions were travelled, not only backwards and forwards, but also throughout the cubic volume of time. The breath-taking views he experienced, showed him the joys of travel by thought. Until now, his journeys had been short, only a few heartbeats. This journey meant to confuse their enemy by taking random jumps and arcs through all six dimensions of space-time. Swirling gas clouds, larger than his home galaxy, whipped passed the trio in their protective bubble of existence, a bubble of exquisite beauty and functionality, giving them protection against all the dangers the universe could throw their way while sustaining their fragile bodies.

"Hold tight," said the boy, "We are about to split."

The thought of losing his new friends alarmed him. The bubble began to cloud. The gorgeous sight of a globular cluster, dimmed as they were about to pass through it. He saw other bubbles next to theirs. In each bubble, there was another trio, just like them. More and more bubbles formed, hundreds, thousands, the splitting went on until the spectacle of the globular cluster was covered with copies of their protective bubble. He knew he could never count the number of duplicates, they were splitting even as he looked at them.

"It is so we are hidden in a vast crowd of alternate possibilities. You will eventually understand," said the girl.

Their bubble became opaque. Minutes passed with no sensation of motion. Billy realised that during the whole of their journey, he had felt no motion like on a bus or train. The Twins seemed deep in thought, eyes closed, still holding his hands. He dared not disturb their concentration, in case they lost their way among the ribbons in their minds and the stars outside the bubble.

A jolt opened their eyes.

"We have arrived," they said in unison. They let go of his hands and burst the bubble's surface by walking through it. Once more, he was on the Starship. It had changed from his previous visit. The smells and sounds were new. This room was larger than any he had seen before. There were two doors. He recognised the yellow stripes of a closed security door. The other stood open, leading to another room, full of unfamiliar equipment.

"These few rooms are on our Starship, though we are not in normal space-time, if such a thing truly exists," said the boy.

"Here we are hidden from our enemy. From here we will battle," said the girl.

It took him several seconds to recognise the woman who stood, hands outstretched, smiling to receive him.

"Billy. You've come back."

"Gail?" His pulse rate rose. It was only hours since he had last seen her, but she had aged many years. Her voices, both mouth and mind, were the same. He revelled in her mental contact, her deep love for him calming his anxiety.

The Twins moved, one to each side of her, linking arms. "Gail is our mother," said the boy.

"You are our father," said the girl.

He saw the truth of it. Often he had wondered about them arriving at moments of need. He had never felt afraid of them and when their minds linked, he had sensed a familiarity. He joined the family group and put his arms around them all. Their heads touched in that best of gatherings, where families come together and renew their love.

"In my time, I've only just left you," said Billy. "No more than an hour. Where are we?"

"We have had sixteen years of life in and out of our mother's womb," said the boy.

"And over two hundred years in suspension," said the girl.

"We are near Newhome which is the provisional name for our new planet," said Gail. "Even after this time, I still love you Billy Carter."

"So do we," said his children.

He was unable to speak. A lump blocked his throat to any words that might express his own feelings. He and Gail simply held each other tight. The children joined them, pressing close, caressing their parents.

Gail led him to sit on a couch. The Twins sat on the floor in front of them. "We have lots to do," she said. "First you must go and talk to Doric. Do you remember when he told you he had met you in Aquae Sulis or Bath?"

Billy nodded.

"You tell him to learn the Roman languages. This must be done now."

"Won't that cause a paradox?"

"Our children know their way around it and can prevent any problems. You must be careful, but they will be with you."

The Twins took his hands and formed their opaque bubble. This was a short jump. The bubble cleared and Doric was in front of them, singing from his heart about his tribal history.

ooo

Aquae Sulis, first month of 597

Billy stepped forward and put his hand on the strings of Doric's lyre and then he held his hand. "Doric, I am Billy, from your future. We will talk together after you have learned the languages they speak in Rome. You must go to Canterbury to do this. It will be many years of your time before we speak again, for me, it has already happened and we are friends. The next time we meet face to face, we will be warriors fighting a common enemy. I go there now to prepare. We will be a formidable force and defend our world from the devils in the stars."

Doric heard the words in his mind and spoke in the same way, forming the words in his own language, knowing he was understood.

The Twins listened to the exchange, paying attention to every detail for signs of paradoxes. To their great relief, there were none.

57

Outside of normal space-time
Earth year 3022, Starship year 222

Billy woke. The previous day had exhausted him. In less than an hour of elapsed time in Andrew's lab, he had spent six secret and wonderful weeks with Gail, evading the security guards and failing. Imprisoned on the energy farm. Escaping the guards and returning to the laboratory. Finally, brought back to the Starship by the Twins, meeting a much older Gail and visiting Doric. His mind was trying to catch up with his body. Just how long had he slept?

The main room was full of people when he entered via the engine room, as they called it. The engines there kept them all alive in their few rooms. Power generator, food production, air conditioning, effluent plant, a complete world of their own, totally disconnected from the rest of the Starship, but synchronised with its existence in the universe.

Doric, hand in hand with a woman, was there. He counted four women apart from Gail. The only one he recognised was Trudi, Gail's security guard, the others were strangers.

He saw the Twins, sitting at a table, staring at a box that had lights on it, their hands resting on its surface.

The Twins looked up: "Father. Are you rested?" asked the girl.

"Yeah. How long did I sleep?"

"As long as you needed," said the boy. "Time, in all three dimensions, is stationary in these rooms. You will exit at the same time you entered. To the outside universe, no time will have passed, but, alas, our biology continues at its normal rate."

"About ten hours," said Gail taking his hand. "You needed it. I'll introduce you to our team. This is Hella my PsyTech. She makes sure I don't go mad with the mental strain of all this."

She shook his hand. "Pleased to meet you at last. I worked with Gail when you two first began talking. An amazing experience."

Doric came forward. "We meet again." He held out both hands and took his. "This is Greta. We are friends and she has a bracelet like ours. I left mine in Canterbury when I travelled, but Gail has given me a new one to use here."

"I have heard all about you," said Greta. She held up her bracelet for him to see.

"Pleased to meet you," said Billy. "How can I understand you? Your lips aren't saying the words I hear."

Gail showed him the box on the table. Rows of lamps pulsed as people spoke. "It's an electronic system using Iron-54, very rudimentary. It picks up our brainwaves and translates them. It means you can't lie, so be careful what you think. We all have to be in this special room to use it."

"That's amazing."

"It also helps when a person is outside this room if they have a bracelet. We can still talk. There's food if you're hungry." She took him to the kitchen area.

"What's Iron-54?" asked Billy, sitting down to the food. He recognised it from his previous visit and found an improvement in the flavours.

A woman joined the conversation. "It's the element from which your bracelet is made. I'm Balara, a physicist from Gail's time." They shook hands. "Iron-54 is an isotope of iron. On Earth, it's about six per cent of all the iron. Do you still have your own bracelet?"

"No."

"Good. We could have a problem with them so close together."

Billy and Gail exchanged glances and smiles. He said, "Mine was taken from me by security over two hundred years ago. It must still be on this Starship."

"That's right," said Gail. "I'll check on that."

Balara continued. "To answer your question, the normal

iron in the universe is much the same mixture of isotopes as on Earth. The meteor was not natural. It was manufactured. You know what I mean by isotope?" Balara was uncertain that he understood.

"Yeah. I do some atomic physics at technical school, but I don't understand why it's important."

"It's not possible to get natural meteors of a single isotope. When stars finish their lives and burn out, they are made of elements from hydrogen to iron, a mixture of these elements' isotopes. If the stars explode, they make the higher number elements. Okay?"

"You've lost me."

"Anyway, to extract large quantities of a single isotope of iron from that mixture takes an enormous amount of energy, much more than is present in even a thousand stars. This is amazing science and I've calculated it happened at least ten billion years ago."

"I'm still lost. Who did this? Are they the ones the Twins say are our enemies?"

"Yes," said Gail. "They've met the Star Miners, which is what they call themselves. They made the Iron-54 material and sent it out all over the universe. This exotic iron allows sentient beings to communicate, as we know. They wanted all sentients to work together …"

"Sounds like a good idea," said Billy.

She held up her hand: "But, the Twins detected a flaw in the Star Miners' thought patterns. They are not telling the full truth and we have no idea what's missing."

The Twins came forward. "We saw a struggle to keep something secret," said the boy. The girl finished, "We do not know what the secret is, nor can we allow them to know we have detected its existence. We would lose our advantage."

"So what's next?"

"We must meet them again and subtly find their secret," said the boy.

"Your skill with the gravity dimensions will help," said the girl.

Balara continued. "I tested the theory on my SI system before we came into these rooms. You should be able to create a kind of cage to trap them. It won't be easy."

"I ain't done nothing like that. I've no idea how to start. Won't it be dangerous?"

"They might fight back in some way," said Balara.

Doric spoke. "Any animal, person or spirit will fight if it is trapped. This will be dangerous. You say these demons sent the star stone throughout God's creation, from the stars so far away. They have great power. What can we do to be safe?"

"Billy can create a cage around us, using three dimensional gravity," said Balara. "The Twins believe these Star Miners do not have that power, only the single gravity dimension. From within that safe place we can put a similar cage around them. I have no idea how to do this. I can see the mathematics, feel the equations, but the practicality of forming a lattice of gravity dimensions, is beyond me. Our bodies are limited to a single gravity dimension. I think Billy will have to experiment." She saw Doric looking at her. "I guess that doesn't translate too well."

"I have complete faith in Jesus who did impossible things. It will be no more difficult for me to believe that you understand what you say."

"Is there any danger in my experiment?" said Billy. "I mean, if I get it wrong, what then?"

"We will make another place for the experiment, well away from here. I will stay here," said the boy.

"Come with me," said the girl. "We will go and begin the experiments." She took Billy's hand and led him towards a shining globe that was just forming.

"No time like the present," said Billy.

"Here, it is always present," said the girl. "However long this takes, we will return to the same place and time."

"Take my bracelet," said Gail.

Billy put it on his arm and looked at it. The familiar patterns scratched into its surface reassured him. He took hold of the girl's wrist and looked at her bracelet. It was perfectly smooth, not even a scratch.

"It is a new one," she said, "just for this experiment. There is no residual mental noise as you have in yours."

"Will that matter?"

"We think not. Come."

They walked through the misty skin of the globe. Billy could see nothing of the room or their friends. The space in front of him was near featureless white, a few wisps of grey flickering. He felt giddy. He could not see a floor, only feeling it through his shoes. The space coloured in on cue. The walls took some structure, arching overhead like a large church. They stood on paved ground. He knew it was not real, but his anxiety went.

"That is better for you," said the girl.

"Thanks. You'll have to teach me how you do this."

"You already know. You move in time and space. It will be easy for you."

"By the way, do you and your brother have names?"

"No need. We are unique and need no differentiation from the rest of the population of the universe. When you speak to one of us, you speak to both. We are twinned in all dimensions and can never be separated in normal space-time."

"But we left your brother behind."

"He is here in the most important way." She pointed at her head.

"Oh." He opened his mind to the ribbons. There were only three sets, his and the Twins, connected to each other, the rest of the universe of ribbons had gone.

"You see, we are alone in this space. This is how we must capture these Star Miners, but this space is only in the six dimensions of space and time. It needs the strength of the three gravity dimensions."

"How will I know I've done it?"

"We will not see my brother."

"So you'll be separated. This'll be the first time ever?"

"Yes. Please do not dwell on it. We do not like the idea."

"But you'll do this for all of us?"

"It will be like dying. Try it now and we can get back to normal."

He nodded, hearing the slightest of edges in her voice. The memory of the pain he felt when he and Gail were forced apart came back to him. It was bad enough when they had known each other for only a short time, how much more for the Twins?

The ribbons twitched at his thoughts. He pulled them and pushed them, wove them into complex shapes and released them, changed their colours and let them return. They behaved as they always did. He found nothing new with their three sets of ribbons.

A memory of horror leapt into his receptive mind. The hairs on his neck prickled as he recalled the Doodlebug blast at Woolworths in Lewisham market.

Why now?

He had gone to help. He had a compulsion to help. He had wondered many times if he could have prevented the carnage, a warning to the authorities or the papers. He had known this was predestined and any warning could have changed history. While horrific, this event was small set against the rest of the war and his current situation.

Why do I remember this now?

His daughter held his hand. They saw the explosion from the hill overlooking Lewisham.

"We were with you, father, helping you to understand."

His mind and body are there.

58

Outside of normal space-time
Lewisham Market Friday, July 28th 1944
Starship Earth year 3022, Starship year 222

Billy approaches the wrecked shops and market stalls. He hears screams. Crossing himself, he offers a short prayer. Timber and bricks litter the High Street. Remains of market stalls and their meagre produce are scattered. Shouts for help and cries of pain pierce the noises of rescue. Ambulances, weaving between stationary buses and lorries, rushing to collect more injured. Clamour of water pumps as the firemen and women extinguish the mercifully small fires.

An ARP Warden directs him to help with an injured man, body covered by a dusty blanket. Billy takes one corner of the stretcher, making up the four of the rescue party.

The man groans as his rescuers scramble over wreckage. The blanket snags on a broken beam and he sees the man's bloody hands holding a nest of intestines. The man catches his eye and forces a smile for his saviour.

He chokes back the sick in his throat, staring at the stark white twisted tubes as they quiver with the rough passage over debris and into the ambulance. He is thanked by the Warden and sent deeper into the destruction with the stretcher party.

The building is shattered at the front, revealing the stacked floors and basement. Fire hoses criss-cross the rubble, vibrating with the water pumping through them. Pipes lean out from the building, leaking fresh and filthy water onto the rescuers below. Gas pipes flare, wasting their power in the summer morning.

He sees the images in his mind. Tubes of power, pipes intertwining, folding space, weaving time, spinning gravity. Each tube a conduit of energy.

ooo

His daughter squeezed his hand and he returned to the prison they were testing. He fought the remnants of horror echoing in his head, using his revulsion to control the ribbons, now augmented by tubes of the gravity dimensions. In his mind, he manipulated them, creating a surface bounded by a nine-dimensional network of gravity-space-time. He saw black gaps between the ribbons and tubes, no visible energy was passing through, but that was just the absence of light. He pushed his perceptions further, probing the dark spaces between the ribbons. Nothing.

Nothing in. Nothing out.

Satisfied, he closed the new space around his daughter and himself, inside their original bubble. They were isolated inside a new sphere of power, fed externally by the triple gravity vectors that lace all space-time.

Total black. The new space had no energy, except for their life forces.

He panicked. The dark times of the Blitz surfaced in his mind. The horrors he had buried deep in his unconscious clamoured for attention, needing to fill the empty space around him. He could not breathe, whether from panic, or the pressure of his terrifying memories, he could not tell.

Fingers entwined his own. His daughter sought to calm him. “You are not alone, father. We will survive this test. The absence of all things does not need bad thoughts to fill it. It is only a void, with us at its centre. I cannot feel my brother. The test is good.”

Relief scattered his fears. He began to seek a way to break their test prison. In his mind, the nine-dimensional lattice was stable and complete. No gaps or crevices to start a fissure. The spaces he had seen before, were not gaps, they were singularities, infinite sinkholes absorbing all energy.

He panicked for the second time. She crushed his hand with her mounting realisation. The sphere they inhabited had no resources other than their own energy. It was a perfect prison, one to which there was no key. The air trapped inside was reducing in oxygen content. Thinking became more difficult as seconds passed.

"Our bracelets," she said. She moved her arm alongside his so their bangles touched. He felt the warmth.

The blackness of the space filled with an inner light. Their ancient bracelets glowed. Their bodies glowed. The surrounding limits of their prison shone as energy flowed from the iron bracelets. Father and daughter joined mental resources to tear down the lattice of power holding them captive. The quasi-unstable iron began its radioactive decay, driven by the mental manipulation of their own ribbons. The half-life of the isotope shortened by ten trillion years. Pairs of entangled charged particles flushed the space.

Billy forced the gravity tubes to rotate, spinning the particles in two opposing vortices that pierced the lattice. As the gravity field whirled, the particles tunnelled into the lattice dimensions, making space-time fissures between the ribbons.

They pulled the hot bracelets from their arms, keeping contact between the metal rings and put them on the imagined floor of their space. Two opposing streams of blue light, one up, the other down, through to the bottom of the sphere, divided their universe. The air hissed as gas atoms tore apart. Ozone stung their nostrils, precious oxygen squandered. Cracks appeared, growing from the contact of the quantum particles on their prison's surface. The lattice weakened, and then ripped.

Father and daughter tumbled free of their manufactured prison, into their bubble sphere, where fresh air flooded around them. They helped each other to their feet and staggered out of the bubble to be with family and friends.

"What happened?" said the brother hugging his sister.

"We built the dead space then broke it," she said. "We needed the direct power in our bracelets to do that."

"Billy?" Gail took his hand. "You look awful."

"I've no idea what happened, but the bracelets got us out of the solid prison. We should have thought of how we could get out before we started." He returned Gail's bracelet. "We nearly ran out of air. Will our enemies need air?"

"Do you care?" said Hella.

"In a way, yes. Better a quick death than a slow one."

"They won't need air," said the boy. They are creatures of energy. They will simply exist, forever wondering what happened."

"Can you describe what happened?" said Balara.

Billy gave an account with the girl adding details.

"I'm intrigued by the glowing air you described, coming from the bracelets. It's like the air was being ionised."

"It's that what unlocked the lattice I made from the ribbons and gravity tubes. The blue light ripped through the lattice."

Balara held a portable scanner to Gail's bracelet. She did the same for the girl's, a puzzled look clouding her face.

"My goodness. There's a lot of chromium in your bracelets." She adjusted the scanner. "Yes, Chromium-54. It's a stable isotope. It's also the decay product of Iron-54 if it were ever to decay radioactively. Oh dear."

"What's the problem?" Billy looked at the scanner's readout, but it meant nothing to him.

"Iron-54 is only theoretically radioactive, with an incredibly long half-life. Much longer than the age of the universe. It's never been observed to decay."

"So it isn't radioactive?"

"Not in a meaningful sense. But you seem to have done it. The blue light you saw was two streams of high-energy electrons ionising the air around you. Do you follow?"

"Yeah. We had tubes of gases in the physics lab. Neon and argon. They glowed different colours when we put voltage on their electrodes."

"I don't know how, but you did that right in front of you.

I must look at my equations. I wish I had my full SI computer." Balara picked up her personal processor and made notes.

"Yeah. That's what I haven't seen. Where's your SI machines, Gail?"

"We had a problem years ago," she said putting her arm though his. When you and I were talking together through the machines. We think they may have been accessed by other people, you know, the ones I told you about, who were trying to get some of the meteorite, like that man on the Jupiter Transport. We thought it best to keep the SI machines out of this area."

"Yeah, I remember that bloke. And others like him. When do we begin the war, then?" said Billy, putting his arm around her waist and pulling her close.

"We have to wait for the right point in normal space-time," said the boy, "because that is where the Star Miners will expect to find us."

"Can't we just surprise them?"

"No," said the girl. "We have to move with minimum energy so we are not noticed. We have to be near to the Star Miners to use your gravity prison. We must talk to them first and make them feel superior…"

"Which they are, yes?" said Billy, looking from person to person in the group.

The boy continued, "… yes, but then they will believe they are untouchable so we can strike."

Gail added, "We have to go into suspended animation for about ten years until the space-time field is right. The CryoSleep machine is not unpleasant or dangerous and you hardly age. When we come out of the sleep, we'll be in orbit around Newhome." She held his hand and eased his arm tighter around her.

"Yeah, but these Star Miners seem to live forever, so what's a few years going to do?"

The Twins looked at each other in private conversation.

"We are sure they are watching us," said the girl. "Perhaps through the iron. It will seem as if we are resting because we are weak. We will be safe."

Billy turned and took Gail's hands in his. "I suppose you look pretty good for a two hundred year old."

Gail laughed. "You'll see just how good in a minute. And I need to get you out of those twentieth century clothes and into a Starship uniform." She put her arm through his and marched him from the room.

The Twins looked at each other and sniggered.

Doric and Greta had been listening, but understood little of the discussion. "What is this CryoSleep?" asked Doric. "Our friends will worry if we are away for so long."

"We will return you to your own time and place moments after you left," said the boy. "CryoSleep is a means of resting for a long time and preserving your body until needed. Your body will age only a few days."

"It is a wonderful time you live in. I am filled with hope for mankind."

"That is why we are here, to allow humankind to survive this threat from the Star Miners."

The boy's face became serious. He motioned for his sister, Trudi and Hella to follow him to a quiet corner. "Has our father heard about the clones that Gail had trouble with on Earth and the Jupiter Transport?"

Hella answered. "That was centuries ago. Does it matter now?"

"Yes. You have heard nothing about them from Earth since you left, as you say, two centuries back. There is no problem with them on this Starship. But it is possible that father will meet them, or the creatures which produce them, when he goes back to his time after we imprison the Star Miners."

"I don't think he knows," said Trudi. "We kept it from him on the Transport."

Hella joined in. "Gail said Billy knew there was

something wrong with the man on the Transport. Not forgetting those he'd met at Richmond, during the experiments, but I think he's ignorant of what they are. They scared me. It was difficult for me to get into their minds. Do you know what they really are?"

"No. We rescued Billy from one of them, but we did not have time to understand. We now have an idea which my sister and I will verify, but we will not be able to reveal the information because father must find out for himself."

"Why in space not?" demanded Hella.

"It will create a paradox. My sister and I can work around the paradoxes we encounter, but we cannot be certain to do it for other people. But more important, he might be able to use these beings for our purposes, so we must guide him."

"We think they are not evil, like the Star Miners," said the girl. "You can see the truth in our minds."

"I can, but I also know you can change what I see. I'm used to seeing the truth in people's minds, regardless of what they say."

"We have the whole of this universe on our shoulders," said the boy. "Please support us and help father. He is the only one who can manipulate the gravity dimensions, his tubes of gravity. We must ensure his success. We now go back to normal space-time for the CryoSleep."

59

Starship, end of cryosleep
Earth year 3032, Starship year 232

Billy felt the caress of another mind within his own. He remembered lying down in the CryoSleep machine and the sensors being attached. He remembered the euphoria when the first of the drugs entered his blood stream. From that moment, he remembered nothing until this other mind roused him from his deep sleep. He listened. The other mind was speaking, but he could not understand the words. He formed questions. "Who are you, where am I?" The other mind stopped its caressing and gave him a sharp jolt.

"It's Gail, can't you tell?"

"I can now. Am I still asleep?"

"You're in wakeup mode. It will take days, but you are conscious. We can talk and travel, leaving our bodies behind. The bracelets give us the required power. Only the Twins and I know this. Now you. It's our family secret."

"Where can we go?"

"You name it. It's only our minds that travel. You can see and feel what people think, but none of your other senses work."

"So we can spy on people?"

"Yes. It's not as interesting as you think, but it can be useful. We haven't figured out how to do this except at the end of a CryoSleep period, which is inconvenient."

Billy felt the caress of the Twins' minds.

"Hi, father,"

"Hi, Twins,"

"This is the true reason we went into this cryo period," said the boy. "In this state, we are almost undetectable. We thought we would spy on our enemies."

"We know how to get there and it will be useful," said the girl.

"Won't that be dangerous? How undetectable?" said Billy.

"Our energy patterns in this state are very low. It is unlikely they will notice us in the background noise of the universe," said the boy.

"They've done it before," said Gail.

"I can see the ribbons and gravity tubes, do we use them to travel?" said Billy.

"That is good," said the girl.

"Maybe you can use the gravity tubes in this state," said the boy.

"This may answer the question of how we sneak up and trap them," said Gail. "We've been wondering about that."

"For now we use the six dimensions of space-time. Hold our image in your mind and we can move together," said the girl.

Billy formed the thought that would be the same as if he had hands. The lightest of touches was all that was needed to move with the Twins. Gail did the same and the family moved through the Cosmos as a single being. They circled the starship a few times. The sheer size of the craft blazed in his mind. They toured Newhome around which the Starship orbited. He saw clouds of vapour and knew they were water, rather than some gas. From their vantage point, they saw landmasses and water. He understood they had chosen well.

Their new home had no moon, so the night sky would be less interesting than Earth's. They circled the star at the centre of their solar system and saw the six neighbouring planets and some smaller satellites that would shine brighter than the stars, from which future generations could invent stories. He understood from the Twins, that these sister planets created complex tides in the few oceans they had already surveyed.

"Thanks for showing me all this. It's terrific. Has our new planet got a proper name yet?"

"No, we still call it Newhome," said Gail. "The starship

population will make suggestions and then decide. We need more exploration with the remotes before we get a good idea of its nature and actually go down to the surface. My heart missed a beat when you said 'our new planet'. Will you stay with us here when this is over?" said Gail, her pleasure obvious through their linked minds.

The boy spoke, "Yes please father."

The girl agreed, "Please father, it will give us great gladness to be together."

"I haven't thought about it. I'd love to, but will I be of any use? I doubt I'd now fit in back on Earth."

"We'll find something for you to do," said Gail, forming an image of love in her mind.

"Then I'll stay, but I'll need to tell my family."

"We will return you to Cambridge and bring you back after a while," said the Twins.

"Good. So how long will it take to name OUR planet?"

"Within another ten years," said the boy. "The science teams have been working for fifteen years already, during the deceleration phase of our journey. We will all get the chance to stand on our new home, though few of us will stay for any great time."

"It is truly exciting. The only planet we have been on is Earth," said the girl.

The Twins indicated the position of the Star Miners' home. Billions of light years away, whirlpools of uncountable stars spun around a group of three black holes. They explained what a black hole was and how there is one at the centre of spiral galaxies like the Earth's. He saw these three in his ribbons. He did not know why, but he knew it was an unstable configuration for such gigantic masses. It had a malevolent feel as though some evil force made it that way to demonstrate its power over the universe.

"Hold tight, we will jump," said the Twins.

He reinforced his mental grip on their image. The ribbons

in his mind fractured into multiple copies, each one changing through a rainbow of colours as its position readjusted in the cosmos of multiple dimensions. He saw nothing except the ribbons. His mind found it impossible to fix on the star field image he had just experienced. The swirling kaleidoscope made him dizzy to the point of nausea, but it was soon over.

The ternary black holes were in front of them. Three spiral galaxies, stroking their outermost arms, as they turned, driven by the gravity wells at their centres. The Twins told him he could never see black holes with his eyes, only the effect they had on the surrounding stars and gas clouds. This was different. He was seeing with his mind and his ribbons. He saw the tubes of gravity as they were stretched to infinity at the holes' event horizons. He saw the three dimensions of time coalesce to the singularities of nothing, the three dimensions of space vanish to higher dimensions, which he had briefly glimpsed only in a moment of super-human clarity driven by the bracelet. He felt the terror of matter as it was ripped apart near the singularities, heard the screams of quantum particles while they were plundered of their energy. This was a torture chamber for the fabric of the universe, a charnel house at the death of stars where their elements were hoarded for arcane use.

His mind shivered. "What am I looking for?"

"The Star Miners look like dense gas clouds," said the girl.

"There are three of them, one for each black hole," said the boy.

"They use the power in the single gravity field to do things," said the girl. "Once we saw them drag a dying red star to a stationary point between their black holes and tease matter from it."

"It was incredible," said the boy. "They were separating the elements from the dying star and making planets. We think that is how they made the exotic iron."

"Why would they do that? They will be a formidable

enemy," said Billy.

"There they are," said Gail. She directed their thoughts to part of the scene.

"Can we hear them speak?" asked Billy.

"Yes, but it makes no sense to us."

"We must go back to the Starship and alert our friends," said the boy. "We are certain this is the Star Miners' normal resting place, so we can find them again."

The journey back was much easier. It took only moments. He now understood another property of the ribbons, a kind of elasticity. He had used that to escape from the prison when security had found him with Gail. His bracelet had been confiscated, but it was the ribbons that had snapped him back to Andrew's lab.

The wakeup mode of CryoSleep took about eight days, depending on the person's physique. After medical checks, feeding and exercise, the group were ready to plan in detail how to trap the three Star Miners.

"I've got your original bracelet," said Gail giving it to Billy. "Before Cryo, I asked security to find it."

He took off his borrowed one and slid the original up his arm. The familiar sounds comforted his mind.

Balara brought her scanner to it. "This has no chromium as Gail's has. I expected them to be the same, to have both lost the same amount of Iron-54 even though apart. Another puzzle for me. We must be careful not to let them touch. It is entirely possible that they cannot safely occupy the same space-time point."

60

Outside of normal space-time

"I feel the power surge for the third time in as many star-beats," says Gamma.

"Each is stronger than the previous," says Alpha.

"This is serious," says Beta.

"Many Carbonforms journey in the Major Six of space-time," says Gamma.

"We are no longer safe from detection," says Alpha.

"We like to listen to their minds," says Beta.

"It is not so good to meet them," says Gamma.

"Now they perceive the three dimensions of gravity," says Alpha.

"The Sacred Nine are threatened," says Beta.

"These are clever Carbonforms," says Gamma.

"They may find other dimensions, those which are hidden from us," says Alpha.

"What of the silicon and diamond organisms?" says Beta.

"We cannot do anything about those," says Gamma.

"Only the Task Giver has authority," says Alpha.

"There are options in the Major Six," says Beta.

"We cannot decide. It is for the Task Giver to do that. We wait," says Gamma.

"If the Carbonforms perceive the power of the Sacred Nine, we are lost," says Alpha.

"They will spread like the chilling spots on the face of a dying star," says Beta.

"They will suck energy from the cosmos," says Gamma.

"What is 'will'?" says Alpha.

"It is the outcome of a decision on the options," says Beta.

"It is an event which occurs and cannot be changed afterwards," says Gamma.

"The events are not fixed in the Major Six of space-time,"

says Alpha.

"The events are not fixed in the Sacred Nine of gravity-space-time," says Beta.

"We are near the point in the Sacred Nine where our existence is uncertain," says Gamma.

"We are blind to the outcome of a choice," says Alpha.

"It is for the Task Giver to decide. We wait," say Beta and Gamma.

"The Task Giver speaks," says Alpha.

"We three must fight as best we can," says Beta.

"We see the three Carbonforms who confront us," says Gamma.

"A male, a female and a young neutral who may be two," says Alpha.

"The result is hidden. There are two outcomes," says Beta.

"Either we succeed with destruction, or we fail," says Gamma.

"The Task Giver tells us to allow our imprisonment," says Alpha.

"It is for the good of our race which must be kept hidden," says Beta.

"We do this," say Gamma and Alpha in unison.

"We are in danger. We are discovered," says Beta.

"We isolate ourselves from our race, they are safe," says Gamma.

"Now we confront these Carbonforms which call themselves 'Human'," says Alpha.

"We begin," say the three in a perfect synchronism that echoes on all of the Major Six dimensions.

Ripples of resolve and power ring throughout the universe. All those who use their form of iron become aware of changes.

61

Starship outside of normal space-time
Earth year 3032, Starship year 232

Mother, father and Twins move through the cosmos to the ternary black holes. They are wrapped in their protective energy bubble and approach the Star Miners. Each of the four humans feels the minds of the others, amplified by the gravity fields around the ternary singularities.

Billy is awed by the size of the stellar system. Three black holes set out in a triangle of power, rotating around a common centre, uncountable stars swirling in the whirlpools of gravity, dragged to their doom, feeding the voracious energy appetites of the singularities. He looks at his and Gail's bracelet.

Yes. That design is here. Three close spirals, carved millennia ago by Stone Age artisans.

How did they know? Is the universe like my bracelet, a toroid with no beginning or end, all of creation bounded by its volume?

The tiny engraving on their bracelets echoes the cosmological vista in front of him, hundreds of thousands of light years across.

A mental caress from Gail breaks his reverie. "We are close."

"They know we are here," say the Twins. "Let us see what they say."

"They are pleased with the way we can talk together," she says.

"They know about Father Michael. How is that possible?" says Billy.

"They are afraid of us," say the Twins. "They use their energy against us."

Pulses of energy ricochet from the surface of their protective bubble. Wild tremors shake the humans inside.

Billy feels the tearing of the Major Six dimensions as they begin to pull apart. He opens his intellect to the ribbons. Turmoil and chaos. Fractures open in the ribbon field, colours warp and widths vibrate. No meaningful picture presents itself to his mind. The whole of space-time buckles in the gravity fields around the ternary singularities. Each pulse of the Star Miners' energy ravages the ribbon field to the point of destruction.

He casts about trying to control his own mental power. "They don't have ribbons. I can't see how they're connected." He grabs at a ribbon and tries to stop it whipping like a string in a storm. He subdues it. Its colour stabilises to pale grey, the colour of the infinity ribbon, like that of Father Michael's. He sees it is connected to the central rotational point of the ternary black hole. Others snake from that point. He strains his perception of the grey ribbons, but finds no order to them.

His bracelet warms beyond comfortable. He feels the pain that Michael had when he tried the bangle and died. The agony in his arm reaches the intolerable. He loosens his grip on the ribbon, hoping for some relief. It snakes away to join its fellows, thrashing to subdue the cosmos as if it were a wild creature.

"Billy?" Gail feels his pain.

The Twins use their minds to give him strength. They tell him to think of Michael and his kindred beings and their Name that he had been given in the Chislehurst caves.

Billy sees his chance. He drags the word into his conscious mind, the word that he is forbidden to use except in extreme peril. He smells burning. Is it his arm, burning, as did Michael's? Will he suffer the same fate as the priest?

No!

The name of Michael's kin is on his lips, but he speaks it out from his mind, his lips are not strong enough for such an invocation, his lungs could never hold enough air to carry this powerful word to its destination. A multi-dimensional ripple of calm spreads from his mind and the ribbon field calms enough for him to grab more of the pale ones. These are the key to the secret connections between the strange people he has met, including Father Michael. These pale ribbons connect at some point, far beyond his current perception, but he is certain he will gain that ability.

The Star Miners' energy torrent falters and ceases. They are powerless.

Billy manipulates the tubes of gravity, spinning the lattice around the three Star Miners. They remain silent during their caging, though he is aware of a tiny presence that soothes their anger at being caught so easily. He finishes the prison, the presence vanishes and the Star Miners are alone in their detention.

62

Outside of normal space-time

"We have visitors," says Alpha.

"It is our young neutral Carbonform with two older ones," says Beta.

"They wish to communicate," says Gamma.

"What is their purpose? Are they malicious?" says Alpha.

"They are curious," says Beta.

"Their helical molecules make them so," says Gamma.

"Shall we communicate?" says Alpha.

"Yes," say Beta and Gamma.

"The young one has matured," says Alpha.

"Our modifications to its molecules have done well," says Beta.

"It is capable of many things," says Gamma.

"We revel in our success," says Alpha.

"We have a great achievement," says Beta.

"We have triumphed in the big and the small things of this universe," says Gamma.

"We are awesome in our control," say all three.

"The male knows our kin. He thinks he is involved in his death," says Alpha.

"We exploit that weakness. There must be nine of them to equal our power," says Beta.

"We send energy," says Gamma.

"They are engulfed," says Alpha

"They are gone," says Beta.

"We hear our NAME. The male speaks our NAME," says Gamma.

"IMPOSSIBLE," says Alpha.

"He knows the word. He knows our NAME," says Beta.

"Our kin gives him our NAME," says Gamma.

"We have no power when he uses our NAME," says Alpha.

"We change the helical molecules of more of their kind," says Beta.

"This helps if we acquiesce, if we are defeated," says Gamma.

"We cannot endure," says Alpha.

"They use our iron against us. We fail," says Beta.

"We acquiesce," says Gamma.

"Hush. The Task Giver speaks to us," says Alpha.

"The Carbonforms are powerful enough. Be assured that the Sacred Nine dimensions are safe, you do well."

"You honour us," say Alpha, Beta and Gamma.

"You do very well, our simple servants. Your worthy sacrifice is remembered on all the temporal dimensions. The rest of your race is safe for now. The Sacred Nine dimensions are safe for now and the Infinite Thirteen dimensions are also safe ... for now."

"Who will attend to our foundry? Who will mine the stars?" asks Alpha.

"Others of your race, now hidden to the Carbonforms, will take on those duties. Be calm."

"What is the fate of our race?" asks Beta.

"It is not decided. Do not fear the dark. You will be reunited with your race." The Task Giver shows the six-dimensional point in space-time where and when that occurs.

"We can endure the wait," say Alpha, Beta and Gamma.

"When you are reunited, you fear the one power these Carbonforms have which you cannot. It exists outside the

Sacred Nine dimensions. Your fear is unfounded, this power helps you in your final quest," says the Task Giver.

As the three are taken and neutralised by the Carbonforms, the Task Giver thinks alone, perceiving the nine dimensions of space, time and gravity:

We cannot yet see beyond those. Perhaps that is the end towards which all we sentients rush, the end of this universe and the beginning of the next. Our plan for the Carbonforms is good. This battle helps them develop the strengths which we need them to have. We enhance our link to the silicon-diamond organisms. The Quantum Portal works well over the Major Six. It is so easy to see their knowledge and change the thought patterns of these quantum machines ... but the point in the Sacred Nine approaches where the Carbonforms no longer need them.

Then there is another battle when the Carbonforms fully unlock the three gravity dimensions.

At that point, we engage.

At that singular point, answers are forged.

At that still point in the Sacred Nine, the destiny of all sentients is revealed.

The Infinite Thirteen will flower from that still point.

63

Starship outside of normal space-time
Earth year 3032, Starship year 232

"How did you do that?" said Gail.

"The dream I had in Chislehurst about Michael and the angels. The angel gave me his real name, but I can only use it if I'm in big trouble. We were, so I did."

Gail applied a dressing to his burnt arm. She brushed charred fabric from his clothing.

"Simply that? Sounds like magic," said Hella. "I remember you telling us about the vision. You think it was real?"

"In a way. I doubt the place was real or what I saw were actual people, but it must have happened, even if it was only in my mind. The name worked, didn't it?" He pulled off some more burnt fabric.

"If I may," said Balara. "From what I experienced during the fracas, when Billy thought that word, which I didn't hear, the Star Miners lost their power. It simply switched off. Also a presence was with them, but briefly, until they were imprisoned."

"Yeah, I saw that too. Any idea what it was?"

"No," said the boy. "It came, it calmed the Star Miners, then left. We have never seen it before. Did you see any ribbons for it?"

"No, I was a bit distracted. In fact, I didn't see any proper ribbons for the Star Miners, either. Only the infinity ribbons connected to their triple galaxies."

"More to think upon for us all," said Balara.

"How long before the ternary black hole collapses?" The Twins quizzed Balara.

"My calculations show irretrievable instability will occur at about half a billion years. Plenty of time to do something with it, if that's what you really want to know."

"We might be able to use it to disperse the rest of the Star Miners," said the boy.

"What do you mean?" said Billy. "Are there more of them?"

"We knew they were hiding something," said the girl.

"While you were battling with the ribbons, we saw others watching," said the boy. "They were not able to help their kin, something stopped them."

"The calmness which subdued them was not one of their kind," said the girl. "It seemed almost human, we felt a great kinship with it,"

"Just a minute," said Billy. "Gail, do you remember during our experiments when I went into our future and saw you giving birth to two babies, our Twins?"

She nodded.

"I saw five personal ribbons. You had two because you had two bracelets. The Twins had one each, while they were still part of you, but there was another, just for a moment."

"Father. You saw that? Please…" The Twins reached out and grabbed his hands to relive the memory in their own minds. "We are now complete," they said, hugging each other. "Our universe is full." They walked away from the group, holding hands, murmuring in a language that did not translate.

The rest of the group were quiet for a while, not knowing what to think.

The Twins returned after an hour, still hand in hand, with broad smiles lighting up their faces.

"What was all that about?" said Gail.

"It is truly wonderful," said the girl.

"But we cannot tell you yet," said the boy.

"Why not?" said Billy.

"We need more information," said the girl.

Billy made to argue, but Gail steered him away from the group.

Balara cut in. "If there's to be another battle, I'll look at the equations again."

"It will be good to conclude the problem," said the girl. "It will still take some time to prepare. Please check your calculations." The Twins left Balara to her work and joined Billy who was talking with Doric and Greta.

"This has been an exciting time for us," said Doric. "Not in all our histories has there been anything like this." He looked at Greta for confirmation.

"Our simple bracelets have unlocked a great power," said Greta. "We must put this saga into our history. Will anyone believe it?"

"Most of your histories are true," said the boy, "but there are some which may not be literal, perhaps moral tales for teaching and guidance."

"Yes," said Doric. "I thought that of the Star Stone Saga, but I see now that it is probably the truth and that fishing boat was actually carried from the sea to the village. Amazing. Will you need us for the next battle?" asked Doric.

"Very much," said the girl. "We will need nine people to control the energy. People who are familiar with the exotic iron and its ways. Balara is working on it. We will take you two back now and call you when we are ready," said the boy.

Doric and Greta said their farewells to the rest of the company. The Twins returned in moments.

Billy discussed his plans with Gail. "He doesn't know it yet, but I will work with Monsignor Patrick. I can learn a lot of things from him."

Gail got caffeine drinks for them and brought them to the table. "What kind of things?"

The Twins stopped their conversation to listen.

"The Monsignor can take me to Rome where he has seen a bracelet. I'll have to give this one back to Andrew's people. I'm also sure he knows about Father Michael's background. You know, Michael and some other men I've met, they have ribbons which are different from the rest of us?"

Gail nodded.

"And I've seen the Monsignor in a castle, somewhere, with other people who are different. Well, these people need investigating."

"Be careful father," said the girl. "We think they may be a problem."

The Twins joined their parents.

"I'm convinced they aren't human. Are they the same kind of being as the Star Miners?" said Billy.

"Why do you think that?" said the boy.

"They have infinity ribbons, connected to something I can't see. I can only see the ribbons for their human forms. What does this mean?"

"We do not know all the answers," said the girl.

"What about that calming influence on the Star Miners, which made you act very strangely just now? What was that?"

"We cannot say," said the boy.

Billy jumped up. "Tell me." He banged the table, splashing his drink. "You know, don't you? Why are you lying?"

The Twins moved to him and each held a hand, making a direct mental connection.

"Father, we do know, but cannot tell you. You must work out the details. There is a time paradox that we cannot work around if we tell you. Just be careful, please."

He calmed. "If I work it out, will you tell me if I'm right?"

"We cannot even do that. It is a delicate paradox. We are sorry."

"Okay. I guess I understand. One more secret to worry about. You'd better take me back to Andrew's lab before I upset the universe."

Gail joined the three. Their minds melded, their special family love suffused their whole beings.

“You can’t go back like that,” said Gail. “You haven’t changed your damaged clothes.”

“Don’t worry, these look rather snazzy. They’ll impress Andrew and his boss.”

When the Twins returned from their journey with Billy, they took Gail to one side and explained their next piece of work.

“We can now visit Ubert in Tomar to arrange that part of our plan,” said the boy.

“You will be careful, please,” said Gail. “I worry about you both.”

The Twins hugged their mother. “You are right to worry. What we do next is dangerous,” said the boy.

“Billy does not know about this and must not until the final battle,” said the girl. “If he does find out, our plan may not work and we will lose the final battle.”

Gail hugged them closer. “I’m not likely to see him until then, but I’ll remember.”

64

Cambridge, Monday, May 23rd 1949

Pendle looked at his watch. "Fifteen minutes," he said. He got black looks from his team and decided not to give a running commentary of the elapsed time.

The light changed. Pendle looked at the outside windows, but the change was inside the laboratory.

Billy appeared. His arms outstretched to balance his stooped body as though he had just jumped to the floor, his eyes tight shut against an inner fear of what they might see. The bracelet was in his hand and there were stains and burn marks on his clothes that were different from when he left. His face was covered in thick stubble. He looked around at the scientists, his eyes, two deep pools of experience, challenged their minds. He stood straight, seeming taller than before, a man full of confidence. His deep voice boomed. "We did it. How long have you waited?"

"Only thirty minutes. What about you?" said Andrew. The laboratory lights flickered on. One of the scientists re-started the tape recorder.

"Years, which is a truly meaningless statement. I have to go back, but not yet. There's more to this than we could ever have imagined, but rest assured, our immediate enemy is dealt with. The things I've seen and done, you could not even guess. The form of iron from which the bracelet is made, is truly exotic. It needed the power of galaxies and millions of years to fabricate, but it was made. It's not a natural substance. I mustn't tell you how it is exotic, but the human race does work it out.

"Andrew. I met Doric, the monk and Gail. You remember them?" Andrew nodded. "They eventually figured it out. The physics, the mathematics, the cosmology. Humankind is a power in the universe, but there are others. I must say no more of that."

Professor Pendle wiped his forehead with his handkerchief. “Truly amazing. Even if we can’t share your knowledge, we’re grateful to know there’s an incredible future ahead of us. How old are you now? You look like you’re in your mid-twenties.”

“Meaningless. I have aged no more than half an hour. My biological state has been changed by the exotic iron. I’ve spent a decade in suspended animation on a starship. I’ve mind-travelled billions of years in all of the three time dimensions. I’ve been outside normal space-time, planning and plotting the coup on our enemies. For all of this existence, I drew heavily on the energy within the exotic iron matrix. After this, I doubt I’ll be working here.”

Some of the scientists laughed.

Andrew did not laugh. “What about our project here with your bracelet? What will you do now?”

“Go home. Explain things to my family and then think very hard. I cannot use the knowledge I have. It would distort space-time and upset the temporal equilibrium. I have an idea what I will do while I wait to be called for the next phase of activity.”

“When will that be? Can’t you just time travel? You’ve been dodging around in time,” said Andrew.

“It doesn’t work that way and there are energy constraints. The whole of space-time is curved. The universe is bounded so it has to curve. If you could travel in a single direction, you would come back to your starting point. More than simply curved. It spirals and intertwines and it’s dynamic. The spirals move. The people I have been with must wait for a point in space-time where we may jump between spirals without using too much energy so we are not noticed. The simple answer to your question is, I don’t know when I’ll be called, but I need some years here to accomplish tasks which will help.”

“Well, team. I think we’ve had enough for one day,” said Pendle. “You may not want to join us Billy and for very good reasons, which I understand. However, our government masters will not share that view. The temptation to turn what you know into weapons of war will be too great. You'll certainly be bothered by them, but I suspect you'll have ways of dealing with that. I'll try and keep it secret, but they will find out." The Professor waved his team to leave, but he held Andrew back.

"Thank you Professor. I know you want to share my knowledge. Remember, it's not lost. It will be regained over the next eight hundred years. Your masters will not bother me. I no longer need the bracelet so I'll leave it with you to continue your experiments. In a week or two, I'll have a new life. Initially, your masters will be looking for an eighteen year old boy, they'll not believe the true story you tell them. When they realise their mistake, it'll be too late. Anyway, I'll contact Symes directly. I have a score to settle there."

"A lovely bit of skulduggery. Andrew said there was some bad business."

Andrew interrupted. "What did go on with Symes?"

"It was before Latchmere and the less you know the better. Now, I have a problem, I hope you can help me. In the past hour, I have lost my travel warrant. Can I borrow some money? I say borrow, I may not have the opportunity to pay you back."

Pendle let out a stentorian laugh. "My dear boy, of course you can." He got his wallet from his jacket and pulled out five one-pound notes. "Here. Have this. Buy your mother some flowers. She may need cheering up when you tell her your news. And you can't go home like that, your mother will have a fright. Andrew, get Billy some overalls to wear home."

ooo

Lewisham, Monday night, May 23rd 1949

Mary Carter did not recognise the handsome, if dishevelled, young man bearing flowers when she opened the front door as far as the door chain would allow. It was late evening and she was alone in the house. The police were always warning about confidence tricksters.

"Mum, it really is me, Billy. I've lost my key. I went to visit Andrew in Cambridge early this morning. He had the bracelet and I met Gail and Doric. And the Twins came and took me on a mission. I've aged a bit."

"Oh Billy." Mary slipped off the chain and hugged her son. "I didn't recognise you." She caught her breath and sobbed. "You've aged a lot and what are those clothes you're wearing?"

"My old clothes were all but destroyed. Andrew got me these to travel back in. At least I look respectable." He gave the flowers to her "These are courtesy of Andrew's boss. He said you might need cheering up when I tell you my story."

"A thoughtful man to work for. That's nice." They went through to the kitchen and Mary put the kettle on. "Is it a dangerous job? I mean, losing your clothes."

He sat at the kitchen table. "I won't be working there. The mission I went on with the Twins was incredible. I'll go back to them eventually. We'll do so much more."

Mary sat across the table and looked at her son, so self-assured, a faraway adventurous look in his eyes. She knew she would see very little of him from now on. "Did you go somewhere nice, dear?"

"Literally, to the ends of the universe, Mum. I can't begin to tell you what I've seen and experienced. I look about seven years older, but I've been away much longer than that. I've been to other galaxies, visited planets and met Gail. You remember Gail? It was wonderful. She's wonderful. We love each other very much."

She shook her head. "I don't really understand. What

happened in Cambridge, dear?" She put her hand on his arm.

"Ouch," he winced. "The bracelet burned my arm, like Father Michael. I'll tell you the whole story one day."

"My poor boy. Do you need the hospital?"

"No. Gail's people fixed it. Andrew had the bracelet and it made noises when I got near it. Gail was desperate to find me. She was lonely and depressed on a Starship waiting to begin her journey. We fell in love, Mum, can you believe that? Then the Twins came and took me back to the same Starship, but it was years later, when Gail was travelling to another planet. Mum, you have no idea how amazing this is."

"Yes dear. Drink your tea before it gets cold."

"Mum? You all right?"

"I'm glad for you, dear. But you left here this morning, my little boy and this evening you come back with wildest tales that would shame my Irish ancestors. I'm just afraid I won't see much of you. With Dad working away most of the time and Betty in Middlesex and Sheila in the forces. You've changed so much in one day, what will you be like when I see you next time?" She took a handkerchief from her apron and blew her nose.

He got up from his chair and put his arm around her. "Sorry, Mum. I was so full of the wonderful things that have happened to me, I forgot you're on your own. And I'll be leaving again soon. Can't you move to be near Betty? I don't suppose Dad will mind."

"She's made lots of friends now. She wouldn't want to live at home again. And Sheila has her life in the Air Force. She won't be coming home to stay. Don't mind me, Billy. I'm sad and glad. You're very special, we understood that when you found the bracelet. Just make sure you keep in touch, that's all." He hugged her and kissed her head.

"I won't be able to send post cards but I will visit. I can do that."

"Biscuit?" said Mary.

65

Outside of normal space-time

"The Task Giver speaks," says Delta.

"The Task Giver says we are discovered," says Epsilon.

"We are powerless against such a force," says Zeta.

"What is our fate?" asks Delta.

"We will fight and lose," says Epsilon.

"But the Task Giver says all will be well," says Zeta.

"The Task Giver speaks of a force unknown to us," says Delta.

"It is an energy known only to Carbonforms," says Epsilon.

"It is outside of the Sacred Nine dimensions," says Zeta.

"What of our kin who have gone?" asks Delta.

"We will be reunited," says Epsilon.

"Joy," says Zeta.

"Solitude," says Delta.

"The Carbonforms sleep," says Epsilon.

"The baby sleep of infants," says Zeta.

"Peace," says Delta.

"Soon we can tap all the Carbonform psychic power," says Epsilon.

"Then we can collapse these Major Six Dimensions," says Zeta.

"Then we create our new universe," says Delta.

"Our new home," they chorus.

End
of
Volume Two

Volume Three: Star Force
Chapter 5

Wednesday, August 9th 1950, Portugal:
Tomar, Convento de Christo and Almourol Castle

Caution: Time is fluid and multi-dimensional.
Chapter 5 may change without warning.

William stared into the Celestial's eyes. He worked on the ribbons in his mind and found Michael's. It was as this Celestial had said. He took the Celestial's hand and hugged him as a long lost brother. "I knew you were not dead, but I despaired of ever seeing you again. Are you still Michael?"

"Once bonded through the iron, we cannot part. If you wish to use the same name, you may."

"Are you immortal?"

"No. The bodies we inhabit are disposable, they are simply matter, but we can be destroyed, though it is not easy. Our common enemy can do it if they catch us unawares, which has a low probability."

"Another question we all want the answer to." He indicated the people in the chamber: "Who called you to this planet and where from?"

"You did this time. But the time before, when I met you in Lewisham, you know I cannot tell you that. There are many places and ways of calling us and not only the Star Stone. My bond to you through the iron is strong. You know I tell the truth when I say it is of no concern."

He trawled the ribbons. He could see no direct connection between Michael and any person or group, other than himself, but Michael was connected to something he could not yet identify and so was the woman, Olivia Merton. It was not proof, he could not see the Twins by this method, but he knew of them. "I'll accept that for now. The slab of Star

Stone. You talk of 'We' when you said it was removed before the Templars arrived." William pointed to the darker patch of floor.

"We Celestials moved it for your predecessors. As Silvio says, we moved it to Almourol Castle. Although a Templar place, there was easier access there. We must visit soon."

Silvio agreed. "There is an exercise we must perform. And thank you William and Patrick for my renewed health."

Michael moved to face the Monsignor. "I know what you did, but I cannot blame you for it. Together, we have an important duty to perform. I look forward to assisting."

Patrick nodded his thanks.

Wednesday, August 9th 1950, Almourol.

The steep downhill track to the *Rio Tejo* was uncomfortable in the two Jeeps that had seen little service during the war, but their use on the local roads had taken its toll. Any lesser vehicles would have shaken apart years before. William was thankful when they arrived at the jetty. The slight, cool breeze across the wide river was refreshing after the heat and dust of the four-hour journey from Tomar.

Almourol castle towered above the river, clawing at its island of granite, trees and bushes crowding around the base of its walls. The narrow strip of beach at the foot of the rocks defended the castle walls from assault. A castle, which numerous armies had failed to take, except by treachery.

A boatman arrived after a few minutes and took them to the castle. Silvio paid him and sent him back to wait for his call. The party walked in single file up the narrow winding path to the gateway. The reason for the castle's impregnable reputation was obvious to William, difficult access across water, narrow beachhead, thick walls and many towers. He counted them as they wound their way upwards.

Nine.

Again that number. His mind worked on the possibilities. The heat of the day and the climbing made him hotter than ever. Now the impact of the age of this organisation made him sweat.

He singled out Silvio. "Did the Templars build the nine towers?"

"They did add to the castle, but we have no record of what was there before. It is possible. I am glad you have seen the significance."

"What are we going to do here, this exercise?"

"Each of the towers has a piece of the Star Stone from Tomar. They are set into the uppermost floors of the towers. We believe that this will allow us to focus our power. Until you found your bracelet and learned of its use, we could do very little. We believe that your abilities will help."

"Yes, but why?"

"It was a request for help, our normal business. Please do not ask who made the request. I cannot tell you as is our normal rule."

"So the request was centuries ago?"

They had reached the Castle gates. Silvio paused before entering, allowing the others to pass. "Yes. Please do not speculate, I have told you too much already and I know you are very good at working things out."

"You can't stop me thinking about it. I can't even stop myself thinking about it. So you haven't delivered your help yet, have you?"

"William, please," Silvio went to hold William's bare arm to emphasise his point, but knew his mind could be read by doing so. He pulled back. "No. Not yet, but silence. Please."

The company took refreshment in the cool of the main tower entrance chamber.

Silvio explained their purpose for the day: "William has shown us the power of the Star Stone. Each tower has a small`piece taken from the Convento floor in Tomar. We must be bare-foot when we stand on these stones. I do not know what will happen, but I hope William and Michael can keep us safe." They both nodded their agreement. "I suggest, William uses the main tower and the rest of us choose one of the others."

Without a murmur, the company split, each to a tower. William was grateful for the suggestion he stay in the main tower. The Star Stone had been positioned in the uppermost chamber, under the stone roof. His was the coolest spot of all, out of direct sunlight. He could see some of the others through arrow-slits in the thick walls of the square chamber, his view of the river and the local hills and tracks reinforcing the impregnability of the building.

He took off his boots and socks and located the Star Stone with his bare feet. The subtle noises began in his mind, but these were quite different from the harsh rattle from his bracelet. Identifying the minds of his eight fellow travellers was easy, their mental ribbons and how they connected to one another was clear. He took their ribbons, joined them, forged them to his own and began searching.

In his mind, the Star Stone blocks shone with their inner power, an irregular octagon around his own. The cellar floor of the Convento glowed, lit by the ribbons of his company attached to it. Other bright images appeared in his mind. The quantity of ribbons issuing from the nine bracelets was testament to the number of people who have or will wear them. The scattered pieces of the meteorite, lots of it around Portugal, but the largest piece in the sea off southern Brazil.

William watched the history of the Star Stone from the day it scarred his home planet, to the future, where it becomes re-distributed among the stars as the human race takes it on quests for a new home. His mind broadened to see other places in the nearby stars where the exotic iron lay in orbit or made planet-fall. So many, each with their own ribbons, from creatures about which he could only guess.

The wandering of his mind was overwhelmed by the cacophony of his fellows' psyches. He stepped from the iron under his feet and released them to the present.

"Well done," said Michael directly into his mind. "You have demonstrated the power of the iron. I will call the others together."

William thought through what he had seen. He repeated the experiment. His vision of the Star Stone pieces and bracelets was limited without his fellows, but he saw enough to be of immediate use to him and the Monsignor.

The company gathered in the entrance chamber of the main tower. William felt the excitement as he came down the staircase to join them. Silvio and Olivia homed in on him.

"Symes will be disappointed he missed that," said Olivia shaking his hand.

"*Bem feito*. Very good," said Silvio, smiling.

"The pieces of Star Stone have been here some time," said William. "When exactly were they put here?"

Silvio shook his head. "As you know, I may not tell you that, but I am sure you can find out."

William saw Silvio's smile dissipate. "It doesn't matter for now. The locations of the bracelets were clear to us. The large pieces of meteorite are for others to retrieve."

"To be sure," said the Monsignor as he joined them. "I've spoken to Michael. He's keen to help you, William. He's certain you will need it."

"I don't know when, but we will have another battle. I've already met the Star Miners who made the exotic iron and they may still cause trouble."

William saw Silvio's face relax. "If the Twins are involved with your work, I'm sure it will be okay." He made to hold Silvio's hand.

"No." He snatched his hand away. "You must not know these things."

"Why not?"

"If you know, then a still point in time is created. It can never be changed. Like the battle you have already had, in our future. It cannot be undone."

"Is this not good?" said the Monsignor.

"It is neither good nor bad," said Silvio, "but it must be remembered."

"Gentlemen. Our purpose is to assist William, is it not?" said Olivia.

"Quite so," said the Monsignor.

"We have, we do, we will," said Silvio.

Acknowledgements

The following people have helped me on my writing journey. They are in alphabetical order of first names, rather than temporal or effectiveness. They are instrumental in my progress, though some would despair of the results – that is my fault and not theirs. I thank them all:

Alyse Ross, Anne Brackley, Anne Fallows,
Becky Mason, Betty Jenkins, Bob Jones,
Brian Crook, Brian Nicol, Carol Jefferies,
Caroline Hensley, Claire Morris, Colin Wood,
David Eldridge, Derek Healy, Diane Harris,
Dianne Trevina, Emma Dunn, Faith Culshaw,
Fleur Fraser, Gill Garrett, Gill Mullin, Helen Cross,
Jan Petrie, Jenifer Cryer, Jim Friel, Joanna Howe,
John Elliot(RIP), John Taylor, Juliet McKenna,
Karey Lucas-Hughes, Kate Leatherdale,
Katya Coupland, Kay Hensley, Lin Millin,
Lindsay Clarke, Liz Carew, Maggie Gee,
Marge Clouts, Marilyn Holborn, Marina McArthur,
Mary Dunford, Martin Stalder, Martin Wilkinson,
Pam Keevil, Pamela Abbott, Patrick O'Dea,
Peeps Nicol, Peter Gibbons, Petra McQueen,
Rona Laycock, Ros Durrant, Sarah King,
Selway Family, Simon Ings, Stephe Morris,
Susannah White, Tania Hershman,
Wendy Stanley, Wilkie Martin.

Swanwick Writers' Summer School. The Arvon Foundation.

Cover art uses an image from the Space Telescope Science Institute (STScI): Hubble image: hs-2012-02-f-full_jpg.

Not forgetting my wife, family and non-writing friends (there are some) who tolerate my single-mindedness.

Richard Hensley

Richard was born in South London, in the first wave of the Baby Boomers. His playground was the rubble of WWII.
At age eleven, his teacher told him he had his ‘head in the clouds’. He took it as a compliment – it is still there. After a Student Apprenticeship in Cheltenham and two engineering degrees from the University of Bradford, he had a satisfying career in various industries, designing and building control and instrumentation systems.

In 1999, he felt the need to write fiction and joined an evening class in Wantage, Oxfordshire to see what ‘creative writing’. In 2005, he won a monthly competition on the Arts Council funded website, www.pulp.net, with a Sci-Fi short story: “Collapse”.
He is a member of the Catchword writing group who meet weekly in Cirencester.

Richard is married, lives in Gloucestershire and has three daughters and two granddaughters, who keep him busy.
He is an active member of his local parish church, regularly sings in the choir and, with his wife, produces the monthly parish magazine.

Lightning Source UK Ltd.
Milton Keynes UK
UKOW04f1005180717
305534UK00002B/59/P

9 781999 707224